Mercer Street

Mercer Street

American Journey Series

Book Two

JOHN A. HELDT

Copyright © 2015 John A. Heldt

ISBN-13: 978-1-09-105483-7

Edited by Aaron Yost

Cover art by LLPix Designs

Novels by John A. Heldt:

Northwest Passage Series: The Mine, The Journey, The Show, The Fire, The Mirror. American Journey Series: September Sky, Mercer Street, Indiana Belle, Class of '59, Hannah's Moon. Carson Chronicles Series: River Rising, The Memory Tree, Indian Paintbrush, Caitlin's Song.

Follow John A. Heldt at johnheldt.blogspot.com

In memory of Grandma, Everett, and Albert

CONTENTS

CONTENTS (CONT.)

CONTENTS (CONT.)

ACKNOWLEDGMENTS

Writing may be a solitary venture, but producing a novel is not. Most authors require the assistance of others to produce works fit for the reading public, and I am no exception. I am deeply indebted to several people who offered their time, talents, and insights.

They include Leslie Teske Mills, Becky Skelton, Christine Stinson, and Kristin Wogahn, who read the early drafts; Cheryl Heldt, Mary Heldt, Cathy Hundley, and Esther Johnson, who read the later drafts; and John Fellows, Jon Johnson, Craig Stoess, and Brent Wogahn, who provided input on topics ranging from military affairs and history to language and medicine.

A big thank you goes to Laura Wright LaRoche for producing the captivating cover. The Indiana illustrator has created or modified the covers of six of my seven novels.

I am also grateful to Aaron Yost for editing the final draft and to several others for providing research assistance. They include staff from the Chicago Public Library, Council on Foreign Relations, Franklin D. Roosevelt Presidential Library and Museum, Grand Canyon (Arizona) Community Library, Historical Society of Princeton, Library of Congress, Miami (Oklahoma) Public Library, Mudd Manuscript Library (Princeton University), Naval Historical Foundation, Navy Department Library, Princeton Public Library, and U.S. Army Center of Military History.

While writing this novel, I consulted several published works, including *Einstein A to Z* by Karen C. Fox, *Einstein: His Life and Universe* by Walter Isaacson, *Fashions of a Decade: The 1930s* by Maria Costantino, five editions of the Princeton University *Bric-a-Brac*, and *The 1930s*, edited by Louise I. Gerdes. I also learned about persons, places, and things in the *Amarillo Globe* (Texas), *Daily Princetonian*, *Hopewell Herald* (New Jersey), *Miami News-Record* (Oklahoma), Newark *Star-Ledger*, *Santa Ana Register* (California), and *Washington Post*.

1: SUSAN

River Run, Wisconsin – Tuesday, June 7, 2016

S usan looked at the lying, cheating bastard in the hospital bed and forgot for a moment she still had a loving husband. It was easy to forget such things after being called to an emergency room and learning that your perfect marriage was not so perfect.

"How do you feel?" Susan asked.

Bruce paused before answering. He turned his head slightly and gazed at his wife with eyes that betrayed more guilt than pain.

"Like you do," Bruce said.

Susan leaned forward in her chair, put a hand on the bed, and smiled at her spouse of twenty-five years. She didn't know what she would do with him after they left the hospital, but she knew any decision on their future could wait.

"We don't need to talk about that now," Susan said. "Get some rest."

Bruce took a breath.

"I'm sorry," he said in a barely audible voice.

Susan fortified her smile, took Bruce's hand, and squeezed it lightly.

"Let's talk about something else."

Susan started to ask Bruce if he needed an extra blanket or something to drink when their twenty-one-year-old daughter beat her to the punch.

"Can I get you anything, Dad?" Amanda Peterson asked.

"No, thank you, honey."

"Then at least let me brighten this place up. A little sunshine would do you good."

"I agree," Bruce said.

Amanda got out of her bedside chair, walked to the window, and adjusted the blinds. Just that quickly, warm, bright, comforting light flooded the private room, which took up a quiet corner of River Run Community Hospital.

"Is that better?" Amanda asked.

"Much," Bruce said.

Susan smiled sadly as Amanda fluffed Bruce's pillows and adjusted his blanket on the way back to her chair. She envied the ease with which her only child could set aside her anger and focus on providing comfort to a man who had betrayed his entire family.

Susan then turned to the older woman sitting in the corner of the room and saw more judgment than forgiveness. She had expected as much from her mother.

Elizabeth Campbell had never warmed to Bruce Peterson, a Chicago developer who seemingly spent more time with female business associates than with his own wife and daughter. She had often warned Susan that powerful men and infidelity went hand in hand and was therefore not surprised to learn that Bruce had conducted an eight-week affair with a buxom staffer he had set up in a high-rise apartment.

Susan thought about the mistress as Bruce again looked at her with repentant eyes. She bore no malice toward the woman who, according to police, had walked away from Saturday night's rollover accident with scratches and a red face. The receptionist was merely a person, a foolish girl who would probably think twice about entering into another adulterous relationship.

What troubled Susan was the nagging suspicion that this mistress had not been the first. Though she had no reason to believe that Bruce was a serial philanderer, she did not know for a fact that he wasn't. A husband who could cheat on his wife for weeks could probably do so for months or years. In fact, he could do just about anything.

The question was not moot. Susan could probably forgive a tryst in the woods that was supposed to be a fishing trip with the boys. She might even be able to forgive a long-term affair. But she could never forgive a lifetime of lies.

Susan thought about the consequences of Bruce's deceit a bit more and then, like Amanda, focused on his recovery. As much as she wanted to scream at this man and put him through a wringer, she wanted to nurse him to health first.

Susan didn't doubt that her husband would return to his feet soon. Despite some internal bleeding and massive trauma to his chest, Bruce was stable, strong, and lucid. Sixty hours after driving his Lincoln Navigator off a winding rural road in southern Wisconsin, he was expected to make a full recovery.

Bruce gazed at Susan for what seemed like an eternity, frowned, and then looked away. He stared at the ceiling, sighed, and turned to face Amanda.

"Did you ever hear back from the think tank?" Bruce asked.

"I did," Amanda said. "The director himself called Friday. He offered me a position in the research department. He said I could start October 3."

"What did you tell him?"

Amanda beamed.

"I told him I could start October 3."

Bruce laughed, or tried to laugh, through obvious pain. He took a deep breath, smiled softly, and placed his hand on his daughter's.

"I'm proud of you, sweetheart. I'm so very proud."

"I am too," Susan said to the recent college graduate.

Susan studied Bruce's face. When she saw more fatigue and weakness in his eyes, she withdrew her hand, checked her watch, and then turned to Amanda.

"Your father looks tired. We should let him rest."

"I'm fine," Bruce said. "You don't have to go."

"We do though. You need sleep," Susan said. "We'll come back. We'll grab some lunch, buy a few groceries, and return this afternoon."

"You don't ..."

"Listen to me for once, Bruce. Get some sleep."

"She's right," Amanda said. "You do look tired."

Bruce sighed.

"All right. I won't argue. Just be sure to ..."

Bruce didn't finish his sentence. He didn't finish anything. He clutched his rising chest, stared at his wife with wide eyes, and then slumped in the bed as he drifted into unconsciousness.

Susan knew something was seriously wrong even before she felt Bruce's hand become cold and clammy. The same heart monitor that had almost put *her* to sleep with its monotonous, rhythmic pings and wavy lines now had her sitting on the edge of her seat. Noises and numbers signaled not health and stability but rather suffering and chaos.

Susan jumped to her feet and leaned over her husband. She called his name and gave him a gentle shake. When that failed to rouse him, she turned to her daughter.

"Get a nurse, Amanda! Get a nurse!"

Amanda raced toward a door that led to a hallway and a nursing station. She didn't take more than six or seven steps before knocking over a twentyish nurse carrying Bruce's lunch on a tray.

The nurse slowly picked herself up. She surveyed the mess on the floor, gave Amanda a withering stare, and then looked at Susan, who tried to revive the patient.

"What's going on?" the nurse asked.

"Everything," Susan said in a panicky voice. "My husband is *failing*."

The nurse glanced at the heart monitor. When it became obvious that she had more than a messy floor on her hands, she returned to the open door, stuck her head in the hallway, and barked an order to people Susan could not see.

The nurse moved quickly to the bed, nudged Susan aside, and began to work on Bruce as the monitor flashed more troubling numbers. She checked the patient's vital signs and shook her head as a doctor and an older nurse rushed into the room.

"Please leave the room," the doctor said.

Susan did not react. She instead stared at the man with the lifeless eyes and pale face, a man she had not yet had the chance to berate, forgive, and perhaps love again.

"I'm sorry, ma'am, but you have to leave," the older nurse said to Susan. "You all have to leave now."

Susan looked at Elizabeth, who stood by the door, and then at Amanda, who stood behind the doctor and tried to catch a glimpse of her father. Even from several feet away, she could see the terror in her daughter's eyes.

Paralyzed by fear, doubt, and guilt, Susan looked on as the medical staff attended to Bruce and prepared a trip to the operating room. She could tell from the grim faces, clipped tones, and frantic pace that the situation was beyond serious. She began to think about her last words to Bruce when the doctor more forcefully repeated his order.

"Please leave the room!"

Susan looked at Amanda. When she saw that she had no intention of obeying the order, she stepped around the bed, put an arm around her daughter, and began to escort her from the room.

"No!" Amanda cried. "I can't leave."

"You have to," Susan said.

"No!"

"Amanda, we *have* to go."

Susan tightened her hold on her daughter when she felt increased resistance. When she realized that she would not get Amanda out of the room by herself, she appealed to the younger nurse with her eyes. Within seconds, the nurse moved toward the Peterson women and helped Susan literally drag Amanda away from the bed.

"Get your hands off me!" Amanda said. "Let me stay!"

Susan ignored the protests and redoubled her efforts as yet another nurse entered the room to assist with Amanda. She fought the urge to throw up as Amanda began to wail.

When the four women finally reached the door, Susan looked back at the bed. The doctor and the older nurse had begun to rush Bruce toward a place where miracles might happen.

She didn't need to look again, however, to know they rushed in vain. There would be no miracles on this or any other morning. Susan Peterson was already a widow.

2: SUSAN

Lake Forest, Illinois — Sunday, August 21, 2016

Susan gazed at the headstone and smiled sadly as she noted the Cubs insignia in one corner and the image of a 1957 Chevy in another. The three-foot-high marker was as impressive as any in the leafy cemetery on the shore of Lake Michigan, but it was not without a blemish.

The man who had engraved the granite slab in a Skokie workshop had botched Bruce Peterson's middle name, spelling Allan with one "l" instead of two.

Susan didn't mind. In fact, she refused the horrified craftsman's offer to correct the mistake. She considered the stone a fitting memorial to a man who was at once beautiful, polished, and deeply flawed.

In the eleven weeks that followed the sudden death of her husband from a ruptured aorta, Susan had had ample opportunity to think about the man, their marriage, and a future she would now have to face alone. She didn't like the idea of navigating midlife without the person who had been her rock, but she wasn't terrified by the prospect either.

Susan sighed and took one last look at the stone. She let her mind drift to the weeks and months ahead until her mother brought her back to the here and now.

"What are you thinking?" Elizabeth asked.

Susan turned to face her questioner.

"I'm thinking about what I'm going to do with my life."

"You'll do what all widows do, dear. You'll move on."

"You make it sound easy," Susan said.

"It's not. It's rather difficult, in fact," Elizabeth said. She placed a hand on Susan's shoulder. "When your father died, I didn't know what I would do either. I had hobbies and activities, of course. I had friends. I had you and Amanda. But I didn't have a *purpose*. Your father had been my 'purpose' for so many years, I didn't know even where to look to find a new one."

"You managed though."

"Yes, I managed."

Susan took a breath.

"Do you miss Dad?"

"That's a silly question," Elizabeth said.

"Is it? I know you two had problems."

"Every married couple has problems. Don't think they don't."

"I know every couple has difficulties, Mom, but not every wife has to deal with an adulterous husband. At least you didn't have to deal with that."

"But I did," Elizabeth said.

Susan stared at her mother like she was a stranger and not someone she had known her entire life. She could not believe what she had just heard.

"What?" Susan asked.

"You heard me. We have more in common than you think."

"Are you telling me that Dad cheated on you?"

"That's exactly what I'm telling you," Elizabeth said. She took Susan's hand. "I'll tell you more on the way back to the car. Let's go."

A few minutes later, as the two walked across the richly landscaped grounds toward the Lexus they had left outside the cemetery gates, Susan resumed the conversation. She had used the silent time to form questions in her mind.

"Why didn't you tell me about this earlier?" Susan asked.

"I didn't tell you because it was none of your business," Elizabeth said. "Would you have shared the news of Bruce's infidelity with Amanda had she not learned of it on her own?"

Susan sighed.

"I don't know."

"*I* know. You wouldn't have said a thing. You would have suffered in silence and let your daughter continue believing that her father was the greatest thing since microwave popcorn."

"You're probably right," Susan said.

"I know I'm right," Elizabeth replied.

"When did this happen? When did Dad cheat on you?"

Elizabeth stopped walking. She looked away for a moment and then gazed at Susan with eyes that reflected sadness, wistfulness, and perhaps some regret.

"He strayed shortly after we lost your brother."

Susan's mind raced to June 1, 1978, the day she had been pulled out of a fourth-grade English class and informed that Jason Campbell, 16, had been killed while driving to school. The high school sophomore had been her only sibling.

"That makes no sense. I remember how we came together after Jason's death," Susan said. "I remember Dad spending more time with me and taking a greater interest in my life."

"You recall correctly. He did all those things and more," Elizabeth said. "What you probably don't recall is the severe depression your father battled in the months that followed. He put on a brave face for a long time, but he couldn't keep it on."

"I still don't understand. Why did he cheat on you?"

Elizabeth clasped her daughter's hand.

"He betrayed me because he was dealing with a lot more than grief. He was dealing with my inability to have another child – a replacement child, if you will."

"You tried to have a baby when I was ten?" Susan asked.

"I most certainly did. I did not want to bear a child in my forties, for all the obvious reasons, but I did want to please your father. When I couldn't conceive, he found comfort in the arms of a younger woman, a woman who presumably could conceive."

"You're not saying I have another sibling, are you?"

"No. I'm just saying that your father was driven to procreate. Grief causes many people to act in ways they normally wouldn't," Elizabeth said. She resumed walking. "Calvin Campbell was one of those people."

Susan took a moment to digest what her mother had said. She had idolized her father and found the revelation that he had cheated on his wife and daughter unsettling.

"How long did the affair go on?"

"It lasted three months. Your father owned up to his misdeeds and sought counseling. When I saw that he was serious about saving our marriage, I decided to give him a second chance. To my knowledge, he never betrayed me again."

Susan stopped walking. She turned toward Elizabeth and gave her a hug.

"I'm sorry, Mom. I know now how difficult that must have been."

"I got through it. That's what matters."

Susan released her mother and looked upon her with new admiration.

"This certainly explains your skepticism of Bruce and maybe even of men in general," Susan said. "A lot of things make sense now."

Elizabeth laughed sadly.

"We women sometimes expect too much of our men and forget they are as weak and fallible as anyone," Elizabeth said. "I loved your father and don't regret staying with him. In spite of his many flaws, he was a good husband and a good father. I think you would agree with that."

"I would."

Susan smiled at Elizabeth and then looked over her shoulder at a group of ash trees in the distance. Unlike many others in northern Illinois, the trees had survived a serious beetle infestation. Like Elizabeth Campbell and Susan Peterson, they were survivors.

"You're thinking again," Elizabeth said.

"I am," Susan replied. "But I'm not thinking about the future. I know I'll be fine. I'll certainly be OK financially. Bruce may have broken his vow to remain faithful, but he didn't break his promise to take care of me. I'm thinking of giving at least half of his assets to charity. I don't need them and would frankly feel better if something good came out of all this."

"If you're not thinking about the future, then what *are* you thinking about?"

Susan sighed.

"I'm thinking about how much the two of us have in common and how life seems to test us when we least expect it," Susan said. "We're a couple of tough old birds."

"Yes, we are."

"I'm also thinking about the trip to Santa Barbara. Do you still want to go?"

"I do," Elizabeth said. "I want to go now more than ever. We could all use a break and a change of scenery. I would go even if you and Amanda did not."

Susan smiled and hugged her mother again.

"That settles it then. California, here we come!"

3: AMANDA

Santa Barbara, California – Monday, September 5, 2016

Amanda set her umbrella drink to the side, leaned back in a padded pool chair, and closed her eyes. She knew the Pacific Winds Resort and Spa wasn't the most relaxing venue on America's Riviera, but it was pretty damn close. It was the perfect place to put a troubling summer in her rear-view mirror and start thinking about a promising fall.

Amanda opened her eyes to the sound of a scream and saw a couple frolicking in the jungle pool, a palm-and-fern-lined tank that dominated the hotel's courtyard. When she was convinced the frat boy posed no threat to his bikini bimbo, she turned her attention to Elizabeth.

The septuagenarian reclined in a chair at Amanda's right. She greeted the sun as she usually greeted it: in a white pantsuit, a floppy hat, and supersize sunglasses.

"Thanks, Grandma," Amanda said. "Thanks for bringing us here."

"You're welcome, dear," Elizabeth replied. She looked closely at her granddaughter and put a hand on her arm. "How are you feeling today?"

"I'm doing better. At least my stomach's doing better."

"That's good to hear."

Amanda cringed as she thought about how the trip had started. Thanks to some dicey deep-fried scallops she had ordered from a beachside vendor, she had spent her first evening in Santa Barbara wrapped around a hotel-room toilet.

"Are you up for a big dinner tonight?" Susan asked.

Amanda looked to her left.

"I think so."

"That's good. Grandma and I would like to try the Thai restaurant across the street. There's also the steakhouse next door, if you want to avoid spicy food."

20

"As long as you keep me away from fish, I'll be fine."

Elizabeth and Susan laughed.

"Do you have a preference?" Susan asked.

Amanda heard her mother's question but did not respond. She had already drifted off to her thinking room where she pondered dead dads, extramarital affairs, and entry-level positions at foreign-policy think tanks.

The dead dad needed no explanation. Amanda missed her father. She missed him so much that she found it almost impossible to think about anything else.

Amanda was mad at him, of course. She could not believe he had cheated on a wife who loved him more than life itself. He had cheated on all of them and done so in a way that would leave permanent marks.

Yet when Amanda reviewed the events of the past few months, she felt more sadness than anger. Bruce Peterson had been the most important man in her life. He had been a friend, a mentor, and a loving father. Even loving fathers, however, were no good when they were dead.

Amanda made a note to visit his grave before she left for her job in D.C. If she did nothing else, she wanted to say goodbye one last time and perhaps find a measure of peace.

As for the job, Amanda could not wait to begin. She would soon start down a road that could lead to many exciting career possibilities, including research, teaching, journalism, and even diplomacy. At least one of her instructors at the University of Illinois had used the think tank, the Foundation for Foreign Relations, as a springboard to a diplomatic career. He was now an assistant to the U.S. Ambassador to Italy.

Amanda sighed. She began to think of diplomatic assignments to sunny countries when her mother rephrased a question that had gone unanswered.

"Amanda? Do you care where we eat dinner?" Susan asked.

"Let's go to the Thai place," Amanda said.

"Are you sure?"

"I'm positive."

"What about after dinner?" Susan asked. "What would you like to do tonight?"

"I vote for cocktails and more pool time," Amanda said.

Susan looked past her daughter to her mother.

"Mom? How about you? What do you want to do?"

Elizabeth lowered a tourist magazine she had been reading.

"I'd like to attend the lecture at seven," Elizabeth said.

"What lecture?" Amanda asked.

"Geoffrey Bell is giving a lecture on time travel in the hotel's auditorium."

"Who is Geoffrey Bell?"

"He's a local professor," Elizabeth said. "The desk clerk I spoke to this morning told me that his lectures are quite popular."

"We're on vacation, Grandma. People don't attend lectures on vacation, particularly in places like Santa Barbara."

"I do," Elizabeth said. "I think a lecture on a topic like time travel would be stimulating – certainly more stimulating than those old goats who were flirting with me in the lobby today."

Susan laughed.

"Men don't flirt after age seventy, Mom. They slobber."

"I'm afraid I must agree," Elizabeth said dryly. "In any case, I'd like to go to this lecture – and I'd prefer to go with my family. This is, after all, a *family* vacation."

"It is, indeed," Susan said with obvious amusement.

Amanda smiled. She knew her grandmother dropped the "F-word" only when she was losing ground in a family discussion and wanted to get her way.

"You're shameless, Grandma."

"I prefer to think of myself as pragmatic," Elizabeth said. She paused for a moment and then looked at Amanda. "I'll tell you what. If this professor bores you to tears, I'll treat you to cocktails afterward and maybe even that male revue in the Lompoc Lounge."

Amanda smiled and shook her head.

"You never cease to amaze."

"Does that mean you'll join me?" Elizabeth asked.

"Yes," Amanda said. "It means I'll join you."

Elizabeth looked at her daughter.

"Susan?"

Susan returned her mother's gaze and tilted her head.

"You really want to go?"

"Yes," Elizabeth said. "I really want to go."

Susan smiled.

"I guess that settles it then. It's time for a blast to the past."

4: ELIZABETH

The woman who had recently told a friend she "had seen it all" in her seventy-eight years admitted to herself she had never seen anything like Geoffrey Bell, at least not in real life. The man on the stage was no boring academic. He was a movie star, a larger-than-life presence who stimulated her senses – or at least the ones that could be stimulated from the eighth row of the Pacific Winds Auditorium.

Elizabeth smiled as she assessed the lively lecturer. With unruly blond hair, wild eyes, and a devilish smirk, Bell looked like Gene Wilder's Willy Wonka. With a biting wit, a debater's command of facts, and an engaging voice, he sounded like him too.

Elizabeth looked at Susan, who sat at her left, and then at Amanda, who sat at her right. She could see from their faces that they, too, were enjoying the show, which was part of a weeklong symposium sponsored by a software company. She tapped Amanda's knee.

"Do you still think lectures and vacations are incompatible?" Elizabeth asked.

Amanda turned her head. She flashed a sheepish grin.

"No. You were right," Amanda said. "This *is* interesting. This guy is good."

"Yes, he is."

Elizabeth returned her attention to the narrow stage, where Bell pranced back and forth and waved his arms like a Southern Baptist preacher. She didn't know if she subscribed to the professor's time-travel theories, but she conceded that his arguments were compelling.

"Just out of curiosity, how many of you folks have seen *Back to the Future*?" Bell asked as he stepped toward his audience. "Let's see a show of hands."

More than ninety percent of the hundred or so people in attendance raised a hand. Most of those who didn't appeared to be under ten years of age.

"That's what I thought," Bell said. "Let me ask another question. How many of you believe it is possible to travel back in time in a DeLorean?"

No one raised a hand.

"How about a spaceship that goes super-duper fast?"

Four teenage boys in the front row threw up their arms and waved them wildly.

Bell smiled at the boys.

"Thank you for the show of support, gentlemen. You can put your arms down."

The audience laughed.

"I like seeing believers and optimists in my audiences, but I can hardly fault those of you who didn't raise a hand," Bell said. "You are right to be skeptical. People don't just hop into cars or spaceships and travel to the past."

Bell returned to his lectern.

"That is not to say that time travel is solely the product of vivid imaginations. Though it is true that scientists demonstrated years ago that a single photon cannot travel faster than the speed of light – thus 'proving' that time travel is 'impossible' – it is also true that our understanding of physics and the world around us is limited. There are powers that we are only now beginning to grasp, including supernatural powers that may someday do for modern science what electricity did for previous generations."

Elizabeth scanned several faces in the crowd and saw that Bell had opened some minds if not won a few converts. Approving nods had replaced skeptical laughter.

The Oxford-educated professor continued to entertain, engage, and inspire his audience for another hour. He finished his presentation at eight fifteen, took a dozen questions, and then asked those in attendance to complete a short questionnaire that two assistants distributed.

Elizabeth looked at the form and saw that it asked three questions. She considered the first question and pondered an answer when she noticed Susan get up from her seat.

"Where do you think you're going?" Elizabeth asked.

"I'm going to the lounge," Susan said. "Didn't you say you would treat us to drinks and strippers after the lecture?"

"I said I would treat you only if Professor Bell bored you to tears. Since clearly he did not, I have no choice but to pull drinks and strippers off the table."

Amanda laughed.

"You should have been a lawyer, Grams."

"I should have. I certainly learned enough from my lawyer husband to know when to hedge my bets," Elizabeth said. "Why don't you stick around a while? I'd like to meet the professor."

Elizabeth glanced at the front of the auditorium and saw that many others had the same idea. More than twenty people crowded around Bell and pestered him for pictures, autographs, and presumably more information on the topic of time travel.

"I think you can handle him by yourself," Amanda said. "I'm with Mom on this one. I'd like to hit the lounge now, even if the boy toys have finished for the night."

Amanda rose from her seat and looked at Susan.

"Are you ready, Mother?"

"I was ready ten minutes ago," Susan said.

Amanda put her hand on Elizabeth's shoulder.

"Excuse me, Grandma."

Amanda stepped around Elizabeth and joined Susan in the aisle. She turned to look back at her grandmother just as a scowl began to form on the old woman's face.

"We'll save you a seat, Grams. If the strippers are still performing, I'll come back and get you myself," Amanda said. She smiled. "Don't stick around too long."

"I'll do what I please, young lady," Elizabeth said defiantly. She lifted her nose. "I will speak to the professor if I have to wait all night."

5: SUSAN

B y the time Susan and Amanda entered the Lompoc Lounge, the five strippers known as the Leather Boys had come and gone. Susan didn't mind. She wanted to talk to her daughter far more than she wanted to watch buff young men take their clothes off.

"How are you doing, honey?" Susan asked Amanda a few minutes later, after their waitress had brought them pomegranate margaritas. "You seem to be feeling better today."

"I am," Amanda said. "I'm still a little weak from all the puking last night, but I feel good. I just needed some rest and a few laughs. I'm really glad we went to the lecture."

"I am too. It was interesting."

Amanda sipped her frozen concoction, put her glass on the table, and settled into her seat in the padded booth. She gazed at her mother.

"Do you believe in all that time-travel mumbo jumbo?"

"I don't know," Susan said. "I suppose anything is possible, but I don't believe we will see time travel in our lifetimes. I think those physicists who tested the possibilities a few years ago are right. We don't have the means to travel through time and may *never* have the means."

"It is kind of cool to think about though."

"It is."

"Grandma is definitely into time travel," Amanda said. "I think she's into Professor Bell too."

Susan laughed.

"I suspect you're right. Thank goodness she's too old to mess around."

Amanda looked away, toward the entrance of the lounge, and broke into a grin.

"Are you sure about that?" Amanda asked.

"Am I sure about what?"

"Are you sure Grandma is too old to mess around? Because if you're not, you may want to warn the man on her arm."

Susan turned her head. She smiled and laughed when she saw Elizabeth approach the booth like a duchess with attitude. Geoffrey Bell, her duke for the night, walked closely at her side.

"There you are," Elizabeth said when she reached her family. "You should have waited for me to order the cocktails. I told you I wouldn't be long."

Susan raised a brow.

"If I recall, Mother, you said you might be gone all night."

Elizabeth lifted her nose.

"Perhaps I did. It doesn't matter. All that matters is that I captured a man and brought him back with me," Elizabeth said. "Susan and Amanda, this is Geoffrey Bell, the professor you abandoned tonight."

"Hello," Susan and Amanda said in near unison.

Bell extended his arm and shook two hands.

"It's a pleasure, ladies."

Susan glanced at Amanda, who mooned over Bell like a star-struck groupie, and then at her mother, who offered a self-satisfied smile. When neither said a peep, she turned to Bell and ended a few seconds of awkward silence.

"Care to join us, Professor?"

"I'd love to," Bell said.

Susan didn't wait for Elizabeth to suggest a seating arrangement. She slid to the end of her bench and patted the unoccupied space at her side. She watched with amusement as Bell filled the space and her frowning mother settled for the seat beside Amanda.

"Can I order you a drink?" Susan asked her neighbor.

"I've already done that," Elizabeth said with obvious irritation. "The professor and I are each having cognac. It's a spirit that lends itself to *serious* conversations."

Susan smiled.

"That's good. We wouldn't want to have a frivolous conversation on vacation."

Bell laughed and looked at Amanda.

"Are they always like this?"

"No," Amanda said. "Usually they get along."

Susan began to say something but stopped when the waitress brought the "serious" drinks to the table. When the server disappeared, she looked at Bell.

"We all enjoyed your lecture, Professor. Please forgive Amanda and me for not sticking around to meet you afterward," Susan said. "I hope you're not offended."

"I'm not," Bell said. "I'm delighted you attended the lecture in the first place. I'm sure you could have done other things tonight besides listen to an academic push far-fetched theories."

"Do you think time travel is far-fetched?"

"I don't. I think it's as possible as a manned mission to Mars. What I'd really like to know, though, is what all of *you* think. I don't believe I received your completed questionnaires."

"That's because we didn't fill them out," Susan said. "Amanda and I escaped to the lounge the minute you finished speaking."

"I take it you caught the featured entertainment," Bell said.

Susan blushed.

"No. We missed it. Which is probably a good thing. We're too old for strip shows."

"Speak for yourself, dear," Elizabeth said.

Bell chuckled.

"That makes me feel even better," Bell said. "It warms my heart to know that three lovely ladies passed up an attraction like the Leather Boys to hear me speak."

"I'd do it again," Susan said. "As I said, I enjoyed your lecture."

"I did too," Amanda added.

Susan sighed.

"I must confess, though, that I didn't give your questionnaire a second thought. What kind of feedback did you want?"

Bell glanced across the table at Elizabeth and Amanda before turning to his right. He already had Susan's complete attention.

"I didn't want feedback at all. I wanted your thoughts on time travel."

"Well, if you want, you can ask us your questions now. We're in no hurry to call it a night," Susan said. She looked at her mother. "At least I'm not."

"Very well then," Bell said. "I'll ask. My three questions are straightforward. The first, in fact, is very straightforward. I simply want to know if you believe time travel is possible."

"I do!" Elizabeth insisted.

"I know *you* do. You said so on the walk over," Bell said. He smiled and looked at Amanda. "Do you feel the same way, young lady?"

Susan watched with interest as Amanda squirmed. She didn't know how she would answer the question, but she was certain she wouldn't describe time travel as "mumbo jumbo."

"I'm open to the concept, Professor. I don't think time travel is possible now, but I do think it may be possible in the future," Amanda said. "Like you said in your lecture, there is a lot we don't know about physics and the world around us."

Bell nodded and moved on to Susan.

"How about you? Do you agree with your daughter?"

"I do," Susan said. "I believe time travel is possible. I just don't think it's something I'll see in my lifetime. I told Amanda as much before you joined us."

"Thank you for the answers, ladies. I can tell they are honest and heartfelt," Bell said. He paused to sample his cognac. "Now let me ask you another question. If you had the chance to travel back to the 1900s and return safely to the present day, would you do it?"

"Why the 1900s?" Amanda asked.

"Let's just say the period is relevant to the question."

"Oh. OK."

"Would you travel back to the twentieth century if given the opportunity?"

"I would," Amanda said. "If I could go back to *any* year and come back in one piece, I would. I can't imagine anything more interesting."

"That's a good answer. It's one I hear a lot," Bell said. He looked at Susan. "Would *you* also participate in such an opportunity?"

Susan looked at the professor and smiled. She could see why this guy packed lecture halls. Geoffrey Bell made even something as frightening as time travel sound like a field trip.

"I would," Susan said. "I would without hesitation."

"I must admit your answer surprises me. Would you not be afraid you might never see your family again?"

"You're looking at my family, Professor. I have one child, no living siblings, and no husband. My husband, Bruce, died in June."

"I'm sorry to hear that," Bell said. "I assume from your answer that if you had the chance to travel to the past, you would take your mother and daughter with you."

"That's correct. Though I would travel enthusiastically, I would not travel alone," Susan said. "I would never do something that crazy without my family."

"I see."

Bell looked at Elizabeth.

"Does the same hold for you?"

Elizabeth nodded.

"It does," Elizabeth said.

Bell turned his head.

"Amanda?"

"I feel the same way," Amanda said. "Even if the time-travel process were a hundred-percent foolproof, I would never travel without my mom and grandma."

Bell smiled.

"I can tell from your answers that there is a lot of love at this table. I appreciate your answers, ladies. They tell me much about you."

Susan put a hand to her chin and studied Bell closely. She wasn't sure where he was going with these questions, but she admitted she was intrigued. She couldn't remember a time, at least not since college, when a man had prompted her to think.

"You said you had three questions," Susan said to the professor. "What's the third?"

"The third question is sort of a follow-up," Bell said. "If you agreed to travel to the twentieth century, *why* would you do it?"

"That seems an odd thing to ask."

"Why?"

"Why? Because the answer is obvious," Susan said. "Traveling through time would be fun. It would be exciting, interesting, and certainly educational."

Bell grinned like a teacher who had just reached a struggling student. He let his eyes linger and then slowly shifted his attention to the youngest person at the table.

"Would you travel for the same reasons?"

Amanda nodded.

"Yeah. I would," Amanda said. "I studied history at Illinois, Professor. I studied the twentieth century. To see it up close and personal would be a blast."

Bell smiled again.

"Elizabeth?"

"I would also do it for the fun," Elizabeth said. She grinned. "Traveling to the 1900s, or any period, would be more enjoyable than dating three men at once."

Bell laughed. When he collected himself, he looked at Elizabeth more seriously.

"Is that your only reason?"

"No," Elizabeth said. She gave Susan a knowing glance. "I would also do it to see people I once knew and perhaps right some wrongs from my past."

Bell gazed at the old woman admiringly.

"That's a lovely answer. I think most of us would correct our mistakes if given the chance," Bell said. "Would you do anything else?"

"Yes," Elizabeth said. "I'd retrieve my wedding ring!"

Bell glanced at Elizabeth's left hand and then at her face. He tilted his head.

"Aren't you wearing it?"

"This is my *second* wedding ring, Professor. I left my first on a picnic table in Miami, Oklahoma, on June 19, 1958, two days after I eloped with my husband."

"This sounds interesting," Bell said. "Please tell me more."

"There's not a lot to say," Elizabeth said. "On our drive to California, Cal and I stopped in Miami for the night. About halfway through our picnic at the city park, a bee stung me on my ring finger. When my finger began to swell, I slipped the ring off as fast as I could. I didn't want doctors to have to saw it off later."

"What happened then?"

"Cal took me to the hospital before I went into shock. I'm about as allergic to bee stings as a person can be."

"Let me guess what happened next," Bell said. "In the rush to get to the hospital, you left the ring behind. Is that right?"

"That's right. We went back for the ring an hour later, but we couldn't find it," Elizabeth said. "Someone had apparently taken it."

"You said this happened on June 19, 1958?"

"I did. Cal bought me another ring, of course. It was bigger and flashier than the original, but it wasn't the same. It wasn't the first."

"What kind of ring was it?" Bell asked.

"It was a diamond solitaire," Elizabeth replied. "What made the ring special though was the inscription on the platinum band. Our jeweler, a good friend, was a one-of-kind artist."

"Did you ask him to engrave the new ring?"

"We couldn't. He died the day we reached Los Angeles."

"How awful," Bell said.

"I was upset, of course, but I quickly put things in perspective," Elizabeth said. "The ring was just a ring. I still had my husband and a promising future. I had fifty-six years with a wonderful man. When I look back at the past, that's what I remember."

"Once again, my dear, you've expressed yourself beautifully."

"Thank you."

"No. Thank *you*," Bell said. "Thank you for being so candid. You ladies have provided me with just the kind of input I was looking for."

Susan smiled as she assessed her charming new acquaintance. In less than an hour, Geoffrey Bell had gone from a stranger on a stage to a person who connected with three women better than their fathers and husbands.

She jumped back into the conversation when it appeared to be veering in a different direction.

"I'm flattered by your interest in our responses to your questions, Professor, but I don't understand why they are so important to you," Susan said. "We're just three people from one of your many audiences. Surely our answers aren't *that* insightful."

"I disagree," Bell said. "They are as insightful and useful as any I've heard. More important, your views on time travel are potentially relevant."

"Relevant? How so? How could our input be relevant to something that even you concede is more fiction than fact?"

"The answer to that question depends on whether you want to continue this conversation. If you do, your insights, opinions, and values could be very relevant. There is more to time travel than I revealed in my lecture. If you would like to hear more, I would be happy to say more."

"Now that's an invitation I can't refuse," Elizabeth said.

"Me neither," Amanda added.

Susan looked at Bell skeptically.

"Just what do you have in mind, Professor?"

"Come to my place and find out. My wife and I maintain a beach house about a mile from here," Bell said. He pulled a pen and a business card from his jacket pocket, scribbled something on the back of the card, and gave it to Susan. "If you're interested in taking this discussion to the next level, please be at this address at noon on Wednesday. Jeanette and I would love to have the three of you for lunch."

Susan furrowed her brows and stared at Bell. When she didn't see him alter his matter-of-fact expression, she broke into a tentative smile.

"All right, Professor. We'll be there, all of us," Susan said. "You have a date."

6: SUSAN

Wednesday, September 7, 2016

The beach house near Shoreline Park was no seaside shack. With windows for walls, lofts for bedrooms, and a stainless-steel kitchen the size of Texas, the octagonal residence was a splashy tribute to glass, metal, and excess.

Susan settled into a white mid-century sofa, which she shared with Elizabeth and Amanda, and took a few sips of French roast. When she finished, she placed her ceramic mug on a walnut coffee table, put her hands in her lap, and smiled at her hosts.

"Thank you for lunch and the tour of your wonderful home," Susan said. "I've seen many lovely houses in my life, but I must admit I haven't seen one like this."

"I'm glad you like it," Geoffrey Bell said. He smiled at his wife, who sat beside him on a couch that faced the visitors, and then returned to Susan. "As I mentioned earlier, though, it's not our home – or at least not our primary one. Our permanent residence is a 117-year-old Painted Lady in the West Adams district of Los Angeles."

"A Painted Lady? Oh, my. I thought only San Francisco had those."

"There are still a few in this part of the state, but their numbers are dwindling. Jeanette and I have done our best to restore our mansion to its original splendor and encourage similar preservation efforts in Southern California."

"Where do you live in Illinois?" Jeanette Bell asked.

Susan shifted her attention to the missus, a friendly, cultured, articulate redhead who bore a striking resemblance to the actress Julianne Moore.

"I live in Lake Forest, a suburb of Chicago," Susan said.

"I know it well. I spent a summer there. It's a beautiful town," Jeanette said. She smiled at Susan and then looked at the senior citizen next to her. "How about you, Mrs. Campbell. Where do you live?"

"I live in Lake Forest as well," Elizabeth said.

"Do you live near the water?"

"I do now!"

Susan and Amanda laughed.

"Did I miss something?" Jeanette asked.

"I'll let my daughter explain," Elizabeth said.

The Bells turned again to Susan.

"Please excuse my mother," Susan said. "She never passes an opportunity to answer a question in an amusing way. She moved into a cottage, behind my home, about six months ago. The cottage is fifty feet from Lake Michigan."

"Did you move to live closer to your family?" Jeanette asked.

"No," Elizabeth said. "I moved because I got tired of stumbling down the stairs of the big house my husband left me."

The Bells laughed.

"That's as good a reason as any," Geoffrey Bell said.

Jeanette offered Elizabeth a kind smile.

"Geoffrey told me that your husband died just two years ago. I'm sorry to hear that," Jeanette said. She turned to Susan. "He also told me that *your* husband died in an accident in June. I'm sorry to hear that as well. That must have been difficult."

You have no idea.

"It was," Susan said. "This has been a difficult summer. That's why we decided to follow through with plans to come out here. We decided that we needed to get away from Chicago and clear our heads before getting on with our lives."

"Have you been able to do that?"

"I think so. I have, anyway. I've been able to put quite a few things into perspective, including my new status as a widow and my fledgling career as a novelist."

The Bells leaned forward.

"You're a *novelist?*" Geoffrey asked.

"I am," Susan said. "Have your heard of the Sinful Spouses series?"

"I can't say I have."

"How about my latest novel, *The Merry Wives of Wheaton?*"

"No," Bell said. "I haven't heard of that either."

"Don't feel bad," Susan replied. "You're in good company."

"What are your books about?"

"They are mostly about life in the soulless suburbs, misbehaving housewives, and the scoundrels who help them misbehave," Susan said.

Laughter filled the room.

"I assume that these misbehaving housewives and scoundrels are solely the products of a vivid imagination," Bell said.

Susan smiled tightly.

They used to be.

"Of course."

Elizabeth put a hand on Susan's knee.

"Your novels sound intriguing," Bell said. He sipped his tea and put his cup on its saucer. "I'll look for them the next time I'm at the library."

"I have a better idea," Susan said. "Let me provide you with signed copies of all of the books before we leave Santa Barbara."

"I like that idea. Thank you for your generosity."

"It's the least I can do for cutting and running Monday night. I should have stayed in the auditorium after your lecture. It was rude of me to leave."

Bell chuckled.

"Don't be so hard on yourself," Bell said. "You did what most people did. You left when the show was over."

"Don't you mean 'lecture'?" Susan asked. "A 'show' is a performance. Don't you believe in the theories you shared with us?"

Bell smiled.

"Oh, I do. Forgive my choice of words. When you give lectures to people who seek your autograph and give you standing ovations, lectures can seem like performances."

"There's no need to apologize, Professor. Even if you are a showman, you put on a good show. I'm glad I attended the lecture. I think time travel is a fascinating topic."

Bell looked at Amanda.

"How about you? Did you enjoy Monday's program?"

"I did," Amanda said. "I admit I wasn't thrilled at first about attending a lecture at the start of my vacation. I had my fill of lectures in college, but I'm glad I went to yours. I liked what you said and how you said it. I would pay to hear you speak."

Bell turned to the senior in the room.

"Elizabeth?"

"You know where I stand, Professor," Elizabeth said. She sipped some tea and placed her cup on its saucer. "I'm your number-one groupie."

The professor laughed.

"I suppose you are. Thank you for the support," Bell said. "That goes for the rest of you too. Thank you for attending the lecture, giving me your thoughts Monday night, and coming here today. I am both flattered and thrilled."

Susan studied Bell as he smiled at his wife and took another sip of tea. She didn't know what to make of the professor, who was equal parts academic, showman, and conversationalist, but she knew she liked him.

What Susan didn't like was the nagging feeling that Professor Bell had invited the visitors into his home for reasons he had not yet shared. She stared blankly out one of the large picture windows and pondered the matter until she heard a familiar voice.

"Susan?" Jeanette asked.

"Yes?"

"Is something wrong? You appear distracted."

Susan smiled at her hostess.

"Perhaps I am. I was just thinking about how my vacation has gone. I never expected to do even half the things I've already done, such as attend your husband's lecture or spend an afternoon in someone's home. I pictured more shopping and beachcombing."

"Oh," Jeanette said. "I hope we're not keeping you from anything."

"You're not," Susan said.

"Well, if we are, please let us know. I often forget that visitors to this area don't have as many chances to see and do what we see and do every day."

"We'll be here eleven more days. I think we'll have ample opportunity to hit all the shopping malls and tourist traps."

Jeanette laughed.

"I suspect you will."

"There is one other thing on my mind though," Susan said. She shifted her attention to Bell. "It's a question for you, Professor."

"Oh?" Bell asked. "What is it?"

"I'm curious as to why we haven't talked more about time travel today. Wasn't that the main reason you wanted to see us again?"

"It was."

"Then why have you asked us more about our backgrounds and interests than about our views on our new favorite topic?" Susan asked. "I thought you wanted to take Monday's discussion 'to the next level.'"

"I do."

Susan looked at Bell with puzzled eyes.

"OK."

"I apologize if I misled you," Bell said. "I *do* want to talk more about time travel. I wanted to talk more on Monday night, but I couldn't. Not until I did some homework. I had to learn more about you and your family before I could continue our conversation."

Susan tilted her head.

"Why would you have to do that?" she asked. "Why are our backgrounds important?"

Bell looked at Susan closely.

"They are important because I have to know if I can trust you with the information I'm about to share with you."

The visitors sat up.

"You have our attention," Susan said.

The professor smiled.

"That's always a plus," Bell said.

"What's this about?"

"Put simply, dear lady, it's about the opportunity of a lifetime."

"You're not peddling property, are you?" Susan asked.

Bell laughed.

"No. I'm not. Though I suspect if I were, I might succeed. It's pretty hard to go wrong selling real estate in this part of the country."

"I won't argue with that," Susan said with a smile. "I've already seen several houses here that meet my standards."

"You have my word that I won't try to sell them to you," Bell said. "You have my word that I won't try to sell you anything."

Susan leaned forward.

"If you're not offering us houses or stock options, then what, precisely, *are* you offering? What is this 'opportunity of a lifetime'?"

Bell glanced at Elizabeth and Amanda. When he was apparently satisfied that their interest in the discussion hadn't waned, he returned to Susan.

"The opportunity I'm offering you is not an asset but an experience. It's a journey of sorts, a journey that few human beings have ever had the chance to take."

"A journey?"

"Yes."

"A journey to where?" Susan asked. "The moon?"

"No," Bell said. He smiled. "The twentieth century."

Silence gripped the room.

"Did you say '*the* twentieth century'?" Susan asked.

"I did."

"People can't send others to another time, Professor."

"I can."

Susan glanced at her couch-mates and saw a mother and a daughter transfixed by what they had heard. Both stared at Bell like he had just said he was God.

Susan looked at the professor.

"You have proof of this, of course."

"I do," Bell said.

"You're full of it," Susan replied.

Bell smiled.

"Jeanette tells me that every day," Bell said. He sipped his tea. "On this particular matter, though, she knows I speak the truth."

Susan turned to Jeanette and watched her nod.

"What kind of nonsense are you peddling?"

"We're not peddling anything," Jeanette said. "We're simply telling you that it is possible to travel through time – at least to the 1900s."

"How do you know this?" Susan asked.

"I know it because I've done it. We both have. Several times."

Susan felt anger build inside her. She didn't know what this was about, but she knew she didn't like it. Her view of this kind and gracious couple was beginning to change.

"Then prove it," Susan said. She turned to Bell. "Show me evidence that the two of you have traveled through time."

The professor sighed.

"There's evidence right over there," Bell said matter-of-factly.

Bell pointed at a dozen or so thinly framed photographs that adorned a nearby wall. Each of the photos was black and white and appeared to feature the Bells.

"Your evidence is a photo gallery?" Susan asked.

"My evidence is a photo within the gallery."

"You'll have to do better than that."

"I will," Bell said. "I assure you. I will."

The professor got up from his couch, walked to the gallery, and removed a single eight-by-ten-inch photograph from the wall. He then walked to the other sofa and presented the picture to the skeptical novelist.

"This is it?" Susan asked. "*This* is the smoking gun?"

Bell answered the condescending statement with a smile.

"It's one of several, in fact," Bell said. "Go ahead. Take a look."

"OK. I will."

Susan watched the professor warily as he returned to his seat. She didn't know where this was headed and wasn't sure she *wanted* to know, but she didn't see any harm in playing along. So she did as her host had instructed.

Susan examined the high-resolution photo for a few seconds and then handed it to her mother. Elizabeth looked at it for a little longer, shrugged, and passed the image to Amanda. When Amanda finished inspecting the object, she returned it to Susan.

"Well?" Bell asked.

"It's a lovely photo, Professor, but it's hardly proof of time travel."

"Take a another look at the picture, Susan, and tell me what you see."

Susan reluctantly complied. She picked up the photo with both hands and studied what appeared to be a recent image of the Bells standing below the awning of an old brick building. Each of the subjects wore stylish 1920s clothing.

"I see you and Jeanette standing in front of what looks like an old restaurant or hotel," Susan said. "You look like you're ready to go to a Roaring Twenties party."

"We were," Bell said.

"Was this taken on your anniversary?"

Bell smiled.

"As a matter of fact, it was. It was taken in San Francisco on October 30."

"So it was taken about a year ago?" Susan asked.

"In a sense, it was."

"What do you mean by that? It was either taken on October 30 or it wasn't."

Bell gave Jeanette a knowing smile and then gazed at Susan.

"Let me help you out."

"Please do," Susan said with an edge in her voice.

"Look at the picture again," Bell said. "Look closely at the items on the sidewalk. Do you see a discarded newspaper?"

Susan inspected the photo.

"Yes," Susan said.

"What does the large headline at the top say?"

"It says: STOCKS COLLAPSE."

Bell glanced at Elizabeth and Amanda before returning to Susan.

"That newspaper was published on Wednesday, October 30, 1929."

"So?"

"The photograph was taken on the same day."

"You're lying."

"I assure you, madam, I am not," Bell said. "Jeanette and I were in San Francisco the day after the markets crashed in 1929."

Susan passed the photo to Elizabeth and gave Bell a hard stare.

"I don't believe you. That newspaper may have been produced in 1929, but this photograph most certainly was not. I could obtain a similar picture from hundreds of studios. With decent software, I could probably make one myself."

Elizabeth looked at the photo and then at her host.

"I'm afraid I agree with Susan. This picture is lovely and compelling, but it is hardly proof that you traveled through time."

Bell gazed at Elizabeth and turned to Amanda.

"I assume you feel the same way," Bell said.

Amanda nodded.

"I do. It's insulting, in fact, that you would try to pass off that image as an original. I've done enough photo-editing work to know that something like that could be produced easily."

Bell smiled.

"You're right, of course. You are all right. I could have easily doctored a photograph using software that is available today."

"So are you admitting that you did?" Susan asked.

"No, Mrs. Peterson, I am not," Bell said. "That photo is quite authentic."

"You're testing my patience, sir. You're going to have to offer more than a bogus photo to get me to believe your claim – or even remain in this house."

"I will," Bell said. "Trust me. I will. I fully expected your skepticism and knew I would have to produce far more than a photograph to address it. That is why I hedged my bets and went on a treasure hunt of sorts. I knew I would need to obtain something particularly compelling to rid you of your doubts."

"What are you talking about?" Susan asked.

Bell sipped his tea.

"Do you know why I invited you to come here today instead of yesterday?"

"I haven't a clue," Susan said curtly. "Did you have a business appointment in 1929?"

The professor chuckled.

"No. I did not," Bell said. He sighed. "But I did have one in 1958."

Elizabeth turned her head.

"I think I've heard enough," Susan said. She looked at her daughter. "Are you ready to go? I'm sure we can find something better to do this afternoon."

"I'm ready," Amanda said.

Susan turned to Elizabeth.

"Mother?"

Elizabeth stared at Bell like she was locked in a trance.

"Mom?" Susan asked. "I'd like to leave now."

"Hold on," Elizabeth said. "I want to hear what he has to say."

Susan sighed. She glared at Bell.

"You have ten minutes, mister."

Bell looked at Susan.

"I won't need five."

40

"Then get on with it," Susan said.

Bell acknowledged the command with a nod and then turned to Elizabeth. He gazed at her like a son might gaze at a mother before sharing some troubling, even disturbing news.

"I wasn't kidding when I said I had business to attend to in 1958," Bell said. "While you and your family enjoyed Santa Barbara yesterday, Jeanette and I went on a mission to the Bible Belt. We went to Oklahoma."

Susan felt her anger rise again as she watched Bell bring up a time and a place that would surely hold her mother's attention. She wanted to leave immediately but decided there was no harm in playing the game a little longer. She jumped back into the conversation.

"You went to Oklahoma?" Susan asked.

"We did. Mrs. Bell and I spent two weeks, in real time, traveling to and from that wonderful state. While we were there, we visited the small town of Miami," Bell said. He looked at Susan and then at Elizabeth. "Perhaps you've heard of it."

"You know I have," Elizabeth said.

Susan grabbed her mother's hand.

"You don't have to put up with this, Mom. We can leave now, if you want."

Elizabeth looked at Susan.

"I want to hear this."

"All right," Susan said. She looked at Bell. "Please continue, Professor."

Bell gazed at each of the women.

"As I was saying, Jeanette and I visited Miami. We spent most of a glorious June day sitting in a large park, where we watched mothers attend to their babies, children play on the swings, and a young couple enjoy a picnic under an oak tree."

"What did the couple look like?" Elizabeth asked.

Bell smiled sadly.

"The man was tall and had a boyish face, a nice smile, and dark, wavy hair. He wore a white, short-sleeved shirt and khaki slacks," Bell said. "The woman was a pretty blonde who wore her hair in a ponytail. She wore a pleated pink dress and carried a white purse. Neither the man nor the woman looked a day over twenty."

"What else can you tell me?" Elizabeth asked.

"I can tell you a great deal. I can tell you that the woman talked a lot and laughed a lot until about thirty minutes into the picnic, when she cried out, shook her left hand, and pulled a ring off her finger. I can also tell you that she appeared to be in considerable pain and that when the pain did not subside, she pleaded with the man to take her to a hospital."

41

As Susan listened to Bell describe a scene he could not have witnessed, she wondered what kind of person could believe his nonsense. Then she looked at Elizabeth, saw a tear roll down her cheek, and concluded there was one.

"Mom? Are you all right?" Susan asked.

Elizabeth nodded at Susan before returning to Bell.

"What happened next, Professor?"

"The man approached an elderly chap who sat on a nearby bench. When the old man pointed north, in the direction of the closest hospital, the young man returned to his lady," Bell said. "He threw his arm around her, guided her to a blue sedan, and drove her away from the park. He did not bother to retrieve any of the items on the picnic table."

"What did you do after they left?" Elizabeth asked.

Bell smiled kindly.

"I think you know what I did, dear. I did what I went there to do."

Susan gasped and put her hand to her mouth as Bell reached into a pocket of his tailored vest and pulled out a ring. She didn't need a second look to know it was the diamond solitaire that had once belonged to her mother.

Bell got up from his sofa and walked around the coffee table. When he reached Elizabeth, he smiled again, extended his hand, and offered the ring to a seventy-eight-year-old woman who had not seen its shine in fifty-eight years.

"My jeweler cleaned the ring yesterday," Bell said. "When he asked if I was giving it to Jeanette, I said no. I said I was returning it to a friend, a friend who deserved to see it at its best."

Elizabeth took the ring, examined the inscription, and turned away. When she looked again at Bell, she did so with eyes brimming with moisture.

"Thank you, Professor," Elizabeth said. "Thank you."

Bell looked at Amanda, who beamed, and then Susan, who fought off her own tears, before returning to Elizabeth. He kissed the old woman on the head, reclaimed his seat on the other couch, and grabbed his wife's hand.

"I'll give you ladies a moment to collect yourselves," Bell said. "When you're ready to talk, just let me know. I think it's time we take this discussion to the next level."

7: SUSAN

An hour after Geoffrey Bell had rocked the world of three Chicago women, Susan looked at two of the women to gauge the fallout. She saw a mother who appeared to be locked in a nostalgic trance and a daughter who smiled like she had just been told that Santa Claus was real.

Susan took a sip of fresh java, placed her mug on the coffee table, and gazed at the man who had surprised her in more ways than one. She wasn't sure where she wanted the discussion to go, but she was sure she wanted it to continue.

"Let me see if I heard you correctly," Susan said. "Did you say that your great-grandfather was the one who discovered the secrets of time travel?"

"I did," Bell said.

"How did this come about?"

"It came about mostly by accident."

"I don't understand," Susan said.

"Then let me explain," Bell said. "It all started in the summer of 1898, when my great-grandfather, Percival Bell, joined a scientific expedition that explored a remote section of the Sierra Nevada mountain range. Percival was forty then and, like me, a man dedicated to science and discovery. He joined the group primarily to gain knowledge of Cretaceous rock formations, but it wasn't long before he gained knowledge of something far more interesting."

"Please continue."

"On the third day of the journey, Percival entered a limestone cave and discovered hundreds of mysterious symbols carved on a wall. With the help of his brother, an anthropologist, he was able to determine that the writing on the wall was a formula – a formula for time travel."

"How come I had never heard of his discovery?" Susan asked.

"You had never heard of it because Percival did not share his find with the others in the expedition or the greater scientific community. He shared the formula only with close family members and people he could trust."

"I see. What did he do when the expedition ended?"

"He returned to Los Angeles," Bell said. "He returned to L.A. and built a very special house, a house Jeanette and I call home. Percival used the formula, limestone bricks, and gypsum crystals he found in the cave to create a tunnel that extended from his basement to his backyard. The tunnel is much like the one he found in the Sierras. By observing astronomical tables and synchronizing crystals in the chamber with ones he carried, Percival was able to turn a limestone tunnel into a portal to the past."

"When did you learn all this?"

"I learned the family secret twenty years ago. When my father died, I inherited, among other things, a detailed journal that Percival had kept. The journal documented the expedition in 1898, the formula, and my great-grandfather's time travels."

"Did he travel a lot?" Susan asked.

Bell shook his head.

"He did not. Percival accessed the portal only three times between January 7, 1900, the day he completed the tunnel, and March 22, 1900, the day he died of a stroke."

"That's sad."

"It *was* sad. Percival left a wife and two children," Bell said. "A few weeks after her husband died, my great-grandmother put the house on the market and returned to her native Boston. She sold the residence, through an agent, in December of 1900."

"You mean the house did not remain in your family?" Susan asked.

"No. Five different families occupied the place between 1901 and 2000, when Jeanette and I purchased it. It wasn't until then that we were able to access the tunnel, test the formula, and prove that Percival Bell was not, as you might say, 'full of it.'"

Susan smiled.

"I'm sorry for doubting you. This is all still very overwhelming."

"There is no need to apologize," Bell said. "I sprung this on you in the middle of your pleasant, carefree vacation. I asked you to believe in something that many of the world's leading physicists have relegated to the heap of science fiction."

"That raises other questions," Susan said.

"Such as?"

"Such as why bring us into this? We're total strangers. If you feel like sharing this secret with others, why not share it with people you know and trust? Or why not share it with the rest of the scientific community? You could change the world."

"You're right," Bell said. "I *could* change the world. I could do a lot of things by traveling to the past. I could cure diseases, prevent wars, and introduce wonderful ideas years before their time. I could do many good things and do them with minimal effort."

"But ..."

"But it's not my place to do so."

"OK. I get that part," Susan said. "But why pick us? Even if you don't want to change the world or turn science on its head, why share your knowledge with us? Why ask us to take a trip that you could just as easily take yourself?"

"There are many answers to those questions, answers I'll reveal over time should you choose to participate in this opportunity," Bell said. "What I can tell you today is that I am driven by the pursuit of knowledge and now wish to gain that knowledge through the assistance of others."

"So why not pick people with suitable qualifications? We're just three average women from Illinois. We're not scientists. We don't have any special skills or knowledge."

Bell smiled.

"That's where you're wrong, my dear. You have exactly the skills, knowledge, and attitude I'm looking for."

"Please explain," Susan said.

"All right. I will," Bell said. "Let's start with you. You're hardly 'average.' You're an educated woman, a novelist, and a trained observer of society and the human condition. You are perfectly suited to interact with strangers in a potentially challenging environment."

Susan smiled.

"I'm not sure about that, but I'll take it."

Bell sipped his tea and continued.

"As for Elizabeth and Amanda, they too are bright, educated women. They too bring valuable things to the table. One lived through most of the twentieth century. The other studied it extensively. They have an understanding of the past that is priceless."

Susan glanced again at Elizabeth and Amanda and saw smiles on their faces. Like herself, they were apparently not immune to flattery.

"Thank you for the explanation," Susan said to Bell. "I understand a lot more than I did a few minutes ago, but I don't understand everything. I don't, for example, understand why we can't do more with this so-called 'opportunity.'"

"What do you mean?"

"I mean why must we travel to the twentieth century? Why can't we go to the eighteenth or the fifteenth or the first? I think running into Benjamin Franklin or Joan of Arc or Pliny the Elder might be kind of fun."

"I'm sure it would," Bell said. "There are two reasons why you can't travel to the distant past. The first is because the tunnel did not exist, at least in its finished form, before January 7, 1900. The second is because the maximum range of the portal is precisely 116 years. I discovered that limitation earlier this year. I believe the stars are to blame, but that's only a guess."

"So what you're saying is that if we accepted your offer – and traveled today – we could not go back to a time before September 7, 1900."

"That's exactly what I'm saying."

Susan settled into her seat and thought about everything Bell had said. She still couldn't quite wrap her head around the idea that time travel, at least to the recent past, was real. She started to raise another matter when her normally talkative mother finally joined the conversation.

"I have a question," Elizabeth said.

Bell looked at his number-one fan.

"Please ask."

"Would we be able to travel to any year in the 1900s?"

The professor smiled.

"The simple answer is yes. The not-so-simple answer is no."

"I don't understand," Elizabeth said.

"Let me put it to you this way," Bell said. "If I did not care about your personal safety, I would let you pick any year. Because I *do* care about your safety, I cannot. As I mentioned earlier, five different families occupied the house in Los Angeles between 1901 and 2000. I have never met these people. I don't know how they would react if they caught three women trespassing in their yard. I don't know if they have dogs or guns or understand the significance of the tunnel. I know only when they occupied the residence and when they did not."

"What does that leave us?" Susan asked.

"It leaves you with nine years," Bell said.

"Just nine?"

Bell nodded. He pulled a piece of paper from his vest pocket and gave it to Susan.

"According to property records, the house was not occupied during the years written on that slip. If you want to travel to the past, you will have to pick a year from that list."

Susan scanned the slip and saw nine numbers ranging from 1900 to 1984. She took special note of the dates 1929 and 1958 and then shared the list with her family. Elizabeth greeted the choices with a smile. Amanda greeted them with apparent indifference.

"Is something wrong with the years?" Susan asked.

"No," Amanda said. "I like most of them."

"Then why the frown. You look a bit troubled."

"I'm just a little concerned about the logistics of all this," Amanda said. She turned to Bell. "I'd like to know more about this process of yours, Professor."

"What would you like to know?" Bell asked.

"Well, for starters, if we went on a trip, would we return to the same time we left?"

"It would depend."

Susan zeroed in on Bell. She didn't expect that answer.

"Depend?" Amanda asked. "On what?"

"It would depend on whether you returned to the tunnel bearing a white crystal or a blue crystal," Bell said. "I would give you one of each before you departed. With the white crystal in your possession, you would be able stay as long as you wanted in the past and return to the present as if you had been gone only a few seconds."

"What if we returned with only the blue crystal?" Amanda asked.

"Then you would return to the present as if time had never stopped. If you left today and remained for a month, you would return to Los Angeles on October 7, 2016. In such a circumstance, you might have to explain your disappearance to others."

"I see."

"There is another consideration as well," Bell said.

"Oh," Susan said. "What's that?"

"The blue crystals have a shelf life of no more than 153 days."

"What does that mean?"

"What it means is that should you lose your white crystal and wait more than 153 days to return to the portal, you may find yourself permanently in the past."

Susan tensed up.

"Oh, my."

"I don't mean to alarm you," Bell said. "In the unlikely event that you lost both crystals or stayed too long, I would still have the ability to bring you back – provided, of course, that I knew where to look for you. That is why I would insist that you create an itinerary and stick to it."

"I think you could count on us to do that," Susan said.

"I'm sure I could," Bell said.

Susan looked at the professor and sighed. She still wasn't sure she trusted him, but she wasn't sure it mattered. She wanted what he was offering. Widowed and unfulfilled at age forty-eight, she needed an adventure like most people needed a car.

"I suppose you have materials for us to consider and a deadline to observe."

"You're right on both counts," Bell said. "I've prepared a packet of papers for you to read, sign, and return. I would like an answer by Friday."

"You'll have one," Susan said.

She glanced at Elizabeth and Amanda, saw that they too were ready to leave, and then returned to Bell. She wanted to say one more thing but couldn't find the words.

"Do you have any more questions for me today?" Bell asked.

"I do. It's not a big deal one way or the other, but it is something I've been thinking about the past ten minutes."

"Then please ask. Tell me what's on your mind."

"OK. I will," Susan said. She took a deep breath and smiled. "I want to know if you've sent any other acquaintances on a time-travel trip."

Bell smiled.

"As it turns out, I have," Bell said. "I sent a San Francisco reporter and his college-age son to 1900 back in April."

"Have you heard from them?"

"No."

"Had you expected to?" Susan asked.

"Yes."

"So they should have returned by now?"

"Yes."

"Oh."

"Please don't read too much into this," Bell said. "I know where they are and believe they are safe, but I don't know for sure."

"Why is that?"

"I don't know because the men in question chose not to follow my instructions. They sought danger where danger lurked. They decided to dance with a hurricane."

8: AMANDA

S itting with her family at a small table in their hotel suite, Amanda Taylor Peterson looked over the papers like an attorney and wondered for the third time in three hours whether she needed this adventure. She agreed with her mother on two counts. Traveling to the past would be fun. Getting stuck there would not.

"What's the matter, honey?" Susan asked. "I see doubt on your face."

"That's because there's doubt in my *mind*," Amanda said. "Look at all these forms. There are at least three separate disclaimers. Do we really know what we're doing?"

Susan laughed.

"No, Amanda, we don't. If we accept Professor Bell's invitation, we will be taking the biggest leap of our lives."

Amanda sighed.

"What do you think, Grandma? Do you think this is worth the risks?"

Elizabeth gazed at Amanda.

"You're asking the wrong person, dear. I'm a woman nearing the end of her life. I look at risk differently than a woman just beginning her life," Elizabeth said. "The only thing I will not do is travel without my family."

"That makes two of us," Amanda said.

Amanda looked again at the scattered papers and laughed to herself. She had to admit that Geoffrey Bell was thorough. He had provided the women with more than a dozen forms to complete and requested everything from their clothing sizes to the names of their closest friends, professional contacts, and next of kin. Bell had also asked the women to release him from any legal liability and commit at least three thousand dollars to the venture. He may have been ready to provide the ladies with the time of their lives, but he was not ready to provide it for free.

"I say we go over the basics one more time," Susan said. "If we can't all agree on what to do and where to go, then we won't take the trip. Period. Does that sound good?"

"That sounds good," Amanda said.

"Mom?"

"You know my answer," Elizabeth said.

"All right then. Let's take it from the top," Susan said. "Do we even want to do this? Do we want to go to a relative stranger's house in Los Angeles, walk through his magic tunnel, and take the chance that we might find something unpleasant on the other end?"

"I do," Elizabeth said.

"Amanda?"

The young woman nodded.

"Then we agree on the big question. I want to do it too," Susan said. "The fact we can return to the same time is key. I don't know if I would be so willing to accept the professor's invitation if we had to explain a long absence to our friends."

"I know I wouldn't," Amanda said.

Amanda smiled. She could just imagine explaining her absence to her boss at the think tank. She could also imagine him calling men in white coats to haul her off to a relaxing sanitarium.

"The next matter is just as important," Susan said. "If we take this trip, we can't just go where we want. We have to select a year from the professor's list. So let's try to find some common ground. Let's start with you, Mom. Make your case for 1938."

"I think I already have," Elizabeth said. "I know it's not as appealing as some of the other years on the list, but it's one that is dear to me. It was the year I was born, the year my parents fled Austria and came to America. I would like to see them again, even as a stranger, and somehow make amends for the choices I've made."

Amanda didn't need clarification. She knew her grandmother regretted the decisions she had made in 1958, when she eloped with a Protestant, abandoned her Catholic faith, and essentially severed ties with her parents. She also knew that Elizabeth had never shaken the guilt that followed their deaths in a car accident four years later and would probably benefit greatly from seeing them when they were young and vibrant and not old and embittered.

"How about you, sweetheart?" Susan asked. "You told me yesterday that you liked 1900 and 1958. Is that still the case?"

Amanda nodded.

"If I had to choose between them, I'd pick 1958. I want to travel as far back as possible, but I also want to go to a time with vaccines and antibiotics."

Elizabeth laughed.

"So polio outbreaks don't appeal to you?"

"Oh, they do, Grandma. They appeal to me almost as much as pneumonia, meningitis, and tuberculosis. I mean what's life without an infectious disease?"

"Are you open to other years?" Susan asked.

"I am," Amanda said.

"That's good to hear," Susan said. "I think you both know I prefer 1929. I love everything about the Roaring Twenties – the music, the fashions, even Prohibition. I think it would be kind of fun to sneak into a speakeasy and listen to some early jazz."

Elizabeth sighed.

"It sounds like we're going to have a dickens of a time agreeing on a year."

Susan smiled.

"We won't if I can get you two to see the light."

Amanda laughed. She liked seeing her mother's playful side. Slowly but surely, Susan Peterson was emerging from the shadow of that awful morning in Wisconsin.

"What about venues?" Amanda asked. "We haven't talked much about *where* we should go. I'd like to travel across the country and then spend some quality time in New York."

"I would too," Susan said. "It sounds to me like you favor a longer trip."

Amanda nodded.

"I do. I want to spend at least six months in the past. We will probably never have the chance to do this again, so why not make the most of it?"

"I agree," Susan said. "If we travel to the past, then we should stay a while. Our friends may notice a few new wrinkles on our faces when we get back, but who cares? If we do this, we should go all out. We should make an adventure of it."

Amanda took a sip from her can of cola.

"We still have to work out the particulars though," Amanda said. "We won't have *any* adventure until we pick a time and a place."

Susan turned to face Elizabeth.

"Are you dead set on 1938 and Princeton, Mom?"

"I am. I know I should be flexible, but I want to see my parents. I want to see them when they were young and happy. I want to see my childhood home," Elizabeth said. She paused for a moment as her eyes began to

51

water. "You two are young. You may have other opportunities to time travel. I won't. I want to do this."

Even before Elizabeth got the words out, Amanda realized that she had no choice but to fall into line. She had many adventures ahead of her. Elizabeth did not. She had an obligation, if not a responsibility, to honor the grandmother who had done so much for her.

Amanda looked at Elizabeth and smiled.

"I have to admit, Grandma, that going to New Jersey in the thirties is not at the top of my list of things to do, but if going there is important to you, then I'll do it."

Elizabeth put a hand on Amanda's arm.

"Thank you, dear."

"I have one request though," Amanda said.

"What's that?"

"If we go to Princeton, I want to drive there. I want to drive on Route 66 and the Lincoln Highway. I want to see the whole country."

"You have a deal!" Elizabeth said.

Amanda turned to face her mother.

"What about you, Mom? Are you OK with 1938?"

Susan sighed.

"It's not my first choice, but it's one I can live with. I don't want to travel with a miserable mama and a grumpy girl," Susan said. "If you two want to go there, then I won't stand in your way. I think we'll have fun no matter where we go."

"Then everything is settled," Amanda said. "So what do we do now?"

Susan smiled warmly.

"We fill out these forms. Then we contact Professor Bell and let him know we've reached a decision. He said he would need at least a week to prepare a trip. That leaves us just two days to spare before we head home."

"Then I guess we had better get busy," Amanda said. She paused for a moment to study her mother's face. "Are you really OK with this, Mom?"

"I'm really OK with it. I'm looking forward to it."

"So am I."

"That makes three of us," Elizabeth said.

Amanda looked admiringly at the two most important people in her life and then reached for her soda. She lifted the can and encouraged the others to follow suit.

"Here's to road trips, depressions, and dust bowls!" Amanda said.

The three women laughed and clinked cola cans.

Susan smiled and raised her can again.

"Here's to a beautiful daughter."

9: SUSAN

Los Angeles, California – Thursday, September 15, 2016

Susan looked at the floral print dress in the bedroom closet and decided she had all the proof she needed. No one would ask another to wear a frumpy thing like this unless she was sending her to a different time.

The author pulled the dress from its hanger and walked toward the others in the spacious room. When she reached them, she held the garment high and grinned.

"I guess I won't be turning many heads," Susan said.

Her hostess laughed.

"You're wrong," Jeanette said. "You're going to turn a lot of heads, but you probably won't turn them until you buy a new wardrobe. At least I hope you won't."

"You want us to keep a low profile. Is that it?"

"Yes. I want you to keep a *very* low profile, at least while you're traveling," Jeanette said. She stepped toward Susan. "Geoffrey told me that you intend to drive to New Jersey. He said you plan to take your time getting there."

"He's right," Susan said. "We may take five or six weeks."

Jeanette nodded and stepped back.

"I thought that might be the case. That's why I picked out modest attire for all of you. I want you to blend in as much as possible. When three attractive women drive across the country on rural roads during hard times, they tend to stand out."

"Are you saying I'm a dish?" Elizabeth asked.

Jeanette laughed.

"Oh, you're much more than that."

Susan laughed at the question and the reply. She wondered if her mother would ever act her age and secretly hoped she wouldn't.

"Thank you for doing all this," Susan said to Jeanette. "I admit I would never have thought about the effect my clothing might have on others."

"That's because you're a product of the modern age," Jeanette said. "You've been told your entire life to flaunt the goods and push boundaries. We all have. In this particular instance, though, I believe modesty is the best policy. If you do nothing else on your journey to New Jersey, you want to arrive safely."

"I can't argue with that."

Susan glanced at the others and saw they had already started to remake themselves. Elizabeth and Amanda straightened their dresses in front of a full-length mirror.

"What do you think?" Susan asked her daughter. "Do you like your new look?"

"I do. This is kind of fun. It's like playing dress-up," Amanda said. She smiled at Susan. "All I need now is a vintage hat and a long strand of phony pearls."

"You'll find them over there, on the sofa, next to your purses," Jeanette said. She laughed. "I thought you should have at least a few 'extravagances' on your trip."

Susan looked again at a woman she had come to admire. She made a note of staying in touch with the inspiring Mrs. Bell when her time-traveling days were over.

"I see three suitcases by the door," Susan said. "I assume they are filled with things we'll need and maybe things we won't need."

"They are filled to the gills," Jeanette said. "I've packed several items for each of you, including more dresses, undergarments, makeup, spendable currency, and documents that may come in handy if you're asked to provide identification."

"Do you really think we'll need ID in 1938?"

Jeanette nodded.

"You'll need it if you want to purchase a vehicle and drive it legally. With the papers I've placed in your bags, you should have no trouble obtaining licenses with the Department of Motor Vehicles. Your permanent address, by the way, is 156 Sea View Lane in Santa Barbara. You might do well to memorize it."

"Is that a real address?" Susan asked.

"It is. It's the address of a beach house built in 1930. The owner is a sixty-year-old man who does not drive and who visits the place only five or six times a year. Geoffrey and I made his acquaintance during a brief trip to 1938 on Tuesday."

"It looks like you've thought of everything."

Jeanette looked at Susan closely.

"We want you to enjoy your trip."

Susan put on her frumpy frock, donned the pearls, and slipped her stockinged feet into a pair of two-tone cutout Oxford shoes. She then placed her hat on her head and turned toward Jeanette.

"How do I look?"

"You look like a woman who may turn heads anyway," Jeanette said.

Susan laughed.

"I suppose that's inevitable," Susan said. She sighed. "No matter what we wear or say or do, we will undoubtedly draw the attention of someone."

"I expect you will."

Susan smiled and then walked to a large paned window that faced the Bells' backyard. She gazed out the window and saw brick steps that rose from the basement to a plush lawn.

"Can I ask you a question, Jeanette?" Susan asked.

"Of course."

"What's it like?"

"What's what like?" Jeanette asked.

"What's it like to travel to a different time?"

Susan turned around the second she finished the question. She eyed the other women in the room and noticed that she had drawn the attention of all three.

Jeanette smiled and sighed.

"What's it like? Well, it's exciting, for one thing. It's very exciting," Jeanette said. "It's like walking through a movie set or a theme park."

"I thought so," Susan said.

"It's also scary."

"Scary? How so?"

"It's scary because you're *not* walking through a movie set or a theme park," Jeanette said. "You're walking through a real world where you are as vulnerable to crime, disease, and events as the people who live there. No matter what you do or where you go, you are always at risk of becoming a permanent part of a new historical record."

"Are you trying to warn us against taking this trip?" Susan asked.

"No. I'm just trying to answer your question honestly."

"Have you ever found yourself in a dicey situation?"

Jeanette nodded.

"I have many times. So has Geoffrey. In fact, we found ourselves in a 'dicey situation' on our last trip to 1958."

"What happened?" Susan asked.

"Geoffrey paid a hotel bill with a twenty-dollar note," Jeanette said.

"So?"

"The note was modern. It had a watermark and a large portrait of Andrew Jackson."

"Oh, my."

"Geoffrey realized his mistake, of course. He even asked the clerk to return the bill."

"Did he?" Susan asked.

"No. He held onto it and summoned his supervisor."

"What happened then?"

"The hotel manager examined the bill, concluded it was bogus, and threatened to call the police," Jeanette said. "He thought Geoffrey was a counterfeiter."

"Are you saying your husband could have gone to jail?"

"He could have gone to *prison*."

"What did he do when the manager threatened to report him?" Susan asked.

"He tried to talk him out of it. Geoffrey argued that the note, an obvious fake, was a gag gift he had received at a party, a gift he had forgotten to remove from his wallet."

"What did the manager do?"

"He kept the bill and picked up the phone," Jeanette said. "He asked the operator to put him through to the police. It looked bleak until Geoffrey did something unexpected."

"What was that?" Susan asked.

"He pulled several 1950-series bills from his wallet and made a generous contribution to the manager's favorite charity."

Susan laughed.

"That will do the trick."

"It did that time," Jeanette said. She smiled and then sighed. "We were lucky though. Things could have turned out differently. You can never be too careful when visiting the past."

Susan tilted her head.

"Do you recommend that we walk on eggshells?"

"No," Jeanette said. "I advise just the opposite. I encourage you to enjoy yourselves. Don't be afraid to take risks or try new things, but never forget that you are a guest of the 1930s – not a resident. If you remember that, you'll have a great experience."

"Thanks for the tip," Susan said.

"You're welcome," Jeanette replied. She smiled at Susan. "Can I answer anything else before we head downstairs?"

"No," Susan said.

Jeanette looked at the others.

"How about you two? Do *you* have any questions for me?"

Elizabeth shook her head.

"Amanda?"

"No," Amanda said. "I think you've covered everything."

"If that's the case, then I believe we're ready for the professor," Jeanette said. "Please grab your hats and bags and follow me. Your adventure awaits."

10: SUSAN

The women in the frumpy dresses and stylish hats followed Jeanette Bell to the main floor of her West Adams mansion and then down a stone staircase that screamed Tower of London.

Susan didn't know much about Painted Ladies or Victorian architecture in Southern California, but she knew enough to realize that the Bell estate in Los Angeles was a very rare bird. She had passed just one other century-old house on the drive through the city – and that was a stucco palace that evoked more images of Santa Fe than San Francisco.

When Susan reached the bottom of the dark, dingy staircase, she expected to walk into a dark, dingy basement. She did not expect to enter a brightly lit, thirty-by-forty-foot space that radiated purity. With white walls, a white ceiling, a plush white carpet, and two large white leather couches, the chamber looked like God's Waiting Room.

"I like what you've done to the place," Susan said to Jeanette as she joined the other women in the middle of the room. "It's positively heavenly."

Jeanette chuckled.

"Geoffrey insisted on remodeling the basement when he discovered that the time tunnel really worked. He wanted the transfer point from this world to the next to be bright and airy," Jeanette said. "Isn't that right, dear?"

"That's right," Bell said.

The professor sat on the nearest sofa about fifteen feet away. He assembled several papers scattered across a glass-and-brass coffee table that stood between the sofas.

"He's been preparing more documents for you," Jeanette said.

"I see the paperwork never ends," Susan said.

"It doesn't in this house," Bell said as he threw the documents into a manila envelope. He placed the envelope next to a book on the table, stood up, and summoned the women with a hand. "Please join me, ladies. We still have much to discuss."

Bell eyed his guests as they followed his wife to the sitting area and set their suitcases next to the far couch. When the three took their places on the sofa and Jeanette returned to his side, Bell sat down and commenced what the visitors had been told would be the last order of business.

"I take it that Jeanette went over some of the particulars," Bell said.

"She did," Susan said. "I appreciate the time and effort you put into our clothes, our documents, and other preparations. I never would have thought of half that stuff."

"You can thank Mrs. Bell for that. She has become quite adept at selecting the right tools for the right trips. I've come to depend on her heavily."

Jeanette beamed.

"She was very helpful," Susan said. "I know more about time travel than I did even an hour ago, but I still have a question. I thought of it as we walked to the basement."

"Oh?"

Susan nodded.

"It concerns money. Jeanette said that our bags contain spendable currency, but she didn't say how much. I'd like to know how much we have on hand and how far it will get us in 1938. We'd like to stay in the past at least six months."

"I can't answer that question definitively," Bell said. "Much will depend on whether you live modestly or lavishly. What I can tell you is that each of your suitcases contains one hundred 1928-series twenty-dollar bills. Six thousand dollars will go a long way in a depression economy if you stay away from Ponzi schemes and poker tables."

"Did you say six *thousand* dollars?"

"I did."

"I'm not a math whiz, Professor, but even I can run the numbers," Susan said. "Six thousand dollars in 1938 would be worth at least fifty today."

"Try a hundred," Bell said.

Susan's eyes lit up.

"A hundred?"

The professor nodded.

"That's funny," Susan said. "I remember writing you a check for only three. Are you feeling particularly generous today?"

"As a matter of fact, I am."

"I don't get it. If you're covering virtually all of our expenses, why would you ask for money from us in the first place?"

The professor looked at Susan thoughtfully.

"I did so because I needed an expression of good faith," Bell said. "Had you balked at a mere three thousand dollars, I would have withdrawn my offer."

"I see," Susan said.

Susan looked at Bell with awe, fascination, and puzzlement. She knew the professor, a multimillionaire, had the means to underwrite the trip. What she didn't know was *why* he would do it. She thought about asking another question but decided that this was not the time or the place to look a gift horse in the mouth.

"Please don't dwell on the money or my reasons for subsidizing your journey," Bell said. "Just hold onto the cash and put it in a bank as soon as you can."

"We will. You know we will," Susan said. She paused to look at her family and then returned to Bell. "You said a minute ago that we still have much to discuss. What more do we have to talk about?"

The professor smiled.

"Let's start with your arrival in 1938. When you three walk out of this house, you will walk into a Los Angeles that has not existed since Elizabeth was an infant. You will step onto an unoccupied property in the middle of a much different city," Bell said. He lifted the manila envelope off the coffee table and offered it to Susan. "The documents in this envelope will make your transition to the past a little smoother."

"What documents? Do you mean more ID?"

"No. I mean bus schedules, maps, a few dollars for minor expenses, and the addresses of places you'll need to visit soon, such as car dealerships and the Department of Motor Vehicles."

"You want us to visit those places today?" Susan asked.

"I think you should," Bell said. "The sooner you establish yourself in the past and take care of the basics, the better."

"OK. What else do you want us to do?"

Bell pulled a slip of paper from his jacket pocket and gave it to Susan.

"I want you to send me a letter to this address."

Susan smiled.

"Why? Do you miss us already?"

Bell laughed.

"I do! I will miss you charming ladies the minute you walk out my door," Bell said. "The point is that I don't want to miss you six months to a year from now. I want you to be able to communicate with me should you run into trouble."

"I want that too," Susan said.

Bell smiled.

"I will periodically visit the main post office in Los Angeles in 1938 and 1939 to check my mail and, by extension, your safety and security."

"You think of everything, don't you?"

"I like to think I do."

"What else is in the envelope?" Susan asked.

"There is a list," Bell said. "Mrs. Bell calls it my Ten Commandments. I call it a piece of paper you should take very seriously."

Elizabeth and Amanda sat up.

"You have our attention, Professor," Susan said.

Bell looked at each of his guests closely before proceeding.

"You already know some of my rules, such as the ones that pertain to personal property. I trust that you left your contemporary belongings in the guest room upstairs."

"We did," Susan said not quite truthfully.

"That's good," Bell said. "I think you'll find time travel less problematic if you leave modern driver's licenses, cell phones, and cameras behind in the present day."

"I agree."

"Then let me get to the two most important items on the list. They are ones I don't want you to forget."

"OK."

"Let me first say that I want you to enjoy your trip," Bell said. "I want you to see the sights, make friends, and participate in activities. What I don't want you to do is bring back a living souvenir or alter the past in any significant way. You will all be traveling to a very dangerous time, a time when the world is on the edge of war. Please don't say or do anything that might result in German textbooks or the loss of freedoms that millions today take for granted."

"I won't," Susan said.

"Elizabeth? Amanda?"

"I'll behave myself, Professor," Elizabeth said.

"I will too," Amanda added.

Bell visibly relaxed.

"I'm glad to hear that. I want to know that I've done the right thing by honoring your request to visit a very perilous year."

"You have," Susan said.

"Before I continue, do you have any questions?"

"I do," Amanda said.

"What's that?" Bell asked.

"You mentioned last week that you recently sent a reporter and his son to 1900."

"I did."

"Have they returned?"

"No. They have not."

"Do you expect them to?" Amanda asked.

Bell smiled.

"I do. The men violated some of the rules I set down for them, but they managed to avoid serious trouble. I expect them to return as early as tomorrow."

"I see."

"Are there other questions?" Bell asked.

"I have one," Susan said. "I sort of asked it earlier. It's been on my mind all week."

"What's your concern?"

Susan sighed.

"Why are you investing so much in three people you still don't know very well?" Susan asked. "You took a big risk in telling us your secret before we even committed to taking a trip."

The professor nodded.

"You're right. I did," Bell said. "I took a huge risk when I told you about Percival Bell, this house, and a secret you could have easily shared with others, but I felt I had to take that risk. I knew you would soon return to Chicago and didn't want you to slip away. I meant it when I said you ladies had the skills, knowledge, and attitude I was looking for. You are perfect candidates for time travel in almost every way."

Susan looked at Bell closely.

"I see the trace of a grin, Professor. That tells me you have more to say."

"I do," Bell said. He laughed. "Do you remember the 1980s adage, 'Trust, but verify'?"

"I remember it well," Susan said. "Ronald Reagan used it frequently when discussing arms agreements with the Soviet Union. He trusted the Russians only as far as he could verify their words and deeds."

Bell smiled.

"You're correct. The president hedged his bets with a party he did not know or fully understand ... and I did the same with you."

"You did what?"

"I had a private investigator check you out. He confirmed what I suspected all along. He said you are all stand-up individuals who are worthy of my trust."

"You checked us out?" Susan asked.

"I checked you out. I hope that doesn't offend you."

"No. Oddly enough, it doesn't. If anything, it makes me respect you more. It makes all of this seem a little more real and legitimate."

"That's good to hear," Bell said. "I felt I had no choice. It's one thing to tell strangers you have a vehicle that could take them to the past. It's another to give them the keys to that vehicle."

"What keys?" Susan asked.

Bell smiled.

"The keys I brought to this gathering."

The professor reached into his left jacket pocket and retrieved two transparent stones. One was white, the other blue. Both were three inches long. Bell then reached into his right pocket and pulled out an old-fashioned skeleton key. He placed all three items on the coffee table for all to see.

"That's quite a collection," Susan said.

"Thank you."

"What's the metal key for?"

"It unlocks the door between the time tunnel and the outside world," Bell said. "You will need it when you return. The lock on the door is the same one Percival Bell installed in 1900."

"I see," Susan said. "I assume the rocks are the infamous gypsum crystals."

"You assume correctly."

"They're beautiful."

Bell handed the skeleton key and the white stone to Susan.

"I'm entrusting you with the more powerful of the two crystals," Bell said. "This stone will allow you to access the portal at any time and return to September 15, 2016, as if you had never been gone. Guard it carefully."

"I will," Susan said.

Susan gazed at the crystal for a few seconds. She couldn't believe something so small and simple could trigger something like time travel, but she could tell from its cut and its shine that it was no ordinary rock.

Bell watched Susan put the white crystal and the key in her purse and then turned to the youngest person in the room. He picked up the blue crystal and offered it to Amanda.

"This is for you," Bell said. He placed the crystal in Amanda's open hand. "It's the backup, the spare, the stone I hope you will never have to use. Please take care of it and keep it separate from the white crystal at all times."

"I will," Amanda said. She put the stone in her purse. "Thank you."

"What about me?" Elizabeth asked. "Do I get a pretty rock too?"

Bell laughed.

"I'm afraid not. I can spare only two," Bell said. "What I can give you is a job. I want you to keep an eye on Susan and Amanda and make sure they act wisely."

"I accept!" Elizabeth said.

Everyone in the room laughed.

The professor looked at Elizabeth with adoring eyes.

"As it turns out, dear, I do have something for you."

Bell grabbed the small book that sat on the table and handed it to Elizabeth.

"What's this?" Elizabeth asked.

"It's a journal, a blank journal I want you to fill," Bell said. "Susan told me that you picked 1938 because you wanted to see your parents and your infant self. I can't say I like the idea, but I understand why you do. So rather than advise you against doing something you'll do anyway, I want to encourage you to make the most of it. I want you to record your experiences in this journal and share them with me upon your return."

Tears filled the old woman's eyes.

"I can do that, Professor," Elizabeth said. "I *will* do that."

"I know you will, dear. I know you will," Bell said. "I believe it's only fitting that we close on that sentimental note. It is time, ladies, for me to show you the door."

"What door?" Susan asked. "I see only four white walls."

"Look again."

The professor turned around and pointed to a faint outline on the far side of the room. The outline framed a white, nondescript door that almost blended into the wall.

"That's the door to the tunnel?"

"That's the door to the tunnel and – for you three – September 15, 1938," Bell said. "Please grab your purses and suitcases and follow Jeanette and me."

Susan, Elizabeth, and Amanda did as requested. They followed the Bells from the sofas to a door that looked like it belonged to a broom closet. They exchanged nervous glances when the professor opened the door, turned to face them, and smiled.

"This is your portal to the past," Bell said. "It is the chamber that Percival Bell built more than 116 years ago and one I want you to know well. Please step inside."

When Bell moved away from the door, Susan motioned Elizabeth and Amanda to enter the tunnel. A moment later, she followed them into the space – a narrow, brick-lined passage about fifteen feet long, eight feet high, and five feet wide. A plain, windowless door at the other end presumably led to the backyard and the outside world.

Susan looked up just in time to see a streak of light race across the ceiling. A strip of glowing white and blue stones, embedded in the bricks, provided welcome illumination.

"I like the lights," Susan said to Bell, who stood next to Jeanette in the doorway. "They give the place a festive feel."

The professor laughed.

"They do. What's more, they match the ones in your purses."

Susan and Amanda reached into their handbags and retrieved their stones. The rocks emitted a soft, steady light like the ones overhead.

"Oh, my," Susan said. "This might start a few conversations."

"Don't worry," Bell said. "The portable crystals and the ones in the tunnel light up only when they have been synchronized and placed in close proximity to each other."

"I must say I'm impressed," Susan said. She looked around and gave the tunnel a cursory inspection. "Is this all there is to it? I don't see any bells or whistles or instructions on the wall. Do we need to do more to complete the process?"

"No," Bell said. "All you need to do is pass through the outer door. When you reach the backyard, take a moment to inspect your surroundings. Look first and foremost for nosy neighbors, people who may wonder why three women carrying suitcases are exiting the basement of an unoccupied house. If the coast is clear, walk as quickly as you can to the street in front of the house. This house is clearly marked on the map in the envelope, as are two car dealerships, a bank, and a nearby grocery store with payphones."

"What if the coast is *not* clear? What if neighbors see us and ask us questions?"

"Use your judgment. If you can talk your way out of the situation, then do so. If you can't, then turn around. Return to the house. The key and the crystals will allow you to reenter the tunnel and the basement."

"What if the nosy neighbors follow us?" Susan asked.

"Don't give them the chance. Enter the tunnel as quickly as you can and shut the door. By the time you dig out your crystals, you'll be back in the present day."

Susan smiled at Bell.

"Thank you, Professor. Thank you again."

"You're welcome," Bell said. "Now do us all a favor and have the trip of a lifetime."

"We will."

Bell stepped into the chamber and shook Susan's hand.

"Remember, Mrs. Peterson, the world you know is only a letter away."

"I won't forget," Susan said.

Bell retreated to the doorway and smiled at the intrepid time travelers one last time. He then stepped into the white room, grabbed the door, and closed it slowly.

Susan felt her stomach drop the second she heard the inner door shut. She didn't know what lay beyond the outer door, but she knew she was about to find out.

"What should we do, Mom?" Amanda asked.

Susan smiled at her daughter through the gloom.

"We should do what the professor told us to do. We should walk through that door and have the trip of a lifetime," Susan said. "Do you want me to go first?"

Amanda nodded nervously.

"Yes."

"OK then," Susan said. "Make way."

When Amanda and Elizabeth stepped aside, Susan walked to the far side of the tunnel that a not-so-mad scientist had built. She put her hand on a sturdy knob, turned it to the right, and opened a door that seemed as old and heavy as the gate to a castle.

Susan stepped outside and quickly shielded her eyes from the sun, which loomed higher in the sky than it had just forty minutes earlier. She took that as a sign that the hour had changed, if not the day, the month, and the year.

Then she looked at a series of rising brick steps and noticed another change. Weeds shot up from nearly every crack in what was once a flawless stairway. If new owners had assumed control of the property, they hadn't kept it up.

Susan ascended the stairs, lowered her suitcase to a weedy lawn, and surveyed her surroundings. She did not see nosy neighbors or neighbors of any kind, but she did see a neighborhood that looked much older than the one she had driven to.

No matter where she looked, Susan saw differences. Victorian mansions stood next to newer Craftsman bungalows. Utility poles lined wider streets and towered over roadsters with rumble seats and white wire-spoke wheels. Even the Painted Lady looked different. With weathered siding and cracked windows, it looked more like a house in need of a wrecking ball than an architectural treasure in need of restoration.

This is real.

Susan glanced at Amanda and Elizabeth, who stood at the bottom of the stairs. She smiled and summoned them with a hand.

"Come on up," Susan said. "It's safe."

"Are you sure?" Elizabeth asked.

"I'm positive. Come on."

Susan watched with fascination as Amanda led Elizabeth up the steps. She could tell just by looking at their faces that they were apprehensive and excited. When they reached the top of the stairs, she stepped back to give them some room.

Amanda didn't wait to ask questions. She dropped her suitcase and walked rapidly to the middle of the yard, where she held out her hands and spun around.

"This is real," Amanda said. "This is freaking real!"

"It sure looks like it," Susan said.

"I can't believe it. I was sure this was a scam. I thought the professor was putting us on, but he wasn't. He wasn't at all. We really did it. We really traveled through time!"

Susan smiled, sighed, and then stepped toward Amanda. She hadn't seen her cynical daughter this excited since she was a young girl and wanted to bask in her joy. She laughed when the college graduate squealed like a first-grader.

"Does this beat a day at the beach?" Susan asked.

Amanda beamed.

"Oh, Mom, this beats everything!"

Susan threw an arm over Amanda's shoulders and walked her back to the stairway. She needed only a second to see that Elizabeth had processed the situation differently.

"Mother? Are you OK? You're crying."

Susan released Amanda and moved quickly to comfort Elizabeth. She put her hands on her mother's shoulders and turned her so that she could see her face.

"Mom? I asked you a question. Are you all right?"

Elizabeth turned away to hide her tears. When she gazed again at Susan, she did so with eyes that revealed happiness, sadness, and understanding.

"I'm fine, dear. I'm fine," Elizabeth said. "I'm just coming to grips with the truth."

"What do you mean? What truth?"

Elizabeth sighed.

"I'm really going to see my parents again. I'm going to see myself."

In that instant, Susan realized that the trip was far more than a vacation to an exotic destination or a spin through a funhouse of time. It was a sentimental journey of the highest order. She smiled, pulled her mother close, and kissed her on the head.

"Yes, you are, Mom. Yes, you are," Susan said. "Now let's go buy a car and get this show on the road. I think we're all going to see a lot of things."

11: SUSAN

Hollywood, California – Friday, September 16, 1938

Susan watched with amusement as four smiling, uniformed men swarmed around her car and fussed over her like servants attending to a queen. Of all the sights she had seen since emerging from the time tunnel, few brought a smile to her face faster than full-service gas stations.

She waved at the attendant wiping the windows of the 1938 Cadillac Sixty Special and then glanced at the ones filling the tank, checking the oil, and checking the pressure of the vehicle's whitewall tires. She turned to the history major in the front passenger seat.

"I think they like us," Susan said.

Amanda smiled.

"I think they like *you*. Even Mr. Squeegee is checking you out."

"He must like my dress."

"He likes something," Elizabeth said from the back seat.

Susan laughed.

"Keep it clean, Mom. You don't want your granddaughter to think you're a dirty old woman, do you?"

"Of course I do."

Susan laughed again. She was happy to see her mother in good spirits. Elizabeth had pretty much kept to herself since arriving in 1938, speaking only about the trip ahead, Princeton, and meeting her parents, who had undoubtedly begun the long process of leaving Europe in the wake of Nazi Germany's annexation of Austria.

Susan stuck her nose out her open window and inhaled the strong but strangely refreshing aroma of oil, grease, and leaded gasoline. She didn't even bother asking the attendants for an unleaded alternative. Alternatives wouldn't appear for another thirty-four years.

Getting used to new smells was just one of many things the women had done since walking out of Geoffrey Bell's mansion. They had also purchased a car, obtained two driver's licenses, and stayed overnight in a Hollywood motor court that looked like the setting for a postcard.

Buying the car, of course, had been the first order of business. After spending an hour walking around Bell's neighborhood and soaking up the sights, the time travelers had walked to a grocery store, called a cab, and asked the driver to take them to Figueroa Street, where more than a dozen auto dealerships awaited their attention.

The women had considered a Plymouth Touring Sedan and a Chrysler Imperial before buying the Sixty Special, a plush, 130-horsepower, eight-cylinder extravagance, from a man with a firm handshake and a warm smile. By five thirty Thursday afternoon, Susan and Amanda had tested their new toy on more than a hundred miles of streets and highways. Elizabeth had wanted no part of driving something bigger than her bedroom.

Susan and Amanda had waited until Friday morning to wander into the Department of Motor Vehicles office on Santa Monica Boulevard and were surprised and pleased to find short lines, pleasant staff, and minimal scrutiny. Getting driver's licenses had been almost as easy as navigating the area's congestion-free roads. The women had needed only one day in Southern California to know that life in 1938 would be different.

Susan glanced at her daughter and watched with interest as she straightened her dress and then checked her face in the rear-view mirror. She laughed.

"Are you primping for our boys in blue?"

Amanda lifted her nose.

"We have a long drive ahead of us," Amanda said in a condescending but playful voice. "You never know who we'll meet."

"She's right," Elizabeth said. "This town is crawling with movie stars. I'd give my right arm to meet Clark Gable or Errol Flynn. Then again, I'd give my right arm for an air conditioner. It's hotter than blazes back here."

Susan looked over her shoulder at the sweaty senior in back.

"We'll keep the windows down, Mom. It's going to get a lot hotter when we drive through the Mojave, so be sure to let us know when you need a break."

"Count on it," Elizabeth said.

Susan laughed to herself. She wondered how her mother would handle riding in a hot car for more than three thousand miles, but she didn't wonder long. She knew Elizabeth Campbell was a tough woman who had faced much worse in nearly eighty years.

Susan straightened the mirror that Amanda had left askew, checked her own appearance, and then waved to Mr. Oil Check as he lowered the hood.

She gazed out the front window. In the distance, about thirty yards out, two men tore up a sidewalk with jackhammers and created more noise than dueling grunge bands. One bore a strong resemblance to Stanley Laurel, the other to Oliver Hardy. Both reminded the novelist that she was in a very different place.

When the chief attendant approached the window and asked for a dollar, Susan smiled, reached into her purse, and pulled out five. She didn't mind giving a large tip for a service that didn't require a gratuity. Her money would go a long way in an age when gasoline was ten cents a gallon.

"Keep the change, share it with the others, and buy something nice for your ladies," Susan said as she handed the bills to the man in the cap. "You boys did a fine job."

"Thank you, ma'am," Mr. Full Service said. "Is there anything else I can do for you?"

Yes. You can make me a latte.

"No. I think we're good to go."

The attendant furrowed his brows.

"I think we have everything we need," Susan said.

"Where are you ladies headed?"

"We're driving to Needles today and to the Grand Canyon tomorrow."

"So you're on vacation?" the attendant asked.

"You could say that."

"Then have an enjoyable trip."

"That's our plan," Susan said. She glanced at Amanda. "That's the plan."

12: AMANDA

Amanda knew she had a problem as soon as she turned off Route 66 and onto a road that looked more like a bike path than the principal highway to Grand Canyon National Park. The needle on the gas gauge had pushed its way left and reminded the driver that even luxury cars with eighteen-gallon tanks sometimes ran out of gas.

She glanced at her mother, who slept at her side, and then at her grandmother, who snoozed away in a back seat that had become her home away from home. She thought about waking them to alert them to the situation but decided to let them sleep.

There was nothing either Susan or Elizabeth could do in a situation like this. The women would either run out of gas before they reached the South Rim or they would not.

So Amanda eased up on the accelerator and tried to squeeze the most out of every drop in the tank. Settling into the seat of a car that drove like a dream, she gazed lazily at the road ahead and thought about the weeks and months to come.

She conceded there was much to think about. In the span of two weeks, she had gone from a college graduate bound for a California vacation and a District of Columbia job to an almost twenty-two-year-old in a frumpy dress bound for New Jersey in the Age of Steinbeck.

Amanda had seen more than a few reminders of that age on the long, hot drive from Los Angeles to Needles. In town after town, she saw the sights that defined a place and a time: antique trucks carrying onions, peaches, and melons to market; migrant workers picking lettuce, strawberries, and potatoes in open fields; and men, women, and children walking into and out of dusty, dilapidated shacks that they called home.

She recalled seeing *The Grapes of Wrath* in high school and writing an essay touting the film's effective use of stark black-and-white imagery. She hadn't seen much in black and white on the journey to Needles, but she had seen a lot that was stark. Even in a state where jobs were plentiful, signs of the Great Depression were everywhere.

Amanda looked out her window and saw that the sun had begun to dip below the western horizon. She had seen a lot of Old Sol on the drive through the desert but not at the end of a day. With a fiery red hue that matched the Cadillac's metallic Oxblood Maroon finish, the big ball was as impressive as any the driver had ever seen.

Then Amanda checked the rear-view mirror and saw something else she hadn't seen, at least not since she had stopped at a vegetable stand near Kingman. She saw a black Ford pickup with a dented left front fender. She didn't need a closer look to know that its operator had scars on his face and suggestive tattoos on his muscular arms.

When the truck picked up speed and approached the Cadillac, Amanda tapped on the brakes and slowed to forty miles per hour and then to thirty. She wanted to make it easy for the driver to pass and was both surprised and unnerved when he didn't.

What are you up to, mister?

Deciding that Scar Face was probably up to no good, Amanda stepped on the pedal and slowly increased her speed to fifty. She started to push it toward sixty when she remembered that she was riding on fumes and that faster speeds would only hasten the moment she ran out of gas.

Amanda glanced again in the mirror and noticed that the truck had pulled to within a few feet of the Cadillac. She also saw that Scar Face had a buddy, a burly, impatient gent who pounded the outside of his door with his open hand.

She grabbed a small carrot out of a paper bag that sat in the middle of the front seat and tried to calm her nerves by chewing it. When that didn't work, she grabbed another and pondered a future where she could summon help and frighten off tormentors with a single cell-phone call.

Amanda peered out her window at the western sky and saw the sun had finally dropped out of sight. Darkness was falling over the vast empty desert and falling at a time that was particularly inconvenient. She tapped the brakes again and slowed to thirty-five as the Cadillac entered a flat, straight stretch.

Amanda breathed a sigh of relief when Scar Face moved into the left lane and proceeded to pass but froze when he pulled even with the Sixty Special to get a better look at the disconcerted blonde. She resisted glancing at either the driver or his passenger but succumbed to curiosity after fifteen seconds.

She turned her head slowly to the left and saw that the passenger was a younger, less appealing version of the driver. Like Scar Face, he wore a white T-shirt, a crew cut, and an ugly smirk. Unlike his friend, he expressed himself with body parts. Junior stuck his closed hand out his window and moved it up and down in a jerking motion.

Amanda reached for another carrot, put it in her mouth, and whittled it down like a beaver gnawing on a birch tree. When she saw a blind curve in the distance, she stepped on the accelerator and forced Scar Face to drop behind her in the right lane.

The reprieve lasted only a minute. When the vehicles entered another flat, straight stretch, Scar Face moved into the left lane and again pulled even with the Sixty Special.

Amanda turned to face the passenger and tried to determine whether he was merely annoying or something worse. She got an answer quickly.

"How about coming with us, doll face?" Junior asked. "We'll show you a good time."

Amanda snapped her eyes forward and stepped on the pedal, but her actions only encouraged the scary young men. She watched with growing concern as Scar Face again pulled even and his sidekick resumed his pursuit of a nervous college graduate.

Junior stared at Amanda for a moment and gave her a sinister grin. Then he flashed her the victory sign and slithered a disgustingly long black tongue between his fingers.

Amanda thought about Jeanette Bell's decision to provide the travelers with modest attire and wondered if there was a dress on the planet frumpy enough to repel these cretins. She glanced again at Junior and decided there wasn't.

She reached to her right and prepared to wake Susan from her slumber, but she withdrew her hand when the pickup suddenly surged forward. When the truck sped away and disappeared into the near darkness, she let out a breath, grabbed another carrot, and returned her eyes to the road.

Amanda checked the gas gauge and saw that the needle had firmly attached itself to the line on the left. She wondered if gauges in 1938 were as precise as those in 2016 and prayed they were not. She didn't want any more excitement on this trip.

As soon as she rounded another bend, however, she got it. Seconds after she passed a pickup parked on the side of the road, the driver of the vehicle flipped on his headlights. Within a minute, Scar Face and Junior were back in the hunt.

Amanda reached again for her mother but pulled back her hand when she saw a green sign in the distance. She sighed and smiled when she drew close enough to read the sign's clear, welcoming message: GRAND CANYON 3 MILES. She was going to make it.

Scar Face wiped the smile from her face. He passed the Cadillac and slowed to thirty miles per hour, forcing Amanda to quickly hit the brakes. When he slowed to twenty, she veered into the left lane and started to pass. She didn't like the idea of driving in the wrong lane in limited visibility, but she liked the idea of stopping even less.

Amanda passed the pickup just as Scar Face attempted to block her way by driving in front of her. She reclaimed the right lane and pressed the pedal to the floor. She felt her heart race when the pickup closed the gap and then skip a beat when she heard a piston pop. She wasn't just driving on fumes anymore. She was driving on air.

Amanda eased up on the accelerator when she saw the lights of the village. She could now measure safety in terms of yards and not miles. When she passed the first of several buildings a minute later, she slowed to thirty and looked for the lodge. She found it immediately.

The time traveler turned into the parking lot of the lodge and watched with relief as Scar Face drove past and headed out of sight. She heard a second piston pop and then another as she navigated her way toward a lighted entry. She felt the car shudder as it rolled to a stop less than forty feet from the office door.

Frightened, relieved, and on the verge of tears, Amanda Peterson lowered her head and rested it on the steering wheel. She did not lift it again until she heard her mother stir and then greet her with a soothing voice.

"Are we at the lodge?" Susan asked.

"We're at the lodge," Amanda said.

"You don't look so good, honey. Are you OK?"

Amanda looked at her mother like she had just asked the dumbest question in history. Then she sighed, smiled, and nodded.

"I've never felt better."

13: SUSAN

Grand Canyon, Arizona – Friday, September 23, 1938

As she trudged up the narrow path three thousand feet above the Colorado River, Susan Peterson reminded herself of two facts. The first was that she was moderately acrophobic. The second was that she was no longer as fit and trim as when she was eighteen years old, when she had first been talked into hiking the Bright Angel Trail in Grand Canyon National Park.

She laughed at the thought of her 1986 visit to the park, which had technically not yet occurred, and picked up the pace. A moment later she caught up to the daughter who had talked her into this latest adventure and tapped her on the shoulder.

"Slow down, cowgirl, or you're going to leave your mama in the dust," Susan said.

Amanda turned around.

"Are you ready for a rest?"

Susan sighed.

"I was ready when we left Phantom Ranch."

Amanda laughed.

"There's a wide spot about a hundred yards up where we can stop and take a breather. Can you make it that far?"

"I've made it this far, haven't I?" Susan asked.

Amanda smiled.

"Let's go."

Ten minutes and *two* hundred yards later, the women climbed on a flat rock, opened their canteens, and replenished their fluids for the first time in nearly an hour. Susan could not remember a time when warm, coppery water tasted so sweet.

"Thanks for stopping," Susan said. "I don't have the energy I used to have."

"You're doing fine, Mom. I'm proud of you," Amanda said. "Next time we'll get Grandma to come. I'll put her on a mule myself if I have to."

Susan laughed when she thought about dinner Tuesday night, when Amanda had first proposed traveling to the bottom of the canyon. Elizabeth had given the idea ten seconds of thought before telling her daughter and granddaughter to "have a nice time." She had remained behind at the lodge to play cards with other seniors and view the world's largest chasm from the relative safety of its rim.

"I would pay to see that," Susan said.

Amanda smiled sadly.

"I'll bet you would."

Susan sipped from her canteen, gazed at the stunning rocks on the northern side of the canyon, and then turned to face her daughter. She was happy to see Amanda in relatively good spirits just days after a frightening encounter with two thugs in a truck.

Amanda had reported the incident to park police but had failed to find justice. Scar Face, Junior, and the dented Ford had vanished from the vicinity as quickly as they had appeared.

Susan studied Amanda more closely and saw her stare blankly into space. She could see that her daughter had moved on to a more serious matter. She was no doubt thinking of something she had not shared on the trip through the canyon.

"Are you thinking about the men who harassed you?" Susan asked.

"No," Amanda said. "I'm thinking about Dad. I'm thinking about how much he would have loved a hike like this."

Susan couldn't take issue with that. Bruce Peterson would have enjoyed the hike immensely and probably found a way to get Elizabeth on a mule. He had been an outdoorsman who rarely passed up an opportunity to see nature up close.

"Do you think about him a lot?" Susan asked. "You haven't talked about him much."

Amanda shifted her eyes from the canyon to Susan.

"I think about him every day, Mom. I think about all the good times we had when I was growing up and the support he provided after Brandon dumped me. I'm sad."

"Your tone suggests you're more than sad. Are you angry?"

"I'm very angry," Amanda said. "I'm angry that I won't have a father to walk me down the aisle or mentor my children. I'm angry I've been denied something so many other women my age take for granted."

"Is that all?" Susan asked.

"No. I'm also mad that Dad threw it all away. I will never understand why he did what he did. He had a family that loved him and supported him. He had everything."

"He did."

Susan paused for a moment to think about the husband she had loved, nurtured, and buried. She thought about the things he had done, both good and bad, and about how her life had changed since that awful morning in Wisconsin. Like many widows who had more living to do than dying, she also struggled with how best to proceed. When you had to reinvent yourself at age forty-eight, there was a lot to think about.

"Why do you think he did it?" Amanda asked. "Why do you think he cheated?"

Susan put her arm around her daughter.

"I don't know, honey. I really don't. I know only that men respond to middle age in different ways. Some count their blessings and embrace what they have. Others ask questions and look for answers in the wrong places. If something was missing from your father's life, it was something he didn't share with me."

Amanda stared at her mother.

"Did you love him?"

"You know I did," Susan said without hesitating. "I often wanted to wring his neck, but I never stopped loving him. I didn't stop loving him even after I learned of his affair. Despite what he did to me, I would have worked to save our marriage because life with him, in my humble opinion, would have still been better than life without him."

Amanda put her arm around her hiking buddy.

"I thought that was the case, but I needed to hear you say it. I needed to know there wasn't more to Dad's affair than a simple error in judgment," Amanda said. She pulled Susan close. "I love you, Mom."

Susan kissed Amanda on the head.

"I love you too, sweetheart."

Susan watched two strapping men in khaki shirts and shorts approach from the trail below. She smiled and waved at the hikers as they passed the rock.

"You're shameless, Mother," Amanda said a moment later. "Those guys are my age."

Susan laughed.

"I'm just being friendly. There's no harm in that, is there?"

"I suppose not."

Susan brushed off her pants, stood up, and gazed at the stunning landscape ahead. She saw sagebrush, switchbacks, and steep terrain but not a whole lot of people. Nearly all the hikers they had followed up the trail had disappeared from sight.

"Do you think we're getting close?" Susan asked.

"We're getting close. We should reach the top in an hour or two," Amanda said. "Why do you ask? Are you in a hurry?"

"I am."

"You're eager to get to the rim?"

"I'm eager to resume our journey," Susan said. "I think we both need to think a little less about the past and a little more about the weeks ahead. There is an adventure waiting for us out there – a big one. I think it's time we gave it a loving embrace."

14: ELIZABETH

Miami, Oklahoma – Saturday, October 1, 1938

Sitting on a bench in Riverview Park, Elizabeth Campbell tried to reconcile what she saw with what she remembered. She succeeded with minimal effort.

She knew, of course, that the scene was not the same. She needed only to glance at the cars in a nearby parking lot to know that she was in 1938 and not 1958.

Yet every time she saw a couple sit at a table or spread a blanket on the grass, she saw a man in khaki slacks and a blonde in a pleated pink dress. She saw birds and bees and a picnic that went awry. She saw one of the most memorable days of her life.

"Does this place look familiar?" Susan asked.

Elizabeth nodded.

"It does. There are fewer trees and picnic tables and not as many paths, but otherwise it's the same park. I'll never forget this place."

Amanda shielded her eyes from the afternoon sun and surveyed the sprawling park, which hugged the Neosho River on the south side of town. She maintained her gaze for a moment, dropped her hand, and turned to face Elizabeth.

"Where did you leave your ring, Grandma?"

"I left it over there," Elizabeth said. She pointed to a table next to three parked cars. "Cal and I sat where that family is sitting now. Had we picked a different table, one farther from the lot, we might have found the ring where I had left it."

Susan smiled.

"It's funny how things work out."

"What do you mean?" Elizabeth asked.

"What I mean is had you not left your ring on that picnic table in 1958, Professor Bell would have never been able to convince us to change our vacation plans. We would all be back in Illinois in 2016 doing the same old things. We wouldn't be here, in 1938, having the time of our lives," Susan said. After a few seconds of silence, she tilted her head and looked at her mother. "We *are* having the time of are lives, aren't we?"

"We are," Elizabeth replied. "I know I am."

Elizabeth meant it too. She admitted she could have done without the hot drives through the desert or the stomach bug she had battled between Albuquerque and Tucumcari, but she could not deny she was having a good time. She was having the kind of adventure most people could only dream about or read about in a science fiction novel.

She laughed to herself as she recalled the things she had done, including teaching hikers how to stretch, drinking whiskey with a sheriff, and singing a duet with a cowboy named Bob. The two had drawn a rousing ovation at a bar in New Mexico.

Elizabeth never could have been so bold in 2016, where her carousing alone would have prompted tongues to wag. In 1938, however, she could do anything she wanted. She was an anonymous free spirit, a woman accountable to no one except a daughter and a granddaughter who would no doubt push their own envelopes in the coming months.

She looked forward to driving the rest of Route 66, visiting Chicago, and settling down in New Jersey. She really looked forward to meeting her parents and younger self, even if she still had to work out the where, when, and how.

Elizabeth did *not* look forward to other things, such as keeping knowledge of future events to herself. When she had read that morning about British Prime Minister Neville Chamberlain signing a peace treaty with Adolf Hitler, she had wanted to call the British embassy and tell the ambassador that it was a bad deal.

She cared about the fate of others, even those in Germany and Japan, but she knew it was not her place to change history or spare any individual from the pain to come. If she honored only one of Geoffrey Bell's Ten Commandments, she would honor that one.

When the family at the picnic table finished their meal and headed for their car, Elizabeth got up from her bench and walked to the table. She did not tell Susan or Amanda what she was doing or why. She simply left.

Elizabeth reached the sacred spot a moment later, brushed some crumbs off the bench with her hand, and sat in a place that had been etched in her mind for fifty-eight years. She smiled at Susan and Amanda when they cautiously approached the table.

"Can't a woman commune with the spirits alone?"

"Do you want us to wait in the car?" Susan asked.

"No," Elizabeth said. "I want you to join me."

She motioned to the others and watched with amusement as they took their places on the opposite bench. Susan and Amanda apparently did not want to disrupt any good vibes by occupying the wrong plank of pine.

"So this is the table?" Susan asked.

"This is the table."

"How do you know?"

"I know because of these initials," Elizabeth said as she pointed to an "E.C." carved in the tabletop. "I remember them because they reminded me of my new name. When Cal and I stopped here, I was no longer Elizabeth Wagner. I was Elizabeth Campbell."

"That's so sweet," Amanda said. "I can't believe you remember things like that. I can't remember where I leave my car keys from day to day."

"You remember a lot of things when you're in love, dear. I know I did."

Amanda settled into her seat and smiled warmly.

"You know, Grams, you've never told me the whole story about your elopement. I've just heard bits and pieces over the years. Why don't you tell me now?"

"Are you sure you want to hear it?"

"Of course I do."

"All right then, I'll tell you," Elizabeth said. "You know, of course, that your grandfather and I were not married here. We were married in Chicago."

"I know," Amanda said.

"What you probably don't know is that we were married by a justice of the peace, a justice we found on a Tuesday morning. We were not married in a church because no priest would marry us and no Protestant minister would marry us on short notice."

"I take it that your parents didn't approve."

"That's putting it mildly," Elizabeth said.

"They didn't like Grandpa?"

Elizabeth shook her head.

"No. That wasn't it at all. They liked him. They liked his intelligence and his kind nature. They liked how he treated me," Elizabeth said. "They did *not* like the fact he was a Lutheran who did not intend to convert to Roman Catholicism."

"So you just eloped?"

"We eloped. When it became clear that my parents would never approve of your grandfather, I made a decision that changed my life. I finished my sophomore year at Northwestern and accepted his proposal."

"He had already proposed?" Amanda asked.

Elizabeth nodded.

"I had what some might call a standing invitation."

"What did you do then?"

"I told Cal that I wanted to marry in June and then drive to California," Elizabeth said. "I told him that if I couldn't have a big church wedding, then I wanted one hell of a honeymoon."

Amanda grinned.

"So you got your kicks on Route 66?"

"I got more than that, dear."

Susan laughed.

"Why don't you tell her about the hobo, Mom?"

"What hobo?" Amanda asked.

Elizabeth smiled.

"Your mother means the 'gentleman' we picked up outside St. Louis."

Amanda stared at Elizabeth with incredulous eyes.

"You picked up a hobo on your honeymoon?"

Elizabeth laughed.

"We did. When we pulled out of St. Louis on our third day, we saw a man on the side of the road who looked an awful lot like Roy Rogers – a young Roy Rogers who sported a knapsack and a ten o'clock shadow and smelled like Trigger."

"You did this on your *honeymoon*?" Amanda asked.

"Yes," Elizabeth said. "I did not want to pick up a hitchhiker, but your grandfather talked me into it. You know how he was. He could never say no to anyone in need. So we put Roy Rogers in back, held our noses, and took off."

"Oh, my," Amanda said. She giggled. "How long did you keep him?"

"We kept him all day. When we reached Rolla, Missouri, our original destination, Mr. Rogers kindly informed us that he really wanted to travel to Amarillo. We drew the line at Miami and left him at the bus station with a ten-dollar bill."

"That's a long drive, Grandma."

"It's three hundred and ten miles, to be exact," Elizabeth said. "We entertained Mr. Rogers for eight hours. I don't remember a longer drive in my life."

Amanda laughed again.

"There's a special place in heaven for you. I know it."

Elizabeth smiled.

"There had better be."

Amanda planted her elbows on the tabletop and rested her chin on folded hands. She looked at her grandmother with eyes that revealed love, admiration, and respect.

"I'm sure the rest of your trip was wonderful."

"It was," Elizabeth said. "We arrived in Los Angeles eight days later and spent two glorious weeks in Southern California. Whatever doubts I had about your grandfather and rushing into marriage dissolved that summer in the ocean surf."

"That's beautiful," Amanda said. "I hope it's that way for me someday."

"It will be, dear. It will be."

"Thanks for sharing the story. I see now why you look at those days fondly."

"It was a happy time," Elizabeth said.

"It still must have been tough though," Amanda said.

"What do you mean?"

"I mean dealing with your parents afterward. I'm sure it was awkward seeing them again after you defied them on something so important."

"It was," Elizabeth said. "When we visited Princeton later that year, my father refused to recognize our marriage. He made Cal stay in a hotel. My mother wasn't much better. She forced herself to be civil and pleasant. I never again slept in my parents' house."

"That's sad. That's really sad," Amanda said. "Did things improve?"

Elizabeth shook her head.

"My parents effectively disowned me and focused their attention on my brother, whom they considered 'salvageable.' They were right too. You probably know that your great uncle Erwin once trained to be a priest."

"No," Amanda said. "I *didn't* know that."

"Well, he did. He completed a full year at a seminary in Philadelphia," Elizabeth said. "He wanted to do missionary work in Africa and Asia, but when our parents died a few months later, he drifted away from the church. Like me, he never really made his peace with the past."

Amanda smiled and took Elizabeth's hand.

"That's going to change on this trip, Grandma. That's going to change real quick."

Elizabeth turned away for a moment as tears filled her eyes. She gazed at the slow-moving river and the swaying trees before returning to her granddaughter.

"I hope so, dear," Elizabeth said. "I truly do."

15: SUSAN

S usan smiled as she watched the natives scatter across an open field. She had seen them in the wild many times and even seen them at night, but in forty-eight years on God's green earth, she had never seen them like this. She had never seen the Chicago Cubs play in the World Series.

"You can pinch me now, Mother," Susan said with a laugh.

"No, dear," Elizabeth said. "You can pinch *me*."

Susan put her left arm around Elizabeth and her right around Amanda. She admitted that her seat in Section 218 was less than ideal. Susan sat behind two obnoxious drunks and a decidedly obtrusive support column. She had to crane her neck to see second base.

That was all right. Even obnoxious drunks and obtrusive support columns could not dampen the moment. Susan was doing something no one born after 1945 had ever done. She was witnessing a special kind of history and doing so with the people she loved.

The three adventurers had come to Chicago after spending four days enjoying the splendors of three more states. Susan had forgotten how beautiful the more rural parts of Kansas, Missouri, and Illinois could be and found towns like Galena, Carthage, and Odell as charming as St. Louis without its signature landmark and Chicago without its glass-and-steel towers.

Susan had forgotten that St. Louis would not open its Gateway Arch for another twenty-seven years, just as she had forgotten that Chicago would not push its already impressive skyline to the stars for another sixty. She liked those differences almost as much as she liked driving through relatively light traffic on the Mother Road. As far as she was concerned, the interstate freeway system and the traffic it carried could wait for another day.

Susan also liked the changes she saw in her traveling companions. Elizabeth had become more daring and vocal on the trip, Amanda more candid and relaxed. Each of the women had used the journey to clear emotional cobwebs, rediscover strengths, and find themselves in ways they could not in the faster, more intense, less personal world of 2016.

Susan was just as pleased to see that other things had *not* changed, such as her family's love for the national pastime. When she had asked Elizabeth and Amanda if they wanted to drive to Chicago a day early to see a baseball game, they said yes. When she told them the game was the second of the 1938 World Series, they said, "Step on the gas!"

By the time the women reached their hotel late Wednesday night, the question was not whether they would go to Wrigley Field but rather how much they would pay to step inside. In the end, they gained admission for a song. They found a scalper on Clark Street who sold them tickets for ten dollars each – or just double their face value.

Susan scanned her surroundings and soaked up the sights. She saw men in wool suits and fedoras, women in long dresses and floppy straw hats, and roving concessionaires in equally snappy uniforms. Even the gentleman manning a hot dog cart a few rows below looked sharp. Wearing spotless white slacks, a crisp white shirt, and a matching soda-jerk hat, he did a brisk business with fans walking to their seats.

Susan turned from the spectators and vendors to the players on the field. Like the people in the stands, the men in baggy pants looked like extras from a movie – a movie that had been playing for three weeks and would likely play for several more months.

The time traveler looked at the visitors first and somehow found them lacking. Though the Yankees featured *six* future Hall of Famers in Bill Dickey, Joe DiMaggio, Lou Gehrig, Lefty Gomez, Joe Gordon, and Red Ruffing, they seemed less impressive in their road grays than in their iconic pinstripes.

Susan thought the Cubs looked spiffier in their home whites with the blue sleeves, socks, and caps, though she freely admitted she was hopelessly biased. She had been hopelessly biased in favor of all things Chicago since 1973, when her father had taken her to her first Major League Baseball game at the tender age of five.

She thought of Calvin Campbell in the bottom of the first, when the Cubs scored a run, and again in the top of the second, when New York answered with two of its own. She thought of how much he would have loved watching Dizzy Dean pitch against greats like DiMaggio and Gehrig in a game as important as this.

Susan also thought about her last visit to the Lake Forest cemetery, when Elizabeth had told her about Calvin's infidelity. She had found the revelation shocking because, like many women, she had viewed her father as an infallible authority figure and not as a man susceptible to weakness, temptation, and errors of judgment.

Susan pondered the fallibility of men and errors of judgment as she watched Dean retire Gomez, his pitching counterpart, to end the second inning. Then she thought of something far more interesting and arguably just as relevant to her life.

Somewhere beyond this stadium filled with *Guys and Dolls* extras was a young Chicago couple celebrating the first birthday of a son named Calvin. The couple would raise him in the suburbs, guide him through the church, and send him to Northwestern University, where he would study history, meet a girl from Princeton, New Jersey, and enter the field of law.

Susan looked at her mother, who seemed transfixed by the Yankees, *her* childhood team, and wondered if she had made the same connection. She decided that she probably had but concluded that it didn't matter.

Elizabeth would not pay a visit to the birthday boy – at least not on this day. She would consider meeting her infant husband bad form, even if she considered meeting her infant *self* the height of good taste. Like Susan and Amanda, she would pick and choose from an array of time-travel options while keeping an eye out for unintended consequences.

Susan gave the matter another moment and then thought of something else. Though that something was less important than family reunions in the grand scheme of things, it was far more immediate. Susan tried her best to contain a smile.

"You're smiling, Mom," Amanda said. "Do you have something good to share?"

Susan laughed.

"I guess I do."

"What's that?"

"I was just thinking it's a good thing we promised Professor Bell that we would behave ourselves on this trip," Susan said.

"Why do you say that?" Amanda asked.

Susan looked at nearby fans before answering.

"I say it because I know who wins this series."

"You do?"

"I do," Susan said. "The Yankees win in four."

She grinned.

"We could have made a bundle."

16: SUSAN

Glencoe, Illinois – Monday, October 24, 1938

As she walked north with her family on the Street of Dreams that locals still called Sheridan Road, Susan realized that French novelist Jean-Baptiste Alphonse Karr got it right. The more things changed, the more they really did stay the same. At least they did in a place that was – and would continue to be – one of America's priciest neighborhoods.

Susan glanced at the Colonial Revival mansion next to her childhood home and saw that it looked a lot like the residence of her future best friend. She had spent many a night in the bedroom overlooking the brick U-shaped driveway and more than a few afternoons in back, where the Mergenthaler family maintained the biggest pool in town.

Susan didn't think she would find Jenny Mergenthaler sunbathing on the porch, at least not until 1980, but she found the possibility pleasing nonetheless. She liked the idea of revisiting her past, even if that past was technically the future. She pondered that mind-twisting fact for a few seconds and then turned to the woman at her right.

"Does this street bring back memories?" Susan asked.

"You know it does," Elizabeth said.

Susan smiled and put her arm around her mother. She wanted to say more but decided to wait until the time travelers reached the next property, the turnaround point in their half-mile walk. She knew that everyone would have something to say there.

Susan stopped in front of a cobblestone driveway a moment later and took a long look at the house her father had bought in 1976. Like virtually every other home on the road, it was large, eclectic, and over-the-top extravagant. Unlike most of the other residences, it celebrated the past more than the present. With dormers, bay windows, and an arched doorway, the gray-brick residence was suburban Chicago's answer to a Yorkshire estate.

"I wonder who lives here now," Susan said. "Do you know, Mom?"

"I don't," Elizabeth said.

Amanda walked fifteen feet to a red mailbox that looked more like a birdhouse than a receptacle for letters and packages. She examined one side of the box and smiled.

"The Petersons live here," Amanda said.

"Are you kidding?" Susan asked.

"I don't kid."

Susan tilted her head.

"Is Peterson spelled with an 'o'?"

"It is," Amanda said. She grinned as she walked back to the others. "Maybe Dad lived here before *you* did. Maybe he came from old money."

Susan laughed.

"I don't think so," Susan said. "Your father didn't have *any* money, old or new, when he was young. Even at Northwestern, he was poor."

"I'll second that," Elizabeth said dryly.

Susan smiled wistfully as she let her mind wander.

The Bruce Peterson she knew in college had not been a man of means. He had been a scrappy student who subsisted on a partial scholarship and a work-study job and counted a squeaky bike, a shoddy wardrobe, and a broken guitar among his worldly possessions. Bruce had not been much better off when he had asked Susan to marry him in the spring of 1991, but he had not seen that as a problem. He had been confident that he would someday be able to provide for her – and he had been right.

Susan remembered arguing with her parents many times about Bruce's prospects for success and, by extension, her own prospects for a comfortable life. She had insisted that money didn't matter. Calvin and Elizabeth Campbell had insisted it did. Susan considered turning Bruce down, but in the end she did what her mother had done. She threw caution to the wind and cast her lot with a boy who made her smile.

She had done what she had wanted to do and would do again if given the chance. She had yielded to her heart and not to her head and followed her dreams. Susan looked away from the house and admired the foliage that lined the street. The trees of Illinois had changed dramatically during her visit. In less than three weeks, they had traded their soothing green coats for ones of yellow, orange, and red. They reminded Susan that a new season was under way and that it was probably time to get moving.

Susan gazed at the trees for another moment and then turned her attention to more important matters. She looked at Elizabeth and Amanda, who gazed at the house.

"Do you want to keep going or head back to the car?" Susan asked.

"I vote for the car," Elizabeth said.

Susan looked at her daughter.

"Amanda?"

"I'm with Grandma," Amanda said. "We've seen what we came to see. We might as well go back to the hotel and pack for the rest of the trip."

"OK then. Let's go," Susan said. "Before we leave, though, I want to mail a letter."

"You want to mail a *letter*? You don't know anyone here."

Susan smiled.

"Of course I do. I know Professor Bell."

Susan reached into her purse. She retrieved a small envelope that was addressed to a post-office box in Los Angeles, a box Geoffrey Bell said he would check periodically.

"You really wrote him a letter?" Amanda asked.

"Yes. I did. I did what he asked me to do. I plan to write more too."

"You're thinking about that reporter, aren't you? You're thinking that maybe he and his son didn't come back from 1900."

"I'm thinking about *us*," Susan said. "I want Professor Bell to know where we are and what we're doing in case we run into trouble."

"Then let's find a post office," Amanda said.

"I have a better idea."

"What?"

"I'll show you."

Susan walked to the mailbox that looked like a birdhouse, opened the door, and placed the letter inside. She shut the door and flipped up the flag.

"Uh, Mom, you can't just put a letter in a private mailbox," Amanda said. "It's illegal."

"You're right, honey. It is. I'll probably do time with Al Capone."

Elizabeth laughed and looked at Amanda.

"Let her be, dear. Your mother is on a roll."

"We'll be fine," Susan said.

Amanda smiled, folded her arms, and gave her mother a scolding glance.

"It's still not right."

"I disagree, Amanda," Susan said. "It's as right as rain."

"What do you mean?"

"What I mean, dear daughter, is that this mailbox belongs to the Petersons," Susan said. She laughed. "Today it belongs to *us*."

17: AMANDA

Mercer County, New Jersey — Sunday, October 30, 1938

Amanda thought of George Washington as she drove across the bridge and entered the last state in her family's twelve-state, forty-five-day tour of the United States.

Like America's Revolutionary War general, she crossed the Delaware River on a cold, dark night with Trenton on her mind. Unlike the Founding Father and first president, she did so in a gas-guzzling Cadillac that was running on fumes.

Amanda felt a sense of déjà vu as she glanced at the gas gauge and then at the road ahead. For the second time in six weeks, she had pushed the Sixty Special to its limit and invited a potentially unpleasant outcome.

She looked in the rear-view mirror, checked the highway for unwanted company, and sighed when she saw a slow-moving sedan and not a fast-moving pickup. She considered that a good thing. The last thing she wanted or needed now was a close encounter with a tattoo-covered bully or a finger-licking cretin.

Amanda knew that most young men weren't boorish, obscene, and obsessed with sex, but she had to admit she was having some doubts. Four of the last five guys she had dated had dumped her when she had refused their advances. The one who hadn't had asked her to "pose" for his "site." When it came to finding men who liked her for her brains, she had more difficulty than a cheerleader in a room full of frat boys and football players.

Amanda set aside her unsatisfactory social life and focused on the task at hand. Following the signs to Princeton, she made her way through Trenton with ease.

She had studied a road map during the last stop, in Norristown, and felt confident she could reach her grandmother's hometown without added

90

assistance. She felt less confident about finding an open gas station at eight fifteen on a Sunday night.

Amanda looked for a port in the storm but found only dimmed signs, empty lots, and closed doors. When she reached the northern fringes of the state capital, she decided to wing it and head straight for Princeton. She figured if the Cadillac could travel twenty miles on empty through the Arizona desert, it could probably do the same through the farmland of New Jersey.

Amanda turned onto Route 583 and then directed her attention to the sleeping beauties in the Sixty Special. Elizabeth snoozed away in the front passenger seat. Susan did the same in back. They snored in stereo and provided the driver with comic relief.

A mile into the fifteen-mile final stretch, Amanda settled into her seat and pondered the weeks ahead. She looked forward to spending some quality time in a college town, making new friends, and witnessing history as only a time traveler could witness it.

Amanda took a moment to examine her surroundings and noticed that the landscape on both sides of the highway had become darker and more remote. Instead of streetlights, business signs, and beams from passing cars, she saw the silhouettes of leafless trees, farmhouses, and barns.

Figuring that she wouldn't see much more the rest of the way, Amanda stepped on the pedal. She pushed the car to fifty when she entered a straight stretch but slowed to forty and then to thirty when she saw a long line of stationary cars. Thirty seconds later, she pulled up behind a yellow coupe and brought the Cadillac to a stop.

"What's going on?" Amanda asked as she pounded the wheel with her hands.

"Did you say something, honey?"

Amanda glanced over her shoulder and saw Susan sit up in the back seat.

"Yes. I did. I want to know why a million cars are stopped in the middle of nowhere on a Sunday night. This road was free of traffic a minute ago."

"I'm sure there was an accident," Susan said.

"I don't think so. There's something else going on."

Amanda rolled down her window and stuck her head into the cool autumn air. She looked ahead as far as she could and saw what she had expected to see: a seemingly endless stream of red taillights. Then she pushed her head a little further out the window and saw something she *didn't* expect to see: oncoming traffic.

Three automobiles emerged from a dip in the road and approached the Cadillac at a brisk clip. Four other cars followed suit. By the time Amanda turned off the ignition to save what little gas she had left, several more vehicles zipped by. If an accident was stopping traffic on Route 583, it was stopping it in only one direction.

Amanda started to say something to Susan but stopped when she saw Elizabeth stir in her seat, sit up, and look around. She appeared as bewildered as the rest of the family.

"Where are we?" Elizabeth asked.

"We're on Route 583 between Trenton and Princeton," Amanda said.

"Why have we stopped? What's going on?"

"I don't know, Grandma. Mom thinks there's an accident ahead, but I think it's something else. The traffic heading to Trenton hasn't slowed a bit."

Amanda returned her eyes to the highway and saw that the stream of cars coming her way had grown. Some moved at a steady pace. Others advanced in fits and starts. A few pulled off to the side of the road for reasons that still weren't clear.

Sounds pierced the night air with annoying regularity. Westbound drivers unhappy with the pace and eastbound drivers unhappy with the stoppage honked their horns, creating a cacophony of displeasure on what was once a quiet rural road.

"Something is definitely going on," Susan said.

Elizabeth glanced at her daughter and then directed her eyes forward. She peered out the front window, shielded her eyes from oncoming headlights, and finally looked at the driver.

"What day is it?" Elizabeth asked.

"It's Sunday," Amanda said.

"I mean what's the date?"

"It's October 30."

"I thought so."

Amanda watched with curiosity as a smile formed on her grandmother's face. The smile quickly grew into a grin.

"Why are you smiling, Grandma? This is not a smiling matter," Amanda said. "We may run out of gas on this godforsaken road."

Elizabeth laughed.

"I don't mean to downplay our plight, dear. It's just that I remembered something."

"What?" Amanda asked.

"I just remembered what happened on this date."

"Stop speaking in riddles, Grams. If you know why we're stuck in a traffic jam, then say something. *What* is going on?"

Elizabeth beamed.

"We're being invaded. The Martians have taken New Jersey."

"The what?" Amanda asked.

"The Martians," Elizabeth replied. She laughed. "We may only have minutes before the little green men have us for dinner. Grovers Mill is just a few miles away."

Amanda needed only a few seconds to figure it out. She turned on the radio, twisted the tuning knob, and navigated a sea of static until she found history on the airwaves.

She listened carefully as an announcer described an invasion that had spread from the hamlet of Grovers Mill to all of central New Jersey. The "journalist" reported details of pitched battles between the army and the invaders from Mars and warned radio listeners that the visiting team was on the move.

"This is the *War of the Worlds* broadcast," Amanda said.

"It certainly is," Elizabeth replied.

"So why is everyone freaking out?"

"They are 'freaking out,' as you put it, because they think the invasion is real."

Amanda turned up the volume on the radio and quickly learned that the situation had worsened. The aliens had cut communications from Pennsylvania to the Atlantic, torn up railroad tracks, and killed several thousand men in Grovers Mill alone.

Amanda looked at Susan and Elizabeth and saw amusement in their eyes. They smiled like women who had bet on the Yankees to win the Series or the Martians to sweep the world in four games. Elizabeth stifled a laugh with a hand.

Others on Route 583 did not share their nonchalance. If they weren't running around like headless chickens, they were driving their vehicles like people possessed.

When Amanda saw a westbound car suddenly veer off the road ahead, she opened her door and stepped outside. A moment later, she stuck her head through the window.

"I'll be right back," Amanda said.

"Where are you going?" Susan asked.

"I'm going to check on that car and make sure no one got hurt."

Amanda stepped away from the Cadillac and started walking down the centerline toward the commotion ahead. What she saw boggled her mind.

Two men argued over a fender bender and threatened each other with fists. A frantic woman carried her baby from car to car. Farther up the road, two more women pleaded with their male companions to "get us out of here now!" Several others honked their horns, swore like sailors, or threatened to call the police.

You people are morons.

Amanda picked up the pace and walked toward the car that had gone off the road. As she drew closer, she saw two dapper young men jump on the hood of a late-model Ford Woody Wagon and pull two bottles from a small brown box. The larger of the two spoke up as soon as she crossed the road and approached the vehicle.

"Hey, sweetheart, you want a beer? We have plenty."

"No, thanks. I just came over to see if you were OK. I saw your car swerve into the field," Amanda said. She raised a brow. "I see you're just fine."

"We're mighty fine," Big Dapper said. He smiled and took a swig. "We just pulled off the road to enjoy the show."

Amanda glanced at the chaos and saw it had not abated. The honking horns barely drowned out the screams and shouts and the radio broadcast that emanated from every vehicle.

"These people don't really believe the Martians are coming, do they?" Amanda asked.

"Some do. Some are pissing their britches," Little Dapper said with a thick Texas drawl. "They heard the big-eyed buggers are coming for the women and children."

Big Dapper laughed.

"What about the people heading east?" Amanda asked. "Why are they driving *toward* Grovers Mill?"

"They want to see the buggers," Little Dapper said. "Some want to see them. Some want to shoot them. We saw at least a dozen rifles coming in."

Amanda laughed.

"This is too much."

"You're not from around here, are you?" Little Dapper asked.

Amanda shook her head.

"No. I'm from Chicago. I'm Amanda Peterson, in case you care."

Little Dapper jumped off the hood and shook Amanda's hand.

"I'm Ted Fiske. It's nice to meet you."

"It's nice to meet you too," Amanda said. "Who's your buddy?"

"He's a Martian I picked up," Ted said. "He goes by Bill Green."

"Green, huh? Maybe he *is* a Martian."

Ted laughed.

"It wouldn't surprise me."

Amanda turned toward the Woody.

"Well, hello, Bill Green. It's a pleasure."

Bill slid off the hood and shook Amanda's hand.

"The pleasure is mine."

"Do you guys go to school around here?" Amanda asked.

Ted nodded.

"We do. We're seniors at Princeton. How about you?"

Amanda sighed.

"I'm just a visitor. I'm visiting Princeton with my family."

"Well, I hope your visit is a long and happy one," Ted said.

Amanda smiled.

She didn't doubt for a minute that these Martian watchers had more on their minds than extraterrestrials, but for once she didn't care. She looked at Bill and Ted and then at the scene ahead. Vehicle traffic had stopped in both directions even as foot traffic had picked up. People continued to run between cars, including a woman who screamed: "We're all going to die!"

"How long do you think the madness will continue?" Amanda asked.

"I give it another hour," Ted said. He smiled. "Even stupidity has a shelf life."

Amanda laughed and looked at her acquaintances.

"In that case, gentlemen, I accept your offer. I think I'll have that beer."

18: ELIZABETH

Princeton, New Jersey — Thursday, November 3, 1938

Elizabeth ran her fingers along the wall and felt a crack. She had found five in the past ten minutes and knew she would discover more. When people rented houses for twenty bucks a month, they found a lot of things like cracks, leaks, and windows that didn't open.

Elizabeth didn't mind. She hadn't come to Mercer Street to find a large and lavish residence. She had come to find one close to her childhood home.

"It's not much to look at, is it?" Elizabeth asked. She walked to the middle of the unfurnished living room. "I recall a fancier place."

"You recall a place that had a live-in *owner*," Susan said. "You can't expect landlords to rent houses to college students and keep them looking like Buckingham Palace."

"I suppose not."

"I like it," Amanda said as she sat on a crate. "It's bigger than the house I had in Champaign and a lot closer to the campus. I have no complaints. You did great, Grandma."

"Thank you, dear. I hope you feel that way when winter comes," Elizabeth said. "This little shack will be our home for at least the next six months."

Elizabeth stepped across the living room to a large window, pulled back the stained and torn cotton sheets that posed as drapes, and allowed the bright morning sunshine to spill across the bare wooden floor. She stared at the imposing green and white colonial across the street. She could almost hear the empty residence call her name.

"When will your parents arrive?" Susan asked.

Elizabeth turned away from the window and stepped toward her daughter.

"They will arrive on December 19. I know that because I have a letter that my mother wrote to her sister. She described our first day in Princeton in great detail. She said it was the day I started crawling."

Amanda stood up.

"This is so weird," Amanda said. She looked at Elizabeth. "I hope seeing yourself doesn't blow a hole in the universe. That would be a nasty way to go."

Susan laughed.

"We'll be fine, honey. Professor Bell would have never allowed us to travel here had he thought we were capable of blowing a hole in the universe or anything else."

"I hope you're right."

"I'm right," Susan said. "I'm sure of it."

Elizabeth smiled at Susan. She didn't think anyone could be sure of *anything* in these circumstances, but she was reasonably certain she would not create a cosmic catastrophe. If she had her way, she would do more than just see her infant self. She would hold her, play with her, and spoil her like she hadn't spoiled a child since Amanda was a baby.

Amanda walked over to Elizabeth and threw an arm around her shoulders.

"I must say I'm envious, Grams. I would give anything to see Dad again – or even Grandpa. You have an opportunity to do something special," Amanda said. She kissed Elizabeth on the head. "Make the most of it."

"I'll try, dear."

Amanda released Elizabeth and stepped to the window. She looked out at the street.

"So what's there to do around here?" Amanda asked. "What does Princeton offer townies with time on their hands? Grandma?"

"You're asking the wrong person," Elizabeth said. "I can tell you what we had in the forties and fifties, but not in the thirties. I barely remember the war."

"Why don't you ask those boys you met Sunday night?" Susan asked. "I'm sure they would be happy to show you some things."

Amanda turned away from the window. She stared at her mother and raised a brow.

"I'm sure they *would*."

Susan put her hands on her hips.

"Amanda!"

"Well? That's what boys do," Amanda said. "They show you their things and not much else."

Elizabeth laughed.

"That may be what boys do, but it's not what *men* do," Susan said with a straight face. "You can't indict half the human race because of a few bad experiences."

Amanda sighed.

"I know. I know. I shouldn't paint with a broad brush, but I'm finding it easy to do. It seems like every guy I meet wants the same thing. Just once I'd like to meet someone who noticed my brain before my other two thousand parts."

"Good luck with that," Elizabeth said.

"What's that supposed to mean?" Amanda asked.

"What it means, dear, is that men haven't changed since the Stone Age," Elizabeth said. "They are drawn to faces and figures. Even if you had an IQ of 170, they would still see you first as a beautiful woman. Your challenge is to find a man who appreciates all of your qualities and not just the ones he can see from the street."

"It doesn't matter," Amanda said. "I don't plan to date here."

"Why not?" Susan asked. "Professor Bell didn't say we couldn't date. He said only that we couldn't bring someone back. I see no reason why you can't have some fun."

"You're right. Maybe I'll look up Bill and Ted and have an 'excellent adventure' – or show up naked at a party. I can't imagine a downside."

"That's the attitude!"

Amanda stared at Susan.

"I'm joking, Mother."

"I know, honey. I'm just teasing."

Amanda shook her head. She paused a moment and then looked again at Susan.

"What about you? What are *you* planning to do here? I know it's too soon to date again, but it's not too soon to make friends – even male friends. Are you going to get out and mingle or spend the next year watching Grandma teach herself to walk?"

"I don't know. I haven't given the matter much thought," Susan said. She sighed. "I guess I'll just see what each day brings and go with the flow."

"That's a good plan," Amanda said.

Elizabeth grinned and shook her head.

"Now that you two have set your social parameters, maybe we can focus on other things."

"Like what?" Susan asked.

"Like making this house a home," Elizabeth said. "It's time to go shopping!"

19: SUSAN

Monday, November 7, 1938

The time travelers spent money like it grew on trees. They bought tables, chairs, and beds on Thursday and Friday, dishes and groceries on Saturday and Sunday, and makeup and clothes on Monday. They didn't stop until Amanda put on a dress at a downtown boutique and proudly declared that the spree was complete.

"Are you sure you want to declare victory?" Susan asked. "There's another store next door and several more on Nassau Street."

"They can wait," Amanda said. "I want to see what more women are wearing before I buy anything else. I think I have enough dresses to get through the week."

Elizabeth laughed.

"You have enough to get through the year."

"I suppose I do," Amanda said.

"There's nothing wrong with that," Susan said. "You want to look your best for all the fine young men who will appreciate your fine young mind."

Amanda smiled.

"You're not helping, Mother."

"Sure I am. I'm providing encouragement."

Amanda stood in front of a full-length mirror and straightened her blue rayon dress, her final acquisition of the day. The pleated garment fell just past her knees.

"I like this one best," Amanda said. She laughed. "I know I like the price."

"I do too," Susan said. "I never thought I'd live to see a two-dollar dress. Then again, I never thought I'd live to see eight-dollar coats and fifty-cent shoes."

Susan shook her head when she thought about how cheaply the three women had filled the rooms and cupboards of their three-bedroom house. They had spent only four hundred dollars on furniture, a hundred on clothes, and less than twenty on food.

"Should I wear this out of the store?" Amanda asked.

"Why not? You don't really want to crawl back into that frumpy sack, do you?"

"No," Amanda said. "I guess not."

"Then let's get it and go," Susan said. "Let's go see the town."

The women paid for their purchases, walked out the door, and headed west toward the university. When they reached the leafy environs of Prospect Avenue, Susan ended several minutes of silence with a question.

"Do you know the college well enough to give us a tour, Mom?"

"I should hope so," Elizabeth said. "I used to walk through the campus at least once a week as a girl to see how the big kids had fun."

"Then maybe you can tell us about some of these buildings."

"Maybe I can. Try me."

"All right. What's this one?" Susan asked. She pointed a narrow, nondescript brick structure. "It looks more like a business than a campus facility."

"That's because it *is* a business," Elizabeth said. "That's Myers, Pendleton, and Simmons, one of the oldest continuously operating law firms in the United States."

"How do you know that?"

"I know it because my brother's best friend, Frederick Price, practiced law there for fifty years. He retired as a senior partner just last summer."

"You mean the firm was still going in 2016?" Susan asked.

"Yes," Elizabeth said.

"Wow."

"Things are old here, dear. They are a lot like me."

Susan laughed.

"What about the other buildings on this street? What about these big houses? They look like people places," Susan said. "Are they dormitories or fraternities?"

"No. They're eating clubs – or at least they used to be."

"Eating clubs?" Amanda asked. "What are eating clubs?"

"They're clubs where people eat."

"You should do stand-up, Grandma. I'm serious."

"I'm serious too," Elizabeth said. "These are the places where students eat their meals, socialize, and study, though I didn't see much evidence of studying when I lived here as a kid."

Susan giggled.

"I'm sure you didn't," Susan said. "Your answer begs a question though. If the students eat and socialize on this end of campus, where do they sleep? Where are the dorms?"

"Most are farther ahead," Elizabeth said. She smiled. "The one I like best, though, is right in front of us."

Susan slowed to a stop to take a better look at an imposing structure that seemed to shoot up out of nowhere. With turrets, arches, and sheer sides, the building looked more like an English castle than a dorm for American college students.

"What's it called?" Susan asked.

"Officially, it's 1879 Hall. I called it the Noise Factory."

"It's *noisy*?"

"It was when I lived here," Elizabeth said. "In fact, at certain times during finals week, it was downright cacophonous."

"I don't understand. I thought people studied during finals week."

"They do. They did here, too, at least until nine o'clock at night. Then the rowdies took a break and gave their more studious peers a Poler's Recess."

"What's a poler?" Susan asked.

"It's a person who studies too much," Elizabeth said. "Some students didn't want others to stick their noses in books all day, so they gave them a recess."

Susan laughed.

"What did they do?"

"They made noise, of course," Elizabeth said. "They beat drums, pounded pans, blew horns, and set off firecrackers for several minutes. No one could study. No one could think. When I was a high school senior, I came here every night during finals week, with my girlfriends, to hear the ruckus and flirt with the boys. We had almost as much fun as the students."

"Did you say this is the 1879 Hall?" Amanda asked.

"I did," Elizabeth said.

"So it was built in 1879?"

"No. It was built in 1904."

Amanda laughed.

"That figures."

"I know the year because my father often shared facts and stories he learned from his colleagues," Elizabeth said. "He loved telling me interesting things."

Susan frowned as she listened. She was sad that Elizabeth had been unable to maintain the happy relationship with her father. She lowered her eyes as she thought about the grandfather she had never known.

"Did Grandpa actually teach at Princeton?" Susan asked.

"He did. He taught over there," Elizabeth said as she pointed to a building in the distance. "Come this way. I'll show you where he worked."

As the women entered the heart of the campus, Susan noted the architecture and apparent age of each building. She could see that Princeton had rushed not to modernize but rather to preserve. It celebrated brick and wood and turned its back on glass, concrete, and steel.

Five minutes later, the visitors gazed at a brick-and-wood building that stood next to a much larger one. With paned windows, arched doorways, and lavish ornamentation, it looked like the kind of place that fostered education.

"This is where my father taught mathematics," Elizabeth said. "He taught math for ten years before taking a job with the government."

"I'll bet he liked it here," Amanda said.

"He loved it. He considered his work at Princeton his crowning professional achievement."

Susan looked at Elizabeth and saw that she was starting to tire. So she guided her clan to a bench that offered a splendid view of a green space called the Prospect Garden.

"Let's sit for a while, Mom. You've done a lot of walking today."

"Yes, I have."

When the women reached the bench, Susan cleared a space by wiping away several red and orange leaves that had settled on the seat. She helped her mother sit down and then picked up a campus newspaper that had fallen to the ground.

"It looks like someone left us a copy of the *Daily Planet*," Susan said.

"Is that the campus paper?" Amanda asked.

"It must be. I see a lot of college news on the front."

Susan examined the paper and laughed when she considered the content. No fewer than five sports articles occupied the front page. Even students and faculty at an academic powerhouse apparently needed to keep up on football.

"What's so funny?" Elizabeth asked.

"Oh, it's nothing. It's just that there's a lot of sports news on the front page," Susan said. "I didn't realize that Princeton was a football factory."

Elizabeth smiled.

"It is now."

Susan laughed.

"I guess it is."

"I mean it," Elizabeth said. "Football is big here. It was big when I was growing up and big fifty to sixty years ago. The Tigers played in the very first game in 1869."

Susan glanced again at the paper, saw a small article she had missed the first time, and shook her head. She looked at her mother.

"You're right. They did play."

"How do you know?" Elizabeth asked.

"I know because this story mentions the game," Susan said. She pointed to the article. "The last member of the team that played in that game just died. He was eighty-seven."

"That's sad," Amanda said.

"The story says that the university will honor him at a game this Saturday. We should go to the game. Princeton is playing Yale."

"Since when did you become a football fan, Mom?" Amanda asked.

"Since I decided to do more than sit around the house," Susan said. "We should go. You want to meet people, don't you?"

Amanda nodded.

"You know I do."

"Then it's set," Susan said.

Susan smiled as she thought about Amanda's question. She was about as interested in football as the King of Siam, but she knew that the game would be a perfect opportunity to get out, mingle, and settle into their new community.

Then Susan looked at Amanda and frowned. She could see from the expression on her daughter's face that she was preoccupied or confused.

"What's the matter?" Susan asked. "You look baffled."

"I guess I am," Amanda said. She turned her head. "I've been watching students go by for the past minute and noticed something."

"What's that?"

"There are no women. I haven't seen one since we left the dress shop."

Elizabeth smiled.

"You won't find any either – at least not on this campus."

"Why? Have they been outlawed, Grandma?"

Elizabeth laughed.

"You might say that."

"I don't get it," Amanda said. "What are you saying?"

"What I'm saying, dear, is that Princeton did not admit women until 1969," Elizabeth said. "In 1938 it was, and is, a male domain."

20: AMANDA

Saturday, November 12, 1938

Fifteen minutes after finding a seat on the forty-yard line in Palmer Stadium, Amanda Peterson turned her attention to a riveting pre-game spectacle. She watched with amusement as Princeton cheerleaders – *male* cheerleaders – carried a tiny Pekinese across the field and prepared to give the lapdog, dressed in Yale blue, to the opposing team.

They didn't get far. Mere seconds after the cheerleaders presented their counterparts with the unimpressive offering, Yale's mascot, a bow-legged, tongue-wagging, happy-go-lucky piece of work named Handsome Dan IV, turned the tables. The bulldog charged at the cheerleaders and the Pekinese and maintained the chase until the students and their mangy mutt beat a hasty retreat to the Princeton sideline.

"This is hilarious," Amanda said as she broke into a laugh. She looked at her grandma, who sat to her right. "Do they do this before every game?"

"I can't remember," Elizabeth replied.

"They do when they can," someone else said.

Amanda looked to her immediate left and saw a young woman look back.

"Did you say something?" Amanda asked.

"I did," the woman said. "I answered your question. The cheerleaders rarely pass up a chance to get the better of the other team's mascot. Sometimes they succeed. Sometimes they don't. They didn't succeed today."

"I guess not," Amanda said. She laughed again. "That was really funny."

"Is this your first football game?"

Amanda nodded.

"It's my first one here."

The woman studied Amanda with curious eyes.

"Are you visiting?"

"I guess you could say that. My family and I just arrived from Chicago. We plan to stay for at least a few months."

"Well, welcome to Princeton," the woman said. She offered a hand. "My name is Dot – Dot Gale. I grew up in Grovers Mill. Perhaps you've heard of it."

Amanda laughed when she saw Dot's wry smile.

"I think half the planet has heard of it. How are the Martians treating you?"

"I wouldn't know," Dot said. "They left in a rush. Invaders tend to do that."

Amanda smiled, took a closer look at her new acquaintance, and did a double take. With green eyes, a pretty freckled face, and shimmering long red hair, Dot Gale looked a lot like Sophie Sanders, Amanda's second roommate at the University of Illinois.

"You're funny. I'm Amanda Peterson, by the way."

"It's nice to meet you," Dot said. She leaned forward in an apparent effort to see the people at Amanda's side. "Is this your family?"

"It is. They are. This is my mom, Susan, and my grandma, Elizabeth," Amanda said. She leaned back in her bleacher seat so that the women could exchange handshakes and pleasantries. "Grandma grew up in this area too. This is sort of a homecoming for her."

"You grew up in Princeton?" Dot asked.

"I did," Elizabeth said. "I spent my childhood on Mercer Street."

Amanda gave her grandmother a nervous glance. She realized that she had given Dot too much information too soon and wondered how Elizabeth would finesse a "childhood on Mercer Street" that technically hadn't started.

"You're pretty close to home then," Dot said. "Where do you live now?"

Elizabeth smiled at Amanda and then looked at Dot.

"We live on the same street."

"Really? Wow. I'll bet that triggers a lot of memories."

"You have no idea," Elizabeth said.

"I would love to live in town and be able to walk to all this. I grew up on a farm and had to drive everywhere, when I could drive at all," Dot said. "My father rarely let me use his car. He rarely let me leave the house."

Amanda laughed. She liked this woman already.

"I take it you escaped the farm," Amanda said.

"I did and I didn't. I left home four years ago when I went to college and came back last June after I graduated," Dot said. "I told my dad I would come back only if he agreed to let me drive the Buick. He did. He trusts me now."

Amanda smiled.

"You went to college?"

Dot nodded.

"I went to Bryn Mawr, the closest of the Seven Sisters and the only one to give me a full ride. You probably passed it on the way here."

"We did. I saw signs pointing to it near Philadelphia," Amanda said. She sighed and looked at her new friend with admiration. "So what are you doing now? What are you doing back here?"

Dot smiled.

"I'm biding my time until the Army decides what to do with this lug," Dot said. She looked at Amanda and then at the large, handsome man at her side. "This is Roy Maine, a Princeton grad, a first lieutenant, and as of Labor Day, my fiancé. We plan to get married next summer."

"Congratulations," Amanda said.

"Thanks."

Dot tapped Roy on the shoulder. She kept tapping until he finally turned his head.

"What?"

"Don't say 'what.' Say 'hello,'" Dot said. "This is Amanda Peterson. She's visiting from Chicago with her mother and grandmother."

Roy smiled and extended a hand.

"It's a pleasure to meet you, Amanda."

"You too."

"That's Mom and Grandma over there," Dot said.

"Hi, ladies," Roy said as he waved to Susan and Elizabeth.

Roy put his arm around Dot and then turned his attention toward the middle of the field, where a few players from each team gathered for the coin flip. All of the players wore leather helmets, sweatshirt jerseys, and bulky, baggy pants.

Amanda paused for a moment to take in the sights and liked what she saw. More than forty thousand boisterous fans of all ages filled the horseshoe-shaped stadium, which opened to the south and offered a splendid view of nearby Lake Carnegie. When Amanda finished surveying her surroundings, she looked again at the girl from Grovers Mill.

"So is Dot short for Dorothy?"

Dot offered a sheepish grin. She paused before answering.

"Yes."

"Oh," Amanda said matter-of-factly. "How are things in Oz?"

"Please don't laugh," Dot said. "People always laugh."

Amanda smiled.

"I won't laugh. I think it's cool. It's not every day I meet a redheaded farm girl named Dorothy Gale who looks an awful lot like Judy Garland,"

106

Amanda said. "You do know she's going to play Dorothy in the movie next year."

"So I've heard," Dot said dryly.

"At least you don't live in Kansas or have a dog named Toto."

Dot smiled nervously.

"You're right about Kansas."

Amanda tilted her head.

"No way. No freaking way."

"Toto the Third is a terrier too," Dot said. "My mother is a huge fan of Frank Baum. I was condemned at birth to be a literary character."

Amanda tried and failed to stifle a laugh.

"I'm sorry. I know I said I wouldn't laugh, but that's too much."

"It's all right. You're human. People laugh at funny things."

"I guess we do," Amanda said.

"What about you?" Dot asked. "What's your story?"

"What do you mean?"

"What brought you to Princeton?"

Would you believe gypsum crystals and a magic tunnel?

Amanda looked to Susan for guidance. When she got it in the form of a smile and a nod, she proceeded to tell Dot a story the time travelers had worked out in October.

"I guess you could say opportunity," Amanda said. "My mom and I have always wanted to visit the place where my grandmother grew up, so when we got the chance we took it."

"Don't you have jobs or school or other family in Chicago?" Dot asked.

"Not at the moment."

"What about your father?"

Amanda started to answer but stopped when the crowd roared in response to a Tigers first down. When the noise subsided, she continued.

"My father passed away in June."

"Oh, no," Dot said. "I'm so sorry."

"Thank you," Amanda said.

"Was he ill?"

"No. He was in a car accident. He died at the hospital."

"That's terrible."

"It is," Amanda said. "I'm still getting used to not having a father."

Dot looked at Amanda with kind eyes.

"So you came out here to get a fresh start?"

Amanda smiled sadly.

"We came out here to do a lot of things. When my dad died, he left us with a lot of time, a lot of money, and a lot of unanswered questions. We decided that the best way to deal with all three was to travel. We decided to see the rest of the country before getting on with our lives. Princeton is just the first stop on what may be a very long trip."

"How long have you been here?" Dot asked.

"Two weeks," Amanda said. "We arrived the night the Martians landed."

Dot laughed.

"That figures. You should have kept driving."

Amanda smiled. She loved Dot's sense of humor.

"No. We made the right decision. We like it here."

"Have you made any friends?" Dot asked.

"Just you," Amanda said.

Dot put her hand to her chin and gave Amanda a closer inspection.

"You probably haven't met any men either, have you?"

Amanda sighed.

Define men.

"No."

Dot flashed a mischievous grin.

"Maybe I can fix that."

"How?"

"I can start by sneaking you into the dance," Dot said.

"What?"

Amanda felt another pang of déjà vu. She recalled the many times that sorority sisters at Illinois had snuck her into one thing or another, with not-so-pleasant outcomes.

"There's a dance tonight at the university gymnasium."

"Don't I need a date or something?" Amanda asked.

Dot nodded.

"That's the fastest way in. The hall monitors who put together these things don't look kindly on party crashers, though I think they would make an exception for you."

"So what should I do?"

Dot grinned.

"You tag along with us," Dot said. She tapped on Roy's shoulder. "I don't think anyone would object to you having two dates tonight, would they, honey?"

"No," Roy said without taking his eyes off the game.

Dot returned to Amanda.

"Roy was a star offensive lineman last year. He can pretty much do what he pleases."

"Are you sure I won't be a burden?" Amanda asked.

"I'm positive," Dot said. "I insist that you come."

Amanda looked again to her mother for guidance. She knew even before she saw her smiling face what Susan Peterson would advise.

"Go with them. Have fun," Susan said. "Have a good time."

Amanda returned to Dot.

"All right. I will. What time's the dance?"

"It's at eight thirty," Dot said. "We can pick you up at eight, if you'd like."

"I'd like that."

"Then I guess we have a date. Do you have a nice dress? If you don't, I can help."

"Thanks, but no thanks," Amanda said. She laughed. "I think I have that covered."

21: AMANDA

Standing near a wall in Princeton's gymnasium, Amanda thought about a novel she had read and decided to take issue with its title. No matter how hard she tried, she couldn't think of even one perk of being a wallflower – at least not at a college dance.

Amanda enjoyed the spectacle, of course. She had enjoyed almost every spectacle in 1938, but she was growing weary of enjoying them as a *spectator*. Amanda caught herself tapping her feet to the beat as she watched couples swing, jitterbug, and jive like they were extras in *Grease*. For the first time in years, she wanted to dance.

She couldn't complain about the music. For more than two hours, Teddy Hill and His Orchestra had kept dancers on the floor and others snapping their fingers with cutting-edge swing and jazz. The Big Band legends shared the stage with a local swing band that had filled in nicely during a long intermission.

Amanda started to head for the ladies' room to check her hair for a third time when she saw four familiar faces. Roy Maine and Dot Gale smiled as they emerged from a moving mass in the middle of the dance floor. Bill Green and Ted Fiske beamed. Each seemed amused to find a blonde in a blue dress standing alone in social Siberia.

"These two characters say they know you," Dot said when the four reached Amanda. "Ted says you had a 'communal experience' on Route 583."

"We shared a beer during the Martian invasion," Amanda said.

"I believe we had *two* beers," Ted said with his infectious drawl. "It does you no good to deny a mighty fine time. I have witnesses."

Amanda laughed.

"I suspect you do."

"I must say, Miss Peterson, that you are the finest thing I've seen tonight."

"Thank you," Amanda said.

Dot looked at Ted and laughed.

"Don't let your date hear you say that."

"You brought a date?" Amanda asked.

"We both did," Ted said. "I considered going stag, but I changed my mind after I met this gal from Philly last week. She's not the kind of woman any rational man would leave home on a Saturday night."

Amanda, confused, furrowed her brows.

"She's Miss Cheesecake 1938," Dot said. "She looks the part too."

"Oh."

Amanda turned to Bill.

"What about you? Did *you* consider going stag?"

"I did," Bill said. "I even told my girlfriend that on Friday."

"What did she do?"

"She guided my thoughts in a more productive direction."

Amanda laughed. She looked at Bill and Ted.

"Where are your dates now?"

"Bill's gal went to the ladies' room," Ted said. "Mine left to make a phone call."

"So when the cats are away the mice will play?" Amanda asked.

Ted laughed.

"You could say that."

"And now you're here."

"Now we're here," Ted said. "Roy told us he brought two dates tonight and that one wasn't getting the attention she deserved. I didn't realize the magnitude of the travesty until we walked this way. I think it's a crime the bozos who came here alone haven't asked you to dance."

"It's not their fault. I haven't exactly made myself visible," Amanda said. She looked at Roy and Bill before returning to Ted. "How do you all know each other?"

"We had some common classes last year," Ted said. "We also joined the same clubs. It's easy to do that in a place like Princeton."

"I believe it."

Amanda smiled at Ted and then took a moment to survey her surroundings. She noticed that many people had left the building since her friends had appeared and that most of those who remained seemed more interested in winning prizes than in dancing. Dozens of couples gathered in a corner of the gym to hear an announcer call out ticket numbers.

Amanda shifted her attention to the other end of the arena, where fewer people congregated, and noticed a man standing under the basketball hoop. Tall, blond, and strikingly handsome, he moved his head like he was looking for someone or something. When he met Amanda's gaze, he smiled warmly, nodded, and resumed his search. The wallflower stared into space and pondered the brief but pleasant exchange. She remained in a daze until Dorothy Gale brought her back from the Land of Oz.

"Have you found your Prince Charming?" Dot asked.

Amanda faced her friend.

"Have I what?"

"Have you found someone of interest? I saw you smile at the blond guy over there."

Amanda eyed the others before responding. Roy, Bill, and Ted appeared to be more into football than into what she might say. They compared notes on Princeton's 20-7 win over Yale.

"I smiled at him because he smiled at me," Amanda said to Dot. "Who is he?"

Dot studied the man closely.

"I'm not sure. I've seen him before, but I don't know his name. Let me ask Roy."

"Wait a few minutes," Amanda said. "Wait until Ted leaves."

Dot raised a brow.

"I see you're not one to burn bridges."

Amanda smiled.

"I'm new here. I have to build bridges before I burn them."

Dot laughed.

"OK. I'll wait."

Amanda returned to Roy, Bill, and Ted as they debated the merits of the forward pass. Only Roy, the former player, thought the pass had a serious future in college football.

"I apologize for my manners," Ted said to Amanda a moment later. "I should be talking to you and not these buffoons. I lose my head whenever a conversation turns to football."

"That's all right," Amanda said. "Boys have priorities, just like girls."

Ted chuckled.

"I can't argue with that. We have lots of priorities, Miss Peterson, and one of mine this evening is to ask you to dance. Would you care for a spin?"

Amanda searched the gym for jealous dates and came up empty.

"Won't Miss Cheesecake object?"

"Nah," Ted said matter-of-factly. "She's an understanding sort. I told her I would dance with others while she made her call. I'll be all right."

Amanda smiled and held out a hand.

"In that case, Mr. Fiske, lead the way."

22: ELIZABETH

Wednesday, November 16, 1938

Elizabeth began her walk down Mercer Street with a walk across it. When she noticed a small sign she had not noticed before, she trotted across the street to her childhood home and saw it had been sold. She looked for other signs, conspicuous and hidden, that suggested change was on the way, but she could not find any. Whoever had planted the sign in the yard had not painted the door or repaired a window or even raked the leaves. He or she had simply hammered a stake in the ground and announced to the world that a special house was no longer on the market.

Elizabeth walked from the yard to the sidewalk and headed southwest down Mercer Street, a stretch of stately homes and landscaped lawns that turned into Route 583 about a mile from the campus. She had traveled the same path every day for the past two weeks in search of things interesting or new and had yet to be disappointed.

She stopped to fasten a button on her red wool coat and then proceeded toward two houses she had always adored. Each stirred memories of a time that seemed impossibly distant and refreshingly close.

Elizabeth smiled as she studied the deeply gabled roof of the first house. She had visited the Cape Cod on countless occasions to share stories and gossip with Penelope Howell, her best friend and confidante from the fourth grade on.

She could almost see Penny stick her head out the front door and beckon her to enter, but she knew that wouldn't happen for another ten years. Like so many others, Penny Howell would not become a part of Elizabeth's life until after the horrible war to come.

Elizabeth found more than ghosts in the brick colonial home next door. She found a living, breathing reminder of a teenage crush.

She watched with amusement as Mason Payne pulled a fully loaded Radio Flyer wagon across his front yard. He wasn't the eighteen-year-old letterman she had fallen in love with as a high school freshman, but even at three he was just as cute.

Elizabeth waved to Mason and then his mother, who sat on the front steps, as she strolled past the house. She wondered what Molly Payne would say if she told her that her son would someday establish a hamburger chain that would become as popular as swing and as enduring as the oak and cedar trees that lined the street.

She didn't have to wonder long. She knew that Mrs. Payne would make a few discreet calls to mental health authorities and report that a kindly old lady who walked the streets every day had lost what was left of her marbles.

Elizabeth smiled as she tried to digest what was still digestible. She was a time traveler, a historical trespasser, and a participant in a drama that had played out once and would play out again. She pondered the mystery of time and wondered whether three ladies from Chicago had already created ripples that would turn into waves.

Elizabeth doubted that they had done that much at this point. In seventeen days the women had done little more than walk around a college town, eat, shop, and set up a surveillance station in a modest house that no one seemed to notice.

She was glad that Susan had started to talk about the future, a future without her husband, and resume favorite activities like reading and walking. She knew that returning to routines was one of the best ways to deal with lingering grief and put a derailed life back on track.

Elizabeth was also happy to see Amanda emerge from *her* shell and make new friends. She worried that she was forming attachments that might later be hard to break, but she was pleased to see that Amanda, too, had started to move forward.

She thought about her family and her own life as she approached yet another house that was fixed in her mind. She gazed at the modest cottage and waved to its owner, a friendly, eccentric, bushy-haired man who walked around his crunchy front lawn in his bare feet.

"Hello," Elizabeth said. "How are you today?"

"I am fine, dear lady," the Old Man said with a thick German accent. "How are you?"

"I couldn't be better."

"That is good. That is good."

Elizabeth watched with interest as the man peeked under a hedge that stood between the yard and the sidewalk. She had seen him do the same thing at least twice since November 3, when she had reintroduced herself to a man she had first met at age six. She smiled as he moved around the yard and continued his dogged pursuit of something or someone.

"Are you looking for something?" Elizabeth asked. "Perhaps I can help."

"No. No," the Old Man said. "She is gone now."

"Who is gone?"

"The cat. She called for me, but now she is gone."

Elizabeth laughed to herself. She vaguely remembered a large tabby that regularly terrorized the neighborhood. The stray would often wander from door to door and meow until beleaguered residents placated her with a tin of tuna or a bowl of milk. She could only imagine the havoc the feline had wreaked today.

"Are you talking about the fat one with the dark stripes?" Elizabeth asked.

"Yes."

"I'll keep my eyes peeled. If I see her, I'll let you know."

"Thank you," the Old Man said. "You are too kind."

Elizabeth waved goodbye and continued on her way. She felt guilty about running off, but not too guilty. She knew she would have other chances to chat.

She smiled as she thought of her many interactions with the man in her youth, which had ranged from selling him Girl Scout cookies to running occasional errands to asking him for help with her math homework. Like Erich Wagner, the Old Man was a whiz with numbers. Unlike her father, he was often home during the day.

Elizabeth walked several more blocks and considered walking farther, but she turned around when she saw dark gray clouds gather to the west. As much as she liked strolling down Memory Lane, she did not want to do so during a heavy rainstorm.

Thirty minutes later she opened the door to her rental house. She entered the living room, sat on a crushed mohair armchair, and let her tired body go.

Elizabeth did not respond to two voices. She had decided long ago that callers, particularly younger ones with fresher legs, could come to her.

"Did you go for a walk, Mom?" Susan asked as she entered the room.

"I did. I just got back," Elizabeth said.

"Did you see anything interesting?"

Elizabeth smiled.

"I did."

Susan walked to the chair and stopped at Elizabeth's side.

"What did you see?"

Elizabeth looked up at her daughter.

"I'll tell you tonight or maybe tomorrow."

"You don't want to tell me now?" Susan asked.

"No."

"No?"

"No," Elizabeth said. She took Susan's right hand and gave it a gentle squeeze. "Go run along. Go fix dinner. Leave your tired old mother to her chair and her memories."

23: AMANDA

Amanda couldn't decide what she liked more – the tavern, the talk, or the company. It was hard to beat a taproom frequented by the Founders or a discussion about Ivy League mating rituals, but Dot Gale came close. In just a few days, she had gone from an interesting acquaintance to the time traveler's BFF.

Amanda took a sip from her pewter mug and then lifted it high. When Dot did the same, she pushed the mug forward.

"Here's to making friends," Amanda said.

The mugs clinked.

"Here's to keeping them," Dot said.

Amanda laughed.

"Are you afraid I'm going to run off?"

Dot giggled.

"Yes."

"I'll try to stick around."

"Please do," Dot said. "You're far more interesting than most of the women I knew in college and definitely more interesting than the girls I knew in high school."

Amanda smiled.

"I accept that endorsement."

"I figured you would."

Both women laughed.

Amanda sipped more lager and then took a moment to assess her surroundings. She liked what she saw. With rustic oak furniture, dim alcoves, a stone fireplace, and a low-raftered ceiling, the taproom of the Colonial Inn looked like the sort of watering hole that would have appealed to eighteenth-century patriots and rabble-rousers.

"Tell me about this place," Amanda said.

"What would you like to know?" Dot asked.

Amanda pointed to a dozen portraits on a paneled wall.

"Let's start with those pictures. Did all those dead white guys actually sleep here?"

Dot smiled.

"They slept in the building. Whether they slept in the rooms upstairs or slept off their ale and punch at these tables is still a topic of debate."

"I thought as much," Amanda said. She ran her hand across her round table. "What about all these tables and chairs? Are they the originals?"

Dot shook her head.

"Most of the furniture is new. The owners have to replace the tables and chairs every few years because the students are so hard on them," Dot said.

"You mean they break them?"

"They break them. They scuff them. They carve their initials in the wood."

"Boys," Amanda said dismissively.

"I know," Dot said. "If we didn't need them to perpetuate the species, I'd favor putting them on a rocket and blasting them to Pluto – or, better yet, Mars. We could repay the Martians for tearing up my neighborhood."

Amanda laughed again. She wondered what Dot would think if she told her that the technology to send men to Mars was closer than she thought.

"Speaking of boys or, in this case, men, where is Roy this weekend?" Amanda asked.

"He drove to Wilkes-Barre to visit his parents," Dot said. "He wanted to see them one more time before starting his next assignment later this month."

"So it's official?"

Dot nodded.

"He leaves on Tuesday for California. He'll spend most of the next year training to be a pilot at March Field, an Army air base near Los Angeles."

"I know where it is," Amanda said.

"You've been to California?"

Amanda smiled.

"I have. I've been there many times."

"I'm envious. I'm *really* envious," Dot said. "I've never been to California. I've never been west of St. Louis. I have a feeling that will change, though, and change soon."

"What do you mean?"

"What I mean is that I plan to join Roy after we're married. If the Army keeps him in California, then California will be my next home. I can think of worse places to live."

"I can too," Amanda said.

"What about you?" Dot asked. She sipped her beer. "What do you want to do after you conquer forty-eight states? Do you have career plans?"

Amanda paused before answering. She wanted to tell the truth but do so in a way that would not invite difficult questions.

"I do. I want to work for a research organization," Amanda said. "I want to study history and foreign affairs and influence policy. I want to build on what I did at Illinois."

"Then do it. Do it now. Do it before you get married and the dishes and diapers pile up."

Amanda smiled.

"I will. Thanks for the support."

"Don't mention it," Dot said. She studied Amanda for a moment. "You know, if you really like history and foreign affairs, you should check out some of the programs here. I know the university sponsors lectures for the public. So does the Nassau Institute."

"What's the Nassau Institute?"

"It's a brain box here in town. It's one of those places where scholars and writers get together and have deep discussions about things like FDR's trade policy with Bolivia or the growing tensions between the Laplanders and the Eskimos."

Amanda smiled. She found Dot's sarcasm both amusing and ironic. She had no idea she was describing what Amanda considered the perfect work environment.

"What about the lectures?" Amanda asked. "When's the next one?"

"December 7," Dot said. "I know that because Roy wanted to attend. The featured speaker is a retired admiral who thinks we should build more aircraft carriers."

"I love stuff like that," Amanda said. "I think we should go."

Dot grinned.

"I definitely think *you* should go."

"You're grinning. Why are you grinning?"

"I have my reasons," Dot said.

"What? Tell me."

Dot laughed.

"It's nothing."

"Yes, it is, or you wouldn't be grinning," Amanda said. "Spill it!"

Dot sighed.

"All right. I will. Do you remember the blond man you ogled at the dance?"

"I didn't *ogle* anyone, but yes, I remember him."

"Would you like to see him again?" Dot asked.

"Of course," Amanda said.

"Then I think you should attend the lecture."

"Why?"

"Why? I'll tell you why," Dot said. "Mr. Tall, Light, and Handsome will be there. He sets up the speeches. He works at the Institute and apparently likes history, foreign affairs, and all that beeswax as much as you do."

"How do you know this?" Amanda asked.

"I had Roy check him out. You wanted his name, remember?"

"I wanted his name, not his FBI file."

"Don't get snippy," Dot said. "Beggars can't be choosers."

Amanda laughed.

"You sound like my grandma."

"I'll take that as a compliment."

"You should," Amanda said.

"In any case, your mystery man will be testing microphones and adjusting podiums two weeks from Wednesday," Dot said. She smiled. "Roy tells me his name is Kurt."

24: SUSAN

Friday, November 25, 1938

Like so many buildings in Princeton, New Jersey, the public library on Nassau Street looked liked something else. With red bricks, white shutters, decorative moldings, and paned windows, it looked more like a Georgian town house or even a small dormitory than a modern repository for books, magazines, and newspapers.

Susan didn't mind. She knew that the collection inside would be as complete and up-to-date as any she had access to in her delightful but temporary hometown.

She walked through the front door and headed up marble stairs to the second floor, where novels shared space with reference books and maps. She browsed the newest offerings for about ten minutes, pulled one from the shelf, and sat at a rectangular table that abutted the back wall.

Susan smiled as she opened the novel and began to read *Rebecca* by Daphne du Maurier for the second time. She found the crisp, hot-off-the-press copy preferable to the tattered, dog-eared, scribble-filled text she had read in high school.

Susan plowed through the first five chapters and started the sixth when an unfamiliar voice pulled her away from her literary escape. She looked up and saw a middle-aged man stare at her with kind and weary eyes.

"I'm sorry," Susan said. "Did you say something?"

"I did," the man said. "I asked if you would mind sharing the table."

Susan looked closely at the man and saw that she would either have to accede to his request or catch some of the dozen or so books that threatened to spill from his arms. She closed her own book, slid it to the side, and motioned with a hand.

"I wouldn't mind at all," Susan said. "Please sit."

"Thank you."

The man plopped his books and a leather portfolio on the table, sat in the only other chair, and quickly arranged the books into three fairly even stacks. Then he opened the folder, pulled a pen from the pocket of his sport jacket, and scribbled a few illegible words on an empty sheet of lined notebook paper.

Susan laughed softly.

"It looks like your teacher gave you some homework."

"Someone did. That's for sure," the man said.

Susan took a few seconds to peruse the titles on the table and found only two things of interest – nonfiction works on early twentieth-century history. She didn't have much use for the automotive manuals or the three books on the mechanics of flight.

"Are you a professor at the university?" Susan asked.

"No. I'm just a retired sailor with a lot of time on his hands."

Susan gave the sturdy, dark-haired man a closer inspection and debated whether to resume the conversation or return to *Rebecca*. She opted for the former.

"Shouldn't sailors read books about ships?" Susan asked. She laughed again. "It looks to me like you're more interested in airplanes."

"I'm interested in both," the man said. He smiled kindly at his tablemate and extended a hand. "I'm Jack Hicks, by the way."

Susan shook his hand.

"I'm Susan Peterson. It's a pleasure to meet you. Do you come here often?"

"No," Jack said. "I rarely come here. I usually go to the university library."

"Is it not open today?"

"It's not open until Monday. It's closed for the Thanksgiving break."

"That figures. I guess there's no point to opening a school library if all of the students have left town," Susan said. She looked again at the books and then at Jack as he jotted a few more lines in his notepad. "Are you doing some sort of research?"

"I am, as a matter of fact. I'm researching a book on naval aviation. With any luck, I'll have something to send to a publisher by the end of next year."

Susan wanted to tell the interesting stranger that she, too, was an author, but she knew that doing so would invite questions about titles that wouldn't be published for another sixty to seventy years. So she asked a question instead.

"Does this library have a lot of books on the subject?"

"No," Jack said. "It has very few. I came here today to grab a few tidbits from books I can use and prepare for a presentation I'm giving next month."

"Oh," Susan said. "Then I guess I had better let you get back to your work."

Jack smiled, put down his pen, and gazed at Susan. He looked at her like a man who was suddenly more interested in a gabby blonde than the finer points of naval aviation.

"There's no need," Jack said. "I could probably use a break."

"Didn't you just get here?" Susan asked.

"No. I've been here since the library opened at nine."

Susan felt guilty about pulling a man away from his work but not guilty enough to shut up or walk away. She had not met someone her age since arriving in Princeton and didn't want to squander an opportunity to make a new friend.

"Do you live here?" Susan asked. "Do you live in Princeton?"

"I have for the past two years," Jack said.

"The only reason I ask is that you don't have a local accent. I can't quite place it, but it's definitely not New Jersey."

"Try Oklahoma. That's where I grew up."

"That makes sense," Susan said. "I heard the same accent coming out here."

Jack tilted his head.

"Is that so? Where are you from?"

Susan paused before responding. If she answered "California," she would have to add another layer to the lie that was her past. If she answered "Chicago," she would have to explain why she drove through the Sooner State on a trip to New Jersey. She decided to keep it simple and stick to the family script.

"I'm from Chicago. I moved here a few weeks ago."

Jack smiled.

"So tell me something," Jack said. "Where does a woman from Chicago hear an Oklahoma accent on her way to New Jersey?"

Think, Susan. Think.

"She hears it in Pennsylvania," Susan said. "I met a nice family from Tulsa on a stop in Pittsburgh. They spoke with the same lovely lilt."

Jack laughed.

"I've heard my accent called a lot of things, but never 'lovely.'"

Susan smiled.

"Well, there's a first time for everything."

Jack laughed again.

"I suppose."

Susan brightened at the sight of his smile. She didn't know where this conversation was going, but she knew she wanted it to continue. She pushed *Rebecca* farther away and directed her full attention to the sailor with the pleasant face.

"So what brings an Oklahoma man to Princeton, New Jersey?" Susan asked.

Jack sighed.

"His wife."

"Your wife's from Princeton?"

"She was," Jack said. "Janet died in January."

Susan took a breath and pulled back. Talk about an answer she didn't expect. In a matter of seconds, a light conversation had turned heavy.

"I'm sorry."

"I am too. We came here two years ago, at her insistence, after I retired. I didn't care much for the East — I'm still not sure I do — but I decided to give it a try. Janet had followed me around for twenty-seven years. I figured it was my turn to follow her."

"Was her passing sudden?" Susan asked.

Jack nodded.

"She was diagnosed with stomach cancer a year ago and died a few weeks later."

"That's terrible."

"It was difficult, to say the least," Jack said. "In any case, our happy retirement was short. I thought about selling our house and moving back to Muskogee, where I grew up, but I changed my mind. I decided I could make more progress on my book right here and maybe find some peace. I think Janet would have wanted me to stay in Princeton."

Susan offered a comforting smile.

"If it's any consolation, I know how you feel. I lost my husband a few months ago. I came here with my mother and daughter to find some peace of my own."

"I'm sorry to hear about your husband," Jack said. "Do you have roots in New Jersey?"

Susan nodded.

"My mom grew up in Princeton. That's why we came here. She wanted to visit her hometown again before we all got on with our lives. We live in a rental house on Mercer Street."

"I see," Jack said. "Do you plan to stick around?"

Susan shook her head.

"We plan to stay through the spring and maybe the summer but not through the fall. We intend to return to Chicago in September at the latest."

"So this is sort of an extended vacation."

"You could call it that," Susan said.

"Well, I hope your stay is a pleasant one."

"Thank you."

Susan glanced at a clock on a wall, saw it was four o'clock, and remembered that she had promised to make dinner. She wanted to continue her conversation with the fascinating Mr. Hicks, but she didn't want to let the others down.

"Is something wrong?" Jack asked.

"No. I just noticed the time. I promised to make dinner for my family tonight, so I had better head home and make it."

"Well, don't let me keep you."

"I won't," Susan said. "I would like to ask you something, though, before I go."

"What's that?"

"Did you say you were working on a presentation?"

"I did. I'm giving a little speech at the Mercer Auditorium on December 7."

"Will it be open to the public?"

"Yes. It will," Jack said. "Why? Are you interested in attending?"

Susan nodded.

"I'm very interested. When does it start?"

"Seven thirty," Jack said. He smiled softly. "The doors open at seven."

25: SUSAN

Thursday, December 1, 1938

Ten minutes after beating her mother in Scrabble, a "new" game she had picked up in a Princeton department store, Susan turned off the first-floor lights of her rental house, ascended the creaky stairs, and headed to bed. Tired from a long day of walking, shopping, and raking leaves, she looked forward to a good night's rest.

Susan walked down the hallway to Amanda's bedroom door, knocked, and waited for an answer. When she didn't get one, she knocked again, opened the door, and peeked inside the dimly lighted room. She saw Amanda sitting upright in her twin bed.

"I just stopped to say good night," Susan said. She paused. "Good night."

Amanda turned to face her mother.

"Good night."

Susan smiled warmly and blew her daughter a kiss. She started to close the door but stopped when she thought she saw a teardrop roll down Amanda's cheek.

"Are you all right?" Susan asked. "You look like you're crying."

Amanda sighed.

"That's because I am."

Susan entered the room, sat on the end of the bed, and put her hand on Amanda's extended leg. She patted the leg twice and looked at her daughter until she met her gaze.

"What's wrong?" Susan asked.

"It's complicated," Amanda said.

"Nothing's too complicated for me. Did something happen today?"

Amanda nodded. She wiped a tear with the back of her hand.

"I met Dot's father. He took the two of us to lunch."

Susan tilted her head.

"That's a good thing. Isn't it?"

"Yes," Amanda said.

"Since when do good things make you cry?" Susan asked.

"When they remind you of the dad you don't have."

Amanda broke into sobs.

"Oh, honey, I'm so sorry."

Susan slid forward on the bed and threw her arms around her only child.

"He looks a lot like Dad," Amanda said. "He even has the same laugh."

"So lunch was difficult?"

Amanda sighed.

"It was really difficult."

Susan pulled her daughter closer. For several minutes, she did nothing but hold Amanda in a gentle embrace and let her release pent-up emotions. She regretted not doing more to address a loss that was obviously still foremost in her mind.

"I know how you feel," Susan said. "I have moments like this too."

Amanda withdrew and stared at her mother with puzzled eyes.

"Do you?" Amanda asked.

"Do I what?"

"Do you have moments like this?"

"Of course I do," Susan said.

"Then how come you never cry?" Amanda asked in a soft but firm voice. "You haven't cried *once* since the funeral."

Susan sighed and looked away. She had no good answer for a question she had asked herself many times.

"You're right. I haven't," Susan said. "I haven't because I've put my anger ahead of my grief. I'm still angry about what your father did."

Amanda stiffened.

"You don't think I'm mad? I'm really mad. I think about his affair all the time, but I'm not going to hold it against him forever. He was a good father and a good man who made a simple mistake. He made a mistake. That's all."

Susan bristled at the word "simple." She wanted to say that there was nothing simple about setting up a lover in a Chicago high-rise for several weeks, but she held her tongue. She saw nothing to gain by pointing out the obvious.

Susan exhaled and then clasped Amanda's hands.

"I want to tell you something," Susan said. "I want to tell you something I should have told you last summer when the wounds were still fresh."

"What?" Amanda asked.

"I loved your father. I loved him even after I learned that he had broken his vows. I think about him every day," Susan said with conviction. "I may not grieve like other wives or grieve like my daughter, but I still grieve. I still care. I want you to know that."

Amanda smiled weakly and hugged her mother.

"That's all I need," Amanda said. "That's all I need to hear."

Susan slid off the bed and stood up.

"Things will get better. I promise," Susan said. She leaned over and kissed Amanda on the head. "Try to think of happier things. Tomorrow is another day."

26: SUSAN

Wednesday, December 7, 1938

Susan needed only seconds to see that the presentation was more than a "little speech" and that Jack Hicks was more than an Okie from Muskogee or "a retired sailor with a lot of time on his hands." Even from her seat in the last row of the Mercer Auditorium, she could see that both the event and the uniformed Navy officer were big-time draws.

She sat in the last row because the last row was all that was available when she walked into the auditorium at seven fifteen with Elizabeth, Amanda, and Dot. She made herself comfortable in a cushioned seat and glanced at the others before directing her full attention to three men sitting together at the back of a brightly lighted stage.

Susan watched closely as one of the men, a fiftyish gent in a gray suit, got up from his chair and nearly tripped over a stray cord as he walked toward the front of the stage. He motioned to his young assistant, who sat next to Jack, and waited for him to retrieve the cord. When the blond man removed the hazard and returned to his seat, the fiftyish man proceeded to a large lectern and turned on the microphone.

"Good evening. I'm Clark Abercrombie, director of the Nassau Institute," the man said to five hundred people. "Welcome to the fourth lecture in the Institute's current series on foreign policy, military affairs, and pressing issues of the day. Our speaker tonight is a man who served this nation honorably for twenty-seven years in the United States Navy. He is a graduate of the U.S. Naval Academy in Annapolis, an author of two books on military strategy, and, if I may say so, a really great guy. Please welcome Rear Admiral John J. Hicks, U.S. Navy, retired, to the Mercer Auditorium."

Jack got up from his chair and walked to the front of the stage to the claps and cheers of an enthusiastic audience. He shook Abercrombie's hand, said a few words, and then replaced his host at the lectern. He waited until the director returned to his seat and then turned his eyes to a gathering that consisted mostly of college-age men.

"Thank you for that kind introduction, Clark, and thank you for inviting me to speak here tonight," Jack said. "As some of you may know, I have called Princeton home for the past two years. During that time, I've had the chance to meet many professors, students, and residents and discuss matters that interest us all in these dangerous times ..."

Susan smiled as she watched her acquaintance from the library speak. He was not just a cookie-cutter retiree looking for a purpose but rather a man of substance who wanted to make a difference in a world that was edging closer to conflict.

The time traveler felt a sense of irony when she remembered the date. A Japanese strike force would attack Pearl Harbor in exactly three years. German forces would invade much of Europe in less than one. By the end of 1941, the greatest war in history, one so many were trying to avoid, would engulf much of the planet.

Susan turned to her left and saw her mother stare at the stage. She could see that Elizabeth was as into the lecture as any professor or student.

So were Amanda and Dot. When Susan turned to her right, she saw two women follow the speaker with rapt attention. They nodded when Jack Hicks outlined his broad theme of military preparedness and smiled when he stated that few had a bigger stake in a strong American military than the young people who might one day be called to serve.

Susan warmed at the sight of her daughter's smile. She worried about Amanda's emotional health in the wake of Bruce Peterson's death and wondered how she would adapt to the loss at an age when many young women needed their fathers most.

She started to return to the lecturer when she saw Amanda tap on Dot's shoulder and point to the blond assistant, who sat in a chair at the back of the stage. Susan laughed. Amanda's unwavering interest in the program suddenly made sense.

Susan smiled at the girls and then returned her attention to the learned Admiral Hicks, who had launched into the meat of his speech. She could see from the ease with which he spoke that he had come prepared and knew his subject.

"Some of you may remember from your studies that aircraft carriers played a small but vital role in the Great War," Jack said. "Great Britain deployed at least six aircraft-bearing ships during that conflict, including the HMS *Ark Royal*, which defended British interests in the Dardanelles, and the HMS *Furious*, a modified cruiser that saw duty in the North Sea and inspired efforts to expand the scope of naval aviation ..."

For the next forty minutes, Jack Hicks, admiral, widower, and library patron, kept his audience on its toes by mixing battle narratives with descriptions of aviation feats. He also paid homage to servicemen in the auditorium, including two Navy flyers who had hunted German submarines in 1918 and a local unit of Army ROTC cadets.

Susan glanced at Dot when Jack mentioned the members of the university's Reserve Officers' Training Corps. She knew that the young woman's fiancé, a product of that corps, had already begun flight training in Riverside, California.

Susan then turned to her mother. She could see by the way she looked at Jack that she was still into his message, but she also knew that Elizabeth had more on her mind than naval aviation. She was counting the days until her parents and infant self completed their journey to Princeton.

Susan turned her attention to the stage just as Jack nimbly shifted from the history of naval aviation to its promise. He said that several new projects were under way but added that recent progress was not enough. He told the audience that the U.S. Navy was not keeping pace with potential belligerents like Germany and Japan.

"We live in a world where a nation's strength is not measured by the size of its economy but rather by the size of its army and the reach of its navy," Jack said. "I hope that my comments tonight will help spur a discussion that is long overdue. I thank you again for the opportunity to speak tonight."

Jack smiled as the audience rose to its feet and gave him a thunderous ovation. He nodded at the ROTC cadets in the front row, took a sip of water, and then yielded the lectern to the Nassau Institute's director.

"I want to thank all of you for attending tonight's lecture and remind you that the series will continue on January 11," Clark Abercrombie said. "Admiral Hicks has informed me that he would be happy to take a few questions from the audience. So, without further ado, I give you back our featured speaker ..."

27: AMANDA

Amanda stood and applauded as Rear Admiral John J. Hicks answered the last of ten questions from his audience and finally called it a night. She admired his passion and eloquence and thought both deserved at least one rousing ovation.

"He's good," Amanda said to Susan as the applause subsided. She looked around to see if others were listening and then whispered in her mother's ear. "The Navy should send him to Pearl Harbor."

Susan looked at Amanda and put a finger to her lips.

"We can talk more about Admiral Hicks later," Susan said.

Amanda nodded.

"Are you in a hurry to leave? Dot and I want to stick around and mingle."

"So do I," Susan said. "I want to say hello to the speaker."

"You know him?" Amanda asked.

Susan nodded.

"I met him at the library two weeks ago. He invited me to come tonight."

"He did?"

"He did."

Amanda raised a brow.

"Suddenly your interest in naval aviation makes sense."

"He's just an acquaintance," Susan said.

Amanda grinned.

"Sure he is."

Susan acknowledged her daughter's comment with a smile and then helped her mother to her feet. She grabbed her purse and looked at Amanda.

"We'll see you back at the house," Susan said.

"OK."

Susan leaned toward Dot.

"It was nice seeing you again, Dot."

"You too, Mrs. Peterson."

Susan returned to Amanda.

"Now go run along and mingle before all the nice young men in this audience find better things to do."

Amanda laughed.

"OK. I will."

"Bye," Susan said.

"Bye."

Amanda watched with interest as Susan guided Elizabeth past several seats to the center aisle. The aisle led to the doors and a lobby where the public could meet and greet Hicks, Nassau Institute officials, and other dignitaries.

She suspected that Susan wanted to do more than say hello to the speaker, but she decided not to make an issue of it. She wanted her mother to get out, socialize, and meet people her own age, even if that meant meeting someone who might someday take her father's place.

Amanda pondered that unsettling possibility as the large hall began to empty. She remained in a daze until her BFF snapped her out of it.

"Well?" Dot asked.

"Well what?"

"Are you going to just stand there all night – or meet Mr. Wonderful?"

"I don't know, Dot. I'm starting to get cold feet."

"Then let me warm them up!"

"I can't do this," Amanda said.

"Sure you can," Dot said. "Just let me do the talking. I know how to handle these things. I have a very subtle touch."

"Oh, all right."

Dot took Amanda's hand and led her to a side aisle and then to the front of the auditorium. They reached their destination just as a young blond man in a crisp white shirt and gray slacks began to push the four-wheeled lectern off the stage.

"Hi!" Dot said cheerfully.

The man stopped to look at the friendly redhead.

"Hello."

"How are you today?" Dot asked.

"I'm fine," the man said. "How are you?"

"I'm fine too. I wasn't fine on Sunday between three and four o'clock or on Monday between six thirty and seven, but I'm fine now. I'm really fine now."

The man looked at Dot like she was an alien from Grovers Mill or a woman fit for a funny farm. He could not have known she was both.

"That's good to hear," the man said. "Can I help you with anything?"

"You can," Dot replied.

"What can I do?"

"You can answer a question."

The man leaned forward.

"OK. What's the question?"

"Will you go out with my friend?"

"Dot!" Amanda exclaimed.

The redhead put her hand to her mouth and tried to stifle a laugh.

"I'm sorry," Dot said. "I couldn't resist."

Amanda glared at her "friend" and turned fifty shades of red. Then she looked at the man and turned fifty shades more.

"Please forgive my friend," Amanda said. "She's not well. She hasn't fully recovered from the science experiment."

The man laughed.

"I suspected as much."

"I'm serious," Amanda said. "She might be nuts for months."

The man laughed again.

"Does your friend have a name?"

"She certainly does," Amanda said. "She's Dorothy Gale, as in *The Wizard of Oz*. She has a dog named Toto and, for all I know, a few witches in her broom closet."

Amanda glared again at Dot. She glared until she realized that the redhead laughing hysterically and holding her sides was immune to harsh glances.

The man looked at Dot and then at Amanda.

"How about you? Do *you* have a name?"

"I do," Amanda said. She sighed. "I'm Amanda."

The man stepped away from the lectern, walked to the front of the stage, and slipped over the edge onto the floor. He smiled at each of his visitors.

"Hi, ladies. I'm Kurt, your entertainment this evening."

"Hi, Kurt," Dot said. "I'm Dot. It's nice to meet you."

She shook his hand.

Amanda, still red-faced, did the same.

"Hi."

Kurt looked at Amanda.

"Is she always like this?"

"I'm not certain," Amanda said. "I just met her."

Kurt turned to Dot.

"Is that true?"

Dot nodded.

"We met last month."

Kurt chuckled.

"You could have fooled me. You relate to each other like old friends."

"It seems that way," Dot said.

Kurt smiled warmly at Dot and then turned to Amanda. He gazed at her for what seemed like an eternity before finally breaking the silence.

"I've seen you before," Kurt said. "I'm sure of it."

"I am too," Amanda replied. "We saw each other at the Yale Ball."

"That's right. I saw you with Dot and two or three men. I assume one was your date."

Amanda smiled.

"You assume correctly. I went to the dance with Dot's fiancé."

Kurt stared at Amanda with wide eyes.

"You did?"

"I did," Amanda said. "What makes it better is that I had Dot's blessing."

Kurt turned to Dot.

"Really?"

"I went to Bryn Mawr," Dot said dryly. "We're very progressive."

Amanda laughed.

"She's just teasing."

"I hope so," Kurt said. He looked at Amanda. "Did you not have your own date?"

"No," Amanda said. "I went with Roy, Dot's fiancé, because it was the only way I could get into the dance. Roy is a Princeton alum."

"I see."

"Are you a Princeton grad?"

Kurt shook his head.

"I attended the University of Virginia. I graduated last spring and moved here in September when I found a job at the Institute."

"Then how did *you* get into the dance?" Amanda asked.

"A friend of mine gave me a ticket. He's a Princeton senior and intern at the Institute."

"So you went stag?"

"I went stag," Kurt said.

Amanda berated herself for not introducing herself at the dance. She liked this soft-spoken blond with the warm smile and the hearty laugh. He seemed like a nice guy.

"So what exactly do you do at the Institute?" Amanda asked.

"I write press releases and assist the senior fellows in the areas of German-American relations, history, and trade," Kurt said. "I studied history and foreign policy in college."

Be still, my heart.

Amanda looked at Dot and saw her flash an I-told-you-so grin.

"Are you working on anything interesting?" Amanda asked.

"It depends on your definition of 'interesting.' I'm currently researching the collapse of the Weimar Republic and its impact on American investments in Europe," Kurt said. "I hope to complete my work before I leave town on Friday."

"Where are you going?"

"I'm going home for the holidays."

"Where's home?" Amanda asked.

"Washington, D.C."

Amanda glanced at Dot again and smiled. She couldn't believe that so many good things could be crammed into one human being.

"You *are* coming back, though, aren't you?" Amanda asked.

Kurt nodded.

"I have to be back in time to help Dr. Abercrombie prepare for the next lecture."

"Oh," Amanda said.

"I return to Princeton on January 9. The lecture is January 11," Kurt said. He looked at the women. "I would love to see both of you then."

"I'm not going anywhere," Dot said with a smile.

"Neither am I. I'll be at the lecture," Amanda said. She looked at Kurt with hopeful eyes. "I'll be there if I have to walk through three feet of snow."

28: ELIZABETH

Elizabeth Campbell stared out her living room window and waited for a family she feared would never come. She had maintained a constant vigil since watching a real estate agent pull a SOLD sign from a frozen lawn at nine fifteen.

She smiled at the thought of her parents buying a house they had never seen. No one jumped into real estate blindly unless they were fools or optimists or had a trustworthy friend willing to minimize the risks inherent in property transactions.

Fortunately for Erich, Ella, and Elizabeth Wagner, they had such a friend in Walter Bauer, a fifty-five-year-old attorney who had left Munich in 1933. Like many other citizens of the late Weimar Republic, Bauer had decided to shift his ample wealth to a country that was free of putsches, purges, and suspended elections. He had come to Princeton in 1935 and founded what had become the township's fastest-growing law firm.

Erich Wagner had contacted Bauer, his godfather, in March 1938, shortly after Adolf Hitler had begun to unify Germany and Austria under a common flag. He had expressed his desire to immigrate to the United States, transfer his own considerable holdings to American banks, and find employment as a professor of mathematics. Thanks to Bauer, his professional colleagues, and a U.S. administration eager to relieve Europe of its brightest minds, he had been able to achieve all three goals by the end of 1938.

Elizabeth glanced at a clock and saw it was three thirty – or about an hour before sunset. She wondered if her parents would arrive before darkness fell on the third shortest day of the year.

Part of her hoped they would not. She was not mentally prepared to meet them or even be in their presence. She did not know what she would do when they arrived.

Elizabeth returned her attention to the street and noticed that snow had started to fall. She had expected as much. Ella Wagner had mentioned snowfall in her written account of the day.

Elizabeth settled into the monotony of her vigil when she heard a noise. She turned her head and saw her daughter walk into the room with a sandwich on a plate.

"I brought you something to eat in case your stakeout runs past midnight," Susan said. She smiled. "I don't want you to waste away."

"I can think of worse things."

"Such as?"

"Such as slipping on that sidewalk and breaking my hip," Elizabeth said. She laughed. "It looks like it's getting slick out there."

Susan looked out the window.

"It does."

Susan walked up to her mother, who sat in a wooden chair, and handed her the plate.

"Thank you, dear," Elizabeth said.

"You're welcome," Susan replied. She stood next to Elizabeth and put a hand on her shoulder. "I take it that no one has even driven by slowly."

"I would have told you if they had."

"Are you sure they will come today?"

Elizabeth nodded.

"I am. Or at least I think I am. I'm not sure of anything anymore."

"We can always visit the realtor tomorrow," Susan said. "We can say we saw him pull the sign out front and ask when our new neighbors are coming."

Elizabeth smiled sadly, grabbed her daughter's hand, and squeezed it.

"I don't think that will be necessary. I have faith they will come today."

"Even if they do, I can't imagine they will spend the night," Susan said. "There is still no furniture in the house. I checked this morning."

"There probably won't be any either until the end of the week. My mother wrote that our first night in the house was Christmas Eve," Elizabeth said. "She wanted my first Christmas in America to be spent in our new home and not in a hotel."

Susan walked to the window and wiped the condensation from two of the panes with the side of her hand. When she was done, she stepped back and gazed at her mother.

"Would you like me to stay?" Susan asked.

Elizabeth nodded.

"I would."

"OK," Susan said. "I will."

"Where is Amanda?" Elizabeth asked.

"She's still out with Dot."

"Those two are becoming as thick as thieves, aren't they?"

"They are," Susan said with a laugh. "They certainly are."

"That's good."

"I think so too. I'm glad to see her make friends here."

Concluding that she might, in fact, waste away before midnight, Elizabeth took a bite of her ham-and-cheese sandwich. She took a second and a third and then decided she needed something to wash the sandwich down. She turned to Susan.

"Can you get me something to drink?" Elizabeth asked.

Susan nodded.

"I'll be right back."

Elizabeth raised her hand as Susan turned around and walked away. She started to ask her specifically for a glass of water when she heard something she would remember for the rest of her life: the sound of a car door closing.

Elizabeth got out of her chair and moved quickly to the window. When she peered across the street to the house that was once her home, she saw a well-dressed man of maybe thirty walk around the back of a Packard taxicab. The man opened the other rear passenger door and helped a young woman holding an infant out of the vehicle.

Susan rushed to her mother's side and looked out the window but did not say a word. She clearly understood the importance and beauty of the moment and did not want to spoil it with questions or small talk.

Elizabeth focused again on the man as he stuck his head through the front passenger-side window and said something to the driver. She could tell from his body language alone that he was instructing the driver to stay.

The man stepped away from the cab, put his arm around the woman, and guided her to the front door of the house. They opened the door with a key, entered the residence, and disappeared from sight.

Elizabeth watched with awe and wonder as the couple reappeared in the large living room window and moved slowly about the room. Even as distant shadows, the man and the woman seemed mesmerizing, haunting, and strikingly familiar.

She sighed when the figures again vanished from sight and became anxious as five long minutes passed. She took Susan's hand and held it until the family stepped through the front door, shut it, and moved carefully down the icy walk to the waiting cab.

Elizabeth moved closer to the window as the man helped the woman with the baby into the back of the taxi, shut their door, and walked to his side of the vehicle. She pressed her face to the glass when he lingered outside his door and looked across the street.

The man put his hand above his eyes and, for several seconds, anyway, seemed to meet Elizabeth's gaze. He then lowered his hand, brushed a few snowflakes from the sleeves of his gray trench coat, and turned away. He opened his door, jumped in the cab, and looked one more time at the rental house on Mercer Street as the taxi drove away.

Elizabeth closed her eyes and smiled as the reality of the moment set in. She had seen more than three people giving their new home a quick inspection. She had seen her parents for the first time in fifty-five years and a baby she knew only from pictures.

She didn't know where she would go from here or how long she would take to get there, but she did know one thing. Life as she knew it was about to change.

29: SUSAN

Wednesday, December 21, 1938

Susan walked along Nassau Street for the first time since Monday, when an afternoon flurry had made walking dangerous, and noticed that Princeton was starting to empty. She saw fewer people, fewer cars, and more shops that had either closed early or restricted their hours as the number of Christmas customers had dwindled.

She didn't mind. She hadn't walked to this part of town to see people, cars, or shops but rather to mail a letter that required extra postage. Susan visited the Palmer Square Post Office every other week to send Professor Geoffrey Bell a reminder that his three lab rats were alive and well and enjoying the good life in 1938.

Susan continued down Nassau Street, taking the long way home, until she reached the Dairy Diner, a tile-covered, art-deco hole-in-the-wall that was typically filled with students. She peered in the front window and noticed that the diner was filled not with students but rather a half dozen older adults who had apparently decided to enjoy one last hamburger and milkshake before switching to turkey, ham, and Christmas cuisine.

She looked at a menu in the window, noted its contents, and debated whether she needed a burger the size of a Buick. Then she noticed a customer sitting alone at a table along a long wall and decided she needed a burger after all.

Susan opened the bell-rigged door and stepped inside the diner. She walked past a clerk at the ordering counter and made a beeline for the table. She smiled when the customer at the table looked up and motioned for her to join him.

Susan laughed to herself when he wiped the corners of his mouth with a napkin and hurried to his feet. She couldn't remember the last time a man had stood up for her when she had approached a table in a restaurant.

"Are the burgers as good as they look?" Susan asked.

"No," Jack Hicks said. "They're better."

"I saw you as I was walking by and decided I had to at least step inside to say hello."

"I'm glad you did. Please join me."

"I think I will."

Susan grabbed the only other chair at the tiny table and sat down. She knew even before she settled into her seat that she would order something decadent but decided to put off ordering anything until she had a chance to chat with one of the most interesting men she had ever met.

"How are you?" Jack asked.

"I'm fine, thank you," Susan said. "How about you?"

"I'm better now that I've had lunch."

Susan laughed.

"I imagine this place would lift anyone's spirits."

Jack pushed his plate away and put his napkin on the plate.

"Where is your mother?"

"She's back at the house," Susan said. "She didn't feel like going for a walk today."

Susan didn't say that Elizabeth hadn't felt like going for a walk of any kind since seeing her parents and infant self on Monday afternoon. She had instead mostly kept to herself and maintained her ongoing surveillance of the house across the street.

"That's too bad. I enjoyed visiting with her after the lecture. She's quite a remarkable woman," Jack said. "Then again, so is her daughter."

Susan smiled.

"You presume a lot, Admiral. I could be a very ordinary woman who has nothing better to do than visit the library and attend lectures."

"There is nothing ordinary about a person who ventures out in pursuit of knowledge," Jack said. "There is nothing ordinary about a person who asks detailed questions about the future of the U.S. Navy. I found your inquiries quite refreshing."

"I take it that you're not used to women asking you about the present capabilities of our standing fleets," Susan said.

"I'm not used to *men* asking me that."

"You find that frustrating, no doubt."

"I find it very frustrating," Jack said. "Far too many citizens believe we do not need a larger navy or a navy with expensive aircraft carriers. They believe that the oceans alone protect us from the reach of potential belligerents like Germany and Japan."

Susan smiled again.

"That's why I found your lecture compelling. You didn't simply demonstrate why expanding the navy is a good thing. You demonstrated why it is an *essential* thing. I personally think you gained a lot of converts to your cause."

"I hope you're right," Jack said. "I suspect that time is growing short for Americans to alter their thinking and recognize the threats that face us."

Susan took a moment to study a man she had first met in the library and quickly concluded that his appeal hadn't lessened in twenty-six days. She saw deep wrinkles around his eyes and a few spots where his black hair had started to thin but nothing to suggest that he was not, in fact, a very handsome man.

The fact he was also an admiral, an author, and a visionary with a delightful twang didn't hurt either. If her new friend had any serious flaws, then he was doing a great job of hiding them.

"I'm surprised to see you're still around," Susan said. "It appears that just about everyone else in town has left for the holidays. Are you going anywhere for Christmas?"

Jack took a sip of water.

"As a matter of fact, I am. I'm catching a train for Maryland later today. I plan to spend the next several days with my nephew and his family. James is an instructor at the Naval Academy. He and his wife, Paula, live on a farm outside Annapolis."

"Do you have any other family nearby?"

"I don't have any other family, period," Jack said. "My parents passed away many years ago. My older brother Roger died of lung cancer last Christmas – just a month before Janet."

"Oh, no. I'm sorry to hear that."

Jack shrugged.

"He'd been very ill for months. In some respects, his death was a blessing."

"It's still hard though," Susan said. "I lost my only sibling, a brother, when I was ten. You never get over things like that."

Jack nodded and looked at Susan sympathetically.

"I suppose not."

Susan pondered the comment before steering the conversation in another direction. She thought Jack seemed oddly indifferent to death and dying, but she saw nothing to gain by pointing that out. She figured that any man who had lost his only sibling and his wife in rapid succession probably understood loss as well as anyone.

"So how is your book coming?" Susan asked.

"It's coming," Jack said with a weak smile.

Susan laughed.

143

"That doesn't sound like you'll publish tomorrow."

"I still think I'll have it out by the end of next year, but I'm not as optimistic as I was even a week ago."

"Why?" Susan asked.

"I fear I may struggle with writing for a general audience," Jack said. "I'm targeting a skeptical public this time and not a sympathetic military. To make a case for a larger, more versatile navy, I'll have to reach out to civilians in language they can understand and appreciate."

"Perhaps I can help."

"How?"

"I could proof your work," Susan said. "I don't know much about the military, but I know a lot about writing for a general audience. I could provide useful input."

"You would do that?"

"Of course."

"I may take you up on your offer," Jack said. "I must write a book that appeals not only to men but also to women. Wives, mothers, and sisters have as much at stake in a strong navy as their husbands, sons, and brothers."

Susan smiled at the understatement of the century.

"I agree."

Jack put a hand to his chin.

"How do you know so much about writing for the public?"

"I did some freelance work many years ago," Susan said truthfully.

"You did?"

Susan nodded.

"I wrote human interest stories for a Chicago paper. I didn't win any awards or land a full-time job, but I learned a lot about writing for a mainstream audience."

"I'm impressed," Jack said. "It appears I've found an assistant."

Susan laughed to herself. She had walked into the diner to find an acquaintance but had found a job instead. She suddenly had a purpose in 1938 that went beyond watching over her brooding mother and adventurous daughter.

"So when do we start?" Susan asked. "Do you have something I can read?"

"I do," Jack said. He laughed. "I have an introduction."

Susan grinned.

"Well, it's a start – literally."

Jack smiled.

"I suppose it is."

"Why don't you drop it off before you leave today?" Susan asked. "I promise I'll read it over the break and give you my thoughts on it when you get back."

"I'd like that."

"Then consider it done. When *do* you get back?"

"I plan to return to Princeton by January 11," Jack said. "I want to be back in time to see my successor in the Nassau Institute's lecture series."

"Oh? Is someone important speaking?"

"You might say that. The featured speaker is Heinrich Schmidt, the military attaché at the German embassy in Washington. He apparently has views on military preparedness that are much like my own."

"I see," Susan said.

"Are you going to the lecture?" Jack asked.

"I wasn't planning to."

Jack sighed and smiled softly.

"Would you go if a washed-up admiral escorted you?"

Susan blushed.

"I would," Susan said. "I'd go if the washed-up admiral simply met me at the door."

30: ELIZABETH

Sunday, December 25, 1938

Elizabeth looked out her living room window at the house across the street and saw two signs of life. The first was smoke pouring out of the chimney. The second was a shadow moving back and forth behind an illuminated, curtained window.

She didn't know whether the shadow belonged to her mother or her father, but she guessed by its movements that it belonged to her mother. Ella Wagner had been a frenetic, busy bee of a woman who rarely sat down unless she had swept every floor and washed every dish.

"Have you spotted Santa yet?" Susan asked.

Elizabeth turned around and saw her daughter and her granddaughter look at her with smiling eyes. They curled up on opposite ends of the sofa and managed cups of tea.

"Have you added comedy to your resume?" Elizabeth asked sharply.

"No," Susan said. "I haven't the time to do stand-up. I'm far too busy helping Admiral Hicks explain Brewster Buffaloes and Grumman Wildcats to duffers and housewives."

"Then perhaps you should return to your hobby and let your mother spy on the neighbors in peace."

Susan laughed. "I would if I thought you would accomplish something. You really should go over and say hi. Your parents are probably very approachable people."

"They are," Amanda said.

Elizabeth looked at her granddaughter.

"How would you know? You haven't met them."

"That's not quite true," Amanda said, drawing out each word. She blushed as she sat up. "I met them this afternoon when the two of you went for your walk."

"You *met* them?" Elizabeth asked.

Amanda nodded.

"I met the baby too. You're cute, Grandma."

Susan grinned.

"Why didn't you say anything?" Elizabeth asked.

"I didn't say anything because I didn't want to upset you," Amanda replied. "I knew you wanted to be the first to welcome them to the neighborhood."

"I do. I did. Oh, it doesn't matter. I'm just a cowardly old woman who can't do what she came here to do."

Amanda smiled.

"You're not cowardly at all. You're prudent. You didn't want to blow a hole in the universe before opening your presents this morning."

Susan laughed.

"Don't you join in," Elizabeth said. She wagged a finger at her daughter. "One tart-tongued person in this family is plenty."

"I wouldn't think of it, Mom. That would be piling on."

Amanda laughed.

"We're just having fun, Grandma."

"I don't need fun," Elizabeth said. "I need courage – and information. Tell me about your visit. I want to hear everything."

Elizabeth did too. She wanted to know as much as possible about the newest residents of Princeton, New Jersey, before jumping into their lives. She knew she would only have one chance to make a good first impression and didn't want to blow it.

"There's not a lot to say," Amanda said. "I knocked on their door around two, introduced myself to Mr. Wagner, and asked if I could borrow some butter for the cookies I was making. He gave me the butter and then invited me into the house to meet his wife and daughter."

"What were they like?" Elizabeth asked.

"He was outgoing. She was more reserved. Both were very friendly. As for the baby, she was just blasted cute. I've never seen a baby that cute or held one that calm."

"You held her? You held *me*?"

Amanda nodded.

"I held you while Mrs. Wagner pulled a pie from the oven," Amanda said. "It's kind of funny when you think about it."

"What do you mean?" Elizabeth asked.

Amanda smiled.

"I mean it's not every day a girl gets to burp her grandma."

Elizabeth laughed heartily and then sighed. She needed to hear an anecdote like that as much as she needed to hear her granddaughter's wit. She was taking this matter far too seriously and really needed to lighten up.

"You're right about that," Elizabeth said.

"Did you tell them about us?" Susan asked.

"I did," Amanda said. "I said I lived across the street with two codependent women who happened to be time travelers and their direct descendants."

Susan smiled.

"I'll bet that broke the ice."

"It didn't," Amanda said. "It only put them off. They didn't believe you were codependent."

Susan laughed.

"You're in a good mood today," Susan said.

"I am," Amanda replied.

"Would your mood have anything to do with a young man?"

"It might."

"Would it have anything to do with a tall, blond lecture assistant?"

Amanda smiled.

"It might."

Elizabeth laughed to herself as she listened to the banter. She didn't know what young man occupied Amanda's thoughts, but she was glad at least one did. She was happy that both Amanda and Susan had apparently developed interests that went beyond dining, shopping, and walking around a college town.

"How come we haven't seen this mystery man?" Susan asked.

"You haven't seen him because he's been in D.C. the past two weeks," Amanda said. "He went home for the holidays and won't be back until January 9."

"Then why are you feeling so good today?"

"I'm feeling good because he sent me a postcard that arrived yesterday. Dot and I each asked him to send us postcards of the Washington Monument."

"That was thoughtful of him," Susan said. "What did he write?"

"He told Dot that he enjoyed meeting her at the last lecture and looked forward to seeing her at the next one."

"What did he write to *you*?" Susan asked.

"He wrote the same thing, but he added a P.S."

"Oh? What was that?"

Amanda smiled.

"He asked me what restaurant I like."

31: AMANDA

Halfway through her third trip down the third aisle in what a sign outside called a liquor store, Amanda stopped, scratched her head, and laughed. In her quest to find a quality domestic whiskey, she had found British gin, Mexican tequila, and Jamaican rum. American distillers had still not fully recovered from the ravages of Prohibition.

Amanda grabbed a fifth of local swill and something better from overseas and joined Dot and Elizabeth near the door. She smiled and held the bottles high.

"Pick your poison, ladies!"

Dot looked at the bottles and laughed.

"I vote for the rotgut."

"Grandma?" Amanda asked.

Elizabeth looked at the bottles and frowned.

"Are those our only choices?"

"They are if you don't want tequila or rum," Amanda said.

"You know I don't like gin, dear. The lighter fluid will have to do."

Amanda laughed.

Five minutes later, Amanda paid for the whiskey, led the others out of the store, and guided them down Nassau Street to Mercer Street. She watched Elizabeth closely as the three women walked across the dark intersection and continued toward the rental.

"How are you feeling, Grams?" Amanda asked.

"I'm feeling well for someone who hadn't planned to walk to a liquor store on a cold winter night," Elizabeth said. "You could have gone without me. I'm sure you would have managed."

Amanda smiled. She was glad to see her grandmother back to her sassy self after watching her slip into a funk of sorts over the past several days.

149

Elizabeth had crawled into a shell each time she had tried and failed to muster the courage to meet the people who had raised her. She had advanced as far as her front door on Monday and the sidewalk on Wednesday but no farther. When Susan had crossed the street on Friday to say hello to the neighbors for the first time, Elizabeth had remained in her room. She had told her family that she simply wasn't ready to close the deal.

"Thanks for agreeing to play cards with us tonight," Amanda said to Elizabeth. "I know you don't like to stay up late and would rather go to bed."

"What I'd rather do, Amanda, is watch my granddaughter leave the house in the company of a dashing young man and not waste a night like New Year's Eve on a relic like me."

Dot laughed.

"You're not a relic, Mrs. Campbell. You're a treasure."

"You're right. I am," Elizabeth said. "I'm a treasure waiting to be buried."

Dot turned to Amanda.

"Is she always this way?"

"No," Amanda said. She giggled. "She's usually worse."

"I mean it though," Elizabeth said. "You should be out dancing and mingling. Surely you have better things to do than play cards with two widows."

"We don't. Right, Dot?"

Dot forced a smile.

"Right."

Amanda looked at Dot with amusement. She knew for a fact that she had better things to do, including attending a Bryn Mawr alumni party in Philadelphia and seeing her favorite jazz band play at a bar in Trenton, but she had given them up to please a new friend. The girl from Grovers Mill continued to impress.

Amanda gave Dot a knowing smile and then returned to Elizabeth. She could see that her grandmother hadn't bought a word the girls had said.

"See, Grandma. It's unanimous. We really don't have better things to do."

"Then you should look for something," Elizabeth said. "These are the years you should seek fun, push boundaries, and step out of your comfort zone. Take it from someone who married far too young. I know."

Amanda turned to Dot.

"Grandma eloped when she was twenty. She and Grandpa spent their honeymoon on Route 66 on their way to Los Angeles."

Dot gave Amanda a funny look.

"Route 66?"

Amanda realized her mistake the second she saw Dot's puzzled eyes. Route 66 did not exist in 1880, the year *this* grandma supposedly got married. She quickly backtracked.

"I'm sorry. I meant to say they took their time traveling to California."

"Oh, how fun!" Dot said. "I want to do that on *my* honeymoon."

"Just don't leave your wedding ring in Oklahoma," Amanda said.

Dot tilted her head.

"What?"

Elizabeth laughed.

"It's a family joke," Amanda said. "I'll tell you later."

"Oh. OK."

"Have you set a wedding date?" Elizabeth asked.

"No," Dot said. "We probably won't set *any* dates before April, when Roy gets his next assignment, but we're still holding out for a June wedding."

Elizabeth smiled.

"June is a good month."

As the trio approached their destination, Amanda looked again at her grandmother. She appeared happier than when they had left the liquor store. She seemed more engaged and more relaxed. She seemed ready for an evening of cards.

Amanda stopped in front of the rental a minute later and surveyed the street. She saw dark houses in both directions and few signs of life. Even the Wagner residence appeared unoccupied. Amanda saw a car in the driveway but no lights in the windows.

She escorted Elizabeth and Dot to the porch and quickly peeked through a small window that was embedded in the door. She saw what she had hoped to see.

"Grandma?" Amanda asked.

"Yes, dear?"

"Do you remember just a minute ago when you told me how important it is to step out of your comfort zone?"

"Of course," Elizabeth said.

Amanda smiled warmly and sighed.

"Well, keep that in mind when we play cards tonight. I have a feeling you're going to do some stepping."

32: ELIZABETH

Elizabeth watched warily as the child wiggled in her high chair, smeared frosting on her face, and flashed a million-dollar smile. She didn't think the baby, a cute-as-a-bug blonde who shared her DNA, could turn her into a toad or blow a hole in the universe with a single glance of her pretty blue eyes, but she knew she *was* capable of charming an old woman to death.

Elizabeth tried to hold herself together as she turned away from the girl and looked again at the people sitting across from her at the card table. Two hours after meeting Erich and Ella Wagner for the first time, at least as a time traveler, she still had difficulty looking them in the eyes. She felt helpless to do anything but sit straight in her chair.

She smiled nervously at the couple, glanced at her worthless poker hand, and decided that she would not be able to think about cards or anything else no matter how hard she tried. It had been that way since Amanda and Dot had led her through the front door and into a meeting that had been put off for far too long.

The first thirty minutes had passed in a blurry daze. Elizabeth had shaken two hands, greeted an infant, and tried to reconcile feelings that ranged from fear and irritation to elation and relief. She had been so taken aback by meeting her original family that she'd had to make two trips to the bathroom simply to throw water on her face.

Elizabeth let her mind drift to a transition that came into sharper focus with each passing minute. She mentally revisited the beautiful, traumatic, unexpected reunion with her parents when the only male in the room brought her back to the here and now.

"Your daughter tells me that you grew up in Princeton," Erich Wagner said with a thick Austrian accent. "Where did you live?"

Elizabeth laughed to herself. She could only imagine her father's reaction if she told him the truth. She instead told him a lie she had long rehearsed in her mind.

"I lived in a large white house on this very street, near the battlefield park," Elizabeth said. "Are you familiar with the area?"

Erich nodded.

"We drove through the neighborhood yesterday. We saw some nice homes there, but I don't recall seeing a large white house."

"That's because it no longer exists. It burned to the ground fifty years ago."

"I'm sorry to hear that," Erich said. "Was anyone harmed in the fire?"

"No. The house was unoccupied at the time."

Elizabeth knew that much was true. She knew from a newspaper article she had read that a home once belonging to a banker named George Pennington had not been occupied when it had gone up in smoke on December 2, 1888.

"That is good," Erich said. "That is something."

Elizabeth relaxed for the first time all night and looked again at the man she had once called Papa. He was as handsome, articulate, and unassuming as she remembered and far more at ease. He looked like a man who had not yet raised a daughter who had renounced her Catholic faith and run off with a Protestant.

"Have you settled into *your* home?" Elizabeth asked.

"We have," Erich said. "We have found it much to our liking. Our house is much larger than the one we owned in Vienna and far more practical."

Elizabeth turned to Ella.

"How are *you* adjusting to life in New Jersey?"

"I'm adjusting," Ella said with a laugh that Elizabeth had loved growing up. "I like it here, but I'm still getting used to America."

Susan grinned at Elizabeth as she dealt a new hand.

"Ella bought groceries today," Susan said. "She saw more food on the shelves than she's used to seeing. She discovered peanut butter, yellow mustard, and ketchup, among other things."

Elizabeth smiled as she pondered the comment. To a twenty-first-century time traveler from Illinois, the grocery and department stores of 1938 were veritable wastelands. To a 1930s refugee from Austria, however, they were consumer cornucopias. They were reminders that even Americans of the Depression years had it better — much better — than the rest of the world.

"Does the baby have everything she needs?" Elizabeth asked.

"I think so," Ella replied. "We plan to buy a new crib and perhaps more clothes for her in the coming weeks, but I believe she has everything she needs for now."

Elizabeth used the pause that followed to study her mother. She saw a woman who was at once practical, prudent, caring, and much more beautiful than she remembered. Like most people, perhaps, Elizabeth thought her mother was the most beautiful woman on the planet. Unlike most people, she had more than one reason to think so.

Ella Wagner was not just a pleasant person with a good heart. She was a strikingly attractive human being. With long curly blond hair, flawless skin, and alpine lakes for eyes, she was a living, breathing thirties cliché, the kind of woman movie producers and magazine editors showered with attention and wealthy men rushed to the altar.

"Do you have a babysitter?" Elizabeth asked.

"A what?" Ella replied.

"Do you have someone to watch Lizzie should you want to run an errand or go out for an evening with your husband?"

"No."

"You do now," Elizabeth said. "I would watch her anytime."

No sooner than Elizabeth the Elder uttered the words, Elizabeth the Younger threw a piece of cake on the hardwood floor. The adults responded with laughter.

Ella smiled.

"Your offer is generous," Ella said. "Are you sure it wouldn't be a bother?"

"I'm sure," Elizabeth replied. "I would consider it a privilege to look after this delightful girl, and I suspect that my daughter and granddaughter feel the same."

Ella glanced at Susan.

"Is that so?"

"It is," Susan said.

Ella turned to Amanda.

"You don't even need to ask," Amanda said. "I would pay *you* to watch her."

"Me too!" Dot said.

Ella laughed and smiled warmly.

"It seems I have found neighbors *and* friends," Ella said. "I was told that Americans were a warm and generous people, but now I see it is true."

Elizabeth gathered the cards and took her turn as the dealer.

"It's true enough," Elizabeth said. "It's true with us. I think the more you get to know us, the more you'll like us and find we have much in common."

She shuffled the cards.

"I must say I feel a connection already," Ella said in a lyrical voice. "I know this sounds silly, but I feel I know you. I feel like I have met my American family."

Elizabeth stifled a laugh, glanced at Susan and Amanda, and saw them smile. She didn't know whether they smiled at Ella's more-true-than-you-can-imagine comment or at her reaction *to* that comment, but she did know that they appreciated the beauty of the moment. They were enjoying the evening as much as anyone.

"It's funny that you say that, Ella. I feel the same way," Elizabeth said. "I feel like I have met my Austrian family."

Susan and Amanda laughed quietly.

"Is something humorous?" Erich asked.

"No," Susan said. "We're just all in a good mood."

"I see."

"We don't entertain much. Please excuse our enthusiasm."

"There's nothing to excuse," Ella said. "Your enthusiasm is uplifting. We would much rather spend an evening in a house of laughter and smiles than in a house of sorrow and tears. We heard precious little laughter in Vienna this year."

"That's understandable," Susan said.

"I suppose it is."

Elizabeth smiled as she soaked up the conversation. She could not have asked for a better evening, even if it was an evening that she had not anticipated or even agreed to.

"I think we're done talking, Mom," Susan said. "You can deal at any time."

"I will in a minute," Elizabeth said. "I will after everyone refreshes their drinks."

"OK," Susan said. "Everyone fill their glasses."

Elizabeth watched closely as Susan poured some Old Jersey No. 10 in her tumbler and started the bottle around the table. When the fifth finally reached the dealer, she poured what was left of the rotgut into her glass and then set the bottle to the side.

Elizabeth looked at Susan, Amanda, and Dot and then at Erich and Ella. She raised her glass to the messy baby and then to the adults.

"Here's a toast to neighbors, friends, and family," Elizabeth said. "May they give us laughter, smiles, and strength and remind us that life is about living."

Six glasses clinked and several people spoke.

"Hear, hear."

33: AMANDA

Wednesday, January 11, 1939

Sitting again in the back row of the Mercer Auditorium, Amanda scanned the public hall for empty seats, found none, and pondered the difference of ten years.

In 1929 the military attaché from the German embassy in D.C. drew an audience of barely a hundred. He did so because he represented the peaceful, predictable Weimar Republic and talked about trade, debt, and other things that put most people to sleep.

In 1939 the same man drew a packed house. He did so because he represented a Nazi regime that had just annexed Austria and parts of Czechoslovakia and talked about treaty violations, miscalculations, and other things that kept most people awake.

Amanda knew that Colonel Heinrich Schmidt had fared poorly in Princeton ten years earlier because she had spoken to a man who had heard him speak. She had learned in a matter of minutes that nothing defined a person or an event like context.

When Schmidt began explaining the reasons for Germany's recent military build-up, Amanda turned away to look at others. She looked at Elizabeth and Dot, who sat to her left, and to Susan and Admiral Hicks, who sat to her right. All seemed riveted to both the speaker and his uncomfortable message.

Amanda didn't need to ask her grandmother why *she* had come to the hall. She knew that Elizabeth wanted to see the face of the regime that had driven her family from Austria and now threatened to disrupt the rest of Europe.

She didn't need to ask Dot why she had come either. Dorothy Gale wanted to see what Amanda wanted to see – a six-foot blond who, for some reason, had exited the stage after Clark Abercrombie, Nassau Institute director, had introduced the speaker.

Amanda knew that Susan and Jack had their own reasons for attending the lecture, ranging from interest in the subject to interest in each other. She figured it was only a matter of time before their working relationship turned into something more personal.

She had mixed thoughts about that. She liked seeing her mother mingling with others, but she didn't like seeing her on the arm of a man who wasn't Bruce Peterson. She had not yet reached the point where she could psychologically bury her father.

Amanda returned her attention to the stage as the speaker, a tall, good-looking man of fifty-two, defended Germany's annexation of the Sudetenland. She didn't know how anyone, in good conscience, could justify Nazi belligerence, but she conceded that Schmidt was doing a fair job. He made even the obscene seem defensible.

Amanda wondered how any German could succeed in peddling such nonsense until she remembered she was in 1939 and not 2016. She lived in an age when news magazines named Adolf Hitler their man of the year and many officials, celebrities, and firms conducted business with the Nazis. Hitler had succeeded in fooling the world because the world did not yet know the depths of his depravity.

The time traveler watched with interest as Schmidt thoroughly and methodically made the case for a stronger, more aggressive, and more independent Germany. For forty minutes she listened to his words, watched the audience, and tried to gauge whether he was making any progress with a group that was arguably brighter than most.

Amanda applauded politely when Schmidt finished his remarks, but she decided she could not let him leave the building without making him sweat. So when Schmidt told the audience that he would field a few questions, Amanda got out of her seat.

"Where are you going?" Susan asked.

"I'm going to ask the speaker a question," Amanda replied.

Amanda looked at the others in her party and saw everything from support to concern to bewilderment on their faces. Admiral Hicks and Elizabeth smiled. Susan frowned. Dot shot Amanda a glance that said: "What in the hell are you doing?"

Amanda stepped around Elizabeth and Dot and continued down their row of seats. When she reached the aisle, she straightened her dark blue dress, smiled at her family, and proceeded toward a microphone that had been set up in the aisle about ten rows from the stage. She reached the end of a short line of questioners a moment later.

Four of the first nine questioners asked Schmidt about Germany's intentions in central Europe. Three more inquired about the nation's defense buildup. Two others asked about prospects for peace in the coming year. All sought answers to questions that related to military and foreign policy. Amanda sought an answer to something else.

She waited for the ninth questioner to return to his seat, sighed, and then stepped to the microphone. She greeted the speaker warmly and then let him have it.

"My question, Colonel Schmidt, is more domestic in nature. Several weeks ago, paramilitary groups in Germany and Austria destroyed thousands of Jewish synagogues, homes, and businesses and killed as many as a hundred innocent citizens in a series of unprovoked attacks. German authorities, I've read, did nothing to stop the attacks and, in fact, may have encouraged them. Why should we trust German leaders to act responsibly toward the world at large when they can't act responsibly toward their own people?"

Amanda smiled as half of the audience cheered wildly. She frowned when she saw many others shake their heads, mutter in disgust, or throw daggers at her with their eyes.

Schmidt turned red. Amanda could not tell whether he was rattled by her question or the audience's reaction to her question, but she could tell he was shaken. He clearly did not expect a five-foot-five-inch blonde who looked like she had just emerged from a sorority function to ask a sensitive question about human rights abuses.

"Thank you for your question," Schmidt said in nearly perfect English. "I appreciate your concern about the events of last November. As a diplomat and a person who has lived in the United States for the past seventeen years, I am neither authorized nor qualified to speak at length about domestic German affairs. I can tell you that I too read the papers and was dismayed by what I read. I hope that you and other Americans will not hold an entire nation responsible for the unfortunate actions of a few."

Amanda started to ask a follow-up question but was cut off before she could utter a word. She watched in frustration as Clark Abercrombie replaced Schmidt at the lectern, thanked the speaker for his time, and reminded the audience about the next lecture.

Amanda sighed as she watched Abercrombie lead the colonel off the stage. She knew they were already headed to a reception where Kristallnacht would not be discussed. She mulled the irritating situation until a woman with a familiar voice brought her out of a daze.

"I must say you know how to liven up a party."

Amanda turned around and saw Dot.

"You didn't like my question?" Amanda asked.

158

"It was OK," Dot said. "You certainly grabbed the attention of the guys in the front row. I think half of them want to marry you for simply showing some spine."

Amanda smiled.

"They don't want a woman with spine. They want a woman who can cook up a storm in the kitchen and the bedroom."

Dot laughed.

"I suppose you're right. It doesn't matter. You didn't come to see them," Dot said. She pointed to the stage. "You came to see *him*."

Amanda turned around and gazed at Kurt, from close range, for the first time in five weeks. She watched intently as he turned off the microphone, wrapped a short electrical cord, and started to push the lectern off the stage.

"You're right," Amanda said. "I came to see him. Let's go."

Amanda grabbed Dot's hand and weaved around several people to the bottom of the aisle. She reached the edge of the stage just as Kurt wheeled the lectern out of sight.

"You think he's coming back?" Dot asked.

Amanda nodded.

"He's coming back. He saw us."

Amanda was right. Thirty seconds after making her bold prediction, she saw Kurt step back onto the stage, pick up a slip of paper, and then walk toward his two biggest fans.

"Hello, ladies," Kurt said.

"Hi," Amanda and Dot replied in near unison.

"I didn't see you in the front row tonight."

"That's because we arrived late again," Amanda said. "How come you didn't sit on the stage with the director and the speaker? We looked for you."

"I had to cater to others offstage," Kurt said. "Our lecturer came with a security detail."

"I can see why."

"What do you mean?"

"I mean he expressed views that didn't sit well with much of the audience," Amanda said. "I don't think many people believe it's OK to annex a country simply because you feel like it."

"So you didn't like his lecture?" Kurt asked.

"I didn't say that. I said I didn't like his message."

Dot tugged lightly on the back of Amanda's dress. She clearly wanted to send a message to her friend that she had come to flirt and not to argue.

"I agree that much of what he said is controversial, but I don't think it was all that much different than what Admiral Hicks said last month," Kurt said.

"Really?" Amanda asked. "I think it was night-and-day different."

Kurt slid off the stage and walked up to the women.

"How so?" Kurt asked. "I seem to recall that Admiral Hicks advocated building up his country's military too. Like Colonel Schmidt and many other speakers we've had, he said the world is a much safer place when there is a balance of power."

"It's not the same thing."

"Why is it not the same thing?"

"Why? Because it's not, that's why," Amanda said. She could feel her blood pressure rising. "Admiral Hicks wants to keep America safe from foreign invaders. Colonel Schmidt wants to keep Germany safe from foreign meddlers."

"He didn't say that."

"He did in so many words. He complained about British and French 'interference' and said that Germany needed a 'sphere of influence' just like America. He said that at least two or three times. I listened to the whole speech."

"So did I," Kurt said. "Trust me when I say that Colonel Schmidt has a broader view of these matters than you think he does."

Amanda ignored another tug on her dress and stepped forward.

"I don't know why you defend him. He didn't say anything I couldn't have read in a German newspaper. He wasn't very candid either."

"You really think so?"

"Yes," Amanda said. "He didn't even try to address my question about Kristallnacht. He just dismissed the event as 'unfortunate' and handed the microphone to Dr. Abercrombie."

"He's a representative of the German government," Kurt said. "What did you expect him to say?"

"I expected him to do more than tout the party line. I expected him to engage his audience – his *American* audience – honestly and responsibly."

"I think he did."

"He didn't," Amanda said. "He didn't at all. He came across as a hack."

"He's not a hack," Kurt said. "He's a diplomat."

"He's a Nazi apologist!"

Kurt sighed.

"He's my father."

34: AMANDA

Thursday, January 12, 1939

Amanda peeked in the window, noted everything she saw, and assessed the situation. She knew she would find Kurt Schmidt inside the Dairy Diner and would probably find him alone, but she wanted to learn as much as possible before approaching him with her hat in her hand.

She surveyed the restaurant and spied him eating a burger. When she was certain that the empty chair at his table did not belong to someone else, she walked to the door, slipped inside, and moved slowly through the diner until she reached the object of her attention.

"Hi," Amanda said.

Kurt looked up and lowered his burger to his plate.

"Hello."

"An intern at the Institute said I could find you here. Do you mind if I join you?"

"I suppose that depends on why you want to join me," Kurt said.

"I want to apologize for my behavior last night."

"Then please sit."

Amanda sat in the empty chair and looked at Kurt for a few seconds as she tried to think of something to say. She found it difficult to maintain eye contact.

"I came here to say that I am sorry for leaving in a huff after the lecture. It was wrong and thoughtless and deeply inconsiderate. I apologize."

Kurt smiled.

"I'm the one who should apologize."

"Why?" Amanda asked. "You did nothing wrong."

"I did though," Kurt said. "I didn't tell you about my father when I had the chance."

Amanda sighed. She couldn't take issue with that. Kurt could have saved them both a lot of grief by sharing a few details about his family.

"Why didn't you?"

Kurt smiled sadly.

"I didn't because I was afraid you would react as you did. Most people treat me differently when they learn I am the son of a 'Nazi apologist.'"

Amanda winced.

"I'm sorry I said that. I could have picked better words."

"There's no need to apologize. You made a judgment based on what you heard in a speech," Kurt said. "My father *is* an apologist for his government, but he is also a capable diplomat, a war hero, and an honorable man."

Amanda widened her eyes.

"He's a *war hero*?"

Kurt nodded.

"He was one of the most decorated pilots in the Luftstreitkräfte, or German Air Force. He downed more than thirty aircraft in 1917 alone. Only Captain von Richthofen, Ernst Udet, and Erich Löwenhardt recorded more kills in the Great War."

Amanda caught only half of the German that whizzed past her ears, but she caught enough to get Kurt's point. Heinrich Schmidt was part of an elite fraternity that included Manfred von Richthofen, the Red Baron, the greatest fighter pilot of all time.

"So how did he end up here?" Amanda asked. "How did he get into diplomacy?"

Kurt took a sip of water.

"My father wanted to make the world a better place. He had grown weary of death and destruction and wanted to promote peace through diplomacy, trade, and mutual understanding. When he had an opportunity to be a part of the Weimar Republic's first diplomatic mission to the United States, he took it. He has served in the embassy in Washington since 1922."

"So D.C. really is your home?"

Kurt nodded.

"I've lived in America since I was six. I went to school here, attended college here, and hope to remain here. In many ways, I'm as American as you."

"That explains a lot," Amanda said. "It explains, among other things, why you don't have an accent and why you seem so at ease in your surroundings. I never would have guessed that you were German or anything other than an American."

"Now you know."

Amanda smiled at Kurt. She liked this guy. She liked him a *lot*, but she felt uneasy about forming a friendship with the son of a man who represented one of the vilest regimes in history.

"Do you mind if I ask you more questions?" Amanda asked.

"No," Kurt said.

"I don't mean to pry. I really don't. It's just that I've never met anyone like you and don't know how to proceed."

"In other words, you're trying to decide whether I'm worth your time." Amanda laughed.

"You might say that."

"Then ask away," Kurt said.

Amanda sighed.

"I guess what I need to know is how you feel about your government," Amanda said. "I'm not like some people in the audience last night. I'm not indifferent toward Hitler."

Kurt did not respond immediately. He instead looked around the diner, as if checking for eavesdroppers, and then paused for a moment before returning to Amanda.

"I despise the Nazis and all they represent," Kurt said in a hushed tone. "They are a cancer on the face of humanity, a blight that must be removed at the earliest opportunity."

Amanda smiled.

"I suspected you felt that way."

"I have hated them since the beginning."

"What about your father?" Amanda asked. "What does he think of the Nazis?"

Kurt sighed.

"My father does not speak to me about domestic politics. He speaks only about his love of Germany and his duties as a citizen and a patriot."

"Is he a Nazi party member?"

Kurt shook his head.

"He declined the opportunity when Hitler assumed power."

"Didn't that tick off the Nazis?" Amanda asked.

"It did," Kurt said. "Some officials wanted to recall my father to Berlin, but they decided to let him stay. They apparently didn't want to explain to their many critics why they removed a war hero from such an important post."

"What does your mother think of Hitler?"

"She is like my father. She does not discuss politics with me."

"How about your siblings?" Amanda asked. "I assume you have some. Are they like you?"

163

Kurt shook his head.

"My brother, sadly, has followed a different path. Like me, he had the chance to attend college in the U.S. Unlike me, he chose to attend school in Berlin. He became a party member two years ago. He is a firm supporter of the changes taking place in Germany."

Amanda closed her eyes. So many things made sense now.

"Is he older than you or younger?" Amanda asked.

"Karl is the same age," Kurt said. "We're identical twins."

"What do your parents think of Karl's choices?"

"My father does not approve of the decisions he has made. My mother has kept her opinions to herself."

Amanda took a moment to process what she had learned. Kurt had a father who worked for Hitler, a brother who *supported* Hitler, and a mother who didn't seem to care. No wonder he seemed reluctant to show her the family photo album.

"That's quite a family you have," Amanda said.

"Have I scared you away?" Kurt asked.

"No. You have, however, given me a lot to think about."

"I understand. You're no different than most of the people I've met," Kurt said. "Be sure to let me know if you want to be seen with me again."

Amanda looked at Kurt with animated eyes.

"Oh, I've decided that."

"You have?"

"I have," Amanda said. "I've decided something else too."

"What's that?" Kurt asked.

Amanda smiled.

"I've decided what restaurant I like."

35: SUSAN

Wednesday, January 18, 1939

"ANTS?" Susan asked.

"Did you find something?" Jack replied.

Susan circled a word on a typewritten page and pushed the sheet across the table.

"I found a lot of things," Susan said. "Every one is cloaked in capital letters and doesn't mean a thing to me."

"You don't like acronyms?"

"No. I don't think many of your readers will either. When I think of ants, I think of little creepy crawlies that infest my kitchen – not Advanced Naval Training Schools."

Jack laughed.

"I can see I was wise to hire you."

"Did you hire me?" Susan asked. "I thought I was your indentured servant."

"You are. You're my servant until the manuscript is completed."

Susan smiled.

"That arrangement sounds slightly illegal, but I'll ignore the legalities if you throw a dinner my way every now and then."

"How does tonight sound?" Jack asked.

"Tonight sounds wonderful," Susan said. She laughed. "That was easy."

Jack smiled and then returned to the book. He had read and reworked many of the pages that morning but not at the expense of ignoring his guest. For more than two hours, he had managed to strike a delightful balance between work and play.

"Would you like some more coffee?" Jack asked. "We may be here a while."

"I'd love some," Susan said.

"Give me a few minutes then. I may have to clean the percolator."

"Take your time."

Susan smiled as Jack stepped away from his dining room table and made a beeline for the kitchen and his coffee pot. She liked hearing the word "percolator" almost as much as she liked spending time with the kind, unassuming widower of 917 Willow Street.

She watched Jack exit the room and then spent several more minutes on the manuscript. When she grew tired of acronyms, statistics, and naval jargon, she got up from her chair and started to inspect something far more interesting: the residence.

Susan walked out of the dining room and into the adjacent living room. She could see from the art on the walls, the books on the shelves, and the sheet music displayed on an upright piano that the house had once been the home of a cultured and educated woman.

She drifted from impressionist paintings on one wall to several framed photographs on another and found Janet Hicks in all but one. The deceased wife of John J. Hicks had been an attractive, dark-haired woman with large expressive eyes and a warm smile.

Susan placed a hand on the largest of the photos and admired a young couple on their wedding day. Jack stood proudly in his Navy whites. Janet clung to his side in a flowing, lacy, pearly white dress. Neither looked old enough to order a drink.

"You like that picture?" Jack asked as he entered the room.

"I do," Susan said. "It's beautiful. You both look like kids."

Jack laughed.

"I guess we do. I was twenty-two at the time, Janet twenty. I had just graduated from the Naval Academy and was awaiting my first assignment."

"Was this taken in Princeton?"

Jack nodded.

"We were married in the Presbyterian church just down the street. We were married there thirty years ago this June. It seems like yesterday though."

Susan sighed as she pondered her own wedding. She had been married at a similar age in a similar dress in a similar church on a day that seemed both distant and close. She smiled at the thought of her handsome, ambitious husband standing nervously at the altar in an ill-fitting tux. She could not believe she had once been so young, naïve, and happy.

"Tell me about Janet," Susan said. She turned to face Jack. "What kind of woman was your wife?"

Jack didn't respond right away. He instead smiled sadly, stared blankly at his guest, and appeared to mull a question that probably had a complicated answer.

166

"I'll tell you in a moment," Jack said. "The coffee is almost ready. I'll bring some out and tell you everything you want to know. Please make yourself comfortable."

"OK."

Susan watched Jack take his leave and then made her way toward a richly upholstered antique sofa. She found a place on the end of the couch, settled into her seat, and resumed admiring a living room that looked like a time capsule from the 1910s.

Jack returned three minutes later bearing a dainty porcelain coffee set on an ornate silver tray. He placed the tray on a mahogany table, poured two cups of coffee, and then placed a cup and a saucer in front of Susan. He took his seat on the sofa and turned toward his guest.

"I ran out of sugar," Jack said. "I hope that's all right."

Susan grinned.

"I'll survive."

Jack smiled. He sipped his coffee, took a breath, and then once again directed his full attention to the woman with the questions.

"What would you like to know about Janet?"

"I don't know. I guess the usual things. What was she like? What were her interests?" Susan asked. "I gather from the things in this room that she was cultured and educated."

"She was," Jack said. "She was far more cultured and educated than me."

"How so?"

Jack laughed softly.

"How much time do you have? When I met Janet in the spring of aught eight, she was an old-money debutante who spoke three languages, played the piano, and studied art history. I was a farm boy who spoke with a twang, played the harmonica, and studied steam engines. If it weren't for the uniform I wore at the time, she wouldn't have given me a second look."

"How did you meet?"

"I met her in Baltimore at a dance sponsored by the DAR. That's the Daughters of the American Revolution."

"I know what it is," Susan said. She smiled. "I know *some* acronyms."

Jack chuckled.

"I suppose you do."

"Please continue."

"OK. As I said, I met her in Baltimore. I was on leave from the academy. Janet was in town to visit a friend. We danced all night, went to dinner the next day, and spent the rest of the weekend arm in arm. Before I knew it, I was writing a lot of letters and traveling to New Jersey every chance I got. I proposed to her that Christmas."

167

"Sounds to me like you were a charmer."

"I don't know about that," Jack said. "I do know I was a man in love. When it became clear to me that Janet saw me as more than a pen pal, I did everything in my power to make her my wife."

"That's sweet."

"I prefer to call it smart. I knew I would never again have the opportunity to win over a woman like that," Jack said. He smiled. "You might say I married up."

"I don't like that term," Susan said. "I think people marry their equals."

She laughed to herself at the boldness of her statement. She knew very well that some people, including Elizabeth, remained convinced that she had married *down*.

Susan didn't share her mother's view. She believed that Elizabeth had been too quick to judge Bruce Peterson by his net worth in 1991 and not his long-term potential. She prided herself on seeing qualities that so many had not seen and still did not see.

Jack sipped his coffee.

"What else would you like to know?"

Susan thought about the question before responding. She wanted to know a lot of things about Janet Hicks, but she didn't want to irritate or bore the admiral by asking too much too soon. So she went with the obvious.

"What was it like for her when you were in the Navy?" Susan asked.

Jack frowned.

"It was lonely. It was lonely because I was gone for months at a time and because she didn't have any children to attend to."

"Did you not want any children?" Susan asked.

"No. We wanted them," Jack said. "We just weren't able to have any."

"Oh. Was the reason medical-related?"

Jack nodded.

"Janet had a condition called endometriosis."

"I know what it is."

"I'm glad," Jack said. "I don't want to have to explain it."

Susan smiled sadly.

"You won't."

"In any case, Janet followed me from Seattle to San Francisco to San Diego. We spent most of our married years in California," Jack said. "Janet entertained a lot and developed interests like painting, but she was never able to do what she really wanted to do. She was never able to raise a family."

Susan could at least partly relate. She had wanted to raise several children but gave up that dream after giving birth to Amanda. Her doctors

168

had told her that her body simply could not withstand the trauma of another pregnancy.

"At least you had many happy years together," Susan said. "That counts for something."

"It does," Jack said with little enthusiasm. "Do you have other questions?"

Susan smiled sweetly.

"Of course. But they can wait for another day. I've pried enough this morning."

"Should we get back to work?"

"We can," Susan said. "Or we can discuss more important things."

"Do you have something in mind?" Jack asked.

"As a matter of fact, I do."

"What?"

Susan grinned.

"Where are we going for dinner?"

36: ELIZABETH

Sunday, January 22, 1939

Elizabeth leaned forward in her chair and extended her arms as the giggling girl crawled her way. She didn't need to do more to encourage the child. Lizzie Wagner already considered the neighbor lady the number-one draw in town.

"She has really taken to you," Ella said from a sofa she shared with her husband. "Lizzie did not warm up that much to my own mother – or to Erich's, for that matter."

"Few people warm up to my mother," Erich said with a laugh.

Elizabeth smiled. She didn't need an explanation. She had her own vivid memories of Gertrude Wagner, a humorless disciplinarian who had joined her son in Princeton in 1946 and become a permanent part of his household.

She recalled the time that she and her brother had given their grandmother – a teetotaler – a birthday cake to remember by pouring schnapps in the batter. Gertrude raved about the cake and recommended it to others until Elizabeth and Erwin told her how they had made it. The woman sentenced the children to six months of peeling potatoes.

Elizabeth picked up Lizzie when she reached the base of the chair. She placed the girl on her lap, lifted her high, and waited for her to squeal. She didn't have to wait long.

"I must say you have the touch," Ella said.

"I think she just likes the attention," Elizabeth said.

"Do you have many children and grandchildren?"

Elizabeth shook her head.

"No. I have just Susan and Amanda."

"Perhaps Amanda will give you great-grandchildren some day," Ella said.

"Perhaps she will," Elizabeth replied. "In the meantime, I guess I'll have to make do with this splendid child of yours."

Elizabeth bounced Lizzie on her knee and smiled when the girl gurgled her approval. She wondered if she had some sort of cosmic connection with the baby but quickly dismissed the notion as New Age nonsense. Lizzie, she concluded, was simply a good-natured infant who had cornered the market on sweetness and light.

"So tell me about your childhood," Erich said. He leaned forward. "I'd like to hear what Princeton was like in the 1800s."

Elizabeth gave Lizzie one more smile before turning to her father and a topic she was not all that eager to discuss. She did not mind rehashing her idyllic childhood, but she did not want to lie. She did not want to tell her parents things that might someday be disproved and threaten a beautiful relationship that was just beginning to bloom.

"It was much different than it is now," Elizabeth said. "There were fewer buildings on the campus and, while I was here, no electric lighting. People lit gas lamps and stoves and moved around in horse-drawn carriages. I moved to Chicago before the first automobiles arrived."

"I see. Tell me about your father," Erich said. "What did he do?"

Elizabeth smiled.

He sat on that couch and taught math at Princeton.

"He was a teacher," Elizabeth said. "He taught mathematics at a local school."

"So he was an educated man?" Ella asked.

Elizabeth nodded.

"He had degrees in both math and science, but he taught only math. He practiced his science in a workshop behind our house."

"What do you mean?" Erich asked.

"I mean he tinkered and invented. He was as intellectually curious as Thomas Edison but nowhere near as successful. He had only seven patents at the time of his death."

"Did he know Mr. Edison?"

Elizabeth smiled. She figured if she was going to create a family history out of thin air, she might as well make it an interesting one.

"He did. My father met him in the 1870s at his home in Menlo Park," Elizabeth said. "That's about twenty miles from here, on Route 1, the road to Newark."

Erich nodded.

"We saw signs to it on our way to Princeton."

"I'm sure you did," Elizabeth said. "The community is more or a less a shrine to the inventor and more prominent than it used to be. Sixty years ago it was mostly a real estate development that never quite fulfilled its promise."

"What about your mother?" Ella asked. "What was she like?"

Elizabeth smiled.

"She was pretty special too."

Ella tilted her head.

"How so?"

"Oh, my. I don't know where to begin. She was special in so many ways. She was fun loving, talented, kind, intelligent, and as beautiful as any actress. My mother was one of the most beautiful women I have ever known," Elizabeth said. She gave Lizzie a funny face and then returned to Ella. "To tell you the truth, she looked a lot like you."

Ella blushed.

"You're being kind."

"I'm being honest, dear. You're a very beautiful woman," Elizabeth said. "Isn't she, Erich?"

Erich chuckled.

"She is, indeed."

"Now you're both being kind," Ella said.

"No," Elizabeth replied. "We're telling the truth."

"Well, whatever you're doing, you're making me uncomfortable."

Elizabeth warmed at the sight of her mother's modesty. She had forgotten that Ella Wagner was self-conscious about her appearance and didn't like to discuss things like the thickness of one's hair, the smoothness of one's face, or the sparkle of one's eyes.

"Perhaps I should speak instead of my mother," Elizabeth said.

"Please do," Ella said. She smiled. "She sounds far more interesting."

Elizabeth laughed.

"All right then. I will."

"You said she was fun loving," Ella said. "How so?"

Elizabeth gave the question some thought. She had a hundred examples to offer Ella and more than a few stories, but she decided to start with something that still warmed her heart.

"Well, for one thing, my mother loved to entertain. When I was young, she used to entertain me with puppets. She put on entire shows using a small stage my father had built."

"That's funny," Ella said with a laugh. "I asked Erich just the other day to build such a stage for Lizzie. I love puppets too. I always have."

Elizabeth chuckled.

"You see? You have more in common with my mother than you think."

"It appears I do," Ella said. She waved at Lizzie and elicited a smile. "Did your parents have other children? Do you have siblings?"

"I had a brother," Elizabeth said. "He died a few years ago."

"I'm sorry to hear that. I hope I have a son someday. I hope I have many children."

Elizabeth winced when she heard the comment. She remembered how her mother had fallen into a funk after giving birth to Erwin. Doctors had told Ella that she would not be able to have more children without risking her health and even her life.

"I hope you do too," Elizabeth said. "I think you would be a wonderful mother to them. I think you are a wonderful mother to Lizzie."

"Thank you," Ella replied.

Elizabeth bounced the baby some more and studied her face as she smiled, giggled, babbled, and did all the things that babies do. She already felt a connection to this child and this family, a connection that grew stronger every day.

She smiled when Lizzie grabbed her right pinky, put it in her mouth, and blew one spit bubble after another. She laughed when the girl squealed in delight.

Elizabeth looked forward to recording the moment in a journal she had opened at least once a week since coming to Princeton. She wondered if there was a word in the English language that described the joy of spending quality time with your infant self.

She encouraged the bubbles and squeals for several more minutes but stopped when Lizzie started to squirm and became visibly restless. She put the girl on the floor.

Elizabeth watched with amusement as Lizzie crawled past her favorite doll and a pile of blocks and raced toward her mother. She watched with interest when Ella popped three buttons on her blouse, pulled the baby from the floor, and plopped her on her lap.

Elizabeth found the scene overpowering. She had seen women breastfeed their babies countless times in seventy-eight years, but she had never seen something like this. She was witnessing a moving episode from her own history, a deeply personal moment, a part of her past that carried as much emotional punch as a primal cry or a first step.

She looked at the mother and the child as long as she could. When the tears in her eyes began to roll down her cheeks, she wiped them with a hand and got up from her chair.

"Please excuse me," Elizabeth said.

Elizabeth walked quickly across the living room to a hallway and the only bathroom on the main floor. When she reached the room, she stepped inside, turned on the light, and shut the door. She lifted her eyes to the mirror and gazed at a very weak woman.

She scolded herself for leaving so abruptly and vowed to do better in the future. She knew she had no choice. She knew that this was only the beginning and that these moments would become more frequent and difficult as the weeks progressed.

Elizabeth returned to the living room a few minutes later with dry eyes and a smile. She reclaimed her chair, threw out her arms, and encouraged a happy baby to return to a woman who had never wanted to let her go.

She picked up Lizzie, put her on her knee, and resumed where she had left off. She let the infant reclaim her finger and reclaim her heart and carry on with the important business of giving an old woman new life.

37: AMANDA

Amanda needed only five minutes in the library to know she had picked the best possible place to spend a Monday. No matter where she looked, she saw something she wanted to read, something she wanted to do, or someone she wanted to meet.

"This place is amazing," Amanda said.

"I spend at least six hours a day in this room," Kurt said. "I can think of no place I would rather be, except in your company, of course."

Amanda looked warily at the flirtatious German. She wasn't entirely sure what to make of him after two dinner dates, several walks around town, and a campus dance, but she did know she liked him and wanted to get to know him better.

"Show me what you have in here," Amanda said. "I want to see everything."

"OK."

Kurt put his hand on Amanda's waist and guided her to the law collection, which took up an entire corner of the Nassau Institute's research center. He greeted several people along the way, including two interns, a noted local writer, and Dr. Clark Abercrombie.

"Do you know everyone here?" Amanda asked.

Kurt nodded.

"I do. I even know the frequent visitors," Kurt said in a low library voice. "A lot of important people use this place."

"Have you met anyone famous?" Amanda asked.

"I guess that depends on your definition of famous."

"Have you met anyone who's in the news a lot?"

"I have," Kurt said. "I met Mr. Hull and Miss Perkins in October. I joined them for lunch after Dr. Abercrombie gave them a tour of the building."

Amanda was impressed. Kurt had met Secretary of State Cordell Hull and Secretary of Labor Frances Perkins, two of Franklin Roosevelt's most powerful cabinet members.

"How about people who aren't in government?"

Kurt paused before answering.

"I've met a few prominent writers and several visiting scholars, but that's about it," Kurt said. "I did see Dr. Einstein in passing the other day, but I didn't get a chance to meet him. He was on his way to a lecture with Dr. Abercrombie."

"Dot told me he lived here in Princeton," Amanda said. "I think that is so cool."

Amanda noticed puzzlement on Kurt's face and realized instantly that she had used a word that was not in his vocabulary. She made a mental note to tuck away "cool" and other contemporary slang until she returned to 2016.

Amanda turned her attention to the nearby shelves, which contained the legal codes of every state and more than a dozen countries. She ran her fingertips along the spines of several volumes, advanced a few steps, and then did the same with more.

"Do you like these books?" Kurt asked.

Amanda laughed.

"I like *all* books. I like libraries. This place reminds me of the academic libraries I used at the University of Illinois. That's where I attended college."

"Are you from Illinois?"

"I am."

"So you're only visiting Princeton?"

"I am," Amanda said. She smiled. "I just haven't decided when my visit will end."

Kurt laughed.

"I see."

Amanda quickly returned to the original topic. She had told Kurt precious little about her past and didn't want to jump into the subject now. All she wanted to do on this January morning was learn more about an amazing facility and perhaps a bit more about her guide.

"What all do you have in here?" Amanda asked. "I see serious materials on these shelves."

"We have just about everything," Kurt said. "We have thousands of books, including hundreds of volumes on economics, industry, history, and the military."

"Do you have any works on treaties and diplomacy?"

Kurt nodded.

"We have an entire section. It's over here."

Kurt guided Amanda along the perimeter of the immense room to a collection of reference books, periodicals, and other materials pertaining to foreign relations. Most of the items looked as though they had been published in the past year.

"I'm in heaven," Amanda said. "I love this stuff. I am so envious."

"Then perhaps you should stick around for a while," Kurt said with a grin. "I'm sure I could help you land a position here in the fall."

Amanda frowned.

"I'm sure you could."

"Then why won't you consider staying?"

"I won't because I have a life in Chicago," Amanda said.

I'm also allergic to world wars.

Kurt looked at Amanda closely.

"I'm sorry. I had to ask. I thought Princeton was growing on you."

"It is," Amanda said. She grinned. "So are some of its residents."

"Is that so?" Kurt asked.

"Yes."

Kurt laughed.

"Then I'll keep trying to persuade you to stay."

"You do that," Amanda said.

"All right. I will."

Amanda smiled and returned her attention to the collection. She pulled a book on Germany from the shelf, opened it to a page in the middle, and stared at her new friend.

"This book is written in German," Amanda said.

"So are most of the works on that shelf," Kurt replied.

"What's with that? Can't you find English translations?"

"We can't for those titles. I know because I looked for them myself."

"Does anyone actually read them?" Amanda asked.

Kurt nodded.

"Most writers and researchers here can read German. So can many of our visitors. Those who can't enlist the help of people like me."

"So there's a lot of interest in German works?"

"There's a lot of interest in *Germany*," Kurt said. "I'm sure you can figure out why."

"I can. I can also figure out why Germany interests *you*," Amanda said. "What I can't figure out is why you're here. I was thinking about that this morning."

"I'm not sure I follow."

Amanda chose her words carefully.

"I don't understand why a person with your education, interests, and connections left Washington, a town with hundreds of research positions, to come to a place like this."

"There's a reason," Kurt said.

"Tell me," Amanda replied.

"I will, but not here. Let's go for a walk."

"OK."

Five minutes later Kurt and Amanda walked out of the Nassau Institute, stepped onto Nassau Street, and headed toward downtown Princeton. They traveled about fifty yards before Kurt resumed the conversation they had started in the library.

"So you want to know why I left Washington to come here?"

"Yes. I do," Amanda said. "Your actions make no sense. I know for a fact there are many more opportunities in D.C. than there are here."

"You're right. There are," Kurt said. "There are a lot of jobs in Washington for people our age. There are not so many for sons of German diplomats."

Amanda started to disagree but held her tongue. She knew that many Americans did not want to give Germans the benefit of the doubt or even associate with them.

Amanda herself had not mustered the courage to tell her family that she was dating the son of a German official. She had told Susan and Elizabeth only that she had formed a friendship with Clark Abercrombie's blond-haired assistant.

"You don't think anyone would have hired you?" Amanda asked.

"I wouldn't say that," Kurt said.

"What do you mean?"

"I mean the German embassy offered me a staff position last June."

"What did you say?" Amanda asked.

"I said, 'Thanks, but no thanks.' I didn't say I would rather die on the spikes than work for Adolf Hitler."

Amanda laughed and took Kurt's hand.

"I'm proud of you."

"I did what my conscience dictated," Kurt said.

"You still did the right thing."

"If you say so."

"I say so. You will never hear me second-guess you or anyone else on something like that," Amanda said. She sighed. "That still doesn't explain why you came to Princeton or, more to the point, why the Nassau Institute hired you. Didn't they consider you a security risk or an awful person or something like that?"

178

"They might have. I don't know," Kurt said. "All I do know is that when I interviewed for the opening here last June, I was treated with courtesy and respect. I suspect I owe a lot to my father. He called Dr. Abercrombie, an old friend, the day before I arrived in Princeton, but he has never told me what he said to him."

"Your dad sounds like a pretty good guy for a Nazi apologist."

Kurt laughed sadly.

"Yeah. He is. It's too bad others can't see past his position."

"I'm sorry now that I didn't meet him after his lecture," Amanda said. "Perhaps I'll have the chance to meet him before I leave Princeton."

Kurt stopped, released Amanda's hand, and turned to face her.

"I'd like that."

"I'd like that too," Amanda said.

Kurt looked at her with probing eyes.

"Is there anything else I can do to convince you that I'm nothing more than a twenty-two-year-old who came to Princeton to find some peace?"

"Yes," Amanda said. "There is."

"What?"

Amanda grinned and clasped Kurt's hands.

"You can kiss me."

38: SUSAN

Friday, February 10, 1939

S usan Peterson liked almost everything about Laurent's. She liked the intimate lighting, the long linen tablecloths, and the landscape paintings on the wall. She really liked the music and an atmosphere that was delightfully festive.

She didn't care much for the pretentious waiter or the poorly designed menu, but she did like how her dinner companion interacted with both. Watching Admiral John J. Hicks order French food was like watching an intelligence officer interrogate a prisoner of war.

Susan stifled a laugh as the waiter walked away. She had done so more than once since arriving at the upscale establishment on Witherspoon Street at half past seven.

"I know what you're thinking," Jack said. "You're thinking I was too hard on him."

"No," Susan said. She laughed. "I'm thinking that you must have been quite a commander in the Navy. You got him to ditch the accent in less than a minute."

Jack frowned.

"I guess I'm not the most polished penny in the drawer."

Susan smiled.

"You're perfect."

"You're kind," Jack said.

"No. I'm honest," Susan replied. "I would much rather be in the company of a man who speaks plainly than one who cloaks his thoughts in fancy words."

Jack laughed quietly.

"I like that comment. I should write it down before I forget it. I might be able to use it in the book you're writing."

Susan put her hand on the admiral's arm.

"*You're* writing the book, Jack. Let's be clear about that. I'm just helping you express your thoughts in language restaurant waiters can understand."

Jack smiled.

"I suppose you are. You're helping me do a lot of things."

"Is that so?" Susan asked.

Jack nodded.

"Among other things, you're helping me adjust to the civilian world. I sometimes forget my manners when I'm out in public," Jack said. "Janet used to rein me in when I started to treat civilians like sailors. I guess I'm one of those men who needs a moderating influence."

"You're fine as you are," Susan said. "Believe me."

"OK."

Susan slid her hand off Jack's arm and reached for her glass of red wine. She took a sip and then gazed at her dinner companion.

"Do you miss it?" Susan asked.

"Do I miss what?" Jack replied.

"Do you miss the Navy? Do you miss commanding men and ships? Do you miss the thrill of the hunt and making life-or-death decisions?"

Jack sipped his wine.

"I might had I ever made such decisions."

"Surely you saw some action in twenty-seven years."

"I didn't," Jack said. "I served aboard a destroyer in the Pacific during the war. The only time I saw a shot fired in anger was when I saw a tavern owner in San Francisco shoot a sailor for running off with his wife."

"Does that bother you?"

"It does at times. I joined the Navy because I wanted to test my mettle. I wanted to see if I was made of the same stuff as my father and grandfather."

"I'm sure you excelled at your job," Susan said.

"I did. I became quite adept at moving men and materiel from Point A to Point B."

"You wanted more though. Is that it?"

"I wanted a lot more," Jack said.

"You'll find more. I'm sure of it. I think you're going to find a lot of satisfaction in writing this book. You're going to change minds at a time they need to be changed."

"I hope you're right."

"I'm right," Susan said. She smiled. "Trust me on this."

Jack nodded and sipped more wine.

"What did you think of the speaker the other night?" Jack asked.

"I liked him," Susan replied. "He wasn't as interesting as the man at my table, but he was certainly worth my time. I liked that he rebutted many of the statements Heinrich Schmidt made last month and drew attention to what's really going on in Germany."

Susan meant it too. She liked watching February's guest lecturer, FDR's Under Secretary of State, denounce Nazi Germany's human-rights abuses and its failure to live up to several international agreements going back to the 1919 Treaty of Versailles. She thought that the lecture audience she had seen in January had been far too indifferent to Germany's military buildup and needed a good old-fashioned kick in the butt.

"I take it you didn't care much for the colonel," Jack said.

"I'm sure he's a nice man," Susan said. "He seemed like a nice man at the reception. I just didn't care much for his message. Did you?"

"I didn't. I thought his message was hogwash and was happy to see the under secretary blow holes in it, but I must admit I admire Colonel Schmidt personally. He fought valiantly for his country in the war and is clearly a patriot of the first order."

"Is that admirable though? Is patriotism a good thing when one's devotion is given to a nation as despicable as Nazi Germany?" Susan asked. "I don't think so."

Jack nodded.

"I suppose not. I will say the colonel gave me the impression he is more devoted to Germany than to the Nazis. I've met quite a few Germans like that. They are more quick to defend their country than the governing party."

"That's not an excuse in my book," Susan said. "Heinrich Schmidt still represents a noxious regime and didn't do a whole lot to distance himself from it last month."

Jack smiled.

"I'm surprised to hear you speak that way about the colonel given that his son is seeing your daughter."

Susan nearly dropped her glass.

"Excuse me?"

"I said I was surprised to …"

"I heard you," Susan said. "I just don't know what you're talking about. Amanda is not seeing anyone's son, to my knowledge, much less the son of a Nazi diplomat."

"Perhaps I'm reading too much into what I saw the other day," Jack said.

"What did you see?"

"I saw Amanda and the colonel's son near the battle monument. They were holding hands and kissing."

"That's not possible," Susan said. "I know Amanda has expressed some interest in Dr. Abercrombie's assistant, the one with the blond hair, but she hasn't mentioned anything about anyone else."

Jack squirmed in his seat.

"I'm hesitant to say more. It appears I've already said too much."

"No. You *haven't* said too much," Susan said. "You apparently haven't said enough. Please tell me what you know."

Jack sighed.

"All right. If you insist."

"I insist," Susan said.

"There's really not a lot to say," Jack said. "I saw two people kissing the other day, two people I've had the opportunity to meet. One person was your daughter. The other was Kurt Schmidt. Heinrich Schmidt's son and Dr. Abercrombie's research assistant are not different people, Susan. They are one and the same."

39: AMANDA

Amanda pondered a few inconvenient facts as she threw her arms around Kurt Schmidt and gave him a gentle kiss. She reminded herself that boys were slugs who wanted only one thing and tended to get it when they asked for it with flowers and dinners. She also remembered she was a time traveler who had to weigh each and every action like it might be her last.

She didn't care. Five months after walking through a magic tunnel and stepping into another world, she was having a good time, a really good time, and she didn't want that time to end.

"Are you enjoying yourself, Miss Peterson?" Kurt asked.

"I'm enjoying myself, Mr. Schmidt," Amanda said as they stood near the intersection of Nassau and Moore streets. "I haven't had this much fun on Valentine's Day since I was twelve."

"I find that hard to believe."

"Why? I haven't had many boyfriends."

"That surprises me," Kurt said. "You're a beautiful woman."

Amanda smiled.

"I'm a *difficult* one. I tend to take a dim view of young men who are more interested in taking me to bed than in taking me to a movie."

"Why do you think I'm different?" Kurt asked.

"I don't," Amanda said. She laughed. "I'm just willing to sct aside my biases until I figure out what makes you tick."

"I see. So you think I have a deep, dark past, after all."

"No. I just think there's more to you than meets the eye, a lot more, and I want to discover what it is," Amanda said. She took his hand. "Come walk with me. You can tell me all your deep, dark secrets on the way to my house."

184

"OK."

Amanda led Kurt onto a campus filled with couples that walked, talked, kissed, and cuddled under a starry sky. When they entered a stretch near the art museum and finally had space to themselves, she opened up and asked questions that had been on her mind all night.

"Tell me about your childhood," Amanda said. "What was it like growing up the son of a diplomat? What is it like being a twin?"

"You don't want to know much, do you?" Kurt asked.

Amanda grinned.

"I want to know what's *important*."

"All right. I'll tell you," Kurt said. "I had a great childhood. I had two parents who loved and nurtured me, a brother for a best friend, and more good times and opportunities than I can possibly count. I was truly fortunate."

"Where did you live?"

"We lived in a row house in Georgetown. My parents still do."

"I thought diplomats lived in embassies," Amanda said.

"Some do. We didn't," Kurt said. "When my father brought us to this country, he knew we might stay a while, so he did everything he could to make us comfortable and happy. He wanted us to feel like Americans."

"You admire him, don't you?"

"I do. He is the best kind of role model: someone who leads by example."

"Are you close to your mother?" Amanda asked.

Kurt nodded.

"I'm closer to her than I am to my father."

"Really?"

"You seem surprised," Kurt said.

"I guess I am. I just assumed that most guys were closer to their fathers."

"I'm not. Don't get me wrong. I love my father and respect him. He is someone I can turn to for advice on many things, but he is not the parent I write to every week. He is not the person I go to when I have problems of a more personal nature."

"So what you're really trying to say is you're a mama's boy."

Kurt chuckled.

"I'm a mama's boy."

Amanda tightened her hold on Kurt's hand. She laughed to herself as she pondered the irony of a Nazi hater falling for the son of a German diplomat.

"Thirties Germans and the time travelers who love them. Next ... on Geraldo!"

"There's nothing wrong with that," Amanda said. "Men who love and admire their mothers tend to love and admire their wives. I read that somewhere."

"You sound like Dr. Freud," Kurt said.

Amanda laughed but did not respond. She did not want to say she had read about the link between mothers and wives in *People* magazine. So she walked with Kurt in blissful silence. A moment later, she raised a new topic.

"You said a minute ago that Karl was your best friend growing up. Is that still true?" Amanda asked. "Are you still close?"

Amanda winced when she saw Kurt frown. She could see she had stepped in something.

"No," Kurt said. "We haven't been close since Karl returned to Germany. I haven't spoken to him in two years. I haven't corresponded with him since May 6, 1937."

"You remember the day?"

"I do. It was the day Karl notified us by telegram that he had joined the Nazi party."

"I'm sorry," Amanda said.

Kurt smiled grimly.

"That wasn't even the worst news of the day."

"What do you mean?" Amanda asked. "Tell me."

Kurt sighed.

"Shortly after I read Karl's message, I packed a bag and drove up here. My father had asked me to pick up my cousin Ingrid when she arrived from Europe. So I hopped in our car and drove five hours to Lakehurst. That's a little south of here."

"I know where it is. Were you supposed to meet her train?"

"No," Kurt said. "I was supposed to meet her airship."

Amanda gulped.

"You don't mean?"

Kurt nodded.

"My cousin, Ingrid Bauer, a promising journalist, was one of the thirty-five people who died on the *Hindenburg*. She had come here, officially, to cover the zeppelin's first voyage to the United States. She had come here, unofficially, to defect. She wanted nothing to do with the Nazis after they started censoring her magazine and her work."

"Were you there when it happened?" Amanda asked.

"I had a front-row seat," Kurt said.

Amanda closed her eyes as images of the disaster ran through her mind. She could picture a burning dirigible falling to the ground. She could not picture one falling to the ground with a relative inside. She felt great sympathy for her new friend.

"I can't imagine how difficult that was."

"It was even harder the next day," Kurt said. "I had to identify Ingrid's body. My parents could not bring themselves to do it."

Amanda looked at him with soft eyes.

"You needn't say more. I think you've satisfied my curiosity about your family. We can talk about something else."

"Maybe we should," Kurt said.

"What do you want to talk about?" Amanda asked.

"How about you? You haven't told me much about yourself."

Amanda smiled.

"That's because I know Dot has told you a few things."

"She has," Kurt said. "She told me that your father died last year and that you took some time off after he died to travel around the country. She said you settled in Princeton because your grandmother grew up here and wanted to revisit her youth."

"She's right."

"Dot also told me that you plan to leave this summer."

"That's not quite true," Amanda said. "We haven't made any definite plans."

"So there's hope for me?"

Amanda laughed.

"There's always hope for you."

Kurt smiled but did not comment. He instead squeezed Amanda's hand and led her westward through the snow-covered campus until they reached Mercer Street. He spoke again when they crossed the street and began the final stretch to the rental house.

"I do have a question for you that I think only you can answer," Kurt said.

"What's that?" Amanda asked.

"Have you told your mother and grandmother about me?"

The question hit Amanda like a bolt from the blue. She considered a few creative lies before settling on the truth.

"I haven't."

"Why?" Kurt asked.

"You know why," Amanda said.

"You don't think they would approve of me?"

Amanda sighed.

"I don't know. I just know I need a little more time before I tell them."

Kurt nodded.

"Then take the time. I don't mind clandestine meetings at restaurants, if you don't."

187

Amanda stopped, turned to face Kurt, and threw her arms over his shoulders. She kissed him gently and then kissed him hard.

"You're a charmer, Mr. Schmidt."

"I try."

Amanda smiled.

"I should probably walk the last block alone. I don't want to give my family or the neighbors something to talk about by kissing a German at my door."

Kurt put his hand to her face and nodded.

"All right," Kurt said. He kissed her softly. "Good night, Amanda."

"Good night, Kurt."

Amanda left her blond-haired suitor and walked the rest of the way to the rental house. She checked for lights in the windows, saw none, and entered the residence as quietly as a burglar.

Amanda went straight to her room, changed into her pajamas, and slipped into a bed that felt surprisingly warm and inviting on a cold winter's night. She closed her eyes as she thought of the boy, their date, and the glorious months ahead.

The trip of a lifetime had suddenly become more than a trip to the past. It had become a journey with options. The question now was what to do with them.

40: SUSAN

Wednesday, February 15, 1939

Susan poured some coffee in her mother's mug and then some in her own. She rarely drank more than two cups after nine o'clock, but she made an exception today. She wanted to be sharp for a conversation she had dreaded for days.

"Did you say she was awake?" Susan asked.

Elizabeth nodded.

"She's taking a bath. I heard splashing in the tub when I went up to get her clothes a little while ago. She'll be down soon."

Susan smiled sadly at Elizabeth, who sat across from her at the dining table, and considered how best to proceed. She hated situations like this. She had hated them since Amanda had begun dating six years ago at the age of sixteen.

Susan pondered two matters she could no longer ignore. The first was her daughter's growing attachment to a boy she would eventually have to leave. The second was her relationship with the son of a man who had Adolf Hitler's ear.

She could relate to the first matter. For weeks she too had struggled with what to do with a man she liked but could not keep. She reminded herself every day that she was a time traveler on vacation and not a single woman who could follow her heart.

Susan could *not* relate to the second matter. She knew that even if she accidentally told Jack Hicks something he wasn't supposed to know, she wouldn't alter history. Jack was an American, an admiral, and a patriot. He could be trusted with anything.

She started to say something to her mother but stopped when she heard the stairs squeak. She looked up just as Amanda walked through the kitchen and entered the dining area.

189

"Good morning," Susan said.

Amanda smiled wearily.

"Good morning."

"Do you want some coffee? I just made a pot."

Amanda nodded.

"I can't stay long though. I'm meeting Dot for breakfast."

"That's all right," Susan said. "We won't be long."

Susan poured a cup of coffee as Amanda pulled out a chair and sat down. She watched with interest as a bewildered expression formed on her daughter's face.

"What do you mean by you 'won't be long'?" Amanda asked. "Do you have something to say?"

Susan sighed.

"We have something to ask you. We have several things, in fact."

"OK. I'm here," Amanda said. She sipped her coffee. "Ask away."

"All right. I will," Susan said. "I guess the first thing I'd like to know is where you went last night. I know you weren't with Dot because she stopped by at seven to say hi."

Amanda stared at Susan.

"Why do you need to know?"

"I need to know because I'm your mother."

"Haven't we had this conversation a few hundred times?" Amanda asked.

"We have."

"I'm not in high school, Mom. I don't have a curfew."

"No. You don't," Susan said. "You don't have a curfew, but you do have an obligation to tell us where you've been going at night and who you've been seeing."

Amanda lowered her coffee cup.

"I've been seeing a boy named Kurt. He's a research assistant at the Nassau Institute, the one you've seen on stage setting up the lectures. Is that a problem?"

Susan paused before responding. She wanted answers from her daughter, but knew she wouldn't get them by plunging headfirst into a heated exchange.

"You needn't get defensive."

"I feel like I do," Amanda said. "I feel like I'm being ambushed."

"Don't be dramatic, dear," Elizabeth said. "We just want some answers."

Amanda stared at her grandmother.

"So you're in on this too?"

"I care about your well-being. I'm just like your mother."

"Well, I'm fine, Grandma. I've never felt better."

Susan glared at Elizabeth and then gazed at Amanda.

"Everyone calm down. There's no need to get contentious," Susan said. "We should be able to have a family discussion without getting on each other's nerves."

Amanda turned her head.

"What do you want to know, Mom? I'm running late."

"I have two concerns, Amanda. The first is that I fear you are forming an attachment that you might find difficult to break when we have to leave."

"Isn't that my problem?"

"No. It's *our* problem," Susan said. "We're in this together."

"You're right," Amanda said. "We're in this together. So shall I ask you whether you'll be able to break your attachment to a certain retired admiral? You spend more time with Jack Hicks than I do with Kurt."

"It's not the same thing," Susan said.

"Why? Why is it not the same?"

"I'm not sneaking off with Jack at odd hours of the day, for one thing."

"So? You like him," Amanda said. "You like him a lot. Don't you think you should end your friendship before it turns into something else?"

"No. I don't. I can manage Jack."

"Are you sure? You didn't manage Dad very well."

Susan bristled.

"What's that supposed to mean?"

"It means you're in no position to lecture me," Amanda said. "You have no more experience in situations like this than I do. You have no more experience with *men*."

Susan took a deep breath.

"That's not true," Susan said. "I have a lot of experience. I know what it's like to date someone and think you have things under control. I've been in your shoes many times."

"Really? When? You've dated one guy, besides Dad, since George Bush was president – the *first* George Bush. I'd say that makes you a newbie in male management."

Susan frowned. She began to regret starting this conversation.

"Look," Susan said. "I'm just concerned, that's all."

"I'm fine, Mom. I'll *be* fine. If I leave Princeton this summer with a broken heart, then I'll just have to find a way to cope. I have before."

Susan smiled tentatively and put a hand on Amanda's arm.

"I know you have."

Amanda visibly relaxed.

"What's your other concern?" Amanda asked.

191

Susan sighed and brought her hands together as she braced herself for more fireworks. She knew that the second matter was far more explosive than the first. She proceeded cautiously.

"I'm just a bit concerned that you might say something to this young man that we will all regret," Susan said. "Jack told me that Kurt is more than just a research assistant at the Institute. He said he's the son of the German military attaché."

"So *that's* what this is about?" Amanda asked. "You're afraid I'm going to spill state secrets?"

"I'm afraid you might do what human beings have done for centuries and invest your trust in someone you really don't know. You're a time traveler, Amanda. You have knowledge of the future, knowledge that people from this time would kill to obtain."

Amanda tensed up.

"I'm not stupid, Mother. I haven't told Kurt anything that would destroy the universe. I haven't even told him much about you. If you're really that concerned about one of us altering the course of history, then perhaps you should talk to Grandma."

"What's that supposed to mean?" Elizabeth asked.

"I'll tell you what it means," Amanda said. "It means you're interacting with your own family. Have you thought about the harm you could do if you dropped Lizzie on her head? Think about *Back to the Future*, Grams. You could make a big mess real quick."

"That won't happen."

"You don't know that. You can't predict the impact you'll have on others any better than I can. You're playing with fire, Grandma. You're playing with fire big time."

"At least I'm not playing with a German," Elizabeth said.

Amanda scooted back in her chair.

"I think I've heard enough."

"Stay put," Susan said.

"No!" Amanda said. "I won't until she apologizes."

Elizabeth stared at Amanda.

"I will not apologize for distrusting one of *them*."

"One of whom?" Amanda asked. "The Germans? Do you even know Kurt Schmidt? Do you know how he feels about his government or what's taking place in his country?"

"I know enough," Elizabeth said.

"You know nothing."

"I know his people forced my family from Austria."

"Kurt didn't force anyone from anywhere," Amanda said.

"He's a German! Hitler is a German."

Amanda glared at Elizabeth as she got up from her chair.

"You're wrong, Grandma. Hitler is *not* a German," Amanda said softly. She leaned forward and got in Elizabeth's face. "Hitler is an Austrian. He was born in Austria. Just. Like. You."

Amanda stepped away from the table.

"Please don't go," Susan said.

"I'm sorry, Mom. I'm out of here."

41: ELIZABETH

Elizabeth walked beside the baby in the carriage and waved to the child when the carriage came to a stop. She had done so three times on the stroll down Mercer Street and had drawn a smile from the infant on each occasion.

"She's in a good mood," Elizabeth said.

"She usually is when you are present," Ella replied. "I mean it when I say that you bring out the best in her. You have a gift."

"I wouldn't go that far. I just know how to make her smile."

Elizabeth frowned as she considered the irony. She could bring a smile to one girl's face with the wave of a hand but couldn't bring a smile to another's with even the profoundest of apologies. She had thought of little else since her falling out with Amanda on February 15. She had *felt* little else except excruciating pain.

"I see why you do this often," Ella said. "This is relaxing."

"It's especially relaxing when the sidewalk is free of ice," Elizabeth said.

Ella laughed.

"I agree."

Elizabeth gazed at Ella for a moment as the two moved slowly on a sidewalk that divided the campus from the busy street. She admired her young friend's graceful demeanor and wondered why she had not noticed it before. Ella seemed more like a princess strolling through a palace grounds than a young mother pushing a carriage.

"Can I ask you a stupid question?" Elizabeth asked.

Ella smiled.

"You can ask me anything."

"Do you like being a mother?"

"I do," Ella said. "Why do you ask?"

194

"I don't know. I guess I'm just curious," Elizabeth said. "You're a woman who could have done many things in life. Yet you chose to be a wife and a mother."

Ella paused before responding.

"I chose to be a wife because I met a wonderful man," Ella said. "I chose to be a mother because I consider motherhood to be my calling. If I do nothing else but raise kind, thoughtful, and considerate children, I will consider my life's mission complete."

Elizabeth felt waves of regret as she heard the words. She regretted everything she had ever done to cause this woman pain and wondered what, if anything, she could do to make amends. Then she reminded herself she couldn't do a thing.

She was a time traveler who had a contractual obligation to leave the world as it was and not as she wanted it to be. She had no right to alter history, even on a micro level, to assuage her guilt, find new meaning, or make her peace with a troubled past.

"That's a beautiful sentiment, Ella. All wives and mothers should be so eloquent."

"Did you not feel the same when you started out?" Ella asked.

Elizabeth smiled.

"I did. I approached marriage and family a little differently than you, but I had the same goals in mind. I wanted to be the best wife and mother I could be."

"Was your husband a good man?"

"He was," Elizabeth said. "He was a very good man. Cal was smart and warm and generous. He was the kind of man I think you and Erich would have liked."

"That is nice to hear. I wish I could have met him."

You will, Mama. You will.

Elizabeth pondered a reply but decided to move on to other things when she saw a friend standing on his porch. She had not seen the Old Man in more than a month. She waved as he tipped his hat to the party of three and wandered back into his house.

"Do you know who that is?" Elizabeth asked.

Ella nodded.

"I do. I met him last month at a reception for new faculty members," Ella said as she handed Lizzie a rattle. "I found him to be charming and engaging."

"Most people do," Elizabeth said. She laughed. "I certainly do."

The women walked in silence until they reached the end of the sidewalk and the turnaround point. They crossed Mercer Street, lifted the stroller onto the other sidewalk, and started back toward their houses. When they passed the home of a prominent Princeton theologian, they resumed their conversation.

"Thank you for attending Mass with us on Sunday," Ella said. "I know it must have been difficult for you to step outside your religious tradition."

"It wasn't difficult at all," Elizabeth said. "I was raised a Catholic."

"Is that so?"

Elizabeth nodded.

"I converted to Lutheranism when I married Cal."

"That explains at lot," Ella said. "You seemed very much at ease in the church."

"That's because I was," Elizabeth said. "I found much to embrace and admire. The two churches are not all that dissimilar."

"You are broadminded."

Elizabeth laughed sadly.

"Amanda might take issue with that statement, but I think it's true. I favor common bonds over differences."

"Are you and Amanda at odds over something?" Ella asked.

Elizabeth nodded and sighed.

"We had a falling out last week over a boy she's been dating. The young man is the son of the German diplomat who spoke here last month."

"Is he a good man?"

"I don't know," Elizabeth said. "I haven't met him. I know only that he is related to a man who represents a regime I deplore."

Ella stopped and frowned at her companion. Then she directed her eyes forward and resumed pushing a stroller containing a baby who babbled and shook her rattle.

"I see," Ella said matter-of-factly.

"Do you think I'm judging him unfairly?" Elizabeth asked.

"I cannot answer that question. I don't know the young man."

Elizabeth looked at her friend.

"Yet I sense you have an opinion on the matter."

Ella smiled.

"I do."

"Please tell me then," Elizabeth said. "Please tell me your thoughts."

Ella sighed.

"All right. I will. When the Nazis moved into Austria last year, they did more than annex a nation. They divided families and neighborhoods," Ella said. "They forced otherwise fair and open-minded citizens, people with little interest in political matters, to choose sides and take rigid stands. They forced them to judge. In a matter of weeks, neighbors became strangers and friends became enemies. Erich and I left Vienna because we did not want to be a part of such a society. We wanted to live and raise our children in a country where people were judged by who they are and not what they are."

"So you think I should give him a chance?" Elizabeth asked.

Ella nodded.

"I think you should get to know him before drawing any conclusions. Many of our dearest friends in Vienna chose to accept rather than oppose the Anschluss. Erich and I strongly objected to their apathy and indifference, but we did not let our political differences interfere with friendships we had enjoyed for years."

Elizabeth wanted to take issue with Ella's accommodating position. She wanted to tell her neighbor that anyone who was indifferent toward a regime that started a catastrophic war and slaughtered millions of innocent people was as much to blame as the Nazis themselves.

She wanted to tell Ella all that and more but knew she could not. She could not because the worst abuses of the Nazi regime had not yet occurred.

As someone who was bound to keep knowledge of the future to herself, Elizabeth was as much a prisoner as those who had been prevented from speaking their minds against mindless actions. So she sighed, kept her opinions to herself, and offered words of praise to a mother she had never cherished more.

"It appears we are broadminded on different things," Elizabeth said. She laughed. "I see beauty in other religious traditions. You see beauty in people you oppose."

Ella stopped pushing the carriage and paused before responding to the comment. She took Elizabeth's hand and smiled warmly.

"Give the boy a chance," Ella said. "Get to know him. Find out who he is and what is in his heart before you make any more judgments. You will be glad you did."

Elizabeth smiled as her eyes began to water.

"You're right. Thank you."

"Thank you for what?"

"Thank you for setting an old woman straight," Elizabeth said. She sighed. "Thank you for speaking to me like a mother."

42: AMANDA

Grovers Mill, New Jersey – Friday, March 3, 1939

Amanda laughed as she released the screen door and heard it slam shut. She had opened the door at least a dozen times, but she had yet to get used to its steel-trap-like snap.

"You really ought to fix that door," Amanda said. She followed Dot Gale through her front porch and into her house. "It might take off someone's arm someday."

Dot giggled.

"What makes you think it hasn't?" Dot asked. "My grandma hates that door so much that she enters through the back when no one's around to hold it open."

"Are you serious?" Amanda asked.

"I'm serious."

Amanda smiled and shook her head. She didn't know if Dot was joking, but she didn't care. She loved hearing these anecdotes about life on the farm.

Amanda followed Dot into the living room, hung her coat on a freestanding rack, and then drifted to a window on the sunny east side. The window offered a splendid view of a grove of leafless trees that, in a few months, would be a thriving apple orchard.

She enjoyed the sight for a moment and then joined Dot on a corduroy couch. The sofa faced a long black coffee table and a stone fireplace in the center of the room.

Amanda settled into her seat and admired the room as Dot set up coffee for two. With a three-foot-high Zenith console radio, a Shaker hutch, striped wallpaper, and two magazine racks filled with issues of *LIFE* and the *Saturday Evening Post*, the living room of Frank and Doris Gale looked like a setting for a Norman Rockwell painting.

Amanda laughed to herself when she saw the radio, which had been the focus of the Gale family's attention on the evening of October 30. Frank, Doris, Dot, and Grandma Marie had listened intently as excited announcers described a Martian "invasion" of their neighborhood.

"Where are your folks?" Amanda asked.

"They went to Trenton for the day," Dot said.

"Where's your grandma?"

"She's playing canasta with the blue-hairs at the church."

Amanda laughed.

"So we have the place to ourselves?"

"We do," Dot said.

"Let me guess. You want to talk."

"Of course I want to talk! I haven't seen you in two weeks, Amanda. That's like four months in dog years."

"We're not dogs, Dot."

"You get my point. We have some serious catching up to do."

Amanda couldn't disagree. They had done a lot since Dot had left New Jersey on February 17. She had flown to Los Angeles to spend twelve days with Roy Maine.

Amanda watched with indifference as Dot lifted a stainless steel pot and poured steaming-hot coffee into two porcelain cups. She watched with amusement as Dot added a generous shot of whiskey to each cup and slid one of the cups in front of her guest.

"I see you made breakfast," Amanda said with a smile.

"I made a Jersey Brunch. Now let's drink and talk."

"What shall we talk about?"

"Let's start with Mr. Wonderful," Dot said. "Is he still floating your boat?"

"We're still together, if that's what you mean."

"The only reason I ask is because you seemed a bit frazzled when I left for California."

Amanda sighed.

"I still am."

"Are things better between you and your grandma?" Dot asked.

Amanda nodded.

"They are. We're talking now. She still doesn't like the idea of me dating a German, but she understands what I see in Kurt and why I won't give him up."

"Have Elizabeth and Kurt met?"

Amanda shook her head.

"No. I'm working on it though. I want to take them to lunch next week. I want Grandma to see that Kurt is a decent, thoughtful *American* man and not a Hitler Youth trying to indoctrinate me or get me into bed."

Dot raised a brow.

"I assume that means you two are still just kissing at the door."

"Yes," Amanda said. "We're still just kissing at the door ... and on benches and under trees and in front of city hall."

Dot laughed.

"You're shameless."

"I'm practical."

Dot grinned.

"So be *less* practical. There's nothing wrong with a torrid love affair."

"I suppose," Amanda said. "I'm just wary about jumping in too deep. We still plan to leave by the end of the summer. There's no point in starting a relationship I can't finish."

"Who says you can't finish it?" Dot asked.

Professor Geoffrey Bell.

"I do," Amanda said. "We're from two very different places. It would never work."

"You're from Chicago, Amanda, not Pluto. I'm sure that if you really wanted to make it work with Kurt, you could."

"I don't know. We'll see," Amanda said. "What about you? Did you have a sinful time in Southern California?"

"I had a pleasant visit with my fiancé," Dot said smugly.

"How pleasant?"

Dot giggled.

"Let's just say I was careful."

"Dot!"

"Well, June is a long way off," Dot said. "I'm getting impatient."

Amanda shook her head.

"I still can't believe your folks let you go. Most parents don't approve of premarital activity."

Dot laughed.

"Mine don't either. They didn't send me to California to stay with Roy. They sent me there to stay with my aunt. She lives in Pasadena."

Amanda smiled.

"You think of everything, don't you?"

Dot grinned.

"I try."

Amanda sipped her coffee. She could already feel the whiskey. She tried to imagine what Dot was like in college and then decided she didn't really want to know. Some mysteries were best kept buried. So she thought of something else.

"Did you say something about June?" Amanda asked.

"I did."

"I thought you and Roy hadn't set a date."

"We hadn't," Dot said. She beamed. "But we have now."

"Oh, that's so exciting!"

"We're getting married June 24 in Princeton. Roy starts his next leave on June 20."

Amanda hugged her friend.

"I'm so happy for you. I know how much you've hated putting your life on hold."

Dot nodded.

"Life will be better now."

"Have you started planning?" Amanda asked.

Dot shook her head.

"I haven't done anything except reserve the church. My mom is going to handle most of the particulars. She considers my wedding her calling."

Amanda laughed.

"I believe that."

Dot put down her cup and looked at Amanda thoughtfully. She grabbed her hand.

"I have decided on one thing though," Dot said.

"What's that?" Amanda asked.

Dot took a breath.

"I want you to be in the wedding party. I want you to be a bridesmaid."

"I would be honored," Amanda said.

"Can you promise me now that you won't leave town before the wedding?"

Amanda nodded.

"I can. I'll be there," Amanda said. She looked at Dot like the sister she never had. "I'll be at your wedding if it's the last thing I do."

43: SUSAN

Princeton, New Jersey – Saturday, March 11, 1939

Susan looked at Jack, apologized with her eyes, and quickly saw that an apology wasn't necessary. The second she caught his playful smile she realized that he was as comfortable participating in someone else's business as he was in sending ships to sea.

She hadn't wanted to drag Jack into a family matter, but she hadn't had a choice. Elizabeth had insisted on having at least two allies at her side when she met Kurt Schmidt for the first time.

Susan rewarded the admiral with a warm smile and then turned her attention to the guest of honor. She had as many questions for the German research assistant as any of the people gathered around her table at Eddy's Cafe, a soup-and-sandwich joint on the north side of town.

"So tell me about your job, Kurt," Susan said. "What do you do at the Nassau Institute?"

"I do a lot of things, Mrs. Peterson," Kurt replied. "I write press releases, set up lectures, and run errands for the director, but mostly I assist senior fellows with their research. I gather a lot of information on foreign relations, trade, history, and military affairs."

Susan saw Jack perk up at the mention of military affairs. She wondered what was going through his head.

"Do you enjoy the work?"

"I do. I love working in an environment where knowledge is prized. I love working with people who are much smarter than I am."

Susan laughed at the self-deprecating comment. She liked humility and genuine modesty and noticed that Jack did too. He smiled and nodded.

Susan then glanced at the others and saw differing reactions. Elizabeth scrutinized Kurt with skeptical eyes. Amanda dug in with a look that said: "Mess with my man at your own risk."

"I'd like to know more about your work in military affairs," Jack said. "What kinds of materials do you peruse when performing research for the fellows?"

Kurt paused before answering.

"As you know, Admiral, we have many military-related resources in the Institute's library, including reference books, manuals, and periodicals. I consult some of these materials and works like *Jane's Fighting Ships* at least a few times a week."

"I see," Jack said. "I imagine you've learned a lot by reading these works."

"I have. I've learned a lot by reading *all* the works. I like learning. I like finishing each day with more knowledge than I started with."

"Do you get along with your colleagues?" Susan asked.

"I do," Kurt said. "I work well with everyone, including those who are very demanding."

Amanda looked at her mother and raised a brow. She obviously saw lunch as a test of sorts for Kurt and believed he was passing with flying colors.

Susan didn't take the bait. She had come to the cafe to facilitate a civil discussion and learn more about a mysterious young man, not to placate her defiant and sometimes difficult daughter.

"Amanda says that you grew up in the District of Columbia," Susan said. "That must have been fun. Tell us about it. Tell us about your childhood."

Kurt sipped some water, gave Amanda a knowing smile, and then looked at her nosy mother with disarming eyes. He clearly understood that Mama Bear wanted more than his resume and knew that the surest way to win her over was to provide it.

"To be perfectly honest, Mrs. Peterson, my childhood was heavenly. I had a loving family, loyal friends, great schools, and all the opportunities I could ask for. I can't think of a single thing I would change. I already miss Washington."

"Do you miss Germany?" Elizabeth asked.

Susan silently praised her mother for asking a loaded question that was surely on the minds of at least three people. She knew she hadn't the guts to ask it herself.

"That's a difficult question to answer," Kurt said. "It's hard to miss something you can barely remember. I was six when I came to this country. I have lived in the United States continuously since 1922 and have never been back to my native land."

"Surely you have some memories of Germany," Elizabeth said.

"I do. I have a pleasant one, in fact."

Elizabeth smiled like she had stumbled onto something big.

"Please tell us."

"All right. It's not much, but it's important to me," Kurt said. "When I was five, I stuttered. I stuttered so badly that my parents feared I would have difficulty making friends and succeeding in school. They took me to several doctors and specialists but were unable to help me until they ran into a retired speech teacher in Berlin."

"I see," Elizabeth said.

"The teacher took me under his wing, if you will, and worked with me every day for nine months – our last nine months in Germany. By the time I came to America, I was able not only to speak without stuttering but also to speak fluent English. The teacher did more than fix an embarrassing problem. He prepared me for life in this country."

"That's a beautiful story," Susan said. "It's hard to believe you ever had a speech impediment or even an accent. You speak more eloquently than most native-born Americans."

"Thank you."

Susan glanced again at Amanda and saw an I-told-you-so glint in her eyes. She couldn't blame her daughter for feeling smug. Amanda had delivered what she had promised to deliver: a charming, intelligent, articulate man who identified far more with the United States and the American way than with anything he had been born into.

Susan wanted to end the probing and move onto other topics but decided to ask a few more questions before the food arrived. She conceded that what really bothered her about Kurt Schmidt was not his background or his views but rather his family connections. She proceeded slowly into dangerous waters.

"Tell us about your father," Susan said. "I met him after his lecture in January, but I didn't have the chance to talk to him long. What's he like?"

Kurt sipped some water and fixed his gaze on Susan. He appeared relaxed, composed, and fully prepared to discuss a diplomat who represented the Third Reich.

"He's like a lot of good men," Kurt said. "He's smart, considerate, principled, and generous to a fault. He can be harsh at times, particularly to subordinates, but he can also be very kind. I found him to be a loving father and an excellent mentor."

Susan forced a smile. She thought Kurt's answer sounded genuine but rehearsed. She turned to her left, saw Elizabeth's disbelieving stare, and guessed that she, too, was having trouble with "considerate," "generous," and "loving." There was nothing considerate, generous, or loving with what Germans were doing around the globe.

"How about your mother?" Susan asked. "What's she like?"

"She's a lot like my father. She's intelligent, generous, caring, and attentive. She's also very religious. My mother is a devout Roman Catholic who is active in the church and in many charitable organizations in D.C."

Susan saw Elizabeth sit up. She wondered how much Mrs. Schmidt had in common with a certain Mrs. Wagner.

"She sounds like a lovely woman," Susan said.

"She is," Kurt said.

Susan noticed that Kurt's easy smile had returned. She had no doubt that he believed everything he had said about his mother.

"I understand you also have a sibling."

Kurt appeared tense.

"I do. I have a twin brother named Karl."

"I see," Susan said. "Does he live in Washington with your parents?"

Kurt shook his head.

"No. He lives in Berlin. He chose to attend college in Germany."

Susan sensed that she had brought up a sore subject. She proceeded cautiously.

"Do you see him often?" Susan asked.

Kurt sighed.

"No. I have not seen him in more than two years."

Susan scanned the faces at the table and saw that the subject of Karl Schmidt had gained the keen interest of three individuals. Elizabeth, Jack, and Amanda looked at Kurt with eyes that reflected vindication, skepticism, and concern, respectively.

"What do your parents think about having a son in Germany right now?"

Susan expected Kurt to respond defensively to a loaded question. She did not expect him to get misty and look away. She had hit the target.

"They don't like it," Kurt said a moment later. "They wish Karl had remained in the United States, like me, and pursued a career in this country. They miss him."

Susan smiled warmly at the man on the hot seat. She now looked at him less like a threat and more like a person trying to cope with family problems at a difficult age. She decided to cease the questioning and offer words of encouragement.

"I'm sure they do miss him," Susan said. "It's hard to watch a child leave the nest. I know I felt that way when Amanda went to college. I almost barred her from leaving."

"She told me as much," Kurt said.

Everyone at the table laughed. The tension dissipated.

"I'm not surprised. She likes sharing family horror stories," Susan said. She looked at Kurt. "Your family sounds nice. I would love to meet them and get to know them."

"Perhaps you can," Kurt said.

"What do you mean?"

"I mean perhaps you can see them later this month. I'm planning to go home in about three weeks. I would love to bring you along."

"You want *us* to go to Washington?" Susan asked.

"I would," Kurt said.

"Won't your parents mind?"

"They won't mind. They want to meet Amanda. They want to meet all of you."

"You know this for a fact?"

"I do," Kurt said. "They wrote as much in a letter this week. They are as curious about you as you are about them."

"I see," Susan said.

"I think you would enjoy the visit. The cherry trees along the Tidal Basin will be in full bloom. It's quite a sight if you've never seen it."

"Let's go, Mom," Amanda said. "You've said you wanted to visit D.C. You've said so on many occasions. Now's our chance."

"I don't know, honey," Susan said. "I don't want to impose on Kurt's family."

"You wouldn't be imposing at all," Kurt said. "My parents live in a five-bedroom house. They would welcome the company. They would welcome all of you."

Susan laughed to herself. She couldn't believe how quickly the conversation had shifted into a dicey direction. She reminded herself to be more selective with her words the next time she uttered a pleasantry.

"Are you sure it wouldn't be a problem?" Susan asked.

"I'm positive," Kurt said.

Susan glanced at her mother and her daughter and saw two predictably different reactions to Kurt's invitation. She saw Elizabeth grimace like she had swallowed a horse and Amanda beam like she had just won the lottery.

"Let us think about it, Kurt," Susan said. "In the meantime, please run the idea past your parents. Find out if they are as open to a visit as you think they are. Will you do that?"

"I will," Kurt said. "It would be my pleasure."

44: SUSAN

Friday, March 17, 1939

A manda recommended this place?" Jack asked.

Susan laughed.

"She did. She said we needed to reconnect with our youth."

"I imagine that won't be difficult in here."

Susan couldn't disagree. No matter where she looked in the taproom of the Colonial Inn, she saw youth. She saw students from Princeton and other colleges run around the room with pewter mugs of lager and noisily celebrate the patron saint of Ireland.

"I like this bar. It's festive and cheery," Susan said. "I need something cheery after the month I've had."

"How are things at home?" Jack asked.

"They are much better. Mom and Amanda still don't see eye to eye on Kurt Schmidt, but they respect each other's viewpoints. They are talking and laughing like they used to."

Jack took a sip of beer.

"What's your opinion of Mr. Schmidt?"

"I like him," Susan said. "I'm not sure he's told us everything we need to know about his family, but I guess that doesn't matter now. We will see for ourselves what kind of stock he comes from when we go to Washington in a couple of weeks."

"So you're definitely planning to go?"

Susan nodded.

"I admit I was hesitant about the whole thing until I received a phone call from Johanna Schmidt last night. We spoke for about ten minutes."

"Did she alleviate your concerns?" Jack asked.

"She did. She extended a warm welcome to my entire family and said that she would do everything in her power to make our stay a pleasant one."

207

"She sounds like a nice woman."

"She sounds like a *mother*," Susan said with a laugh. "I think she wants to make sure her baby hasn't fallen in with the wrong crowd."

Jack chuckled.

"How long do you plan to be gone?"

"We plan to drive to D.C. on March 30 and return on April 5," Susan said. "So we'll be gone a full week. Why do you ask? Will you miss me?"

"I'll miss you," Jack said.

"You mean you'll miss your editorial assistant."

Jack reached across the small table and took Susan's hands.

"No. I mean I'll miss *you*."

Susan gazed at him with serious eyes.

"I like hearing that. I like it a lot," Susan said. "It's been a long time since a man said he would miss me."

Jack took a breath.

"I mean it. I know I haven't suggested as much these past few weeks, but I do see you as more than just a colleague. I see you as a friend – and I'd like to see you as more."

Susan frowned. She knew this moment would come sooner or later and secretly hoped it would come later. She liked Jack and wanted to see him socially as well as professionally, but she didn't want to head down a road that could only lead to heartbreak.

"I see," Susan said.

"Did I say something wrong?" Jack asked.

"No."

"You just don't feel the same way. Is that it?"

"No," Susan said. "That's not it at all. I feel exactly the same way."

"Then why the glum face?"

Susan sighed.

"I guess I don't see the point in starting something I can't finish. I plan to leave Princeton by September. I don't think it would be fair to either one of us to get involved right now."

Jack withdrew his hands and brought them together under his chin.

"I see I've misread your interest in this community."

"I like living here," Susan said. "We all do. We just can't stay."

"In other words, Chicago is home."

Susan forced a smile.

"Chicago is home."

"For what it's worth, I'm no more attached to Princeton than you are," Jack said.

Susan winced. She didn't know how to respond. She had clearly underestimated Jack's interest in her and found herself with yet another time-travel-related problem.

"Give me your hands," Susan said.

Jack laughed.

"Do you promise to give them back?"

Susan smiled.

"I do."

"All right then," Jack said.

He pushed his hands forward.

Susan took the hands and held them as she assembled a message in her head. She knew she would get only one chance to say this right and didn't want to blow it.

"Let me first say that I like you. I like you and respect you as much as any man I have ever known, which is why I'm finding this difficult," Susan said. "I want to continue seeing you. I want to strengthen what I think is a very special friendship."

"I sense a caveat coming up," Jack said.

Susan laughed.

"It's more like a statement of understanding."

"I'm not sure I follow," Jack said.

"I want to approach each day like it's our last. If it is, it is. If it's not, it's not. As long as you understand that I can't promise you a thing, we can move forward."

"Moving forward is still moving."

"It is," Susan said. She smiled warmly as she squeezed his hands. "Let's move, Jack Hicks. Let's move forward, but let's do it slowly."

45: AMANDA

Saturday, March 25, 1939

Amanda looked at the grinning baby and the dirty diaper and shook her head. She didn't care how much Lizzie smiled. No smile could put a bloom on this rose.

"What's wrong?" Kurt asked.

Amanda sighed.

"I'm just trying to figure out how a baby this cute could produce a toxic waste site after only one feeding. This child is the Incredible Pooping Machine."

Kurt laughed.

"Are you new at this?"

Amanda shook her head.

"No. I watched a lot of babies when I was in high school, including twin boys, but none that crapped like this one. She's a modern marvel."

Lizzie squealed.

"Yes, I'm talking about you," Amanda said. She smiled and rubbed noses with her favorite infant grandmother. "I swear you'll be the death of me."

Amanda wiped Lizzie's bottom, set the dirty diaper to the side, and grabbed a fresh one from a stack. She pinned it into place, picked up the baby, and walked across her neighbors' living room to their sofa. She handed Lizzie to Kurt.

"Hold her. Sing to her. Teach her German. I don't care," Amanda said. "Just don't let her crawl into the kitchen. That place is as baby-proof as a minefield."

Amanda returned to the scene of the crime, grabbed the dirty diaper with her fingertips, and headed into the bathroom. She shook the diaper

210

over the toilet, placed it in a hamper, and washed her hands twice before returning to the living room.

Where are Pampers when you need them?

"I see you survived," Kurt said with a smile.

"I'm walking, yes, but my olfactory nerve has been compromised," Amanda replied.

Kurt laughed.

"Something tells me you're going to be a great mother."

"You're an optimist, Mr. Schmidt."

Kurt looked at her more seriously.

"Don't you *want* to be a mother?"

Amanda sighed. She had never given the matter much thought. She had always assumed she would build a career first and worry about raising little people later.

"I suppose I do," Amanda said. She took Lizzie from Kurt and returned to a padded rocking chair. "It just seems like a lot of work."

"Where are Lizzie's parents?"

"Ella is shopping. She'll be back in an hour. Erich is at a retreat for math professors. He'll be back on Monday."

"I see," Kurt said. "They are fortunate to have neighbors willing to change dirty diapers on a moment's notice."

Amanda gave him a death stare.

"Did you come here to mock me?"

"No. I came here to update you on the trip. I spoke to my mother this morning."

"What did she say?" Amanda asked.

Kurt smiled warmly.

"She said she's looking forward to meeting you. She's looking forward to meeting the Chicago girl who has bewitched her son."

Amanda laughed.

"Did she really say that?"

Kurt chuckled.

"She did. My mother is direct. It is one of her most appealing qualities."

Amanda gazed at the man on the couch.

"So is it true?"

"Is what true?" Kurt asked.

Amanda raised a brow.

"Is it true that a Chicago girl has bewitched your mother's son?"

Kurt blushed.

Amanda warmed at the sight of Kurt's red face. She couldn't recall the last time she had made a boy blush, though she was fairly certain it was July

4, 2006. That's when she had kissed fellow eleven-year-old Evan Iverson behind a dunk tank at an Independence Day picnic.

"I see I've found your soft spot," Amanda said.

"I guess you have," Kurt replied.

"So is it true? Have I bewitched you?"

Kurt sighed and nodded sheepishly.

"You have. I find it hard to get through a day without thinking about you."

Amanda beamed.

"It sounds to me like the universe is in proper alignment."

Kurt chuckled.

"I suppose it is."

Amanda held up Lizzie and studied her smiling face. She could not believe the child never fussed. When it came to bewitching females in Princeton, New Jersey, no woman held a candle to this little fart. She kissed Lizzie on the head, put her back on her lap, and looked again at the German boy who was still getting his emotions under control.

"So what do your parents have planned for us?" Amanda asked.

"They want to do the usual things," Kurt said. "They want to visit the memorials, the capitol, and the blossom festival, of course. We really couldn't be going at a better time. The city will be ablaze in color."

"I've never been to Washington in the spring. I'm looking forward to seeing the trees."

"I've seen them every year since 1922 and still never tire of them."

"What about the accommodations?" Amanda asked. "Are you sure you don't want us to stay in a hotel? You know what Ben Franklin said about fish and visitors."

Kurt tilted his head.

"No. I don't."

"He said they both start to smell after three days."

Kurt laughed.

"I'll take my chances."

Amanda smiled.

"Are you sure though? Are you sure we won't be imposing?"

"I'm positive," Kurt said. "There will be plenty of room for the eight of us."

"Eight?"

"Eight."

"I'm not a math major, Kurt, but even I can count," Amanda said. "You, your parents, and my family add up to six people."

Kurt took a breath.

"Things have changed since I spoke to you last."

212

"Changed? How?"

"My brother is back in the States," Kurt said. "He's in New York."

"New York?"

Kurt nodded.

"He left Germany in February but didn't tell a soul. I guess he's been looking for work and found a job with the German American Friendship Federation. He called my parents yesterday to tell them the news. He wanted to surprise them."

Amanda felt her stomach sink. She remembered reading about GAFF in a college history class. It was a prominent Nazi front organization.

"So Karl is coming to Washington?" Amanda asked.

"He'll be there next week. He's leaving New York on Friday and bringing a friend," Kurt said. "I'll understand if you decide to cancel your trip."

Amanda sighed.

"No. I'll go. I *want* to go," Amanda said. "Whether my family will still want to go is a whole other matter."

46: ELIZABETH

Washington, D.C. – Friday, March 31, 1939

E lizabeth walked slowly along the long south wall of the Georgetown row house and gazed at photographs that repulsed, intrigued, and inspired. If photos were a reflection of a family's values and priorities, the Schmidt clan was a complicated lot.

The repulsive shots were easy to find. Pictures of German military units on parade took up much of the right side of the gallery and hung next to images of the 1936 Summer Olympics, the shiny facade behind which Nazi Germany so recently tried to hide.

The intriguing photos included images of Heinrich Schmidt posing with celebrities like German President Paul von Hindenburg, U.S. President Calvin Coolidge, Charles Lindbergh, and Babe Ruth. They did not include images of Schmidt standing next to members of the Nazi party.

The inspiring photos celebrated nature and included shots of the Alps, the Danube, and what looked like the coast of Maine. Pictures of European settings outnumbered pictures of American settings two to one.

"Do you see anything you like?"

Elizabeth turned around and saw Johanna Schmidt enter the lavish living room, which took up half of the residence's first floor. She smiled politely when the matron of the house, a pretty, fair-haired woman of fifty, joined her in front of a photo of an alpine meadow.

"I like this one," Elizabeth said. "It reminds me of a movie I saw once, a musical with singing and dancing, a musical set in Austria."

"I'm not surprised," Johanna said with a faint German accent. "That photo was taken near Austria, in the Bavarian Alps, near the town of Kempten. Heinrich took our family there the summer we came to the United States. He wanted the boys to remember the best about their native land before they adopted a new one."

214

"Have they?" Elizabeth asked. "Have they adopted this country as their own?"

"They have to a certain degree," Johanna replied. "We all have."

Elizabeth wondered about that. She didn't doubt that Johanna and Kurt had developed an affinity for the U.S. She could see their happy American memories plastered all over the wall. She wasn't as sure about Heinrich Schmidt, who kept his views and his loyalties to himself, or the mystery son who had just arrived from Germany.

Elizabeth stepped away from the photo of the meadow and moved toward one of the Schmidt family in New York. She was immediately drawn to the twin boys, who stood between their parents in front of the Statue of Liberty. One of the boys smiled. The other did not. Elizabeth didn't have to guess who was who.

"What was it like raising twins?" Elizabeth asked. "I imagine you have many stories."

Johanna smiled.

"I have more than I could possibly share."

"Tell me one."

"All right. I will," Johanna said. She paused for a moment. "One of my favorites is not that old. Five years ago, when the boys were high school seniors, Kurt began tutoring a freshman girl in German. He tutored her once a week in the fall and the winter and had planned to help her through the spring, but he stopped when he turned out for track."

"Let me guess," Elizabeth said. "The girl needed more help."

Johanna nodded.

"She needed a lot more help. She had just begun to master the basics of the language when Kurt decided to focus on other things."

"Did Kurt tell her why he had to stop?"

"No," Johanna said. "He had planned to. He had planned to go over to her house and tell her in person until Karl offered to take his place and continue the tutoring."

"That was nice."

"There's more. When Karl went to the girl's house, he did not identify himself as Karl. He pretended to be Kurt. The girl knew the difference, of course, but her parents did not. Karl asked the girl to keep the secret to herself and continued the lessons as if Kurt had never stopped."

"I'm not sure I see where this is going," Elizabeth said.

Johanna looked closely at her guest.

"Karl knew his brother needed prestigious references to get into the college of his choice and wanted to make sure that Kurt got full credit for tutoring the girl, the daughter of the Spanish ambassador. So he made it appear as though Kurt had tutored the girl for the entire year."

"I take it that Kurt got into his college."

"He did," Johanna said. "The ambassador wrote Kurt a letter of reference that we believe made a difference."

"What about Karl?" Elizabeth asked. "Did he get credit for anything?"

"No. He didn't ask for it either. He didn't think he needed the same kind of references to get into the college of *his* choice."

"I'm guessing he did."

"He did," Johanna said. "When the number of colleges to turn him down reached five, he decided to continue his education in Germany."

"Why are you telling me this?" Elizabeth asked.

Johanna frowned.

"I'm telling you this because I know you've already formed opinions about my family and particularly the son you have not met," Johanna said. "I don't expect you to agree with Karl's choices or the views he may express while you are here, but I do want you to know that he was once a young man worthy of even a critic's admiration."

Elizabeth smiled.

"My daughter was right about you."

"How is that?" Johanna asked.

"She said you were very supportive of your sons. She could tell what kind of woman you were simply by speaking to you on the telephone."

"I'll take that as a compliment," Johanna said.

"You should," Elizabeth said. She looked at Johanna with kind eyes. "I'm sure we have many differences, Mrs. Schmidt, irreconcilable differences, but I'm comforted to know that we have at least one thing in common."

"What's that?"

"We are women who care about our families. That may not seem like much now, but it's something. It's something I can hold onto this weekend."

"I'm happy to hear that," Johanna said.

She started to say something more but stopped when the sounds of car doors shutting and men talking reached the living room. She put a hand on Elizabeth's shoulder.

"It sounds like the men have returned," Johanna said. "We should prepare for dinner."

47: AMANDA

Amanda stared at the men and laughed at her luck. Thanks to a series of unfortunate circumstances, she had the pleasure of dining with two Hitler Youths instead of one.

She had expected Nazi blather from Karl Schmidt and, in fact, had mentally prepared for it all week. She had not expected the same from Max Becker, a native New Yorker who had been described only as Karl's new American friend.

Amanda pondered her lot for another moment and then returned to her meal. She and Kurt sat between Elizabeth and Susan on one side of a long mahogany table. Karl and Max sat between Heinrich and Johanna Schmidt on the other.

The diners ate in peace for twenty minutes and discussed nothing more controversial than the weather, the blossom festival, and the Washington Senators. That changed when Max, a svelte man of twenty-five, decided to inquire about one of his fellow guests.

"Miss Peterson, I'm told you have a keen interest in history, politics, and international affairs," Max said. "Is that true?"

"It's true," Amanda replied.

"I see. Do you plan to pursue a career in one of those fields?"

"I do."

"Which one?" Max asked.

"I haven't decided yet."

"Have you given any thought to working for an organization that educates the public in areas such as international or cultural relations?"

"I have," Amanda said. "Why do you ask?"

"I ask because I know there are many opportunities in these organizations for bright, educated, and principled women like yourself."

Amanda stared warily at Max.

"I suppose you have such an organization in mind."

217

"As a matter of fact, I do. I know of several current openings at GAFF," Max said. "That's the German American Friendship Federation."

"I know what it is," Amanda said.

"I thought you might."

"Tell me, Mr. Becker, what exactly do you and others do at the German American *Friendship* Federation?"

Max smiled.

"We do many things," Max said. "We promote better relations between the two countries, address misconceptions about Germany, and educate the American public on a variety of issues."

"I see. Do you think Americans need to be educated about why Germany annexed Austria last year or forcefully occupied Czechoslovakia just two weeks ago?"

Amanda glanced at Heinrich, Johanna, and Karl and saw differing reactions to the polite barbs. Heinrich maintained his familiar stoicism, Johanna grimaced, and Karl smiled. He seemed a little too eager to please his fellow fly in the ointment.

"I see you do not care for the policies of the Third Reich," Max said.

"You're right," Amanda replied. "I don't. I don't care for them at all."

"Would you care to elaborate?"

"I'd be happy to, Mr. Becker. I take great issue with what Germany is doing not only to its neighbors but also to its own people. I think what Hitler and his supporters did to the Jews last fall was appalling."

"Do you know all the details behind that unfortunate series of events?"

"I know enough," Amanda said. "I know that even now, four months later, Jews continue to be treated like third-class citizens. That is inexcusable and unprecedented."

"Unprecedented?" Karl asked.

"Yes," Amanda said.

Karl laughed.

"We're sitting in the most segregated city in the world, the capital of a nation that has persecuted ten percent of its population for centuries," Karl said. "Can you honestly say that what's going on in Germany today is worse or different than what's going on in the South? Can you say that America has treated its blacks, Jews, and indigenous peoples any better?"

Amanda winced. She knew that the comparisons were not fair, but she also knew she could never win an argument over human rights records when the U.S. was still enforcing Jim Crow laws and was just three years away from interning its Japanese citizens.

She knew as well that it was pointless and even dangerous to suggest that Germany's treatment of Europe's Jews was about to go from appalling to evil. She may have had knowledge of places like Auschwitz, Buchenwald,

218

and Dachau, but the rest of the world, at least in early 1939, did not. She felt angry, frustrated, and helpless.

"I don't believe the situations are comparable, but even if they were that would not excuse what Germany is doing to its neighbors," Amanda said. "It has become a bully among nations."

"What would you have Germany do?" Max asked. "The nation is constantly pestered by meddlers and troublemakers who wish to undermine its interests."

Amanda looked at Susan, saw a frown, and decided to behave. Then she looked at Elizabeth, saw a smile, and decided to press on. She simply could not let Max's nonsense stand.

"Who are these 'meddlers' and 'troublemakers,' Mr. Becker? The British? Americans? Jews? I don't see troublemakers from where I stand," Amanda said. "I see people who want to keep Nazi Germany from acting on its worst impulses."

"You have strong opinions about Germany," Max said. "I'm curious as to how you arrived at them. Have you ever been to Germany? Have you been there *recently*?"

Amanda sighed.

"No. I have not."

"I see. So you really don't know what you're talking about."

"That's not true," Amanda said. "I do know what I'm talking about. I know because I read. I read articles by people who *have* been to Germany and other places in Europe where the Nazis are creating chaos and mischief."

"Are you referring to the Sudetenland?" Max asked.

"Of course I am. Germany has no more right to meddle in Czechoslovakia than it does in Austria or Poland or Lithuania or anywhere else."

"So you believe a nation should not assert control over areas it considers its own?"

"Yes!"

Amanda realized her mistake the second she saw Max grin. He smiled like a cat that had just cornered a mouse, a mouse that suddenly found herself in over her head.

"I take it then that you oppose America's annexation of Hawaii and the Southwest," Max said. "I assume that you oppose its occupation of Puerto Rico, Guam, and the Philippines and its outright theft of this entire continent from the Indians."

"That's not the same thing," Amanda said.

"It's not?"

"No."

"I think it is," Max said. "I think it's exactly the same thing, except that Germany has restricted its 'meddling' to its own backyard."

Amanda saw an opportunity and seized it.

"Really?" Amanda asked. "Does Germany's backyard extend to Spain?"

"I don't know what you're talking about."

"You know exactly what I'm talking about," Amanda said. "Germany has actively supported the Nationalists since the beginning. It has provided Franco with soldiers, tanks, and planes and done so at the expense of a growing democracy."

"You overstate Germany's influence, Miss Peterson."

"I don't think so," Amanda said. She sighed. "Not that it matters. Madrid has fallen. The Republicans have surrendered. The war is over."

Amanda sank in her chair when seven people looked at her. She knew even before Elizabeth put a hand on her knee that she had stepped in it again.

She had assumed that it was April 1 – the day Francisco Franco had claimed victory over government forces in the Spanish Civil War. When she remembered that it was March 31 and that Franco had not yet spoken to the world, she braced for the worst.

"I've heard no word of a surrender," Max said. He turned to Heinrich. "Have you?"

The colonel shook his head.

"I've heard nothing either," Heinrich said. He looked at Amanda. "Where did you hear this news?"

Amanda took a breath. She had just seconds to dig herself out of a hole and move the conversation in a less dangerous direction.

"I heard something on the radio just before dinner, Colonel," Amanda said. "I can't remember the station, but I definitely heard it. The Republicans have surrendered."

Amanda put on a brave face as Heinrich Schmidt, Karl Schmidt, and Max Becker looked at her with skepticism, suspicion, and contempt, respectively. She didn't think any of the men would investigate her claim in a serious way, but she didn't really know.

All Amanda Peterson knew was that she had put herself and her family at risk. She vowed to do better. She didn't have a choice.

48: AMANDA

Amanda swept the landscape with her eyes and beheld a sight she would never forget. No matter where she looked, she saw green grass, blue sky, and an arresting riot of pink. Spring had come to the nation's capital and had announced itself with a shout.

She gazed at the far reaches of the Tidal Basin, a reservoir between the Potomac River and the Washington Channel, and then slowly returned her attention to the man at her side. She could see that he was enjoying the moment as much as she was.

"I must admit I'm envious," Amanda said. "Chicago has nothing on this. I don't think *any* city has something on this."

"I take it you like cherry blossoms," Kurt said.

"I like heavenly scenes, and this, Mr. Schmidt, is heavenly."

Amanda leaned into Kurt's side as they sat on a small wooden bench. Despite the presence of thousands of people, who had come to D.C. from all over the nation to see the changing of the seasons, she felt like they had the place to themselves.

"I assume it's more heavenly than a dinner at my house," Kurt said.

"You assume correctly."

Kurt smiled.

"Don't be too hard on yourself. You defended your principles Friday night. You raised points that needed to be raised," Kurt said. "I admire that."

"Does anyone else though? Your parents haven't said more than a few words to me in the past two days. I suspect they weren't too thrilled with my theatrics."

"My father is a German diplomat, Amanda. You can't expect him or my mother to openly rush to your defense when you criticize their country in their own home."

"I suppose not," Amanda said. "I'm still not sure they like me."

"They do," Kurt said. "I know that for a fact."

"They told you this?"

Kurt nodded.

"They each said something yesterday."

"What did they say?" Amanda asked.

"Let's see. They said you're a beautiful, charming, intelligent woman that I should cherish, nurture, and hold on to if it's the last thing I do."

"They didn't say that."

"No," Kurt said. He laughed. "They didn't. I did."

Amanda smiled.

"You're terrible!"

Kurt sighed.

"No. I'm a man who's very fond of you."

Amanda burrowed further into Kurt's side.

"So did your parents say *anything* about me?"

"They did. They said they like you and want to see more of you. They asked me to invite you back to Washington for another visit this summer."

"I'm sure your brother will love that," Amanda said.

"Karl won't be here," Kurt replied. "He'll be in New York stirring up trouble."

Amanda lifted her head, gazed again at the sea of pink, and mentally revisited her contentious first meeting with Karl Schmidt. She could not believe that the strident Nazi and the man she adored had come from the same womb.

"What's the deal with him, anyway?" Amanda asked. "I'm serious. What does he see in those nasty bigots? I don't get it."

Kurt sat up straight and looked at Amanda.

"Karl has always preferred order and clarity to chaos and ambiguity. He likes simple answers to complicated problems. When he watches American politicians debate issues, he does not see a healthy exchange of ideas. He sees discord. He sees weakness. When he watches the Nazis, he sees strength. He sees people who get things done."

"He must like Mussolini then," Amanda said. "It's hard to imagine someone more appealing than a man who gets the trains to run on time."

Kurt smiled.

"I see you brought your wit to the park."

"You like it?" Amanda asked.

"It's one of your most appealing qualities," Kurt said.

"What else do you find appealing?"

Kurt put a hand to his chin.

"Let me think. This might take a while."

Amanda glared at her companion.

"It had better not!"

Kurt laughed.

"You're right. I shouldn't need much time."

"Well?"

"Let's see," Kurt said. "I like your intellect, for sure, and I'm definitely warming up to your blond hair and blue eyes. I really like your eyes."

"That's a good start. What else?"

Kurt looked at her thoughtfully.

"I like your perceptiveness."

"What do you mean?" Amanda asked.

"I mean I like how you see things that others don't. I like how you *know* things that others don't. I'm still trying to figure out how you knew that the Nationalists had captured Madrid a day before anyone else."

"I heard something on the radio. I told you that."

"I know," Kurt said. "I also know that I didn't hear the news, from an official source, until this morning when I picked up a paper."

"Are you accusing me of something?"

"No. I'm just saying that either you heard something no one else did or you have some sort of gift. I like to think it's the latter. I like to think I'm dating someone who's gifted."

Amanda laughed.

"I guess I just pay attention to things, that's all. Has your dad said anything to you about my revelation at dinner? Does he plan to say anything to me?"

"No," Kurt said as he shook his head. "He hasn't – and he won't."

"Why is that?"

"He won't because he's not the kind of person to put someone on the spot," Kurt said. "When he wants information, he finds it himself. He's very good at that."

49: ELIZABETH

Princeton, New Jersey — Saturday, April 8, 1939

For the first time in weeks, Elizabeth Campbell, walking machine, strolled down her street alone. She didn't mind walking alone. She liked it, in fact. She liked it because it gave her the opportunity to think, and on this sunny spring day, she had much to think about.

Elizabeth thought about the trip, of course. It was hard not to. She had seen Congress in session, met an interesting couple, and watched the world's most famous cherry trees come to life. People didn't forget things like that in the course of a week. Nor did they forget watching a granddaughter take on two Nazis in a dining-room debate.

Elizabeth felt bad about the weeks she had lost fighting with Amanda over something as trivial as her boyfriend's ancestry.

She realized just in time that what mattered was what Kurt Schmidt did and thought and not who he was. She had told Amanda that she approved of her companion before they left Washington.

The time traveler also thought about her family, her original family, and what they had come to mean to her in just a few months. She wondered how she would ever break a bond that was growing stronger every day or refrain from meddling with a future she had no right to change. On more than one occasion, she had considered writing a letter to Geoffrey Bell and asking him for permission to break a commandment or two.

Elizabeth sighed when she thought of that long-ago night in Santa Barbara. Had she not taken the time to meet the professor after his lecture, she would be playing cards with the same old crowd in 2016 and not having the time of her life.

She continued south on Mercer Street and noticed a few new sights. People worked in their gardens, mowed their lawns, and threw baseballs around. If spring had come to the District of Columbia in a blaze of color, it had come to Princeton, New Jersey, with a flurry of activity.

Elizabeth waved to a young woman who played with her toddler on the front porch of a house that had just been sold. She didn't know the name of the woman or the child. She knew only that the two were part of a family that was on its way out. They hadn't been a part of her life the first time around and wouldn't be a part of it the second time.

Elizabeth continued walking and kept to herself until she came upon a scene she had hoped to find. She found the Old Man in a sweatshirt and baggy pants wandering around his yard as though he had lost a cat – or perhaps his mind. She waved when he waved and smiled when she finally met him at his gate.

"How are you this morning?" Elizabeth asked.

"I am fine, dear lady, albeit a bit distracted. I seem to have lost my keys."

"I didn't know you drove."

"I don't," the Old Man said. "I have lost the keys to my house."

Elizabeth laughed to herself. She never tired of seeing a side of a man that many others did not. She would definitely put this in her journal.

"Have you locked yourself out of your house?" Elizabeth asked.

"No. I have just lost my keys. I know they are here somewhere."

Elizabeth started to ask if she could help with the search when she saw objects in the grass that reflected the bright morning light. She pointed at her discovery.

"Are those your keys over there?" Elizabeth asked.

The Old Man turned around and looked at the spot on the lawn. He walked slowly to the location, picked up the keys, and held them up.

"There you are, my friends."

Elizabeth smiled.

"I think they were just playing hard to get. You know how keys are."

The Old Man turned to face Elizabeth.

"Thank you. Your eyes are as sharp as they are bright."

"I'm glad someone thinks so," Elizabeth said with a laugh.

The resident returned to his gate.

"I should reward you with a cup of tea. That is the least I could do."

Elizabeth thought about the invitation. She had spoken to the Old Man on many occasions during her second tour of the thirties but had never done more than exchange a few pleasantries.

Perhaps it was time to change that.

"I think I'll take you up on that," Elizabeth said.

"Splendid," the Old Man replied.

"I have just one condition."

"Oh. What is that?"

"I'd like to return the favor," Elizabeth said. "I'd like to have you over for tea and perhaps breakfast. I'd like you to meet my family."

The Old Man smiled.

"I would be honored. I believe that is something I'll do."

50: SUSAN

Friday, April 14, 1939

Susan pondered the question as she sat in a car parked in front of her house. She didn't mind the question or how it had been asked, but she admitted she didn't know how to answer it. She thought about the matter a little more and then turned to face the driver.

"So you want to know about Bruce?" Susan asked.

Jack nodded.

"I do. I don't mean to pry. I'm just curious. I can't figure out why you haven't talked about him more often. He must have meant a lot to you."

"He did," Susan said.

"We can discuss something else. I sense he's an uncomfortable subject."

"My husband is a complicated subject."

"The difference is the same," Jack said. "If you don't want to talk about him, then we can talk about something else. We can always discuss cruisers and destroyers."

Susan laughed.

"I think I'd rather talk about my husband."

"I'm sure you would," Jack said with a smile. "We've had a long week."

Susan glanced at her dark house. She surmised that her mother was asleep and that her daughter was still out on her date with Kurt.

She thought about inviting Jack in for a drink but decided that the front seat of his open 1937 Plymouth Roadster convertible was as good a place as any for a potentially delicate conversation.

"What would you like to know about Bruce?" Susan asked.

"The usual things, I guess," Jack said. "What did he do for a living? What were his interests? What activities did you enjoy together?"

Susan gazed at the starry sky and considered the questions carefully. She knew she would have only one opportunity to provide meaningful answers and wanted to make the most of it.

"The first question is an easy one," Susan said. "Bruce was a developer. He developed commercial real estate in Chicago and northern Illinois."

"What about his interests?"

"He loved sports, hunting, and fishing, like most men. He also enjoyed collecting things, such as autographs, baseball cards, and old recordings."

He liked young receptionists too.

"I see," Jack said. "He sounds like someone I would have liked."

"I think you would have."

"How about your common interests?"

Susan frowned.

"That's a hard question to answer. We had many common interests in the beginning and for most of our marriage. We both liked baseball, tennis, art, and the theater. We even developed a mutual interest in fancy cars. Bruce would have loved this vehicle. He had a special fascination with convertibles."

"Why is the question difficult?" Jack asked. "It seems to me that the two of you had a lot in common, certainly more than most married couples."

Susan sighed.

"The question is difficult because we drifted apart toward the end. Bruce immersed himself in his work. I pursued other interests. We did not treat our marriage like a garden that needed to be watered and nurtured. We took each other for granted and broke the promises we had once made to each other."

"You're not suggesting what I think you are, are you?"

"I am," Susan said. "Bruce had an affair with one of his subordinates last spring. I didn't learn about the relationship until just before he died."

"You don't need to say more," Jack said.

"I do, though. I do. You've asked honest questions and deserve honest answers. I haven't said much about my husband because he is still a painful subject. I'm still coming to grips with his deceit and my own shortcomings as a wife."

"You'll get through it. I'm sure."

Susan laughed.

"Is that the glass-is-half-empty admiral talking or the more optimistic retiree?"

"It's neither," Jack said. "It's a man who knows exactly what you're going through."

Susan sat up in her seat.

"You may have to elaborate. I'm getting a little slow in my old age."

Jack smiled sadly.

"I know what you're going through because I went through the same thing."

"Your wife had an affair?" Susan asked.

Jack nodded.

"Janet didn't call it that. She called it a 'mistake,' but it was an affair just the same."

"You don't need to say anything."

"I think I do," Jack said. "If we're going to share skeletons, we should share all of them."

"You're probably right."

"I know I am. Honesty really is the best policy."

Susan looked at Jack Hicks with new admiration. She saw not only a sailor who had defended America's interests abroad but also a sensitive man who had fought his own battles at home. She wondered what other surprises he had for her.

"When did all of this happen?" Susan asked.

Jack sighed.

"It occurred in 1919 when I was away at sea."

"Were you two having problems?"

"No," Jack said. "We were doing well, at least in my opinion, for a couple that had been married ten years. We had just moved to San Diego and had looked forward to finally settling down after living out of suitcases in Seattle and San Francisco."

"What happened?"

"Two things happened. The first is that Janet saw a series of doctors and learned why she could not bear children. The second is that my six-month tour of the South Pacific turned into a twelve-month tour. I was not at her side when she needed me most."

"I see," Susan said.

"Janet turned to her friends for comfort but found misery instead. Most of the women she knew had children," Jack said. "Whenever she visited their homes, she saw what she did not have. She saw what she could *never* have."

"I'm so sorry."

"She eventually found solace in the arms of a Navy captain. She carried on with him for about six weeks. When my ship returned to San Diego, she confessed everything."

Susan reached across the seat and put her hand on Jack's arm.

"That must have been hard."

"It was difficult," Jack said. "I considered divorce, of course. I considered divorcing Janet for several weeks, but I concluded I would be happier with her than without her. We eventually worked out our differences with the help of a Navy chaplain."

"Do you regret staying together?"

"No. What I regret was putting her through several weeks of hell while I decided whether or not to continue our marriage."

"I admire what you did," Susan said. "Forgiveness is hard."

Jack laughed sadly.

"It may be hard, but it's also liberating. I became a better husband after that episode. Janet became a better wife. We enjoyed eighteen more years together, good years, years that I would have never known had I succumbed to bitterness."

Susan smiled. She remembered her mother saying something similar after she had revealed her own struggle with an adulterous spouse.

She considered Elizabeth and Jack better people for passing a test that she had not even been required to take.

"Thank you for sharing that," Susan said.

"You're welcome."

"I should probably head into the house. If I stay out here much longer, my mother may turn on the front lights to see if I'm up to no good."

"Do you feel like a teenager, Mrs. Peterson?"

"No. I feel like a forty-nine-year-old woman who's too old to be parking in the dark with a boy I barely know," Susan said. She laughed and then looked at Jack seriously. "Thanks for the lovely evening. I enjoyed the show tonight. I enjoyed our conversation."

"I did too," Jack said. He sighed. "Let me at least show you to the door."

"All right."

Jack opened his door, stepped out of the Plymouth, and walked around the back of the vehicle to the passenger side. He opened Susan's door, helped her out of the car, and escorted her up the walk.

He took her hands when they reached the door of the rental.

"Thank you for a memorable evening," Jack said. "I'd like to do this again."

"I would too."

Jack leaned forward and gave Susan a gentle kiss.

"Good night, Susan."

"Good night, Jack."

Susan watched intently as Admiral John J. Hicks returned to his car, turned on the ignition, and drove out of sight. She didn't know what to make of her interesting evening, but she did know it had given her food for thought.

She had completed a Masters course on love, betrayal, and forgiveness and concluded something she should have concluded long ago. She realized that life was not about looking backward but rather forward. She vowed to look forward the rest of the way.

51: AMANDA

Saturday, April 15, 1939

Amanda opened her eyes, stared at the ceiling, and started to sweat. She realized it was April 15 and that she had not paid her due. Then she remembered she had not earned an income in 1938 and would still have plenty of time to file a 1040EZ for 2016 when she returned to the future and the wonderful world of taxes.

She rolled onto her side and laughed. She wondered how she had ever made it this far in a world where everything she did, or didn't do, was a potential cause for concern. She started to drift back to sleep when her mother disrupted her tranquility with a knock.

"Are you awake, Amanda?" Susan asked from behind the bedroom door.

"I'm sleeping. Go away."

"I made breakfast and coffee."

"I'll be down in a bit," Amanda said. "I want to think about the IRS for a while."

"What?"

"Eat without me, Mom."

Susan opened the door halfway and stuck her head through the opening. She smiled at Amanda when her daughter returned her gaze.

"We have a visitor who wants to meet you," Susan said.

"Who?" Amanda asked.

"Why don't you come down and see?"

"Oh, all right. Give me five minutes."

"Great," Susan said. She beamed. "I'll tell him you're coming."

"Him?"

Amanda tried to make sense of the exchange as she cleared the remaining cobwebs from her sleepy head. She wondered who could possibly want to see her, without her make-up, at eight on a Saturday morning. She was almost certain it wasn't the fair-haired boy who had kissed her at the door at midnight. She rolled out of bed and walked to her closet. Deciding that her male caller was probably someone more significant than the milkman, she pulled a bright cotton dress off a hanger, threw it on, and walked out of her bedroom and into the bathroom.

Amanda ran a brush through her thick blond hair, splashed water on her pretty face, and checked her breath for halitosis. When she was satisfied that she wouldn't scare the visitor away, she flipped the light, exited the bathroom, and headed down the hallway.

She stopped at the top of the stairs, listened for voices, and frowned when she heard nothing more than the clattering of dishes. She figured the least her mother could do was to start a lively conversation that might give her a better idea of what awaited.

It didn't matter. Amanda needed only to whiff the air at the bottom of the stairs to know that the meal was no ordinary breakfast. She smelled pancakes, sweet rolls, and coffee, among other delightful things.

Amanda proceeded through the kitchen. When she walked into the dining area, she saw a smiling mother, a talking grandma, and something she would remember for the rest of her life. She saw the world's smartest man.

"It's you," Amanda said as her eyes grew wide. "You're … you're *him*!"

The old man shrugged.

"Most people call me Albert, but 'him' will do."

"Dr. Einstein, this is my granddaughter, Amanda," Elizabeth said. "She is a recent graduate of the University of Illinois and a big fan of yours."

Einstein stood up and extended a hand.

"It's a pleasure to meet you, Amanda."

Amanda took the hand and gave it a tepid shake. She wasn't sure she had the strength to do more than remain on her feet.

"Take a seat and grab some coffee, honey," Susan said with a laugh. "Dr. Einstein has graciously agreed to join us for breakfast. He'll be here a while."

Amanda snapped out of a stupor as she digested her mother's words. She watched Einstein sit down and then pulled up a chair opposite him at the table for four. She took a moment to study the man and found him to be exactly as advertised: disheveled, uncombed, and a little distracted. He wore a shaggy blue sweater, baggy gray pants, and hair that wouldn't quit. Even at age sixty, he looked like his caricature. Amanda couldn't see if he had worn socks, but she was pretty sure he hadn't. She had heard stories, even from Kurt, that the famed scientist never wore them.

233

"So tell me, young lady, what did you study at the University of Illinois?" Einstein asked with a thick German accent.

"I studied history and political science," Amanda said.

"I see. What do you hope to do with such an education?"

"I want to work for a research organization and then go from there. I haven't decided what I want to do in the long term. I need to think about it more."

Einstein nodded.

"Research is good. Thinking is good. As I tell my colleagues at the Institute, we need more thinkers and fewer talkers."

Amanda laughed at the observation. She had been told that Einstein had a sense of humor and was delighted to learn that she had not been misled. She didn't need to ask where he worked. She already knew he was a fixture at the Institute for Advanced Study, a postdoctoral research center in Princeton that rivaled the Nassau Institute and offered programs in historical studies, mathematics, natural sciences, and social sciences.

"My mom thinks that too," Amanda said. "She thinks the world needs more people who use their minds and fewer who flap their gums. Did she tell you she's a writer?"

"No. She did not," Einstein said. He turned to Susan. "What do you write?"

Susan shot her daughter a thanks-for-putting-me-on-the-spot glare. She sipped her coffee, took a breath, and then smiled sweetly at her guest.

"I write steamy romances," Susan said.

"Is that so? I will have to look for your books."

"Let me know when you find them," Susan said. She laughed. "I haven't published them yet."

"Oh."

"She's also helping an admiral write a book on the U.S. Navy," Amanda said.

"Really?" Einstein asked.

Susan nodded.

"I'm assisting Jack Hicks with his latest work. Perhaps you've heard of him."

"I have," Einstein said. "How are you assisting him?"

"I'm reworking his prose to make it more understandable to a general audience. He's the actual writer," Susan said. "I'm more like a volunteer editorial assistant."

"I am impressed," Einstein said. "You are giving and not taking. Most writers I meet only want to take. Take. Take. Take. They pester me endlessly."

"How do they pester you?"

"They write to me asking for help. Some come to my door."

"What kind of help do they want?" Susan asked.

Einstein buttered a roll. He had eaten three since Amanda had entered the room.

"They wish to know about time travel, of course," Einstein said. "They all want to know about time travel. They want to know if it is really possible."

Amanda sat up in her chair and watched Elizabeth and Susan sit up in theirs. She could see that the professor had everyone's attention.

"*Do* you think time travel is possible?" Amanda asked.

Einstein shrugged.

"Yes. No. Maybe. It is all relative."

Amanda laughed.

"That's pretty funny. You should work the clubs."

"Hmm?"

Amanda smiled and shook her head. When she saw that Einstein seemed more interested in his next roll than answering her question, she tried again.

"I thought your special theory of relativity proved that time travel, at least forward time travel, was possible."

"It *is* possible," Einstein said.

"Do you believe that backward time travel is possible?" Amanda asked.

Einstein shook his head.

"No. I am afraid that is a horse of a different color."

Amanda smiled. She didn't know which was more impressive: Einstein's incorrect answer or his command of American idioms.

She liked both. She had learned more about the man in ten minutes than she had learned in the previous ten years. Amanda glanced at her mother and her grandmother and saw grins on their faces. She could only imagine what they were thinking.

"Do you think backward time travel will *ever* be possible?" Amanda asked.

"I do not," Einstein said.

"Even in the very distant future?"

The visitor again shook his head.

"Sadly, I think even that is unlikely," Einstein said. "If men of science possessed such power a hundred years from now, then surely they would be with us now."

Amanda looked at the physicist and smiled.

"I think you're right, Dr. Einstein. They would," Amanda said. "They most certainly would."

52: ELIZABETH

Sunday, April 23, 1939

Elizabeth aimed her Brownie Special at the baby in the high chair and snapped five pictures. She took five because she didn't trust a camera without a digital display. She took pictures, period, because she wanted the memento of a lifetime.

"How did I do, Lizzie?" Elizabeth asked. "Did I take a winner?"

The baby squealed and pounded her fists on her tray.

"I think you have your answer, Mom," Susan said with a laugh. "Why don't you take more pictures just to be safe?"

"No," Elizabeth said. "Why don't *you* take more? I want some pictures with the princess."

"All right."

Elizabeth handed the camera to her daughter, showed her how to use it, and then walked to the back of the high chair. When Susan lifted the camera, Elizabeth leaned close to Lizzie, smiled, and said "cheese" on command. She repeated the process four times and then listened as Susan, Amanda, Erich, Ella, and Kurt sang "Happy Birthday" to one girl marking her first birthday and another her seventy-ninth.

"Now that's what I call singing," Elizabeth said.

She kissed Lizzie on the head and joined the adults at a picnic table on the back patio. She tried to remember if she had photos of her first birthday but ultimately decided it didn't matter. She had new pictures now and new memories and would hold onto them for as long as she lived.

Elizabeth sat with Susan and Amanda on one side of the table, which Erich had built in March. Ella, Erich, and Kurt faced them on the other side. Lizzie sat in her high chair a few feet from her mother. She tore into a piece of chocolate cake that Ella had put on her tray.

"I would love to borrow the negatives if your photos turn out," Ella said to Elizabeth. "Would you provide them to me?"

"I'll do better than that. I'll order prints. I want you to have at least a few pictures of us."

"Thank you."

"Don't mention it," Elizabeth said. "It's the least I can do for you for allowing me to be a part of your wonderful child's life."

Ella reached across the table and put her hand on Elizabeth's arm.

"I am the one is who is indebted. I do not know how I would have managed to get through these past few months without your help. I feel blessed to have family here."

Elizabeth smiled as she pondered Ella's words. She wondered how Ella Wagner, the *original* Ella Wagner, had managed to get through the first few months of 1939 without the active and eager assistance of three time-traveling neighbors. She imagined that she had simply tapped into her bottomless reservoir of patience, strength, and understanding.

"How are you adjusting to Princeton?" Elizabeth asked.

"We are adjusting well," Ella said.

Elizabeth turned her head.

"Erich?"

"I agree with Ella. I feel like we have finally found a home," Erich said. "I feel like we are Americans now and not simply Austrians shuffling from place to place."

"It sounds to me like you want to stay."

"We do," Erich said. "Whether we can, of course, depends on whether I am hired as a full-time professor in the fall, but I am optimistic. I believe I will get the position I seek and that we will be able to remain in Princeton for many years."

"I'm happy for you," Elizabeth said. "I'm happy for all of you. I admire your ability to integrate yourselves in a new country and a new community so quickly."

"Thank you."

"I also admire how you and Ella have worked as a team. You haven't disagreed once on a matter of importance."

Erich laughed.

"That is not quite true."

"What do you mean?" Elizabeth asked.

"We disagreed on a matter of importance just this morning," Erich said.

"Oh? What was that?"

"Ella and I disagreed on what kind of pet to get for Lizzie. She would like to get her a cat. I would like to get her a dog."

Elizabeth laughed. If Eric and Ella Wagner could find nothing better to argue about than the choice of a pet, they were doing as well as anyone.

Elizabeth turned to Ella.

"Why do you want to get a cat?"

Ella smiled.

"They are less work. They are also cleaner, friendlier, and much better with children."

"I see," Elizabeth said. She turned to Erich. "Why do you want to get a dog?"

Erich laughed.

"That is a silly question. I want to get a dog for the same reason that most people want to get a dog. They are superior pets. They are perfect companions."

Elizabeth glanced at Susan. She wanted to see if she was following the Great Pet Debate and was disappointed to see that she was not.

Susan discussed another matter with Amanda and Kurt. The three went over the details of a multi-family trip to the World's Fair in New York the following week.

Elizabeth let her mind drift. She thought about the things she wanted to do on that trip when Ella brought her back to a more pressing concern.

"Do *you* have an opinion?" Ella asked.

"What?" Elizabeth replied.

"Do you prefer cats or dogs?"

"I would like your thoughts too," Erich said. "What do you suggest?"

Elizabeth cringed. She didn't want to answer the question. She didn't want to come between her parents, but she knew she didn't have a choice. Ella and Erich would press her for an opinion until she provided one.

Elizabeth knew the right answer. The right answer was a golden retriever that had just been born in Princeton Junction. Elizabeth remembered that her parents had adopted the puppy shortly after her first birthday and kept him as a pet for fourteen years. She couldn't imagine Lizzie going through life without the dog.

"I suggest that you compromise," Elizabeth said. "I advise that you get a dog first and then a cat. Give Lizzie the best of both worlds."

Erich beamed.

"You are wise beyond your years."

Elizabeth laughed.

"That's saying a lot since I'm older than half the buildings in town."

"I mean it though," Erich said.

Elizabeth acknowledged the compliment with a nod. She paused for a moment to consider what she had done and then turned to her mother.

"Does that solution work for you?" Elizabeth asked.

"It does," Ella said. She sighed. "You are right. Lizzie should have a dog and a cat."

Elizabeth smiled. With a few choice words, she had offered a constructive solution, resolved a family dispute, and given Lizzie Wagner something that Elizabeth Wagner had always wanted growing up: a cat.

"What kind of dog do you suggest?" Erich asked.

"I recommend you get a golden retriever," Elizabeth said. "They are excellent family dogs. I know because I had one growing up."

"What a coincidence. I was considering that very breed. Do you know where we can find one in this area?"

"You can find them in a lot of places. Check the classified ads in the paper. Check them today. I suspect you will find something worthwhile very soon."

"I will do that," Erich said. "Thank you."

"You're welcome."

Elizabeth smiled at Erich and Ella and then turned to the girl in the high chair, a girl who had smeared chocolate war paint on her cherubic face. She laughed to herself when the baby, her diaper-wearing soul mate, answered her grin with one of her own.

We did well today, Little One. We did very well.

53: SUSAN

Queens, New York – Sunday, April 30, 1939

S usan could barely see the lectern, much less the man behind it, but she could see enough to know she was seeing something special. The speaker was no mere policy expert on loan to the Nassau Institute. He was the president of the United States.

She settled into her folding metal chair, closed her eyes for a moment, and did nothing but listen. Even through a rudimentary amplification system, the clipped, aristocratic voice of Franklin Delano Roosevelt sounded like music.

"I have seen only a small fraction of the fair; but even from the little I have seen, I am able to congratulate all of you who conceived and planned the fair and all you men and women who built it . . ."

Susan put her hand on Jack Hicks' knee, patted it twice, and whispered into his ear.

"I feel like I'm watching a newsreel," Susan said. "This is amazing."

"It is," Jack said softly.

A fortyish woman sitting one row up and two seats down turned her head and glared at the gabbers. The woman, attired in a velvet suit and a lace-netting pillbox hat, stared at Susan like she was a noisy tramp from Brooklyn or, worse yet, a Republican.

Susan politely smiled, gently waved her gloved hand, and then stuck out her tongue. When the woman huffed, turned up her nose, and returned her attention to the speaker, Susan laughed quietly, took Jack's hand, and spoke again into his ear.

"I seem to have stirred a bee in a bonnet."

Jack smiled.

"It appears so."

Susan focused again on the stage. She couldn't make out the dignitaries seated on each side of the lectern, but she knew from the introductions that they included Mayor Fiorello La Guardia, Governor Herbert Lehman, and the estimable Dr. Einstein. Though all were men of stature, all seemed insignificant compared to the man behind the microphone.

Susan leaned toward Jack.

"Have you met FDR in person?"

Jack nodded. He leaned toward Susan.

"I met him once when he was Assistant Secretary of the Navy and again last year at a reception in Washington. He's even more impressive up close."

"I believe it," Susan said.

Susan scanned the crowd in the Court of Peace, the large plaza with the ironic name, and beheld the witnesses to history. She saw men in suits and fedoras and women in dresses and berets. She saw America in its Sunday finest on one of its finest days.

Then she looked closer to home, in her own row, and saw a group of family, friends, and acquaintances that only a fiction writer could love. Amanda, Dot Gale, and the entire Schmidt family sat to her left. Jack, Elizabeth, and the entire Wagner family sat to her right. Ella kept Lizzie quiet with a bottle the size of Newark.

The journey to the World's Fair had begun Saturday afternoon when the Mercer Street families and Dot had driven to their hotel in midtown Manhattan. They joined Jack for breakfast the next morning and then proceeded together to the fairgrounds in Flushing Meadows, where the Germans and thousands of others from around the world awaited.

Susan planned to make the most of the fair's opening day and the four that followed. She had talked Elizabeth, Amanda, and Dot into staying the week by arguing that they would never again have the chance to see an exposition as magnificent. Only Elizabeth offered even a feeble objection. She didn't care much for crowds.

Susan could relate. She didn't care much for crowds either and typically put up with them only at Cubs games, parades, and significant public events. She had long decided that the New York World's Fair, the first held in the nation's largest city, was significant enough to merit several days and many dollars.

If she had one regret, it was that she would not have the chance to see Jack again until Friday. She wanted to get back to working on his book. She wanted to get back to *him*.

She had thought about Jack a lot since he had revealed his painful past, kissed her for the first time, and indicated that he wanted their friendship to be more than a friendship. She thought about what he had done, what he was doing, and what he wanted to do.

Susan knew the future was the problem. She could no more start a long-term relationship with a man now, at least in good conscience, than she could start a long-time job. She was a time traveler, a woman with a secret, a person who would disappear from 1939 in less than five months. At least that's what she thought she would do.

She hated this part. She hated knowing that she would have to walk away from people she had come to know, respect, and even love. She once again tipped her hat to Geoffrey Bell, who had warned her against getting too involved with the people she met.

Susan thought about her uniformed admiral for a moment and then thought about his predecessor, a man who still haunted her thoughts. She liked to think that her problem with Jack was simply a chronological one, but she knew it was more than that.

She still had not removed the clutter in her heart to make room for someone else. She still had not come to grips with her past, her dead husband, and a life she missed.

"Are you all right?" Jack asked. "You seem preoccupied."

"I guess I am," Susan said.

"Can I help?"

No. You're doing enough already.

"No. I'll be fine. I'm just a little distracted."

Snooty Lady looked over her shoulder and issued another ten-dagger glare. She did not appear to care about Susan's preoccupations or distractions.

Susan smiled warmly and put a finger to her lips. She tried to tell the woman that she, Susan Peterson, would stop talking if she, Snooty Lady, got a life. She laughed to herself as she pondered the odds of either happening before Roosevelt finished his speech, which commemorated the 150th anniversary of George Washington's first presidential inauguration.

She didn't laugh about Bruce Peterson, Admiral John J. Hicks, or the current state of her personal life. Each subject left her wistful, depressed, and frustrated but not hopeless. She didn't need to decide anything today.

She needed only to keep all of her options open and be prepared to make a decision – The Decision – when the time came. Susan tightened her hold on Jack's hand, gave him her best smile, and returned her eyes to the thirty-second president. It was time, she thought, to enjoy a handsome man, a sunny afternoon, and a memorable moment in history.

54: AMANDA

Monday, May 1, 1939

By the end of the second day of her first world's fair, Amanda Peterson, time traveler and thrill-seeker extraordinaire, decided that she liked three things. She liked Dot Gale's reaction to television, her reaction to camel rides, and at least her initial reaction to a towering amusement called the Parachute Jump.

"I don't know about this," Dot said.

"You'll be fine," Amanda replied.

"No. I mean it. I'm terrified of heights."

Amanda laughed.

"So am I."

Dot clutched her friend's hand.

"What if the chute doesn't work?"

"It will," Amanda said. She smiled. "It's already open."

"You owe me."

"You're right. I owe you forty cents for the ride."

"You're awful!" Dot said.

Amanda laughed.

"Relax. We'll be fine."

In fact, Amanda knew no such thing. From the moment a ride attendant buckled the two women in a canvas seat that hung from their chute, she knew only that her faith in 1930s engineering was about to be tested.

Amanda threw her arm around Dot's shoulders and held her closely as a cable pulled the chute, the seat, and the passengers skyward. She felt a little guilty about teasing her friend but not enough to stop. She was enjoying the moment immensely.

As the chute rose higher, Amanda looked down at the fairgrounds and saw many of the attractions she had enjoyed for two days. She saw amusements that entertained, public art that inspired, and pavilions that showcased the best of several very different countries.

Amanda the Kid had gravitated toward the train rides and spectacles like an exotic animal park and a music-dance-and-swimming show in an aquatic amphitheater. She had also marveled at "new" inventions like air conditioning, television, fluorescent lamps, color photography, the View-Master, and a movie special effect called Smell-O-Vision.

Amanda the Adult had sought more cerebral attractions. She had flocked to the transportation exhibits, Vermeer's painting *The Milkmaid*, and a copy of the Magna Carta that she knew would remain in America, for safekeeping, during the coming war. She pondered that war until Dot brought her out of a daze with five attention-grabbing words.

"Oh, Lord. Here it comes!"

Dot covered her eyes when the chute reached the top of the 250-foot tower and screamed when she heard a click. Then she pulled her hands, opened her eyes, and shouted in glee as the women floated slowly and safely toward the base of the tower and not the top of a tree, a bevy of power lines, or a watery grave in Long Island Sound.

Amanda laughed when they hit spring-loaded shock absorbers ten seconds later.

"See? We made it," Amanda said.

"We did!"

"I'm so proud of you, Dot. Your therapy is complete."

Dot glared at Amanda.

"Give me my money."

"Why?" Amanda asked.

Dot smiled.

"I want to ride this again!"

Amanda laughed.

"Maybe later. I want to talk first."

"You're no fun," Dot said.

"A minute ago I was awful. Now I'm no fun?"

Dot laughed.

"Perhaps you're both. Let's go."

"All right."

Amanda and Dot unbuckled their seat belts, got out of their seat, and stepped away from the tower. They walked slowly past the Hawaiian Village and Old New York but picked up the pace near the amphitheater. Five minutes later, they crossed World's Fair Boulevard, left the family attractions behind, and resumed their conversation.

"So what do you want to talk about?" Dot asked.

Amanda tilted her head.

"Oh, I don't know. How about your *wedding*?"

Dot beamed.

"I thought you'd never ask. I have so much to tell you."

Amanda laughed.

"Let me guess. You rented the Empire State Building."

"Try the Morris House in Trenton," Dot said.

"I thought you were getting married in a church."

"I am. The reception is at the Morris House."

"Oh."

"We've invited two hundred guests. I wanted three, but my dad drew the line at two," Dot said. She grinned. "He wouldn't sell any acreage to pay for the extras."

Amanda laughed.

"Good for him. I wouldn't either."

"You wouldn't sacrifice a few apple trees for your daughter's happiness?" Dot asked.

"Nope."

Dot frowned.

"You're a regular Scrooge."

"I suppose I am," Amanda said. "Are you still getting married next month?"

Dot nodded.

"The rehearsal is June 23. The wedding is the next day at five."

"You still want me in it?"

"Of course I want you in it," Dot said. "Don't be silly."

"Should I start shopping for a dress?"

"No. My mom's got that covered. She's making all the dresses."

Amanda smiled. This really was a different time.

"What do I need to do then?" Amanda asked.

"You don't need to do anything," Dot said. "No. That's wrong. You need to do three things. You need to give me your measurements, tell me that you really like pink taffeta, and promise me that you won't run off with a dashing German in the next eight weeks."

"I think I can manage that."

Dot stopped walking. She grabbed Amanda's hand, turned to face her friend, and looked her in the eyes.

"I'm serious about the last thing," Dot said. "I want you to promise that you'll stick around."

"I can do that."

Dot sighed.

"OK. I just have the feeling that your attachment to New Jersey is a bit tenuous now. I don't want you to do anything reckless, like leave, before I get married."

"I won't," Amanda said. "I promise."

Dot smiled.

"Then it's set. You're a bridesmaid!"

"I thought that was already settled," Amanda said.

"Nothing is *ever* settled in a wedding."

Amanda laughed.

"I guess not."

The two women resumed walking.

"Does this mean you don't plan to run off with Kurt?" Dot asked.

"We're not eloping, if that's what you mean."

"You're thinking about it though. I can tell."

"I'm thinking about a lot of things," Amanda said.

That much was true, Amanda admitted. She had thought about many things in the past several weeks, including her growing affection for Kurt Schmidt, his complicated family ties, and what, if anything, she would do when the time came for her to leave the thirties.

"How are things going between you two?" Dot asked.

"They're going OK."

"The only reason I ask is because your mom told me that things got a bit tense in D.C. She said that your first dinner there was very contentious."

"It was," Amanda said. "I didn't care for Kurt's brother. I didn't care for his Nazi friend either. I found them obnoxious and arrogant and their views toxic."

"Do you like his folks?"

Amanda sighed. That was a tougher question but one she could answer honestly.

"I do. I still don't know them very well, but I like them. They treated me well. They seem decent, too, even though they represent a regime I despise."

"I told Roy about Kurt's family connections when I was in California," Dot said.

"What did he say?" Amanda asked.

"He said you should be careful. He said a lot of Germans in America right now are spies trolling for information. He hasn't heard anything bad about Kurt or his family, but he still thinks you should be careful. He said you should watch what you say."

"Thanks for the timely advice."

"What do you mean by 'timely'?" Dot asked.

"I mean that I'm meeting the Schmidt family for dinner tomorrow night."

"You're what?"

"I'm meeting Kurt, his parents, and his brother at a restaurant in Manhattan," Amanda said. "We have a reservation at six."

55: AMANDA

manda read the front of her menu, looked around the room, and smiled. She had been in a lot of fancy restaurants in her life but never one that had once housed sheep. She tipped her hat to the city's parks department for turning an agricultural building on the south side of Central Park into one of the most celebrated eateries in the world.

"You seem amused," Heinrich Schmidt said.

Amanda looked across her round, linen-covered table.

"I guess I am," Amanda said. "I was just reading about this place. It has an interesting history. I like places with interesting histories."

Heinrich nodded.

"I'm glad you approve. I selected this restaurant because it is close to the park and to a natural setting. I wanted you to be relaxed and comfortable."

"Is there any reason why?" Amanda asked.

"Yes," Heinrich said. "I wanted to get to know you better as a person and hopefully avoid some of the difficulties of our first dinner together."

Amanda smiled.

"In other words, you want to avoid politics tonight."

Heinrich smiled warmly.

"You are as keen as you are lovely."

Amanda laughed.

"Thank you, Colonel," Amanda said. "I'll try to behave myself."

Amanda studied Heinrich and wondered which man she would get tonight: the war hero, the aloof diplomat, the friendly host, or perhaps something else. She decided to set aside his resume for one evening and give him a chance as a human being.

Amanda didn't doubt she could do the same for Johanna Schmidt, who sat to her left. She genuinely liked the woman and wanted to find out if there was more to her than a warm smile and a caring nature that had impressed even Elizabeth.

She *did* doubt she could do the same for the young man who sat between Kurt and his father. She didn't like Karl Schmidt. She didn't like his attitude or demeanor and certainly didn't like the fact he was a card-carrying member of the National Socialist German Workers' Party.

Amanda vowed to be pleasant anyway. She knew she would never succeed in diplomacy, journalism, or any other field unless she learned to get along with people she despised and figured that dinner with a Hitler acolyte was a good place to start.

"Where is your family this evening?" Johanna asked.

"Grandma is at our hotel. Mom is with Dot," Amanda said. "She took her shopping as sort of an early wedding present. Dot is getting married next month."

"Kurt told me that. He said you are one of the bridesmaids."

"I am."

Johanna smiled sadly.

"I envy your friend's mother. I would love to fuss over a daughter on her wedding day."

"You might change your mind if you knew all the work she is doing," Amanda said. "She's planning the entire reception and making dresses for five bridesmaids."

"I suppose you're right," Johanna said.

"I think the best way to get married is to elope. That's what my grandma did. She ran off with a boy from Chicago."

Johanna laughed.

"I can picture that. Elizabeth strikes me as a spontaneous type of woman."

"She is," Amanda said. "Believe me. She is."

"I enjoyed visiting with her on Sunday," Johanna said. "We have much in common."

"Such as?"

"We were both born in Austria, for one thing. Elizabeth told me that she was born in Vienna. I was born in Innsbruck. She also told me that she likes pinochle and schnapps. *I* like pinochle and schnapps."

Amanda smiled. She could see that Johanna Schmidt hadn't lost an ounce of her warmth or her wit in the past four weeks.

Then she looked at her again and noticed something she hadn't seen all week. Johanna seemed paler and weaker than she had in D.C. Was she ill?

Amanda made a mental note to ask Kurt about her health at the earliest opportunity.

"You're right," Amanda said. "You do have a lot in common. Perhaps you two should get together tomorrow. I think she'd like that."

"I would too," Johanna said. "Do you plan to stay in New York for a while?"

Amanda nodded.

"We do. We'll be here until Friday morning. I want to see more of the fair and figure that this is the time to do it. I have a feeling the crowds this summer will be too much."

"Have you enjoyed the fair?" Johanna asked.

"I have, Mrs. Schmidt. I really have," Amanda said. "I must admit I've spent more time in the amusement section than in the pavilions, but I've enjoyed everything."

Amanda glanced at Kurt and exchanged a knowing smile. She could see that he was probably not going to say a lot. Nor did she want him to. She was more than capable of holding her own.

"Which pavilions have you seen?" Heinrich asked.

"I've seen the ones relevant to our times."

"I assume you mean the exhibits sponsored by Czechoslovakia and Poland."

"Yes," Amanda said. "I started with those."

Amanda glanced at Karl and looked for a reaction. She didn't see anything that suggested more than mild fascination. Perhaps he, too, was trying hard to get through the evening.

"What others have you seen?" Heinrich asked.

"I visited the British and Russian pavilions, of course, and also the ones from Japan, Italy, France, and Palestine. I made a special trip to see the Jewish Palestine exhibit."

"That's quite a lineup," Karl said. "A typical girl would have gone to the cosmetics, fashions, and home furnishings pavilions."

Amanda smiled. She had to give Karl credit. He had crammed at least three insults into one sexist sentence without appearing to be unpleasant.

"I'm not a 'typical' girl, Karl. I care more about how the world looks than my face or my body. I visited the pavilions in question because I have a hunch their sponsoring countries will play vital roles in the 'World of Tomorrow,' which, as you know, is the theme of the fair."

"Is this hunch similar to the one you had on March 31 when you announced Franco's victory in Spain thirty-six hours before the American media?" Karl asked.

Amanda felt her blood boil. She wanted to put the Hitler Youth in his place but reminded herself that she was Colonel Schmidt's dinner guest and had told him she would behave.

"I guess it is," Amanda said. "You might say I have a feel for these things."

"Really?" Karl asked. "Are you saying that you're some sort of seer?"

Be careful, Amanda.

"I'm saying that I have hunches and that sometimes these hunches turn out to be accurate," Amanda said. "That's all."

Heinrich smiled politely.

"I'm sure Karl meant no offense. I was very impressed by your declaration at dinner that day. Your sources were far more reliable than mine. I didn't get word at the embassy about Franco until early Sunday morning."

"Like I said, I had a hunch," Amanda said.

"Do you have any more 'hunches' you would like to share with us?" Heinrich asked.

Amanda looked around the table and saw four people return her gaze. She felt like a person in the know in a television ad for a brokerage firm. It was time to bring this discussion to a close.

"I don't, Colonel. But I'll tell you what," Amanda said. "If I have a hunch about a horse race or a baseball game in the next few weeks, I'll be sure to let you know."

"Fair enough," Heinrich said. He laughed. "Now let's turn to a more important matter."

Heinrich picked up his menu.

"Let's order."

56: ELIZABETH

L izzie walked to the no man's land between the sofa and the chair and then paused to weigh her options – or perhaps fill another diaper. Erich and Ella encouraged her to join them on the sofa. Elizabeth begged her to walk to the chair.

The toddler, who had stood without help for weeks, hesitated for a few seconds and then wandered the greater distance to the chair. In the process, she provided her parents with a laugh and an elderly woman with a memory to treasure.

"It appears she has made a choice," Ella said.

Elizabeth lifted Lizzie from the floor, held her up, and then plopped her on her lap. She looked at Erich and Ella with sheepish eyes.

"I think she just wanted to show off," Elizabeth said. "I was farther away."

Elizabeth laughed to herself. She didn't have the slightest idea why the baby chose to reward the neighbor lady, rather than her parents, with her first lengthy walk, but she didn't care. She was delighted to be a part of another magic moment.

"Or maybe she just loves her grandmamma," Ella said.

Elizabeth hoisted Lizzie again.

"Is that so, Little One? Is that so?"

Lizzie smiled and babbled in agreement.

"I am so glad she has taken to you," Ella said. "I think it is important for children to form attachments to older adults. I was very close to my grandmother."

"Is she still alive?" Elizabeth asked.

"No. She passed away years ago."

Elizabeth had no memory of three of her four grandparents. Erich's father and both of Ella's parents had died in Austria before the end of World War II. She had memories only of Gertrude Wagner — and most of those were not positive.

"I'm sorry to hear that," Elizabeth said.

"I believe you would have liked her," Ella said. "You have much in common."

Elizabeth nodded but did not reply. She instead lowered Lizzie to the floor and instructed her to walk to her mother. She smiled when the girl did just that.

"You see? She just needed encouragement," Elizabeth said.

Elizabeth thought of the word "encouragement" as Ella put Lizzie on her lap and started to feed the child. She remembered the many times she had wanted encouragement growing up but had not received it — at least for certain things.

Erich and Ella had not pushed Elizabeth to reach her full potential. They had encouraged piano lessons, choir, and class plays but not tuba lessons, golf, and tennis. They had wanted their daughter to have an education much like their own.

"I have a question for both of you," Elizabeth said.

Erich sat up.

"Please ask."

"What do you want Lizzie to do when she gets older?"

"What do you mean?" Erich asked.

"What activities do you want her to participate in? Music? Drama? Sports? Debate?"

"I suppose music and drama," Erich replied. "That is what Ella and I did in Austria. They were pleasant diversions from our studies."

"I see," Elizabeth said.

"Why do you ask?"

"I'm just curious. I know that Lizzie may have opportunities here that you did not have and want to know if you have given much thought to those opportunities."

"I have not," Erich said. "Do you have any suggestions?"

"I don't now, but I might later."

"Then inform me when you think of them."

"I will," Elizabeth said. She got up from her chair. "Please excuse me."

Elizabeth started toward the bathroom but didn't get far before she experienced a tightening in her chest and a shortness of breath. She paused, put a hand on her chest, and turned to face her hosts. Both looked at her like worried parents.

"Are you all right?" Ella asked.

253

Elizabeth felt her strength return.

"I'm all right. I just had a senior moment."

"A what?"

"I had a reminder from God that I'm seventy-nine years old," Elizabeth said. She took a deep breath. "I'll be fine."

57: SUSAN

Prior to stepping into Geoffrey Bell's time tunnel, the closest Susan had come to Asbury Park was the weathered cover of a Bruce Springsteen album she had purchased at a garage sale. For a quarter she had picked up a piece of pop art that became the main attraction in her dorm-room art gallery at Northwestern.

She thought about the postcard-like album cover as she strolled arm-in-arm with Jack Hicks on a four-year-old boardwalk. As much as she loved seeing Asbury Park in art, she loved seeing it in person even better.

"Thank you for bringing me here," Susan said.

"Thank you for coming," Jack replied. "I wasn't sure you would."

"Why do you say that?"

"I say it because you've seemed distracted lately. I figured you might have more important matters to attend to."

Susan winced. She *had* been distracted. She had focused more on Elizabeth's dizzy spells, Amanda's social life, and even the World's Fair than on the one person in Princeton who had given her his undivided attention.

"I guess I have been distracted," Susan said. "I'm sorry."

"You're here now," Jack replied. "That's all that matters."

Susan scanned her surroundings and soaked up the sights. To her right, she saw restaurants, amusements, and shops that catered to every taste. To her left, she saw vendors, sunbathers, and a white sandy beach that matched any in the state.

She also saw the ocean. Susan didn't care whether the ocean was the Atlantic, the Pacific, the Mediterranean, or the Caribbean. Water was water. She loved it all.

"Kurt Schmidt told me there's an ice cream shop here we have to try," Susan said.

"He's right. It's in Ocean Grove, about a mile down the road, but it's worth a visit. If you want, we can go there later."

"I'd like that."

"How is Kurt?" Jack asked. "You haven't mentioned him lately."

"That's because I haven't *seen* him lately," Susan said. "Amanda usually goes to his place. He has an apartment on Moore Street."

"Their friendship sounds serious."

"It is."

"Is that a concern?" Jack asked.

"Yes."

"Why?"

Susan sighed. She knew there were few ways she could answer the question without inviting unwanted scrutiny. She tightened her hold on Jack's arm and paused a moment before speaking.

"I'm still troubled by Kurt's family ties," Susan said. "He's a pleasant young man who has shown me nothing but courtesy and respect, but he comes from a very different background."

"Is that all?"

"No," Susan said. She looked at Jack. "I'm also thinking about our pending departure. I'm concerned that my daughter is starting something she can't finish."

"I see," Jack said. "Are you also concerned that *you* are starting something you can't finish?"

Susan smiled sadly.

"I suppose I am."

"Do you want to talk about it?"

"Yes. I do," Susan said. "Let's find a place to sit though. My feet are killing me."

"How about there?" Jack asked.

He pointed to a bench at the edge of the boardwalk. It faced a steel pipe fence, the beach, and a relatively tranquil stretch of the Atlantic.

"That would be perfect," Susan said.

Jack escorted Susan to the bench and sat down beside her. He extended his arm around his companion's shoulders and gazed at the ocean but did not say anything until a brown-and-white bird flew twice around the bench and finally settled on a log about twenty yards away.

"Do you see that bird over there?" Jack asked. "The one on the log?"

"I do."

"It's a sooty shearwater. It's one of several species of seabirds that migrates from the Southern Hemisphere to the Northern Hemisphere and back each year."

"That's interesting," Susan said.

256

"The reason I mention the bird is because it's mobile and adaptable. It doesn't hang a shingle in a single location," Jack said. "It finds contentment in many places. Home for the shearwater is wherever it happens to be."

Susan smiled. She could see where Jack was going even before the bird flew off the log and headed north for points unknown.

"People aren't birds, Jack. They don't migrate several thousand miles a year."

"I suppose they don't. They do move around, though, and some find happiness in the unlikeliest of places."

"I'm sure they do," Susan said.

"I believe you could be one of those people if you just give it a try."

"I'm sure I could. I'm sure I could find happiness in a lot of places."

"Then why won't you?" Jack asked. "Why won't you consider staying in Princeton?"

Susan sighed. For the first time since stepping into the 1930s, she was tempted to tell a resident of the time the truth about who she was and where she had come from.

"I won't because I can't," Susan said. "I know that's not a great answer, but it's the best I can give you now."

Jack smiled.

"Mrs. Peterson, you are indeed a woman of mystery."

"Is that a good thing?"

"It's not a bad thing," Jack said. "It's more of a frustrating thing."

"Does that mean you're going to keep me?"

Jack nodded and pulled Susan close. He kissed the top of her head.

"It does. It would take more than a mystery to drive me away."

58: AMANDA

A manda turned the doorknob and smiled when she heard a click. She did not believe Kurt when he had told her that he kept his apartment unlocked, but she did now. She liked that he had told the truth. She liked that he trusted her.

Kurt had sent Amanda to Moore Street after she had paid an unexpected visit to the Nassau Institute. He had promised to join her after completing a press release that could not wait.

Amanda walked into the one-bedroom apartment, which she had visited at least a dozen times, and moved quickly toward the kitchen. She pulled a glass from the cupboard, filled it with tap water, and then sat in one of four padded chairs at Kurt's dining table. She glanced at the tabletop and saw two things of interest: a short stack of newspapers and a shorter stack of mail. She started with the newspapers. What better way to kill time, she thought, than to read last week's news today?

Amanda found the headlines intriguing, inspiring, and depressing. Spain had left the League of Nations. A five-year-old girl in Peru had given birth to a boy. Pan-American Airways had begun transatlantic mail service. Germany and Italy had signed the Pact of Steel.

She moved on to the mail and noticed two bills, a letter from the German embassy, and a letter from a familiar address in Georgetown. She wanted to know the contents of the letters but not enough to break their seals. She held the second letter, from Kurt's mother, up to the ceiling light and examined it until she heard a male clear his throat.

"Find anything interesting?"

Amanda dropped the letter and looked to her left. She saw Karl Schmidt standing in the doorway that separated the kitchen and the living room.

"What are you doing here?" Amanda asked.

"Perhaps I should ask *you* that question," Karl said.

"Kurt sent me here. Did he send you?"

Karl shook his head.

"No. I'm paying him a surprise visit."

"Do you often pay him surprise visits?" Amanda asked.

Karl stared at Amanda.

"Do you often ask a lot of questions?"

"Yes. I do," Amanda said. "It's my nature to ask questions."

Karl smirked and walked across the kitchen to the table. He pulled up a chair, opposite Amanda, and made himself comfortable.

"Then perhaps you should ask," Karl said. "I'm sure you have many questions for me."

"I think I should leave," Amanda said.

She got out of her chair, pushed it away from the table, and grabbed her purse. She started to depart but stopped when Karl spoke again in a softer voice.

"Please stay. I insist."

Amanda paused to consider her options. She could stay and spar with the Nazi. Or she could leave and save herself a lot of grief. She decided to stay.

"All right. I'll stay," Amanda said. "If you want to answer questions, I'll ask them."

Karl extended a hand and invited her to reoccupy her chair.

"Please sit."

Amanda sat in her chair, scooted up to the table, and glared at Karl. She tapped her fingers on the tabletop for a moment as she considered where to begin. She finally decided to start with a question that had been on her mind for weeks.

"I know one thing I'd like to ask you," Amanda said.

"What's that?" Karl asked.

"How did you become you?"

"What do you mean?"

"I mean how did you turn out to be different? You and Kurt are twins. You had the same parents, friends, and interests growing up. You grew up in the same towns and attended the same schools. How did you become a Nazi and Kurt a thoughtful, caring, freedom-loving man? How did that happen? Tell me."

Karl chuckled.

"You really despise me, don't you?"

Amanda nodded matter-of-factly.

"Yes, Karl. I do. I despise you and everything you stand for."

259

Karl sighed.

"Fair enough. If you want an answer, I'll give you one. You are right about one thing. My brother and I did have a lot in common growing up. We still do. The difference is that when it came time to leave home and see the world, Kurt stayed home, and I saw the world."

"You moved to a fascist state," Amanda said. "That's hardly seeing the world."

Karl leaned forward.

"When my family left Berlin seventeen years ago, Germany was a nation in ruins. The inflation rate was three *million* percent. Women sold their children in alleys. Men pushed wheelbarrows full of worthless currency to stores to buy a single loaf of bread. Germans were dispirited, humiliated, and hopeless. They had no hope because American, British, and French politicians chose to punish their country rather than rebuild it. When I returned to Berlin five years ago, things were different. Germany was different. People had jobs and purposes. They had pride. They had hope. Remember that the next time you call Germany a 'fascist' state."

Amanda took a breath and dug in.

"None of that excuses the excesses. Hitler has done more than create jobs. He has violated the rights of an entire nation. He has persecuted minorities, crushed dissent, and brought out the absolute worst in his people. His rhetoric alone is sickening. He's evil."

"Evil, huh?" Karl asked. "Is Hitler any worse than a president who restricts commerce, goes after his opponents, and tries to make himself king by packing the Supreme Court?"

"Yes. He is," Amanda said. "He's a lot worse. When Roosevelt restricts commerce, he does so with our consent. When he tries to pack the court, he follows the law. When he 'goes after' his 'opponents,' he criticizes them in the papers. He does not round them up, put them in camps, and kill them with gas."

"Camps? Gas? What are you talking about?"

Amanda kicked herself. She had done it again. She had revealed a fact known only to a few. Most of the world would not learn of the Holocaust until the liberation of Europe in 1945.

"Never mind," Amanda said.

"No," Karl replied. "I want to know. Where did you hear of these 'camps'?"

"I just heard about them. OK?"

"I see. Is your source the same one that told you Franco would capture Madrid a day before he did? If so, I'd like to meet him."

Amanda stood up.

"I'm leaving."

"Sit down!" Karl said. "We're not done."

"Yes, we are."

"Please sit. You may want to hear what I have to say."

Amanda slowly returned to her chair.

"Say your piece and leave," Amanda said.

"I'd be happy to."

Karl stared at Amanda for a moment but did not speak. He apparently wanted to size her up before going in for the kill.

"Well?" Amanda asked.

Karl flashed a smug smile.

"Do you know what I did last week?"

"No."

"I checked you out, that's what," Karl said. "I contacted the University of Illinois and learned that no one named Amanda Peterson attends the school. No one named Amanda Peterson has *ever* attended the school. Shall I tell my brother that you lied? Shall I tell him that the woman he loves is a fraud?"

Amanda sank in her chair as she digested the disturbing information. She pondered her options, concluded she had just one, and stood up.

"Tell him what you want. I don't care."

"You *do* care though. You do," Karl said. "You love my brother as much as he loves you. I can see it in your eyes."

"You can't see a thing," Amanda said. "You don't know anything about me."

"Tell me how you learned about Franco and these camps, and I'll leave you alone," Karl said. "I'll leave your life forever."

Amanda pushed her chair back, collected her purse, and stepped away from the table. She stopped in the middle of the kitchen, turned around, and stared at her tormentor.

"I would rather sacrifice a relationship than tell you a thing," Amanda said.

Karl got up.

"Don't go."

"Sit, Karl. Sit and stew in your hatred," Amanda said. "You think you have the answers, but you don't. You never will either."

"Amanda?"

"You've cast your lot with the wrong people. This won't end well for you."

Amanda gazed at Karl for a few more seconds and turned around. She left the apartment on Moore Street and hoped she would never see him again.

59: AMANDA

Tuesday, May 30, 1939

Amanda watched with awe as the single scull emerged from under the Harrison Street Bridge and headed into a smooth, uncluttered expanse of Lake Carnegie. The rower moved as quietly, rhythmically, and gracefully as a synchronized swimmer and with as much determination as a water bug stretching its legs on a pleasant spring morning.

"Do you think he's a member of the crew team?" Amanda asked.

Kurt nodded.

"He wouldn't be out this early if he wasn't," Kurt said. "The casual rowers are still sleeping."

"I guess that makes sense. It *is* a holiday."

Amanda looked at Kurt, who stood next to her on the bridge, and then gazed again at the still gray water. She couldn't see the rower. He had disappeared into a thick patch of fog that covered much of the lake like a soft white blanket.

"Are you ever going to tell me what happened at the apartment?" Kurt asked.

"Hasn't Karl filled you in?"

"No. He told me only that you're not who you say you are."

"He's right about that," Amanda said.

Kurt turned to face Amanda. When she turned to face him, he put his hands on her shoulders, looked her in the eyes, and lowered his head.

"I don't know what that means," Kurt said. "Have you lied to me?"

"I have," Amanda said. "I've lied about a lot of things."

"I don't understand."

"I haven't told you the truth about who I am, where I come from, and why I need to leave Princeton – and you – in a few months."

262

"You're not from Chicago?" Kurt asked.

"Oh, I am. I'm just not from the Chicago you know."

"That makes no sense to me."

"I know it doesn't," Amanda said. "I wish I could tell you more, but I can't. I can't because of promises I made to my family and to a man who sent us here."

"Does Karl know these secrets you won't tell me?" Kurt asked.

"No. He suspects things, but he doesn't *know* anything."

Kurt looked at Amanda closely with eyes that revealed everything from curiosity and compassion to frustration and fear. He frowned.

"He got to you, didn't he? Karl got to you."

Amanda looked away as her eyes started to water.

"He did."

Kurt turned Amanda back toward him.

"I'm sorry. I'm sorry I wasn't there to deal with him. I had no idea he had come to town."

"That's all right," Amanda said. She sighed. "I'm actually glad we had the chance to talk. We cleared the air and set a few things straight."

Kurt put his hand under her chin and lifted it.

"I don't know what he said to upset you. I'm not sure I *want* to know," Kurt said. "What I do know is that Karl will not have the chance to upset you again."

Amanda looked at Kurt with puzzled eyes.

"What do you mean?"

"He's leaving for Berlin next week," Kurt said. "He's returning to Germany with my mother."

"Why?" Amanda asked.

"My mother is ill. She has a rare form of cancer."

"Oh, Kurt. I'm so sorry."

"I know. I am too," Kurt said.

"Can't doctors treat her here?"

Kurt shook his head.

"They can treat her pain but not her disease. Her physicians give her three months."

"Then why is she going to Berlin?" Amanda asked.

"It's simple," Kurt said. "There's a doctor there who says he can cure her cancer if he can see her right away. We want to at least give him a chance."

Amanda wanted to say the doctor was a quack stringing the family along. She wanted to tell Kurt that a cancer diagnosis in 1939 was a death sentence and that it would be better for Johanna to die in America, surrounded by loved ones, than to return to Germany, but she couldn't do it. She couldn't deny anyone the peace that comes with hope.

"What does this mean for your father?" Amanda asked. "What does it mean for *you*?"

"We will both remain here, in the States, until Karl summons us to Berlin," Kurt said. "Our relatives there have already rented a flat for the family."

Amanda took a breath.

"Karl said nothing about this when I saw him. He didn't mention your mother at all."

"I'm not surprised," Kurt said.

"What do you mean?"

"I mean you're an outsider and – to Karl – a meddler. I'm surprised he took the time to talk to you at all."

"I wouldn't say we talked," Amanda said. "We argued."

"It doesn't matter," Kurt said. "He wouldn't have told you anything under any circumstances."

Amanda looked again at the lake. She could see the rower in the distance. He had moved beyond a bank of fog that was fading into thin tendrils of dissipating cloud.

"Do *you* consider me a meddler?"

"No," Kurt said. "I consider you a mystery I want to unravel. I hope that at some point you will trust me enough to tell me the things you can't tell me now."

Amanda smiled sadly.

"I hope so too," she said.

"Do you have any more questions for me?"

Amanda gazed at Kurt.

"I do. I have one."

"What?" Kurt asked.

"When Karl was badgering me, insulting me, and trying to get under my skin, he told me something I hadn't heard before. He said you loved me. Is that true?"

Kurt blushed.

"It is. I think I've loved you since the night you called my father a Nazi apologist."

Amanda laughed softly and then looked at Kurt with wistful eyes.

"Me too," Amanda said. "I don't know what I can do with this feeling, but I feel the same way. I love you, Kurt Schmidt. I have for a very long time."

60: ELIZABETH

Wednesday, June 7, 1939

Elizabeth heard the sound before she saw the sight. Walking up the stairs she cursed on a daily basis, she heard what sounded like sobs.

She wasn't sure who might be crying. She considered Amanda's voice and mannerisms to be indistinguishable from Susan's at times and, for that reason, considered them peas in a pod.

Elizabeth went first to Amanda's bedroom. She put her ear to the door, listened carefully, and heard nothing. She expected to hear nothing. Her granddaughter was usually out of the house by ten in the morning.

So she continued to the other bedroom. When she heard more sobs, she turned the knob, gently pushed open the door, and looked inside. She saw two things she hadn't seen in months: a daughter in tears and a sparkling white crystal.

"Susan? Are you all right?" Elizabeth asked.

"No," Susan said. "I'm not."

"Do you want to talk about it?"

Susan wiped her eyes with a tissue and nodded.

"I think I do."

Elizabeth walked to the far side of the room and joined her daughter on a bench seat cushion. The bright blue cushion formed part of a window nook that measured six feet by eight and dominated an otherwise drab living space.

Elizabeth sat on the right side of the nook. Susan sat on the left. Professor Geoffrey Bell's white gypsum crystal occupied a space in the middle.

"What's wrong?" Elizabeth asked.

"A lot of things are wrong, Mom."

"Be specific."

Susan looked at her mother through red, watery eyes.

"I woke up this morning and realized what day it is. It's June 7. Bruce died a year ago today."

"He did," Elizabeth said.

"I've been crying for an hour. I couldn't figure out why until just a minute ago," Susan said. "I've never moved past that day. I've never really mourned my husband."

Elizabeth leaned forward and gave her daughter a hug.

"No. You haven't," Elizabeth said. "I've been waiting for these tears."

Susan pulled back and wiped her eyes again.

"I don't get it. I can go days without thinking about him, weeks even, and when I *do* think about him, I get angry. I get bitter. I think about what he did to me. So why am I crying now?"

Elizabeth put a hand on Susan's knee.

"You're crying now because you have to. This is the price of moving on."

"The what?"

"Listen to me, Susan. Listen to your mother, for once," Elizabeth said. "You had a husband. You loved him and cared for him for twenty-five years. You made a beautiful child with him. That kind of person does not just disappear from your heart or your mind overnight."

"I suppose you're right," Susan said.

"I know I'm right. It's hard to bury a husband. It's even harder to bury one who cheated on you. You have mixed emotions."

Susan took a deep breath.

"Sometimes I wonder if I could have saved my marriage. I wanted it to work. I really did. I don't know why it didn't. What did I do wrong?"

"You did *nothing* wrong," Elizabeth said. "You were a good wife. You did all the things a good wife should do and more. Bruce brought this on himself."

"Then why do I feel so bad?"

"You feel bad because you lost a spouse. Now you have to figure out a way to move on. You have to decide what you want to do with the rest of your life."

Susan smiled sadly.

"I guess I do."

Elizabeth pulled her hand from Susan's knee and picked up the crystal. She held it up to the light and admired its sparkle for a moment before putting it back on the cushion.

"I see you brought out your rock," Elizabeth said.

Susan nodded.

"I do every once in a while to remind myself that our stay here is temporary."

Elizabeth brought a hand to her chin.

"That's what's really bothering you. It's not Bruce or your alleged failings as a wife but rather that we will soon have to leave this place – a place where you've found a measure of happiness."

"That's part of it," Susan said.

"Does your anxiety about leaving have anything to do with a retired admiral?"

"You know it does."

"Do you like him?" Elizabeth asked.

"Yes. I like him."

"Do you love him?"

"Yes. No. Maybe. I don't know," Susan said. "All I know for sure is that Jack really likes me and can't understand why we can't continue our relationship into the fall."

"Has he hinted at anything serious?"

"Yes. He has. Jack has all but suggested that he would be willing to move to Chicago to keep me. He just has no idea of what that really means."

Elizabeth frowned.

"Do you think he'll propose?"

"I do. We're moving slowly but surely in that direction," Susan said. "Jack Hicks is an old-fashioned man, Mom. If he thinks the only way he can keep me is to propose before we leave, then he'll do just that."

"Have you told any of this to Amanda?" Elizabeth asked.

"No. I'm not going to either. She has her own problems. This is something I'm just going to have to work out by myself."

Elizabeth leaned forward and gave Susan another hug.

"I'm proud of you. You get smarter and wiser every day."

"I had a good teacher," Susan said.

Elizabeth smiled and retreated to her side of the nook. She put a hand to her heart when she felt a sharp pain ripple through her chest.

"Are you all right?" Susan asked.

"I think so," Elizabeth said. "I feel a little weak, that's all."

"Shall I call a doctor?"

"No. I'm sure it's just a passing thing."

61: SUSAN

Thursday, June 15, 1939

Susan opened the text to the bookmarked page, found six paragraphs on naval aviation, and started copying the paragraphs, word for word, on a yellow legal pad.

She didn't mind the work. She found it educational. What she didn't like was taking four hours to do what a modern photocopier could do in four minutes. She stopped writing after the third paragraph, put her pencil down, and stretched her fingers like she was counting by fives.

"Is your hand getting sore?" Jack asked.

Susan laughed.

"It was sore an hour ago."

Jack stopped writing. He set his pencil aside and leaned back in his chair.

"Then let's call it quits. It's getting close to dinner time."

"I know it is, but let's finish," Susan said. "We have only two more books."

"Are you sure you want to continue?" Jack asked.

"I'm sure."

"OK."

Susan grabbed one of the two remaining unopened books and pushed the other toward her partner. She sat opposite him at a wooden table in the small study room of the Nassau Institute. She gave Jack a fleeting glance before returning to her work.

"When does this place close?" Susan asked.

"Five."

Susan scribbled a few lines.

"When does our favorite restaurant open?"

Jack laughed.

"Five."

Susan smiled.

"Then I guess we had better get moving."

Susan picked up the pace with her pencil and her pad. She needed only the promise of French food on a Thursday night to boost her productivity and her spirits.

She copied essential information on two more pages, grabbed the last book, and opened it to the first bookmarked page. She frowned when she saw more acronyms than verbs.

Susan started to ask Jack a question about a reference she didn't understand when she heard a knock on the closed door. She looked up just as Clark Abercrombie opened the door slightly and stuck his head through the gap.

"Am I interrupting anything?" Abercrombie asked.

"No," Jack said. "We're just finishing up. What do you have?"

"It's not what I have, but who. *You* have a visitor."

"Is it someone who can wait twenty minutes?"

Abercrombie laughed.

"No. I don't think so."

Susan lowered her pencil. The director of the Nassau Institute had her attention.

"Then send him in," Jack said.

Abercrombie smiled.

"I'll send *her* in."

Abercrombie opened the door and stepped aside to make way for the visitor. When the visitor entered the room with two official-looking men, the director joined them and closed the door.

"I'm sorry to impose, Admiral," the visitor said. "I just couldn't leave town without saying hello. Dr. Abercrombie told me you were in the building."

Jack shot up from his chair.

"I'm glad you didn't leave," Jack said. "It's a pleasure to see you again."

Susan rose from her seat and watched in awe as Jack stepped forward and shook hands with the visitor, a tall, stately woman in her mid-fifties. She couldn't believe what she was seeing.

"I see you're busy," the visitor said. "Are you working on your next book?"

"As a matter of fact, I am. I'm about halfway through it. What brings you to town?"

"I came to Princeton to dedicate a building at the university. I came *here* to see how Clark is spending the grant money we sent him."

"Has he squandered it already?" Jack asked.

"Thankfully, no," the visitor said. She smiled. "But he still has another year."

Several people laughed.

Susan cleared her throat.

Jack turned to face Susan, blushed, and then returned to the visitor.

"I'm sorry. I forgot to introduce my editorial assistant. Mrs. Roosevelt, this is Susan Peterson. She has been helping me with the book since December," Jack said. He looked at Susan. "Susan, this is the First Lady of the United States."

Susan stepped away from the table and shook Eleanor Roosevelt's hand.

"It's a pleasure, Mrs. Roosevelt."

"The pleasure is mine."

Susan paused for a minute and then spoke.

"How do you two know each other?"

"I met Jack at a fundraiser for literacy in San Diego five years ago," Eleanor said. "His late wife organized the event. We have corresponded regularly ever since."

Susan looked admiringly at Jack.

What else haven't you told me?

"He is quite the writer," Susan said.

"How about you?" Eleanor asked. "How did you meet our earnest author?"

"I met him at the library."

Eleanor laughed.

"I'm not surprised. He has a fondness for books. In fact, I believe the last time I saw him he was carrying a stack of military journals through the Library of Congress."

Jack chuckled.

"You don't forget a thing."

Eleanor smiled.

"I didn't forget that."

"Are you staying the night in Princeton?" Jack asked.

"I'm afraid not," Eleanor replied. "I must return to Hyde Park this evening. I have a speaking engagement there tomorrow morning."

"Do you have time for dinner? Susan and I were about to leave for a restaurant. I would love to have you join us."

"Perhaps next time. I will be back in the fall. We can catch up then. In the meantime, keep up the good work. The president is aware of your book and is willing to provide any assistance you need to get it published. We both look forward to reading it."

"I appreciate that," Jack said. "It means a lot."

Susan watched with interest as one of Mrs. Roosevelt's aides checked his watch and then whispered in the First Lady's ear. The other opened the door and walked into the hallway.

"Well, I guess it's time for me to go. My plane is waiting," Eleanor said. "It was a pleasure seeing you again, Admiral. It was a pleasure meeting you, Susan."

"Give my best to the president, ma'am," Jack said.

"I will."

Mrs. Roosevelt shook two hands and then exited the room. The second aide and Abercrombie followed. Silence quickly filled the fifteen-by-twenty-foot chamber.

"Wow," Susan said. She laughed. "I didn't see that coming."

"Neither did I," Jack said.

"I'm impressed, Admiral Hicks, *very* impressed."

"You shouldn't be. She's that way with a lot of people."

"I don't care about them," Susan said. "I care only about the man in this room."

Jack smiled and nodded.

"You want to finish our work?" Jack asked.

The editorial assistant shook her head.

"No. I'd much rather get an early start on dinner," Susan said. She grinned. "I want to talk. I want to learn more about someone I'm just getting to know."

62: AMANDA

Trenton, New Jersey — Saturday, June 24, 1939

D o you know the history of this place?" Kurt asked.

"No, Mr. Schmidt. I don't," Amanda said. "Are you going to give me a history lesson on a night we should be snuggling under the stars?"

"Yes."

Amanda laughed.

"OK. Fire away."

Kurt slid closer to Amanda on their bench in a square brick gazebo. He pulled her close, kissed her head, and pointed to a two-story Georgian residence about thirty yards away.

"The Morris House was the de facto capital of the United States in 1798. Federal officials relocated most of their offices to this building when yellow fever swept through Philadelphia."

"Now how do you know that?" Amanda asked.

"I know it, Miss Peterson, because I read and because I have a deep and abiding love of this country," Kurt said. He smiled. "I love some of its citizens too."

Amanda kissed Kurt on the cheek and burrowed into his side.

"I hope so."

She gazed at the former capital of the United States and noticed that it was holding up nicely as a reception venue. More than a hundred people danced, talked, and laughed inside and outside the Morris House as they celebrated the union of Roy Maine and Dorothy Gale.

"Did you enjoy the wedding?" Kurt asked.

"I did. It was simple but elegant. I liked it."

Amanda meant it too. She didn't care for the stifling heat in the church or the hideous bridesmaid dresses, but she liked just about everything else.

She particularly liked where Roy and Dot exchanged humorous vows and then lit candles in memory of beloved grandparents.

She had also enjoyed the reception. She had enjoyed eating cracked crab and baked salmon, sipping pink champagne, meeting Dot's friends from Bryn Mawr, and dancing to the lively music of the Franklin Four, a swing quartet from Philadelphia.

Amanda tightened her hold on Kurt. She had enjoyed him most of all. She liked seeing him in a setting away from think tanks, guest speakers, and even relatives. She liked seeing him in a dark blue suit that fit well on his athletic frame.

"What are you thinking about?" Kurt asked.

Amanda smiled.

"I'm thinking about a lot of things."

Kurt laughed.

"That's not very helpful."

Amanda sighed.

"I know."

"Are you thinking about things you can't tell me?" Kurt asked.

Amanda nodded.

"I am."

"Can I ask *why* you can't tell me these things?"

"You can ask," Amanda said. "I just can't give you an answer."

"Are you in trouble with the law?"

"No. It's nothing like that."

"Then what is it? Surely your situation can't be so terrible that you can't explain it to someone you love and trust," Kurt said. "Can it?"

Amanda looked at Kurt.

"My situation isn't terrible. It's complicated. It's more complicated than you can possibly imagine."

"Is that your way of saying you won't ever tell me the truth?"

"No," Amanda said. "It's my way of saying I need more time."

Amanda frowned at the understatement. She needed more than time. She needed guidance. She would have to make the most important decisions of her life in the coming weeks and do so without an instruction manual.

"I see," Kurt said.

"Let me ask you a question," Amanda said.

"OK."

"What if I asked you to give up everything to follow me?"

"What do you mean by 'everything'?" Kurt asked.

"I mean your family, your friends, and your job. Would you do it?"

Kurt relaxed his grip.

"I don't know. I'd have to think about it. Are you asking me to do this?"

"No," Amanda said.

"Then why ask?"

"I ask because I have to know what you would be willing to do before I can decide what *I* would be willing to do."

"The plot thickens," Kurt said.

"Don't joke. This is difficult."

"I'm sorry. I just don't understand why you can't level with me. I mean it, Amanda. I would love you even if you told me you were a bank robber."

Amanda laughed.

"You probably would."

Kurt kissed her head again.

"I would."

"You still didn't answer my question," Amanda said.

"Then ask again."

"Could you possibly give up everything for me?"

Kurt sighed.

"I suppose I could. It would depend on the circumstances."

Amanda nodded. She could work with an answer like that. She pondered possible responses when she saw a woman in a white dress rush out of the Morris House. She smiled as the bride strode purposefully toward the gazebo.

"Have you left the groom already?" Amanda asked in a playful voice.

"No," Dot said. "Roy left me. He's drinking with his Princeton buddies and talking about the '37 Harvard game. I can't very well train a husband if all he thinks about is football."

Amanda laughed.

"I suppose you can't. Come sit with us."

Dot stepped into the gazebo. She gave her fifth bridesmaid a hug and sat at her side.

"I hope I'm not interrupting anything," Dot said.

"No," Amanda replied. "We're just talking. We're saving the heavy petting for later."

Dot looked at Kurt.

"Do you always let her talk that way?"

Kurt nodded.

"She's a free spirit," Kurt said. "I can no more tame her than I can tame the wind."

Dot looked at Amanda.

"I see you've trained him. I see many happy years in your future."

Amanda laughed.

"I hope so."

"I really came out here to see how you were doing," Dot said. "We haven't had a chance to talk much today. Are you having fun?"

Amanda gazed at her friend.

"I am having the time of my life."

"That makes my day," Dot said. "I'm so glad you could be a part of this. I'm also glad your mom and grandma could attend the wedding. Thank them for me when you have the chance."

"I will."

"Are you coming to breakfast tomorrow?"

"I wouldn't miss it. *We* wouldn't miss it," Amanda said. "It's at eight, right?"

Dot laughed.

"It's at eight. I doubt even a quarter of the people here now will make it to the farm. Most will be sleeping off their hangovers."

"We'll be there. What more do you need?"

Dot smiled and hugged Amanda.

"Nothing."

"So what's next for the newlyweds?" Amanda asked. "Are you taking a trip?"

Dot nodded.

"We're going to Montauk on Monday. We found a beach house there we can rent for a song. We'll stay on Long Island a few days, head back to New York, and then fly to Los Angeles."

"So is this it?" Amanda asked. "Is this goodbye?"

"No," Dot said. "It's not. At least I hope it's not."

"What's going on?"

"Roy gets another leave in September. We plan to fly back here, say goodbye one last time, and then have a second honeymoon on Route 66."

"You're going to drive across the country?" Amanda asked.

Dot beamed.

"We're going to buy a car first. I've already picked one out."

Amanda laughed.

"You amaze me."

"You have only yourself to blame, missy. When you told me all those stories about canyons, deserts, and cowboys, you made an impression on an impressionable young woman," Dot said. She held her nose up. "I have no choice but to see if the Old West is everything you say it is."

Amanda laughed.

"When do you expect to return?"

"We'll fly back on the seventh or the eighth. Promise me you'll stay until at least the ninth."

"I promise," Amanda said.

"I'll hold you to that," Dot said.

Dot slid off of the bench, straightened her lace wedding dress, and stepped in front of her friends. She grabbed one of Kurt's hands and then one of Amanda's.

"What are you doing?" Amanda asked.

"I'm motivating my guests."

"You're what?"

Dot stared at Amanda.

"I'm providing encouragement where encouragement is needed," Dot said. She smiled. "Get off your duffs and start mingling. Enjoy my reception."

63: ELIZABETH

Princeton, New Jersey – Friday, June 30, 1939

Elizabeth pulled the envelopes from her mailbox and waved at the postman as he walked away from the residence. She liked getting mail in a time and a place where she did not officially exist – or at least not as more than a toddler in the house across the street.

She entered the rental and walked through the living room to the dining area. She sat at the table, took a bite out of a ham sandwich, and examined what the postman had delivered.

Elizabeth opened the envelopes and discarded the first three letters. She had no interest in buying life insurance, joining a service club, or giving generously to the New Jersey Wildlife Foundation. She could find plenty of wildlife in Princeton on a Saturday night.

She did not dismiss the fourth letter. She couldn't. It was virtually impossible to dismiss a handwritten letter from someone who lived seventy-seven years in the future.

Elizabeth thought at first that Professor Geoffrey Bell had written only to Susan, his faithful pen pal of the past nine months, but he hadn't. He had addressed his letter to the entire family.

Elizabeth put on reading glasses she had purchased in May, pushed the other mail aside, and started reading the letter from Bell. It was short and to the point.

Dear Elizabeth, Susan, and Amanda:

I hope this letter finds you in good heath. I received your correspondence of May 23 and noted the progress you have made as friends, family members, and colleagues. I encourage each of you to make the most of the opportunities Princeton and 1939 have to offer, but I also advise you to be mindful of your special responsibilities as tourists of time.

277

I am particularly concerned about Amanda's growing relationship with the son of Germany's military attaché. My research on the diplomat suggests that his family is about to undergo a serious transition – one in which allegiances and possibly friendships will be sorely tested.

I recommend that all of you exercise caution when interacting with Heinrich, Johanna, Kurt, and Karl Schmidt in the days and weeks to come. I look forward to hearing more about your adventures and preparing your return to 2016.

Elizabeth read the letter a second time and then a third. She leaned back in her chair as she tried to figure out what the professor was attempting to say.

One thing was obvious. Bell wanted all three women to read the letter and abide by his advice. Even though he had corresponded exclusively with Susan for months, he did not want her to keep the contents of *this* letter to herself.

Another thing was not so obvious. What did he mean by a "serious transition"? Was the Schmidt family moving? Was someone ill? Was someone's luck about to change?

Elizabeth also wondered which allegiances and friendships would be "sorely tested." She pondered how the German family's fortunes could be related to her own.

Then there was Bell's advice. Elizabeth understood the need to exercise caution when interacting with Germans in 1939. She didn't understand why the threat level with this particular family had been raised. What did Bell know that she didn't?

Elizabeth got up from her chair, walked into the kitchen, and grabbed a bottle of orange juice from the noisy four-legged refrigerator. She poured herself a glass, looked out a small window, and pondered all the possible ways she could handle the letter.

She lifted the glass, sipped some juice, and returned to the dining area. She reclaimed her chair, picked up Bell's letter, and started to read it a fourth time when Susan entered the room.

"Did the mailman bring us something good today?" Susan asked.

Elizabeth forced a smile and pushed the opened letter across the table. "I'll let you decide."

"What's this?"

"Take a look," Elizabeth said.

Susan pulled up a chair, grabbed the letter, and started reading. She put the letter back on the table a moment later and looked at her mother.

"He knows something important," Susan said.

278

"Of course he does."

"Then why doesn't he share it with us?"

"I don't know," Elizabeth said.

"Has Amanda seen this letter?"

"No. I'm not sure she should either."

"Why not?" Susan asked.

Elizabeth leaned forward.

"I'll tell you why. It would only make her angry and irrational."

"So?"

"If she's angry and irrational, she can't do what Professor Bell wants her to do. She can't engage Kurt and his family with a clear head."

"You're reaching, Mother."

"Am I?" Elizabeth asked. "The professor didn't advise us to avoid the Schmidts. He advised us only to 'exercise caution' around them."

"So?"

"He has a purpose. I know he does. He wants us to act cautiously but independently."

"You're speculating," Susan said.

"Why else would he give us the freedom to associate?"

"I don't know. I just know we can't keep this from Amanda."

"We can and we will," Elizabeth said.

"Mom!"

"Trust me, Susan. Trust me on this."

64: SUSAN

Susan looked at the humble man at home plate, wiped her eyes, and squeezed the hand of the retired admiral who stood at her left. She never cried at baseball games unless the Cubs blew a lead in the ninth, but she cried now. She couldn't help but get caught up in the moment as she watched a dying Hall of Famer declare himself the "luckiest man on the face of the earth."

Susan gazed at Amanda, who stood at her right, and saw that she, too, was a weepy mess. She threw her free arm around her daughter and pulled her close.

"Isn't this better than Coney Island?" Susan asked.

Amanda nodded and wiped her eyes.

"I'm curious about something though," Amanda said.

"What?"

"You bought these tickets two months ago, but the Yankees didn't schedule this event until two weeks ago," Amanda said. "How did you know today was the day?"

"I remembered that he gave his speech on a Fourth of July. I confess I had forgotten the year, but I remembered the day," Susan said in a quiet voice. "When I read that he had benched himself in May, I knew this was the year. I bought tickets early to beat the rush."

Susan glanced at Jack Hicks and then at Kurt Schmidt, who stood at Amanda's right, and checked to see if her comment had raised any brows. It hadn't. The men appeared to be too caught up in the spectacle to notice that a time traveler had made a subtle slip.

She returned her attention to the infield and watched history unfold. New York Yankees first baseman Lou Gehrig stood before a bevy of microphones and elegantly delivered one of the most memorable speeches of the twentieth century. He dismissed his battle with amyotrophic lateral sclerosis as a "bad break" and praised team owners and relatives as officials, teammates, opponents, and sixty thousand sobbing fans looked on.

Susan scanned the faces of those closest to the speaker and saw people she recognized: Mayor LaGuardia, Manager Joe McCarthy, and members of the 1927 Yankees. The dignitaries stood at the head of two lines that stretched from the pitcher's mound to home plate.

Several had already taken their turns as orators and paid tribute to a man who seemed as unassuming in real life as he did in legend. Each had stoked an emotional fire that had burned slowly and steadily for more than thirty minutes.

Susan reached for her handkerchief one last time when Babe Ruth stepped forward at the end of Gehrig's remarks. The burly legend hugged his former teammate and whispered something in his ear. The two friends had not spoken since a falling out six years earlier.

"I wish I had a camera," Amanda said.

"I wish I had a *good* camera," Susan replied.

Susan didn't mean it. She could just imagine the buzz she would create by whipping out her Nikon D750 and snapping dozens of digital color images in the age of black-and-white photography. She would replace the Iron Horse as the main event in Yankee Stadium.

Susan applauded as Gehrig walked off the infield with most of the others and then redirected her attention to the people in her own circle. Each represented a seemingly unsolvable problem.

Jack needed no introduction. As her friend, colleague, and nominal boyfriend, he was never far from her person or her mind. He embodied all Susan wanted and all she could not have.

Susan pondered her tearful conversation with her mother. She had hoped to find answers in June, but she had not. She was as undecided as ever about how to handle her growing affection for the admiral and how to find peace with a dead husband who still haunted her dreams.

She also thought about Kurt, his family, and the letter she and Elizabeth had kept to themselves. For four days, she had obsessed over Professor Bell's warning, his ambiguity, and his intent. She didn't buy her mother's theory that Bell had something up his sleeve, but she couldn't dismiss it either.

Susan knew only that Bell's warning had started to lose its punch. Johanna and Karl Schmidt had already left America for Berlin. Heinrich Schmidt remained at his post in Washington.

"How is you mother doing, Kurt?" Susan asked. "Have you heard anything from Germany?"

Kurt leaned forward, looked to his left, and nodded.

"Karl sent a telegram yesterday. He said she's doing well despite the circumstances. He said she began her treatments on the tenth and that her doctor remains optimistic."

"Do you expect to see her soon?" Susan asked.

"It depends," Kurt said. "If her condition improves, I'll visit in the fall. I've already requested time off. If her condition worsens, I'll leave immediately."

"That's prudent."

Susan forced a smile. She had hoped for a different answer. Though she wished the best for Kurt and his family, she wanted him on the first boat out.

She knew a difficult goodbye might turn into an impossible goodbye if his relationship with Amanda lasted even another month. She knew because she faced a similar situation with Jack.

"How about your father?" Jack asked. "Will *he* return to Berlin?"

Kurt leaned further to his left.

"He will," Kurt said. "He'll return in September unless summoned earlier."

"I see," Jack said. "Well, please give your parents my best."

"I'll do that. Thank you, Admiral."

"You're welcome."

Susan pondered Kurt's comment as the Yankees finished their pregame warm-up and took their positions. Two minutes later, starting pitcher Monte Pearson went into his windup and fired the game's first pitch past Washington Senators center fielder Sam West.

"Kurt?" Susan asked.

"Yes?"

"I'm curious about something."

"What?"

"Does your father plan to leave in September or arrive in September?"

"He plans to leave in August and arrive in September," Kurt said.

Amanda turned her head.

"Did he tell you *which* day he planned to arrive?" Susan asked.

Kurt nodded.

"He did. He plans to arrive in Berlin on September 1."

Susan looked at Amanda and saw her return a knowing frown. Both women had apparently drawn the same conclusion about two men and a looming date.

Heinrich Schmidt planned to be in Berlin on the date Germany would invade Poland and start World War II. Kurt Schmidt did not. Life for both was about to get worse.

65: ELIZABETH

Princeton, New Jersey – Wednesday, July 5, 1939

T hank you for spending the day with us yesterday," Ella Wagner said. "I so wanted Lizzie's first Independence Day to be spent with an American."

Elizabeth laughed.

"You're an American too."

"You know what I mean. You grew up in this country. I did not," Ella said. "Erich and I want to learn as many customs as we can so that we can embrace them and make them a part of *our* heritage."

"Then you're off to a good start," Elizabeth said. "Fireworks are easy to embrace."

Elizabeth smiled as she walked with Ella and Lizzie on Nassau Street. She had thoroughly enjoyed the fireworks show at Palmer Stadium and so, apparently, had Lizzie. The toddler squealed with delight with each pop and flash in the indigo sky.

"I am sorry Susan and Amanda could not join us," Ella said.

"They thought about it."

Ella laughed.

"I doubt for very long. I understand their game was quite significant."

"It was," Elizabeth said. "It's hard to beat Lou Gehrig's retirement party."

Ella smiled.

"Some American customs are more sacred than others, it seems."

Elizabeth chuckled.

"They are on the Fourth."

When Ella stopped for traffic at the intersection with Bank Street, Elizabeth stopped to greet her favorite one-year-old. Lizzie Wagner, God's gift to happiness, sat up in her stroller seat and waved her hand around like she was John Philip Sousa. She smiled when her nana smiled.

"Did you say you had a card to mail?" Ella asked.

"I did," Elizabeth said. "I want to drop it off at Palmer Square so it goes out this morning. It's a very important card."

"Who is it to?"

"It's to an old friend in Los Angeles. I haven't corresponded with him in a while."

"It must be nice to have friends all over this wonderful country," Ella said as they crossed the street. "Most of our American friends are right here in Princeton."

"I guess that's one of the perks of getting old. You collect a lot of friends and acquaintances along the way."

Elizabeth laughed to herself. She had collected more than a friend when she had walked into the Pacific Winds Auditorium on September 5, 2016. She had collected a year full of trouble.

She patted the front pocket of her dress and felt the greeting card inside. It was as rigid and crisp and ready to go as it had been when she had stamped and addressed it three hours earlier.

Ten minutes later, Elizabeth, Ella, and Lizzie reached the three blue boxes outside the Palmer Square Post Office. The first had a collection time of 11:15 a.m.

Elizabeth pulled the envelope from her pocket and checked the address one last time. She wanted to be doubly sure that the card went to a time-traveling professor and not a time-wasting salesman. She didn't need to double check what she had written. She had that script memorized.

Dear Professor Bell: Thank you for your letter of June 22. I shared it with Susan but not with Amanda. I want to know the particulars of the Schmidt family's "serious transition" before showing the letter to my granddaughter. I suspect you are up to something. Please respond as soon as you can. Regards, Elizabeth Campbell

Elizabeth paused as she stood in front of the box. She didn't like sending important messages behind her daughter's back, but she saw no harm in doing it just this once.

She was requesting potentially vital information at a critical moment. She would have all the time in the world to share the professor's reply.

Elizabeth glanced at Ella, who looked at her with curiosity, and then at Lizzie, who looked at her with amusement. She smiled at both and walked to the box. She dropped the card in the slot and corresponded with the twenty-first century for the first time in nearly ten months.

66: AMANDA

Amanda knew something was wrong the moment she approached the bench in the center of the leafy Princeton campus. Kurt did not stand to greet her, kiss her, or even acknowledge her. He instead sat motionless on the bench and stared blankly into space.

Amanda didn't wait for Kurt to budge. She sat next to him, lowered her purse to the ground, and extended her arm across the back of the bench.

"What's up?" Amanda asked.

"My father's been summoned to Berlin," Kurt said. "I spoke to him this morning."

Amanda put a hand on Kurt's knee.

"You knew Karl might call sometime soon."

Kurt slowly turned his head and looked at Amanda.

"Karl didn't call. Von Ribbentrop did. He ordered my father to return to Germany by the end of the month to report on his activities at the embassy."

Amanda frowned. She knew that Joachim von Ribbentrop, Foreign Minister of Germany and one of Adolf Hitler's closest advisors, was not a person that anyone could ignore.

"What's your dad going to do?"

"He's going to go back, of course," Kurt said. "He has no choice."

"Has he done something wrong?"

Kurt stared at Amanda with sad, vacant eyes.

"You ask a lot of questions."

"I ask because I want to know what's going on. I care about your father," Amanda said. "Why do his superiors want to talk to him?"

Kurt sighed.

285

"He didn't say why. I don't know why. I know only that he has never been recalled in the seventeen years he has served in Washington."

"Can he refuse to go?" Amanda asked.

Kurt looked at Amanda like she had asked a stupid, naïve question, the kind of question only a clueless American could ask. He turned away when his eyes began to moisten.

"My mother is in Berlin, Amanda. So is my brother," Kurt said. "The Nazis have all the leverage they need to compel my father to return."

Amanda scolded herself for not seeing the obvious. She wanted to comfort Kurt and perhaps make amends for asking pointless questions, but she didn't know how.

"Is he still in Washington?" Amanda asked.

Kurt nodded.

"He leaves next week. I will drive to D.C. on Wednesday to see him off."

Amanda sighed.

"I'm so sorry, Kurt. I don't know what to say."

Kurt smiled sadly.

"You don't need to say anything."

Amanda leaned back on the bench and gazed at a building in the distance. She saw several young men exit the structure and quietly disperse. She assumed that they were among the few hundred students who attended Princeton during the summer.

"What does this mean for you?" Amanda asked.

Kurt paused for a moment, as if to collect his thoughts. When he finally spoke, he did so clearly, joylessly, and matter-of-factly. He delivered a message Amanda did not want to hear.

"It means I give my notice, pack my bags, and return to Germany."

Amanda pulled her arm from the back of the bench. She clutched Kurt's hand.

"You don't have to go. You can stay here. You can stay here with me."

Kurt looked at Amanda with incredulous eyes.

"Until when? Until you leave for Chicago? I can't stay," Kurt said. "I can't abandon my family any more than you can abandon yours."

Amanda took a deep breath as nausea gripped her midsection. She had no right or reason to feel jilted or blindsided, but she felt that way just the same.

"What are you saying?" Amanda asked. "Are you leaving me?"

Kurt nodded.

"I board a ship in two weeks."

Amanda turned away as tears began to flow. She could not process Kurt's comments. He had hit her too hard and too fast. She needed time to think, to reason, to persuade. She needed an opportunity to save a relationship that had become the most important in her life.

"You could come back. I would wait. I don't have to leave in September."

"Coming back is not an option," Kurt said. "My father will never leave Germany. Nor will my mother. I have no choice but to join them and stay with them. I'm sorry. I love you. I want to be with you, but I can't. We have to end this now."

Amanda wiped away her tears and tried to think. She had come to the campus expecting to meet Kurt for lunch. She had not come expecting to see him for the last time.

"Give me a chance to work something out," Amanda said.

"There's nothing to work out," Kurt replied. "Prolonging the inevitable will only make matters worse. We have to say goodbye."

Amanda tightened her hold on Kurt's hand, got up from the bench, and gently pulled him to his feet. She grabbed his other hand, turned him toward her, and looked him in the eyes.

"You're right. You have to see your family," Amanda said. "I won't try to stop you. I'll let you go without a fight if you agree to do one thing."

"What's that?"

"Go to Cape May with me."

Kurt frowned.

"I don't think that's a good idea, Amanda. It will only make parting more difficult."

"Please come with me. If we really have to say goodbye, then I want to do it right."

"Is that all you want to do?"

Amanda sighed.

"No."

"What else then?" Kurt asked.

"I want to do something I should have done weeks ago," Amanda said.

"What's that?"

"I want to come clean."

"Come clean?"

"Yes. I want to tell you who I am, where I'm from, and where I belong. I want to tell you all the things you need to know," Amanda said. She sighed. "I want to tell you the truth."

67: ELIZABETH

Thursday, July 20, 1939

Elizabeth smiled as she watched her favorite girls do their favorite thing. She was glad that Amanda had the strength to hold Lizzie high and spin her around. She knew she could not do the same without dropping the toddler on her head.

"You two look like skaters on ice," Elizabeth said.

"Did you hear that, Lizzie?" Amanda asked. "Grandma said it's time for a throw jump."

"Don't even think about it!"

Amanda lowered the girl and glared at her grandmother, who shared a couch with her mother in Erich and Ella Wagner's spacious but cluttered living room.

"You're no fun."

"I'm responsible," Elizabeth said. "That's better than fun."

"It isn't in my book," Amanda said. "When does Ella get back?"

"Two," Susan said.

Amanda held up Lizzie and rubbed noses with her.

"Then we have an hour to play out front."

"Enjoy yourselves," Susan said.

Amanda secured Lizzie with one arm, picked up a Raggedy Ann doll with the other, and headed for the front door. She opened the door a moment later and disappeared from sight.

"She's in a good mood," Elizabeth said.

"She's in a *funny* mood," Susan replied.

"What do you mean by that?"

"She's not acting like a girl who's breaking up with her boyfriend."

"Do you want her to whine and wail all week?" Elizabeth asked.

"No," Susan said. "I want her to tell me what she's planning to do."

"You already know. She's planning to do what lovers have done for centuries."

"That's what I'm afraid of."

"She's a grown woman, Susan."

"I know. I'm just afraid that sex will make it harder to move on."

"She'll be fine," Elizabeth said.

"Since when did my elderly mother become a champion of free love?"

Elizabeth sipped tea from a glass, looked at Susan, and smiled.

"Since when did my steamy-romance-writing daughter become a prude?"

Susan laughed.

"Touché."

"Let her have her fun," Elizabeth said. "She's invested more than six months in the boy. She's entitled to a meaningful goodbye."

Elizabeth laughed to herself. She didn't favor free love any more than she favored rabid dogs, but she did favor happy granddaughters and smooth transitions. She wanted Amanda to put Kurt Schmidt behind her as soon as possible and start preparing for the long trip home.

She had nothing against the Schmidt family – at least three quarters of it. She had come to like and respect Heinrich, Johanna, and Kurt and wished them the best. She was truly baffled over the colonel's recent change of fortunes and wondered if she had prejudged him in any way.

Elizabeth regretted sending Geoffrey Bell the greeting card of July 5. She now knew that the German family's "serious transition" was Johanna's illness and Heinrich's transfer to Berlin. She had meddled without cause and hoped she had done nothing more than irritate a professor.

"You're right," Susan said. "Amanda's entitled to handle things her way."

"Is that my daughter talking or the girlfriend of Admiral Hicks?"

"Both."

Elizabeth laughed.

"That's good," Elizabeth said. "I just hope the two women are on the same page in seven weeks. I would hate to see my daughter go through the same pain."

Susan sighed and looked at her mother seriously.

"What makes you think she has to?"

"What are you saying, Susan?"

"You know what I'm saying, Mother."

"We can't take him," Elizabeth said.

"Why not?" Susan asked. "It's not like he has a family or any meaningful ties."

Elizabeth leaned forward.

"That's not the point."

"What *is* the point?"

Elizabeth sighed.

"The point is that we promised Professor Bell to leave the thirties as we found them. We have an obligation to keep that promise."

"Says who?" Susan asked. "The woman who is altering her own family history?"

"I am doing no such thing."

"How do you know? How do you know you haven't already influenced Erich or Ella or Lizzie in ways that will change their lives?"

"I don't," Elizabeth said.

"That's right. You don't."

"That doesn't mean we can bring someone back."

"You're right. It doesn't," Susan said. "I don't know that this will even be an issue in September. Jack and I have a lot to sort out. I just don't want to rule out anything in advance."

Elizabeth stared at her daughter.

"Just don't say or do anything without talking to me first."

"I won't," Susan said.

"Do you promise?"

"I promise."

"Fair enough," Elizabeth said.

"Do you feel better now?"

"I feel better."

"Then we both feel better," Susan said. "Now let's go check on Lizzie. I suspect your soul mate is due for a diaper change."

68: AMANDA

A manda took Kurt's hand as she gazed at the entrance of Delaware Bay. She looked first at a trawler returning to port and then at a reddish sun. Old Sol had begun to set on the bay, the First State, and a nation enjoying one of its last peaceful summers.

"It's beautiful, isn't it?" Amanda asked.

"It is," Kurt said. "I'm glad you brought me here."

"Are you glad I brought you here because of the scenery or because of what I have planned for you later this evening?"

Kurt laughed.

"Both."

"That's a typical male answer," Amanda said.

"Am I a typical male?"

"No. I can honestly say that you're not."

"Why *did* you bring me here, Amanda?" Kurt asked. "I'm not complaining. I love you and want to spend as much time as I can with you, but all this seems rather pointless now."

"It doesn't have to be."

"What do you mean?"

"I'll tell you in a minute," Amanda said. "Let's walk first."

"All right."

Amanda led Kurt westward along the strip of sand that divided Beach Avenue and the water. To her right lay scores of amusements, hotels, restaurants, and colorful Victorian houses. Though hundreds of tourists from Philadelphia, New York, and elsewhere flooded the streets, Cape May felt like a sleepy seaside town that time had forgotten.

Amanda didn't rush into what she suspected would be a difficult discussion. She wanted to consider every statement and every possible

291

response before saying a word. She knew she would never get another chance to make her case for a shared future.

"Do you remember our conversation at Dot's reception?" Amanda asked.

"Of course."

"Do you remember the question I asked?"

"I do," Kurt said.

"Do you remember your answer?"

Kurt slowed his step.

"I do."

"Do you still feel that way? Could you give up everything for me?"

"I could under the right circumstances."

"That's what you said before," Amanda said.

"I know."

"That's what I want to talk about now."

"What do you mean?" Kurt asked.

"I want you to define the 'right circumstances.'"

"I'm not sure I can."

"Try," Amanda said.

"Why? The question is hypothetical."

Amanda stopped, took a breath, and prepared to cross the line. She turned to face Kurt.

"It's not hypothetical anymore."

"What do you mean?"

"I'm a time traveler, Kurt."

"You're a what?"

"I'm a time traveler. I'm from the future. I'm from a time so different than this one it would make your head spin."

Kurt laughed.

"You're from the future?"

"I am," Amanda said.

"Is this a joke?"

"No. It's *not* a joke. I'm from the year 2016. I walked through a magic tunnel in California ten months ago and popped out in 1938. I was born on September 18, 1994. I grew up in an age of cell phones and computers and drones and things people today can't even imagine."

"You can't be serious," Kurt said.

Amanda looked at Kurt and sank when she saw the amusement on his face. She didn't know why she had expected a different reaction, but she did. She felt stupid, silly, and lost. When she glanced again at Kurt, she realized the futility of her mission and dissolved into tears.

"I *am* serious. Would I be crying if I wasn't?"

"No. I suppose not."

Kurt said no more. He instead pulled Amanda close, wrapped her in his arms, and held her tightly for the next few minutes. He released his grip when she gently pushed him away.

"You don't believe me, do you?" Amanda asked.

Kurt sighed.

"I believe that you believe."

"That's not the same thing."

"No. It's not," Kurt said.

"What can I do to make you believe me?"

Kurt smiled kindly.

"You could start by offering proof."

Amanda sighed.

"I don't *have* proof. That's the thing. I left everything I had from 2016 in 2016. That was one of the conditions of coming here. I had to leave my belongings behind. We all did."

Amanda lamented that decision. She had left her phone, her Illinois driver's license, and her laptop at Professor Bell's house. She wished now that she had brought them all.

Kurt took Amanda's hands and kissed her forehead. He studied her somber face for a minute, sighed, and smiled.

"What did I do to deserve you?"

"You sent me a postcard," Amanda said. She laughed through her tears. "I'm an easy date."

Kurt gazed at his companion.

"No. You're a worthy date. You're a kind, intelligent, beautiful woman that I'm going to miss and never forget. That makes you much more than an 'easy date.'"

Amanda looked up at Kurt.

"What can I do make you believe me?"

Kurt sighed and frowned.

"I doubt you can do anything," Kurt said. "Put yourself in my place, Amanda. Would you believe me if I told you I was from Mars?"

"I might. I know for a fact Dot is."

Kurt laughed.

"I guess I should have used another example."

"Yeah."

Kurt kissed Amanda again, this time softly on the lips, and wiped the remaining tears from her cheeks. He took a deep breath, tightened his hold on her hands, and looked at her closely.

"There is one thing you can do," Kurt said.

"What?"

"It should be obvious."

"Tell me," Amanda said.

"If you really are a time traveler, you can tell me about things to come."

Amanda's eyes lit up.

"I can!"

"Then enlighten me," Kurt said. "Tell me something only a time traveler would know."

Amanda smiled.

"I already have."

"What do you mean?"

"I told you that Franco had captured Madrid before Franco had captured Madrid."

Amanda watched with interest and satisfaction as Kurt released her hands, widened his eyes, and stepped back. She had his attention.

"So you knew all along?" Kurt asked.

Amanda nodded.

"I knew all along. I knew when the war would end months ago."

"What else do you know?"

"What else do I know about *Spain*?"

"No," Kurt said. "What else do you know about the future?"

"How much time do you have?" Amanda asked.

"I have all night."

Amanda raised a brow.

"You have *all* night?"

Kurt blushed.

"I have five minutes."

"I thought so," Amanda said.

"Can we move on?"

Amanda laughed. "We can move on."

"Thank you," Kurt said.

"So you want to know more?" Amanda asked. "Well, I'll tell you more. I know that *Gone with the Wind* will win Best Picture. I know the Cubs will return to the World Series in six years and then go into hiding. I know that men will walk on the moon in 1969 and that televisions, those boxes you saw at the fair, will someday be as large as buildings."

Kurt smiled.

"I'd love to see them."

You can!

"What else do you want to know?" Amanda asked.

"Tell me about the things you mentioned earlier," Kurt said. "What are cell phones? What are computers? What are drones?"

Amanda sighed.

"You want long answers or short?"

"I'll settle for short ones," Kurt said.

"All right. Cell phones are easy to explain. They are wireless telephones you can take anywhere. Most aren't any bigger than a box of cigarettes, but they are very powerful. They can transmit text, pictures, and sounds anywhere in the world in a matter of seconds."

"Go on."

"Computers are like large cell phones," Amanda said. "They have screens like televisions and keyboards like typewriters. People use them to write papers, play games, watch movies, and do a thousand other things."

"What about drones?"

"Drones are like little helicopters."

"What's a helicopter?" Kurt asked.

Amanda smiled sheepishly.

"Something that's still in the works."

Kurt rubbed his chin.

"What about people? Who will be famous in the future?"

"Can you be specific?" Amanda asked.

"All right. Who will be the next president?"

Amanda decided not to answer. It was one thing to explain a cell phone. It was another to reveal Franklin Roosevelt's successor with a war looming. "I think I'll pass on that one."

"Why?" Kurt asked.

"I have my reasons."

"What about foreign leaders?"

"I think I'll pass on that too," Amanda said.

Kurt frowned.

"Does that mean you can't say anything about other countries?"

Amanda put her hands to Kurt's face.

"It means I won't say anything tonight," Amanda said.

"Will you tell me some things?"

"I will. I promise."

Amanda smiled as two thoughts hit her at once. The first was that she had finally opened Kurt's mind to time travel. The second was that their weekend was about more than just that.

"When?" Kurt asked.

"You'll see."

Amanda took Kurt's hand, kissed him softly, and gently tugged him toward the setting sun. She led him westward to a sixty-year-old hotel, an empty suite, and a long-overdue appointment. Affairs of state, she reasoned, could wait until morning. Affairs of the heart could not.

69: AMANDA

Sunday, July 23, 1939

Amanda had picked the Taylor Inn because of the charm it exuded in a brochure. The Victorian hotel at the corner of Congress Street and Beach Avenue boasted wide verandas, dormers, a red mansard roof, landscaped grounds, and an unfettered view of the ocean.

She had picked Suite 17 because it was all that was available when she scrambled to find a room in one of the busiest resort towns on the eastern seaboard. She did not bother to ask for the room rate when she made the reservation. She knew she would pay it.

Amanda fluffed a pillow behind her back, sat up in the large bed, and nudged the lightly clad young man to her left. When he didn't respond, she nudged him again.

"Wake up," Amanda said. "I ordered breakfast."

"You what?" Kurt asked.

"I ordered bacon, eggs, and pancakes for two people who aren't dressed to go out."

Kurt rolled over, wiped the sleep from his eyes, and smiled.

"That was very thoughtful of you, Mrs. Schmidt."

Amanda giggled at the reference. She had not become Kurt's wife in a quickie wedding, but she had become his weekend spouse in a dime store on Decatur Street.

The two had purchased rhinestone rings at one thirty and exchanged vows of secrecy before engaging the desk clerk at the Taylor Inn. They needed only to flash the bands a few times to convince the balding man that they were married and not mischievous.

"It *was* thoughtful of me," Amanda said. "I figured it was the least I could do for you after you so thoughtfully attended to my ... um ... vacation requirements."

Kurt blushed.

"If you say so."

"I say so," Amanda said with a smile. She let the tender moment linger before changing the subject. "Someone will bring us breakfast at ten. I guess the kitchen is a little busy this morning."

Kurt leaned to his right and kissed Amanda on the cheek.

"I'm not going anywhere."

"That's good, Mr. Schmidt, because we have a lot to talk about."

Kurt nodded and sighed.

"OK. Where should we start?"

"Let's start with the big question," Amanda said.

"You want to know what it would take for me to 'give up everything'?"

"Yes. I want to know."

"It would take a lot, Amanda. It would take an awful lot."

"Can you be more specific?"

Kurt did not answer right away. He instead stared blankly at the far wall, took a few deep breaths, and tapped his fingers on his thighs. When he finally looked again at Amanda, he did so with eyes that revealed frustration, resignation, and more than a little sadness.

"What's the point?" Kurt asked. "It won't change anything."

"You don't know that," Amanda replied.

"I think I do. I think I know myself."

Amanda kicked herself for not picking up *How to Win Friends and Influence People* at the library. She was sure Dale Carnegie's classic had a chapter on dealing with difficult Germans.

"I just want an answer to the question," Amanda said. "I want to know what it would take for you, Kurt Schmidt, to leave your home, your country, and maybe your family and follow me, the woman you say you love, into the twenty-first century."

Kurt sighed.

"All right. I'll give you an answer."

"Thank you," Amanda replied.

"Like I said, it would take something big. It would take a crisis or a catastrophe or something I can't even fathom. It would take a war. Is that want you want to hear?"

Amanda smiled sadly.

"That's exactly what I want to hear."

"I thought so," Kurt said. He grabbed Amanda's hand and kissed it. "I wish I could give you more, but I can't. I can't order a catastrophe to save our relationship. I can't order a war."

Amanda gazed at Kurt with watery eyes.

"You can't . . . but I can."

297

Kurt tilted his head and stared.

"You can what?"

Amanda sighed.

"I can give you your war."

"Are you telling me a war is coming?"

Amanda nodded.

"It's almost here, Kurt. It's so close I can smell the smoke. It's going to be a big war, too, a conflict that will affect the whole planet and both of our families."

Kurt released Amanda's hand and turned away. He stared blankly at a wicker dresser for about a minute before returning to the time traveler in his bed.

"Why didn't you tell me this earlier?" Kurt asked.

"I didn't because I promised others I wouldn't. I also counted on your family staying in D.C. I had hoped to keep my options open. Now it appears I have just one option left."

"What are you saying?"

Amanda leaned back against her pillow. She finally had Kurt's attention on the only matter that mattered. The question now was how to proceed.

"I'm saying I love you and want you to come back with me. I want to build something with you in the future," Amanda said. "I'm also saying that if you go to Germany now you may never get out. Europe is about to become a war zone."

"I have to see my family. You know I do."

"I know."

"Then say what you have to say," Kurt said. "I'll listen. If I can find a way to come back to you, I will. I love you too. I don't want to leave you either."

Amanda gazed at the fair-haired man with the blue eyes and wondered if she could do it. She had hoped to dissuade Kurt from leaving the country with vague warnings of wars to come. Now she had to do more. She had to wander into the dangerous realm of specifics.

"Do all Good Germans look like you?"

"What?" Kurt asked.

"Never mind."

"What are you thinking, Amanda?"

"I'm thinking I'm going to have to do something I didn't want to do. I'm going to have to trust you completely with information I have no right to share."

"You can trust me."

"Look at me," Amanda said.

"Why?"

"I want to see your eyes when I say this."

"All right," Kurt said.

Amanda grabbed his hand.

"Promise me that you will never repeat what I'm about to tell you."

Kurt met her gaze.

"I promise."

"I trust you, Kurt, and I want you to trust me," Amanda said. "So I'm going to tell you something that should leave no doubt in your mind that everything I've said is true."

"OK."

Amanda took a breath.

"In exactly one month, Germany and Russia will sign a non-aggression pact."

"That's not possible," Kurt said. "Hitler hates Stalin."

"You're right. He does. He despises him, in fact. But he's not going to sign this treaty to placate his enemy. He's going to do it to buy time."

"I don't understand."

"Hitler plans to use the pact to build up his defenses," Amanda said.

"You don't mean?"

Amanda nodded.

"He's going to invade the Soviet Union in 1941. He's going to be at war with Russia, Britain, America, and half the world in just two years."

"Good God," Kurt said.

"Don't worry about Russia. Worry about getting out of Germany alive."

"All right."

"I want you to remember two dates," Amanda said. "OK?"

"OK."

"I want you to first remember August 23. That's when the foreign ministers of Germany and the Soviet Union will sign the treaty. It will be in the news."

"I'll look for it."

"Most people will react to the treaty with concern but not alarm. That's because they won't know about a secret protocol that carves up Poland, Finland, Romania, and all of the Baltic States. They won't know that Hitler is preparing for war."

"What about the war?"

"It will start on September 1. Hitler will invade Poland. He'll declare war on the British and the French, they will declare war on him, and six years of slaughter will be under way."

"How do you know this?" Kurt asked.

"I'm a history major, Kurt, a history major with hindsight. I studied this period. I studied it for years. I know every detail. That's why you have to listen to me."

"I'm listening."

"That's good because I think you'll like this part," Amanda said.

"What part?"

"I want you to try to save your family. If you do nothing else, get them to Britain, France, or Switzerland by August 31. Then get back to this country as soon as possible."

"What if they resist?" Kurt asked.

"Then do what you can to persuade them. Beg. Bribe. Lie. Coax. It doesn't matter. Just say something to get them on a boat or a plane in August. You won't have another chance."

Kurt gazed at Amanda.

"I'll try. I'll do all I can to get them out."

"I know you will," Amanda said.

"I have two questions though," Kurt said.

"Ask."

"What can you offer my family in 2016?"

"I can offer a lot," Amanda said. "I can help your mom find a treatment for her cancer. I can help your dad and brother get a new start. I can help all of you find a better life."

"I see."

"What's the second question?" Amanda asked.

"*Why* should they leave Germany?"

Amanda stared at Kurt.

"Are you kidding?"

"No. I'm not," Kurt said. "I may need more than your promises to get them on a boat. Even if they believe a war is coming, they may choose to ride it out. Why should they leave?"

"They should leave because Germany's going to lose!"

Kurt tensed up.

"Hitler's going to lose?"

"Yes. Hitler is going to lose. Europe is going to lose. Sixty million people are going to lose. Your family is going to lose. They will have nothing to ride out but endless Allied bombing runs."

"I don't see how," Kurt said. "Hitler has the world's strongest army."

"He won't in six years. He will lose it all."

"Tell me how."

Amanda sighed. She didn't want to say another word but knew she had to finish. It was time to put this conversation to bed.

"I can't say much except that Hitler is going to have a bad time in places like El Alamein and Stalingrad and Normandy. The Germans who survive the war will inherit a nation in ruins. Many of those who still have homes will face joblessness and starvation. There's no upside to staying in Germany, Kurt. There's a big upside to following me."

"When will you leave Princeton?"

"We plan to catch a train to Los Angeles on September 10. I will wait for you at our house until noon. If I don't see you by then, I'll assume you didn't make it," Amanda said. She leaned forward and kissed Kurt lightly. "I hope that you make it."

"I'll be there. I promise," Kurt said. "Wait for me."

70: SUSAN

Princeton, New Jersey — Wednesday, July 26, 1939

Susan held on tightly as the sailor navigated an unfamiliar vessel through unfamiliar waters. She had faith in his ability to guide the boat to a safe location, but she didn't breathe easily until he stopped the craft, dropped anchor, and set up a dinner for two.

"Are you this kind to all the girls?" Susan asked.

Jack Hicks smiled.

"I am to the ones who can spell."

Susan laughed.

"You set the bar high."

"I suppose I do."

Susan could not complain. She could not imagine a better way to spend a lazy summer evening than dining with a handsome man in a rowboat in the middle of a placid lake.

"What do you have in the basket?"

"I have a lot of things, Mrs. Peterson," Jack said. "I have roast beef sandwiches, potato salad, Swiss cheese, and cherry pie, of course."

"Did you bake the pie, Admiral?"

"No. Your daughter did."

Susan giggled. She remembered seeing her date's co-conspirator preparing the dessert at ten that morning and had not given the act a second thought.

"I'll be sure to thank her tomorrow," Susan said.

Susan watched with admiration as Jack loaded the plates, lit a short candle, and then dug out a bottle of merlot. She found the dinner as impressive as the view to her right, where a saffron sun touched the tips of dogwood and sycamore trees on the west shore of Lake Carnegie.

"Has Amanda said goodbye to Kurt?" Jack asked.

"No. Not yet," Susan replied. "She'll say goodbye this Friday in New York."

Jack nodded.

"I see. Then how did her weekend go? Did she enjoy Cape May?"

"She must have. She returned with a smile."

"That says something. I must admit you're more progressive than most mothers I've known. Most wouldn't have let their daughters even leave the house."

"I trust Amanda," Susan said. "I trust her to make good decisions."

"I admire that."

"You just admire freethinking women."

"They *are* more interesting," Jack said.

Susan laughed.

She liked laughing. She liked being around a man who made her laugh and put her at ease. She wondered what it would be like to be with such a man for the rest of her life.

"Thank you for taking me out here," Susan said.

"You're welcome."

"I mean it. Dinner in a rowboat shows imagination."

"Is this a first for you?" Jack asked.

"Oddly enough, no. Bruce took me out once."

"Is that right?"

Susan nodded.

"He took me out on Geneva Lake, in Wisconsin, when I was twenty-three," Susan said. She sighed. "He took me out on the night he proposed."

"He sounds like a romantic man."

"He wasn't," Susan said. She laughed. "He wasn't at all. Like most men, though, he could sometimes be tender, sensitive, and creative."

Jack poured two glasses of wine. He handed one to Susan.

"Do you miss him?" Jack asked.

Susan grabbed the glass and forced a smile. She didn't know how to answer the question. She *did* miss Bruce Peterson. She missed the life they had together, but she didn't miss how Bruce had treated her at the end and certainly didn't want to discuss either subject with Jack.

"I do," Susan said.

"There's nothing wrong with that, Susan. I'd think less of you if you didn't."

"You're very gracious. Many men would think less of me. They would wonder why I have any lingering feelings for a husband who betrayed my trust."

"You forget that I've been in your shoes," Jack said. "It's easy to remember the worst in a person when that person has hurt you deeply.

What's difficult is putting that hurt aside and remembering why you were attracted to that person in the first place."

Susan smiled.

"It seems I'm dining not only with an admiral but also a poet."

Jack laughed softly.

"If I were a poet, I wouldn't need your help on the book."

"You might," Susan said. "Even poets need feedback."

"I suppose."

Susan gazed at the modest man. She admired someone who recognized his own strengths and weaknesses. Jack Hicks may have downplayed his talents as a writer, but that didn't change the fact he was a great writer. Susan had seen his work. She knew that he was as capable as anyone of communicating a complicated message to an uncomplicated public.

"How much further do we have to go?" Susan asked.

"Do you mean on the book?"

"Yes."

Jack paused.

"I estimate thirty to forty pages. We're getting close to the end."

Susan sighed.

"Do you think we'll have a first draft ready by the end of August?"

Jack nodded.

"I'm sure of it," Jack said. "Why do you ask? Are you planning to leave me in September?"

Susan smiled. She had wondered when Jack would acknowledge the 800-pound gorilla sitting in the rowboat. She didn't blame him. There really was no point in ignoring a subject that was never far from their minds.

"Let's just say I'd like to finish the draft before I make any big decisions."

Jack smiled sadly.

"I guess I can live with that."

Susan regretted her answer the second she saw the shine go out of Jack's eyes. She hated stringing along this kind, thoughtful, patient man with evasive comments. She studied his face for a moment, put down her glass, and leaned forward.

"I mean it when I say I haven't committed to leaving Princeton or you," Susan said. "I just need more time to think things through. Can you understand that?"

"I can," Jack said.

"That's good because I'm going to ask for more understanding in the coming weeks."

"You are?"

"I am," Susan said. "I'm going to ask you to be understanding, patient, open-minded, and perhaps even a little reckless."

"That's a tall order, Mrs. Peterson."

"It is. Right now, though, I don't need any of those things."

"You don't?" Jack asked.

"I don't," Susan said. She leaned forward a bit more. "All I need now is a kiss."

The admiral fulfilled the civilian's request. When he was done, he put down his glass, leaned forward himself, and fulfilled it again.

Susan studied the happy widower in the short-sleeved shirt and khaki pants. She liked this man. She loved him too. The question now was what to do with him.

She had forty-six days to make the call of her life, seven weeks to choose a new path. The day of resolution drew closer. The time for action neared. The Decision loomed.

71: AMANDA

New York, New York – Friday, July 28, 1939

The passenger terminal on Pier 86, at the foot of West Forty-Sixth Street, was huge. High, wide, long, and open, it was as big as an aircraft hanger, as light as a shopping-mall atrium, and as functional as Grand Central Station. It wasn't the most private venue in Manhattan, but it was more than suitable to say goodbye to someone Amanda Peterson hoped to see again.

"Do you have everything you need?" Amanda asked. "That suitcase seems small."

"It's big enough," Kurt said. "I like to travel light."

Amanda leaned forward and put her mouth to Kurt's ear.

"Why don't you say goodbye to my family?" Amanda whispered. "This would probably be a good time. I'll walk you to the gangway when you're done."

"All right."

Amanda released Kurt's hands and stepped back. She watched closely as the German who was an American in all but name moved on to the next woman in his receiving line.

"Goodbye, Mrs. Campbell," Kurt said.

Elizabeth smiled.

"Please call me Elizabeth."

"OK. Goodbye, Elizabeth. I know we haven't always seen eye to eye, but I want you to know that I respect your views, your skepticism, and your willingness to see me as a person."

"It wasn't hard, Kurt. You made it easy."

"In any case, thank you."

"You're welcome."

Kurt gave Elizabeth a gentle hug. When he was finished, he smiled, took a breath, and then moved down the line to a tearful middle-aged mother.

"Goodbye to you, too, Mrs. Peterson ... Susan," Kurt said. "Thank you for your kindness and understanding. Thank you for allowing me to get to know your wonderful daughter and bringing me into your family. I hope to repay the favor some day."

"There's no need," Susan said. She wiped her eyes with a handkerchief. "Please give my best to your family. Tell your mother I will pray for her every day."

"I'll tell her that."

Susan took Kurt's hand and gently squeezed it.

"Please be safe. We will all sleep better knowing that you are looking out for yourself as well as those you love. Promise that you'll be careful when you get to Germany."

"I promise," Kurt said.

Susan dropped the hand, leaned forward, and smothered Kurt with a hug. She held onto him until a man spoke over a crackling public address system and announced a passenger liner's pending departure to Cherbourg, Southampton, Rotterdam, and Hamburg.

"Goodbye, Kurt."

"Goodbye."

Amanda wiped away a few tears of her own, walked to Kurt's side, and took his hand. She gave him a reassuring smile and then turned to face her mother.

"We won't be long," Amanda said.

Susan smiled softly.

"Take your time, honey."

Amanda acknowledged the comment with a nod and then led Kurt to the boarding area about thirty yards away. More than twenty people waited patiently to show their tickets to an attendant and ascend a steep gangway that shot through the side of the building.

When they reached the back of the line, Kurt released Amanda's hand, lowered his suitcase to the ground, and straightened his tie. He glanced at Elizabeth and Susan and then at Amanda.

"They don't think I'm coming back, do they?" Kurt asked.

"They don't *know* you're coming back," Amanda said. "I haven't told them."

"When are you going to tell them?"

"Next week. That way they can't ship me out with you."

Kurt laughed.

"You think of everything."

Amanda put her hands to Kurt's face.

"Right now I'm thinking only of you," Amanda said. "Don't take any unnecessary chances over there. Do what you have to do, save your family if you can, and get your butt back here before all hell breaks loose."

"I will. Even if I have to return alone, I will. I'll return to Princeton before you leave."

Amanda kissed Kurt gently.

"I'm counting on that."

"Is there anything I can bring you?" Kurt asked.

Amanda smiled.

"As a matter of fact, there is. Bring me an edelweiss."

"You want a flower?"

Amanda nodded.

"I don't care if its fresh, dried, or squished in waxed paper. Bring me a flower. Bring me something beautiful from a place that's about to get ugly."

Kurt laughed and smiled.

"OK. I will."

Amanda took a deep breath.

"I guess this is it."

"I guess it is," Kurt said.

Amanda wiped away a fresh tear and then placed her hands on Kurt's shoulders.

"I love you."

She kissed him longer and harder.

"I love you too," Kurt said.

Amanda lowered her hands and smiled sadly.

"Come back to me. I'll be waiting."

Kurt nodded, picked up his suitcase, and then looked over his shoulder at a nonexistent line and a ticket attendant that called out to late boarders. He smiled at Amanda.

"That's my cue," Kurt said. "Goodbye."

"Goodbye."

Kurt walked to the attendant, showed him his ticket, and ascended the gangway. He took about ten steps, stopped, and turned around to face Amanda. He blew her a kiss.

Amanda returned the kiss and watched closely as Kurt advanced through the opening in the terminal wall and disappeared from sight. She had said her first goodbye to the only boy she ever loved. She hoped it wouldn't be her last.

72: ELIZABETH

"You did *what?*" Susan asked.

"I told him," Amanda said. "I told him we were time travelers."

"You had no right to do that."

"I had every right."

Elizabeth put a hand to her temple to stave off a headache that had suddenly grown worse. She hated family fights as much as she hated rap music.

"No. You didn't," Susan said. "You had no right to tell Kurt a thing."

"Don't get all high and mighty on me, Mother. You're planning to do the same thing with Jack. I know you are."

"You know nothing."

"Will you two stop it?" Elizabeth asked. "You're giving me a migraine."

Amanda turned toward the woman in the living-room recliner.

"I'm sorry, Grandma, but I have to get this out. I told Kurt about us because I want him to come back with us. I love him and want to build a life with him."

Susan stepped forward until she, too, was about eight feet from Elizabeth. She looked at her mother and then at Amanda. Like Amanda, she appeared to be spoiling for a fight.

"What exactly did you tell him?" Susan asked.

"I told him a lot of things," Amanda said.

"That's not an answer."

"I told him to return by September 10. That's when we're leaving, isn't it?"

"What did you say about us?" Susan asked. "What did you say about the future?"

"I told him enough to get a commitment. That's all you need to know."

309

"I've heard enough," Elizabeth said. "I'm getting a glass of water."

Elizabeth got out of her chair, stared at each of the combatants, and walked shakily to the dining area and then to the kitchen. When she reached the refrigerator, she pulled out a pitcher of ice water, carried it to the counter, and grabbed a glass from the cupboard.

She sank when she heard the voices in the living room grow louder. She understood why Susan and Amanda had to talk, but she didn't understand why they had to fight.

Elizabeth poured herself a small glass of water and drank it quickly. She repeated the process twice until the throbbing pain in her head finally began to subside.

She put the pitcher away, placed the glass in the sink, and walked out of the kitchen and into the dining area. She stopped when she reached the arched doorway that divided the dining area and a living room that had become increasingly noisy.

"I want to know!" Susan demanded. "I want to know exactly what you said."

"What difference does it make?" Amanda asked.

Susan put her hands on her hips.

"It makes a huge difference. What did you say?"

"I said we could help his mother."

"What do you mean?" Susan asked.

"I said we could help her find cancer treatment."

"What else?"

"That's mostly it," Amanda said.

"There's more," Susan said. "I know there's more."

"I said we could find jobs for Heinrich and Karl."

"Try again."

"What do you want from me, Mom?"

"I want the truth!"

"I've told you the truth," Amanda said.

"You've told me part of the truth," Susan said. "There is no way Kurt would have agreed to come back here and leave 1939 unless you told him more. Tell me what you said."

"No."

"Amanda?"

"No!"

Elizabeth stepped into the living room.

"Tell her, Amanda," Elizabeth said. "Tell us both."

Amanda sighed.

"I told him about Molotov-Ribbentrop."

"What?" Susan asked.

"I told him about a treaty Russia and Germany will sign in three weeks," Amanda said. "I had to give him a prediction. I had to give him proof."

Susan tapped her foot.

"What else?"

"Don't push me, Mom."

"I'll push you until I get everything. What else did you tell Kurt?"

Elizabeth walked to Susan's side. She did not want to jump into this scrap any more than she wanted to jump into Lake Carnegie, but she did want answers.

"Tell us," Elizabeth said.

"No."

"Tell us!" Susan said.

"I told him war was coming!" Amanda said. "OK? I told him war was coming September 1 and that he had to get out of Germany before then or he would never get out."

"Amanda!"

"I had no choice. I had to tell him if I wanted to see him again."

Elizabeth felt her head swim as she considered what she had just heard. She reached out to Susan just as her daughter moved toward Amanda.

"What else?" Susan asked. "What else?"

"I told him about El Alamein and Stalingrad. I told him about Normandy."

"No! No!"

"Yes! Yes!"

"You didn't," Susan said. She shook her head. "You didn't."

"I did, Mom. I did," Amanda said. She dissolved into tears. "I told him too much. I said the world was about to explode. I told him Hitler would leave Europe in ruins."

"No."

"I said Germany was going to *lose*."

Elizabeth heard "Stalingrad" and "Normandy" and some of the rest but not "explode" or "Hitler" or "ruins." By the time Amanda Peterson had spilled the rest of her beans, Elizabeth Campbell had dropped to the floor.

73: AMANDA

Wednesday, August 2, 1939

Amanda gazed at the woman in the hospital bed and then at the one sitting on the other side of the bed. She couldn't speak to the first and didn't want to speak to the second, but she knew at some point she would have to answer to both. Such was the case when one acted selfishly, recklessly, and provocatively and drove another person to death's door.

Amanda started to speak but stopped when a nurse entered the room. She watched closely as the caregiver checked Elizabeth's pulse, put a hand on the patient's forehead, and then made a few notations on a clipboard attached to the footboard of the bed.

When the nurse finally exited the room, Amanda gazed again at Susan, gathered her courage, and prepared to engage. Small talk, she concluded, was better than no talk.

"Did you get any sleep last night?" Amanda asked.

"I got a little," Susan said.

Amanda knew for a fact that Susan had slept less than four hours. She had heard her mother go to bed at midnight, get up at four, and clean the upstairs bathroom between five and six.

"You don't look like you did," Amanda said.

"Are you saying I look haggard?"

Amanda sighed.

"No. I'm saying you look tired."

"I guess I am," Susan said.

Sleep had not been a high priority for either woman after they had called an ambulance and followed the emergency vehicle to Mercer County Hospital. Neither had food. Both Susan and Amanda had found it impossible to eat even as much as a sandwich after returning home at eight.

Amanda studied her mother's eyes as the two exchanged stares. She looked for warmth, forgiveness, and even lingering anger, but she found nothing except indifference and fatigue.

"Do you want to get lunch?" Amanda asked.

Susan sighed.

"Let's wait."

"You're not saying much."

"I have nothing to say," Susan said.

"Are you mad at me?"

"No. I'm not mad at you."

"Are you disappointed in me?"

"Let's talk later."

Amanda looked away, toward a window, as tears flooded her eyes. She didn't need a direct answer to her question. She could hear her mother's answer in every clipped response.

"I'm sorry, Mom," Amanda said. "I'm so sorry."

Susan smiled softly.

"Don't be sorry."

"Why not? I made a mess of everything."

Susan shook her head.

"We don't know that. We don't know that you made a mess of *anything*."

"What do you mean?" Amanda asked.

"I mean we don't know," Susan said. "We don't know for a fact that Kurt has violated your trust. For all we know, he is exactly what he appears to be: a kind, thoughtful, trustworthy young man who loves you and plans to return to you."

Amanda took a moment to get it together. She hated crying. She hated showing weakness and vulnerability, but she hated failing people even more. She grabbed a few tissues from a box on a bedside table, dried her eyes, and looked again at her mother.

"What about Grandma?" Amanda asked in a soft voice. "What about her?"

"What about her? I knew she had dizzy spells weeks ago," Susan said. She offered another comforting smile. "I could have insisted that she see a doctor. I could have taken her to a doctor, but I didn't. If anyone deserves blame for her current condition, it's me."

Amanda settled into her chair and lowered her eyes. She no longer cared about blame or mistakes or missed opportunities. She cared only about the woman in the bed.

"What did the doctor tell you this morning?" Amanda asked.

"He didn't say much," Susan said. "He doesn't know much."

313

"Why not? He's a doctor."

"He's a doctor in 1939, Amanda. He doesn't have access to twenty-first-century technology. He doesn't even have a conscious patient. Until Grandma wakes up, he won't be able to determine whether she had a stroke, a heart attack, or something else."

"So what do we do?" Amanda asked. "What *can* we do?"

"We sit. We wait. We pray," Susan said. "There's not much else we can do."

Amanda didn't like that answer. As a product of the digital age, she was used to getting diagnoses and prognoses in hours and not days. She didn't like walking through the darkness. She feared the unknown.

"What will we do if she doesn't get better?"

"Let's cross that bridge when we come to it," Susan said. "There's no point in worrying about something we don't know or can't control."

Amanda nodded and mustered a weak smile. She agreed with the comment. She knew she would accomplish nothing by obsessing about things that might happen.

She thought about the encouraging exchange with her mother and then directed her full attention to the patient. She scooted her chair closer to the bed.

Amanda took Elizabeth's left hand, gazed at her bony fingers, and pondered all the things she had done with those fingers in seventy-nine years. She thought of all the letters she had typed, pots she had made, flowers she had planted, and even diapers she had changed.

Elizabeth had lived an active life. Even if it had been domestic by modern standards, it had still been active. She had not wasted a moment in eight decades on earth.

Then Amanda looked again at the hand and noticed something else. She saw that Elizabeth had replaced her second wedding ring with her first. Grandma Campbell had gone retro. She had embraced her past in a tangible, meaningful, surprising manner.

Amanda gazed at the diamond in the platinum band and noted the irony. This rock had started it all. Had Professor Bell not retrieved the gem from 1958, three women would have never agreed to travel to 1938. They would have never agreed to safeguard two other stones, put their lives on hold, and bravely test the boundaries of the human experience.

Amanda massaged Elizabeth's hand for a minute and then finally let it go. She figured if she couldn't coax her grandma into consciousness, she should at least let her rest peacefully.

"Have you told Jack about Grandma?" Amanda asked.

"No," Susan said. "I will later today."

Amanda stared at her mother. She was surprised to hear that she hadn't told him. She had assumed that Susan Peterson had Jack Hicks on speed dial or whatever amounted to speed dial in an age when telephones looked like little Liberty Bells.

"Was I right about you two?" Amanda asked.

"What do you mean?"

"Are you planning to tell Jack who we are? Are you planning to gain his trust, win him over, and persuade him to come back with us?"

Susan looked at her daughter.

"I'm thinking about it."

"So I *was* right."

"You were right," Susan said.

"I'm not judging, Mom. I know you like Jack. You may even love him. I just want you to understand that I didn't ask Kurt to return with us on a whim. I thought about it for weeks. I thought about the promises I had made and the consequences of saying too much. I agonized a long time before deciding I couldn't leave Princeton without him."

"I know."

"So why haven't you taken the same step?" Amanda asked. "Why haven't you asked Jack to join us? It's not like he has a family or strong ties to this time."

"I haven't taken the same step because I'm not ready," Susan said.

"Are you waiting for a proposal?"

Susan sighed.

"I'm waiting for a sign."

Amanda tilted her head.

"Are you becoming psychic?"

Susan smiled.

"No. I'm becoming cautious."

"I don't understand," Amanda said.

"I'm reluctant to take a big step until I've cleared the emotional clutter I left behind," Susan said. "I can't ask anything of Jack until I've made my peace with the past."

"Are you talking about Dad?"

"Yes."

"What does Dad have to do with this?" Amanda asked.

"He has a lot to do with it. You'll understand someday," Susan said. "When you've been married to someone as long as I was to your father, you'll understand."

Amanda disagreed but conceded she was in no position to argue. She had never been in a relationship that lasted twenty-five months, much less twenty-five years. Most of her affiliations with men could be measured in news cycles.

"I suppose," Amanda said. "Just don't take too long to clear that clutter. We have only six more weeks in the thirties. That's not a lot of time."

"It's not … but it's enough."

"You really think so?"

"I do," Susan said. "If there's one thing I've learned to do in forty-nine years, it's how to clear clutter. I'll be ready to go when the time comes – and so will you."

74: SUSAN

Wednesday, August 9, 1939

Susan pushed through the doors of the diner, hurried past a blur of booths, and looked for a reason to smile. She found one in the form of a friend.

"I'm sorry I'm late," Susan said.

"You're right on time in my book," Jack said.

The admiral slid out of his booth, rose to his feet, and greeted Susan with a kiss on the cheek. He looked at her for a moment, smiled warmly, and then motioned for her to join him.

"Please take a seat."

Susan sat in the seat opposite Jack and put her purse on the bench. She grabbed a menu, gave it a quick scan, and then placed it on the table.

"Have you ordered yet?" Susan asked.

"No," Jack replied. "I knew you would show up."

"I like your optimism."

"How is your mother?"

"She's conscious," Susan said.

"That's a good thing, isn't it?"

Susan frowned.

"It's a good thing if a patient wants to live. It's a bad thing if she doesn't."

"What did you learn at the hospital?" Jack asked.

Susan sighed.

"I learned she had a stroke."

"Is she all right?"

"She's stable," Susan said.

"Is she able to speak?"

Susan nodded.

"She's able to speak and eat and follow commands. She's able to do a lot of things. She's *unwilling* to do any of them."

"Give her time," Jack said. "She'll bounce back."

"She might. She might not."

"You have to be positive."

"Are you a doctor now?" Susan asked.

"No," Jack said. "I'm a man who's been in your shoes. I went through the same thing with my own mother several years ago. I know what you're up against."

"I suppose you do."

"How is Amanda doing?"

"She's hurting," Susan said. "She thinks she's at least partly responsible."

"Why is that?"

"We argued in front of my mother before she collapsed."

"I see," Jack said. "What did you argue about?"

Susan sighed.

"We argued about a lot of things. It doesn't matter. Amanda's not to blame."

Jack nodded.

"No. She's not. I can relate to how she feels though. I felt a lot of guilt when my mother had her stroke. We had argued over some fairly trivial things beforehand."

"Did your mother recover?" Susan asked.

"She did. She recovered fully. That's why I'm optimistic about Elizabeth's prognosis. If she's able to speak and eat and follow commands, she's more than halfway there."

Susan leaned forward.

"Let's talk about something else."

"OK," Jack said. "What would you like to talk about?"

Susan turned her head as a thin man in an apron entered the room.

"How about sandwiches?"

"Do you see the waiter?" Jack asked.

"No. I see a man who wants to clear this booth of loiterers."

Jack smiled.

"Let's talk about sandwiches then."

Susan opened her menu a second time. She examined her options, requested input from Jack, and settled on the Princeton Pastrami. She didn't know if it had anything on the Trenton Turkey, the Camden Club, or the Hoboken Ham, but it did look more interesting than a bowl of soup.

"What are you going to get?" Susan asked.

"I was thinking of a hot dog."

Susan laughed and then looked at Jack with deep affection. She couldn't help but admire a man who could take her mind off an ailing mother, a troubled daughter, and a world war that only three time travelers, a German research assistant, and perhaps a few others saw coming.

The waiter came to the table a moment later. He took two orders, grabbed two menus, and then escaped to the front of a diner that had become noticeably busier in the past ten minutes.

"How is the book coming?" Susan asked.

"It's coming," Jack said.

"Is that your way of saying, 'I miss my assistant'?"

Jack smiled.

"Yes."

"I'll try to help you more this week," Susan said.

"You take care of your family. I'll be fine."

"No. I want to help. I committed to this project. I want to finish it."

"OK. Let's meet next week," Jack said. "I'll have more work for you."

"How does Thursday at my place sound?"

"It sounds perfect. We have a date."

Susan smiled as she pondered the definition of "date." With Jack Hicks, it could mean anything from a baseball game to a lecture to a dinner in a rowboat.

"Did you ever hear from Admiral Jones?" Susan asked.

"No. He's still on vacation."

Jack had tried twice in July to reach Sidney Jones. The two-star admiral, a professor at the U.S. Naval Academy, was among a handful of senior officers who had spoken publicly in favor of rebuilding the nation's outdated fleet.

"What will you do if you can't reach him?" Susan asked.

"I'll quote Bill Franks instead. He's an old friend who works in the War Department. I spoke with him at a luncheon in Philadelphia on Monday."

"Does he know a lot about naval aviation?"

"He does," Jack said. "He knows more than I do."

"Then your problem is solved."

"I suppose it is."

Susan tilted her head.

"You don't sound very excited."

"Oh, I am," Jack said. "I'm very excited about using Bill as a source in the book."

"Then why the frown?" Susan asked.

Jack smiled.

"Am I frowning?"

"Yes. You are. Or at least you were."

"I guess it's a good thing we're not playing poker then," Jack said. "I would never be able to bluff my way through a bad hand."

"No. You wouldn't," Susan said. "Now tell me what's wrong."

Jack sighed.

"I'm not sure that anything is wrong. I'm just a little troubled by something Bill told me as I was leaving the luncheon."

"What's that?" Susan asked.

"Can I trust you to keep a secret?"

"No."

Jack laughed.

"I thought so."

"I'm kidding, Jack."

"I know you are."

"What did Bill tell you?" Susan asked.

Jack took a deep breath.

"He told me, in no uncertain terms, that Hitler is preparing for war. He said Germany has redeployed several Panzer divisions and other assets to its border with Poland."

"How did you respond?"

"I told him I didn't believe him," Jack said.

"You did?"

"Of course. I said there was no way Hitler would be so stupid or brazen. I said if he moved troops to the east, he would only invite a reciprocal move by Stalin."

Susan felt a knot form in her stomach.

"What did Bill say to that?"

"He agreed with me," Jack said. "He said Hitler would never act so provocatively unless he was certain the Russians would not respond in kind."

"So what are you saying?"

"I'm saying that a man I trust, a man I've known for twenty years, believes the Germans and the Russians are about to sign a non-aggression pact."

Susan recalled her argument with Amanda. She remembered that her daughter had mentioned a treaty called Molotov-Ribbentrop.

"What do *you* believe?" Susan asked.

Jack laughed.

"I think Bill Franks is henhouse crazy," Jack said. He sighed. "I also think he's right."

75: AMANDA

Monday, August 14, 1939

Amanda Peterson could read eyes like Boy Scouts could read signs on a trail. She could tell whether a boyfriend had cheated, a girlfriend had blabbed, or a coworker had lied simply by looking at their pupils, irises, and lids. Once, as a college freshman, she had forced a boyfriend to confess to infidelity by looking him in the eyes and reciting the lyrics of a song by the Eagles.

For twenty-two years she had been able to read her grandmother's eyes too. She had been able to tell whether she was mad, sad, or happy simply by looking at her peepers.

For the past ten days, however, she had not been able to read anything at all. When she looked at Elizabeth Campbell's eyes, she did not see anger, sadness, or joy but rather vast reservoirs of disinterest. She saw a woman who had given up on life.

Amanda pondered that change as she entered Room 220 at the Mercer County Hospital, glanced again at the eyes she could not read, and put a vase of fresh flowers on a table. She greeted Susan with a nod and then sat in a chair that had become her home away from home.

"How is she doing?" Amanda asked.

"She's doing all right," Susan said. "She asked for a glass of juice about a half hour ago. I guess that's something."

"I guess."

Amanda looked at her grandmother and watched her eyelids flutter and shut. She had hoped to say a few words to her but saw that the words would have to wait.

"Where did you go?" Susan asked.

"I went back to the house to pick up the mail," Amanda said.

"Did Mr. Postman leave anything good?"

321

"He did for me."

"Oh?"

Amanda reached into her purse.

"I found this in the box," Amanda said.

She handed Susan a postcard from Southampton, England. The front featured an image of an Edwardian couple strolling down a boardwalk. The back contained an August 3 postmark, a stamp bearing the likeness of George VI, and the handwriting of a homesick man.

Susan gave the sepia photograph on the front of the card a quick examination and then flipped to the back. She read the short message, smiled, and returned the card to its owner.

"He misses you," Susan said.

"I sure hope so," Amanda replied.

"He does."

Amanda settled in her chair, closed her eyes, and thought of the boy who had undoubtedly reached his destination. She wondered what had gone through his mind as he traveled to the Third Reich. She opened her eyes, held up the card, and read it again.

Dearest A: I miss you! I need your laugh and smile. So does England. People are gloomy. I will stay here a day and move on. Give my best to your family. Love, K

P.S. – I left two boxes in my closet. Please discard by August 30.

Amanda smiled as she pondered the message. She couldn't think of another man who could present his romantic, observant, thoughtful, and practical sides in less than fifty words.

She made a mental note to visit Kurt's place before August 30. If she did nothing else in the next sixteen days, she would clean out his apartment, prepare it for the next renter, and take care of any paperwork he had neglected in his rush to leave the country.

Amanda slipped the postcard back into her purse and smiled at Susan. She was happy she could once again talk to her mother about her boyfriend without getting into an argument.

Amanda snapped the purse shut, put the bag on the floor, and glanced again at Elizabeth. She saw that her fluttering eyes had fluttered again and this time remained in the ON position.

"Hi, Grams," Amanda said. "Are you awake?"

"What time is it?" Elizabeth asked.

"It's about two."

"Oh. Is it time for breakfast?"

"No, Grandma. It's not."

Elizabeth gazed at Amanda and then at Susan before resuming her favorite hospital activity. She laid her head back on her pillow, took a deep breath, and fixed her gaze on white perforated ceiling tiles that were as interesting as egg yolks.

Amanda glanced at her mother and saw that she too was on the verge of tears. She hated what strokes did to people and to the people who loved them. They didn't just strip the victims of their ability to function and reason. They stripped them of their souls.

Amanda looked around the room for a newspaper. She figured if she was going to spend another day in a hospital room waiting for a miracle to happen, she might as well put that time to good use. Perhaps she could learn something new about a world that was set to detonate.

"Did you buy a paper this morning?" Amanda asked.

"No," Susan said. "Do you want one?"

"Yeah. I do."

"Let me get one then."

"I can get it," Amanda said.

"No," Susan said. "Let me. I need to get up and stretch."

"OK."

Susan got up from her chair.

"What do you want?"

"Get the *Times*. I want to read about Hitler. I suspect he's up to no good."

Susan smiled.

"I suspect you're right. Do you want anything else?"

"No," Amanda said. "Just get me something to read."

"All right."

Susan gazed lovingly at Amanda and Elizabeth and then headed for the door. She walked out of the room a few seconds later and left her daughter and her mother to themselves.

Amanda closed her eyes and let her mind drift to the days and weeks again. She got as far as early September when she heard a knock on the door. She opened her eyes.

"Mom? Is that you?" Amanda asked.

"No. It's Ella. May I come in?"

"Of course," Amanda said. "Let me get the door."

Amanda got up from her chair and walked across the room. She reached the door just as the person on the other side slowly pushed it open.

"Have I come at a bad time?" Ella Wagner asked.

"No. You've come at a good time. Grandma is just waking up."

Amanda opened the door wide and took a closer look at her neighbor. She saw Ella holding a diaper bag in one arm and a fifteen-month-old tornado in the other.

"The nurse said we could visit now," Ella said.

"You can," Amanda replied. "Come on in."

Ella and Lizzie entered the room.

"Where is your mother?" Ella asked.

"She went to the newsstand to buy a paper. You just missed her."

"Will she be back soon?"

"She should be," Amanda said.

"I see. Do you mind if we sit?"

"Of course not. Take my seat."

Amanda raced to the side of the bed, retrieved her chair, and positioned it so that Ella could sit in it with a minimum of effort. She took the diaper bag from Ella, placed it on the floor, and helped the young mother into the chair.

"Thank you," Ella said.

"Is there anything else I can do?" Amanda asked.

"Yes," Ella replied. She laughed. "Take Lizzie off my hands. She's been extremely restless since we walked into the hospital."

"I would be happy to take her."

"Thank you."

Amanda took Lizzie from Ella and walked to an open spot in the middle of the room. She gave the toddler a hug and a kiss, rubbed noses with her, and held her high.

"Have you been 'restless,' Miss Lizzie?"

Amanda expected the World's Happiest Baby. She got the World's Grumpiest Toddler. Lizzie cried and fussed and tried to squirm her way out of Amanda's arms.

"I wasn't joking," Ella said.

"I guess not," Amanda said. She laughed. "Let me take Lizzie for a walk in the hallway. Then you can visit Elizabeth in peace. Is that OK?"

"Yes."

"All right then. We're off."

Amanda lowered Lizzie to the floor, grabbed her hand, and led her out of the room and into a hallway that stretched the length of the building. She released the toddler's hand the moment they reached the long corridor.

Amanda was sure that all Lizzie wanted to do was to run around and burn off excess energy. She was wrong. All she wanted to do was run back into Room 220.

Lizzie had no interest in running the length of the hospital. She had no interest in meeting the staff at two nursing stations or a nice old man who

324

waved to people from a wheelchair. She just wanted to return to the room she had left and presumably return to her mother.

Amanda fought the good fight for ten minutes. She didn't like giving in to someone who crapped her pants three times a day, but she did like doing favors. She liked giving Ella at least a few quality minutes with an elderly woman she had come to revere.

Amanda lifted Lizzie, kissed her on the nose, and carried her back to Room 220. When she opened the door, she found a scene that tugged at her heartstrings. Ella kneeled at Elizabeth's side, clasped her rosary beads in her folded hands, and prayed for the restoration of her friend's body, mind, and spirit.

"Would you like more time with her?" Amanda asked.

"No. I am finished," Ella said as she rose to her feet and made the sign of the cross.

Amanda tightened her hold on the squirming child and entered the room. She stopped when she saw the concern, unease, and fear in her neighbor's eyes.

"Did Elizabeth respond to you?" Amanda asked.

Ella shook her head.

"She did not even acknowledge me."

"Don't feel bad," Amanda said. "She doesn't acknowledge *us* half the time."

Lizzie tried to wriggle free.

"How did your walk go?" Ella asked.

"It didn't," Amanda replied. She stared at Lizzie when the toddler pushed away and started to cry. "Will you simmer down?"

"Perhaps we should go," Ella said. "I can come back later."

"Are you sure? My mom will be back any minute."

Ella nodded.

"I am sure. We should go."

"OK."

Ella pulled a greeting card out of the diaper bag, placed it on the table next to the bed, and lifted the bag from the floor. She pushed her chair against the wall and walked toward the door.

"Thank you for watching her," Ella said.

Amanda handed Lizzie to her mother.

"It was my pleasure. She's the best."

Amanda meant it too. Even at her worst, Lizzie Wagner was ten times more charming and appealing than the average one-year-old. She was simply having a bad afternoon brought on by the stifling heat, too much excitement, and perhaps not enough sleep.

She assumed Lizzie would calm down when she went to Ella and was mildly surprised when she did not. The girl was as fussy in her mother's arms as in her big sister's.

Amanda noticed that Lizzie fought off every effort to calm her down. She pounded her fists, spit out her pacifier, and resisted everything from soothing voices to gentle pats.

Then Amanda noticed something else. She noticed that Lizzie looked repeatedly at the bed. She seemed determined to visit the one person she had not yet seen.

"I will bring her by tomorrow when she is feeling better," Ella said. "I am sure she will be calmer. Give your mother my best."

Ella started to leave.

"Wait!" Amanda shouted.

Ella turned around.

"Is something wrong?"

"I'm not sure," Amanda said. "Do you mind if I hold Lizzie again?"

"Of course not."

Ella handed Lizzie to Amanda.

"Thank you."

"What do you have in mind?" Ella asked.

"You'll see."

Amanda did her best to get Lizzie under control and then carried her slowly toward the bed. She could feel a change in the baby's mood with each step. Lizzie stopped crying, kicking, and wiggling and started smiling, cooing, and gurgling. By the time Amanda reached the bed and placed Lizzie on Elizabeth's chest, the toddler was in a state of rapture.

"She is happy," Ella said.

"She's more than happy," Amanda said. "She's in nirvana."

Lizzie wasn't alone either.

Elizabeth too had responded to the contact. She had lifted her arms and brought them around her younger self. She had smiled and started to talk. She had laughed.

"Grandma? Grandma?" Amanda asked. "Are you feeling better?"

Elizabeth didn't answer at first with words. She smiled and laughed. She smiled and laughed when Lizzie cooed and gurgled and smiled and laughed when she didn't. She responded to pure love with pure joy and gave it back in spades.

"I can't believe this," Amanda said as tears began to flow. "You're getting better. You're coming back, Grams. You're coming back!"

"I never went away, dear," Elizabeth said.

Amanda took a deep breath as she tried to reconcile what she saw and heard with what she believed was possible. She was watching a recovery unfold in real time.

"Are you OK, Grandma? Are you OK?" Amanda asked.

Elizabeth laughed.

"I'm fine."

"Are you sure?"

Elizabeth smiled.

"I'm positive. Just leave me with my baby."

Amanda pulled a blanket over Elizabeth and Lizzie and then wrapped them in her arms. She held them like puzzle pieces that could never again be separated.

"Get my mom," Amanda said to Ella. "Please get my mom!"

"Are you sure?" Ella asked.

"I'm sure," Amanda replied. "I want her to see this."

"I already have," another woman said.

Amanda turned her head and looked at the open door for the first time in minutes. She saw her mother, cheeks streaked with tears, standing next to her smiling neighbor.

"I already have," Susan repeated.

76: SUSAN

Thursday, August 17, 1939

Susan read the typewritten sheet – the *final* typewritten sheet – one last time and scribbled a note in the margins. She wrote her initials at the top of the page, placed the sheet atop a small stack in the middle of the dining room table, and awaited her reward.

She expected Jack to nod or smile or perhaps even grin. She did not expect him to get up from his chair, walk to the other side of the table, and kiss her tenderly on the lips.

"Thank you," Jack said.

"You're welcome," Susan replied.

"I mean it. Thank you for sticking it out."

Susan laughed.

"Did you think I would leave you adrift, sailor?"

Jack smiled.

"I wasn't sure. I knew you had better things to do this summer than correct the manuscript of a three-hundred-page book."

Susan took Jack's hands.

"That's where you're wrong, Admiral Hicks. I *didn't* have better things to do."

"You're being kind."

"I'm being honest," Susan said. "It has been my pleasure to help you complete this work. I can't think of one thing I've done that's more important."

Jack laughed.

"I can."

"What's that?" Susan asked.

"You raised a wonderful daughter."

"You know what I mean."

"I do," Jack said. He kissed Susan's hands. "I do."

Susan smiled and shook her head as Jack returned to his seat. She wondered if it were even possible to admire anyone more than she admired this admiral, widower, author, and friend.

"So what's next?" Susan asked.

Jack folded his hands atop the table.

"I submit the manuscript to some publishers and wait."

"Do you think they will take it?"

Jack nodded.

"I know they will. Someone will," Jack said. "Two publishers have already contacted my agent. The First Lady apparently put in a good word when she made her rounds last month."

"It's nice to have friends in high places."

Jack sighed and gazed at Susan.

"It's nice to have friends in this *room*."

"Are you getting fresh, Admiral?"

Jack laughed.

"I'm getting something."

"Perhaps it's good then that there's a table between us," Susan said. She smiled. "I'd hate to think what might happen if there wasn't."

Jack blushed.

"I think it's time we talked about something else."

Susan giggled.

"I agree."

"How is your mother?" Jack asked.

"She's good and getting better. She had a breakthrough the other day."

"She did?"

Susan nodded.

"It seems all she needed was a little quality time with the neighbor girl," Susan said. "She's talking and eating and laughing now. She's laughing a lot."

"That's great news. Where is she now?"

"She's still at the hospital."

"Is she all right?" Jack asked.

"She's fine. She's just recovering. She'll be home on Monday."

"I'll be sure to stop by and say hello."

"You do that," Susan said. "I know she'd like to see you."

"Where is Amanda today?"

"She's at the hospital too. She's giving me a break."

"That was nice of her," Jack said.

"It was."

Jack gathered the papers on the table and brought them together in a tidy stack. He placed the stack inside a manila folder and then inserted the folder into a well-worn leather briefcase.

"Do you mind if I help myself to a glass of water?" Jack asked.

"Of course not," Susan said. "Let me get it."

"No. You sit still. I can manage."

Susan started to object but stopped when she heard a familiar sound. She heard someone step onto the front porch, open the squeaky mailbox door, and slam the door shut.

"OK. You get your water," Susan said. "I'll get my mail."

Susan got up from her chair, walked across the living room, and opened her front door to the sight of neighborhood kids having a water-balloon fight in the street. She watched as they made a mess of themselves and their surroundings but kept delightfully cool. She smiled when she remembered the many times she had beat the heat the same way as a girl.

Susan reached into the vertical mailbox and pulled out three letters. She waved to the kids, told them to watch out for cars, and then retreated to the cooler, drier confines of her house. She reached the dining room table just as her guest finished a glass of iced tea.

"The tea looked better," Jack said. He smiled. "I hope you don't mind."

Susan laughed.

"I don't mind. Amanda might though. She made it."

"It's delicious," Jack said. "What's in it?"

"Oh, I don't know. Mint. Ginger. Eye of newt."

Jack smiled.

"I'm sold. Tell Amanda I'll pay her to make more. It's perfect."

"I'll pass along your review," Susan said.

Susan reclaimed her seat and quickly scanned the mail. She found a bill from the hospital, a fundraising postcard from the Friends of Princeton, and a small letter from G.B. in Los Angeles, California. The letter was addressed to Elizabeth Campbell.

Susan sank in her chair. She could not imagine why Geoffrey Bell had written to Elizabeth unless Elizabeth had written to him. She tried to recall the specifics of a letter Bell had sent to all three women. One passage came to mind:

I am particularly concerned about Amanda's growing relationship with the son of Germany's military attaché. My research on the diplomat suggests that his family is about to undergo a serious transition — one in which allegiances and possibly friendships will be sorely tested.

"Is something wrong?" Jack asked. "You seem distracted."

"I am," Susan said.

"Can I help with anything?

"I don't know."

Susan sighed as she considered her options. Several questions hit her at once. Should she open someone else's mail? Should she open it now? Should she share the letter with Jack? Should she share the letter with *anyone*?

Susan pondered the matter for a minute and decided she couldn't wait. She had to know what Bell had written and had to know it now. She opened the letter and started reading.

Dear Elizabeth: I was dismayed to learn of your decision to withhold my last letter from your granddaughter. By ignoring my warnings, acting independently, and taking matters into your own hands, you may have put lives at risk. Please cease communications with the Schmidt family and return to Los Angeles immediately. Regards, Geoffrey Bell

"Susan?"

Jack's matter-of-fact voice snapped Susan out of a daze.

"Huh?"

"I asked you a question," Jack said.

"Yes?"

"I asked if I could help with anything. You said, 'I don't know.'"

"I was wrong," Susan said. "I do know."

"You know what?"

"I know you can't help. You can't help with this," Susan said. She sighed. "No one can."

77: ELIZABETH

Tuesday, August 22, 1939

Elizabeth looked at the reply to the reply to the letter she didn't show Amanda and shook her head. She had no words to justify her actions.

"I'm sorry. I should have leveled with you," Elizabeth said. "I should have leveled with both of you. I should have trusted your judgment."

"You made a mistake, Mom. So did I. So did Amanda," Susan said. "We have all acted in ways that were selfish, shortsighted, and even dangerous."

"Don't forget stupid," Amanda said. "Stupid deserves at least an honorable mention."

Susan laughed.

"You're right. We've been stupid too."

Elizabeth sipped her coffee and looked at her two favorite people. She regretted letting them down and vowed to do better in the future.

"What do you suggest going forward?" Elizabeth asked.

"I thought you'd never ask," Susan said. "I've given this a lot of thought and can think of at least three things we need to do."

"OK."

"The first thing we need to do is put all our cards on the table. I'm going to start by showing you the letters I've received from Professor Bell."

Elizabeth watched closely as Susan placed a stack of letters and postcards on the dining table and spread them out. She had seen most of them but not all.

"How many are there?" Amanda asked.

"Twenty," Susan answered.

Amanda picked up a letter, scanned it, and put it down. She looked at Elizabeth for a moment, as if trying to read her thoughts, and then returned to her mother.

"What if I don't have letters?"

"Then tell us about your conversations," Susan said. "If you think of something you told Kurt but haven't shared with us, then tell us. Even if you think it's unimportant, tell us."

"OK."

"That brings me to the second thing."

"What's that?" Elizabeth asked.

"We need to figure out what Professor Bell meant when he said your letter 'may have put lives at risk,'" Susan said. "I know Kurt and his family may be at some risk in Germany, but I have a feeling the professor was referring to someone else."

"Why didn't he tell us then?" Amanda asked. "Why wasn't he specific?"

"I don't know. He may not *know* who's at risk. Or maybe he doesn't want us to know."

"You sound like a conspiracy theorist, Mom. You sound like Grandma."

Susan smiled.

"Don't get carried away."

Elizabeth laughed.

"So what can we do?" Elizabeth asked.

"We can think," Susan said. "We can try to reach conclusions and, if necessary, act on them. I don't think any one of us wants to leave 1939 knowing we put others in harm's way."

Elizabeth lowered her eyes. She thought about the letter she had withheld from Amanda and wondered if the girl would have told Kurt less had she seen it.

"I think we can handle that," Elizabeth said. "What's the third thing we need to do?"

Susan sipped her coffee.

"We need to be honest about our intentions."

"What do you mean?"

"You know exactly what I mean, Mom. We've all formed deep friendships here. We may not want to end those friendships when the time comes."

"Are you saying we should end them now?" Elizabeth asked.

"No," Susan said. "I'm saying we should be forthright. If we're thinking about breaking one of Professor Bell's Ten Commandments, we should discuss it first. We owe it to each other."

"That's fair," Amanda said.

"Then let's start with you," Susan said. "What are your plans? What are your plans with Kurt, Heinrich, Johanna, and even Karl?"

"I already told you. I gave Kurt until September 10 to return. If he comes back to Princeton, I want to bring him to Los Angeles. I don't care what Professor Bell wrote. I'm waiting until at least the tenth. I'm not leaving now."

Elizabeth thought about the man who had sent them to the thirties. She wondered what he would think of all this plotting and planning. She knew the answer.

"I'm not asking you to leave now," Susan said. "No one is ready to leave now."

"Then what *are* you asking?"

"I'm asking you to tell me your plans. I want to know, for example, what you plan to do if Kurt returns with his parents or even his entire family. What will you do?"

"I don't know," Amanda said. "I haven't thought about it."

"Well, think about it. Think about it now," Susan said. "We can't bring people back with us unless we are prepared to take care of them. Do you want that responsibility?"

Amanda lowered her eyes.

"I don't know."

"That's my point, Amanda. You *have* to know. We all do," Susan said. "We have to think this through. We have to be prepared to make decisions when the time comes to leave. There's more to consider than your feelings for one young man. There's a lot more."

"I know," Amanda said.

Susan looked at Elizabeth.

"What about you, Mom?"

"What *about* me?" Elizabeth asked.

"What are your plans with your family?"

"I'm not planning to kidnap Lizzie!"

Amanda laughed.

"I know you're not," Susan said softly. She smiled. "At least I hope you're not."

"Then what are you getting at?" Elizabeth asked.

"I'll tell you. I'd like to know if you're planning something else. Do you intend to tell Erich and Ella who we are? Do you intend to invite them to come with us?"

Elizabeth looked at Susan with eyes that started to water.

"No," Elizabeth said. "When I say goodbye to them, I'll say goodbye for good. I don't want to mess with the past any more than I have."

Elizabeth admitted that the temptation to do otherwise was great. She wanted badly to tell her parents about a disobedient daughter, a family rift, and a car accident in 1962, but she knew she had no right to do so. She had an obligation to leave the past as she had found it.

"I think that's best," Susan said.

"What about you?" Elizabeth asked. "What about Jack? What are your plans with him?"

Susan smiled.

"I guess I'm in the worst position of all. Unlike you and Amanda, I haven't decided what to do with my special friend."

"Do you think Jack is going to propose?" Amanda asked.

Susan nodded.

"I'm sure of it."

"Then why don't you say yes? I wouldn't mind."

"Neither would I," Elizabeth said.

"I know you wouldn't," Susan said. "I appreciate the support too."

"Then what's the problem?" Amanda asked.

"The problem, honey, is that I haven't reconciled my past with my present. Nor have I placed a value on my happiness."

"What does that mean, Mom?"

Susan reached across the table and touched Amanda's arm.

"What it means is that, like you, I have to make a decision," Susan said. "I have to figure out my life. I have to choose a path."

78: AMANDA

Monday, August 28, 1939

Amanda knocked on the door twice. She didn't want to bother the manager or anyone else, but she knew she would have to bother someone in 1A to gain access to 10B. For the first time in months, Kurt Schmidt had locked his apartment.

She lowered a bag of cleaning supplies to the ground and knocked again. She knocked until she heard a man mumble an obscenity and something about patience.

A moment later, a middle-aged man sporting a five o'clock shadow, a beer belly, and a wife-beater undershirt opened the door. He looked at Amanda like his ship had come in.

"Who are you?"

"I'm Amanda Peterson. I'm here to collect a few things from Apartment 10B."

"That place is empty," the manager said.

"It isn't according to its tenant," Amanda replied. She pulled a postcard from the pocket of her frumpy housedress and handed it to the man. "Kurt Schmidt asked me to pick up some boxes. I'm here to get them."

The manager looked at the card and returned it.

"What's in the bag?"

"Cleaning supplies," Amanda said. "I figured I might as well clean the place while I'm here. I don't want Mr. Schmidt to lose his deposit."

The manager laughed.

"What are you? His dame?"

Amanda sighed.

"I'm a person who doesn't want to spend all morning standing in front of your door. Are you going to let me into the apartment or not?"

"Hold on a minute."

"OK."

The manager closed the door halfway and retreated into his lair. He returned a minute later with a set of keys, a broom, a dustpan, and a smirk that Amanda didn't like. He gave her the goods but kept the smirk.

"Bring back the keys when you're done," the manager said.

"What about the broom and the dustpan?" Amanda asked.

"Bring them too."

"All right."

"There's one more thing," the manager said.

"What's that?"

"Don't steal anything."

Amanda stared at the halfwit and forced a smile.

"I won't. I promise."

"Good."

The manager grunted, frowned, and shook his head. He gave the pretty cleaning lady one last look, closed the door, and returned to his cave.

Amanda laughed as she picked up the bag, turned around, and walked across a small parking lot to a building that contained the other half of the complex's twenty apartments. She couldn't believe the things people did for love. Then she reminded herself that Kurt Schmidt was worth it.

When she reached 10B, she opened the door, pushed her way in, and gazed upon a furnished living space she hadn't seen in weeks. She saw a soda bottle on a table and a wad of paper on the floor but few other signs of neglect. Kurt had done a fair job of cleaning up before packing his suitcase, shutting his door, and leaving Princeton for the most dangerous nation on earth.

Amanda walked to the kitchen and went to work. She swept the floor, emptied the garbage can, cleaned the sink, and wiped the counters, cabinets, and refrigerator. She cleaned most of the bathroom but drew the line at the toilet. She didn't have a toilet brush or a burning desire to clean something that the manager probably wouldn't notice anyway.

Amanda dusted the furniture in the living room, shook the drapes, and wiped spots and smudges wherever she found them. She kept it up until she was convinced that even the throwback in 1A would give his seal of approval.

Amanda placed the cleaning supplies, the broom, and the dustpan next to the front door and walked to the main attraction. She smiled when she considered the irony of entering her longtime boyfriend's bedroom for the very first time.

She opened the door and found two things she expected to see and one thing she didn't: a double bed, a dresser, and a roll-top desk with a lockable top. She ignored the furniture and walked straight to an open closet that faced the end of the bed.

Amanda peeked in the closet and saw the boxes on the floor. She carried both to the bed, lifted their tops, and inspected their contents. She found magazines in the first, stationery in the second, and nothing of interest in either. She could see why Kurt had wanted to discard them.

Amanda placed the smaller box atop the larger and started to lift them off the bed, but she stopped and released the boxes when she glanced at the roll-top desk. She stood up, pulled the keys out of her dress pocket, and walked to the desk.

She inserted the key in the keyhole, turned it until she heard a click, and then pushed the top open. She checked several small drawers and found them empty. Then she opened the large center drawer and found it stuffed with knickknacks and correspondence. She grabbed more than thirty letters, jumped up on the bed, and rested her back against the headboard.

Amanda needed only a minute to determine that the letters were keepers. They included a birthday greeting from Heinrich Schmidt, a supportive message from Johanna Schmidt, and a fragrant love letter from a University of Maryland coed named Deborah.

She sighed when she saw a note from Johanna that referenced her cancer and laughed when she discovered another perfumed plea from Debbie. She didn't sigh or laugh when she stumbled upon dozens of handwritten letters from Karl Schmidt. She sank.

Amanda quickly thumbed through the dates: 14 May 1937, 26 August 1937, 4 October 1937, 14 December 1937, 12 February 1938, 18 April 1938, 7 July 1938, 10 September 1938, and 22 November 1938. She then remembered what Kurt had told her on Valentine's Day.

"We haven't been close since he returned to Germany. I haven't spoken to my brother in two years. I haven't corresponded with him since May 6, 1937."

Amanda picked up a letter dated January 27, 1939, that referred to a Princeton girl and a February 2, 1939, offering that mentioned Amanda by name. Karl had known about his brother's girlfriend two months before meeting her.

Amanda moved on to four letters Karl had sent from New York in 1939. In the letters, written on April 10, April 25, May 4, and May 27, Karl drew attention to statements Amanda had made in Georgetown, the restaurant in Manhattan, and Kurt's apartment.

Three of the letters referred to comments by Kurt. All focused on his "pretty new friend with the curious mind." One raised questions about the Peterson family's "true background." In his correspondence of May 27,

Karl described his argument with Amanda in great detail. The letter triggered memories of Amanda's conversation with Kurt on the Harrison Street Bridge.

"Are you ever going to tell me what happened at the apartment?"
"Hasn't Karl filled you in?"
"No."

Amanda dropped the letters and lowered her hands to the bed. She tried her best to remain steady as waves of nausea, fueled by lies, swept through her body.

She examined the recent letters from Karl and saw more troubling details. Karl had reminded Kurt of "our common interests" on April 25 and "our unshakable bond as brothers" on May 4. On May 27, Karl Schmidt, Nazi party member, had advised Kurt to remain vigilant against those who would "undermine the family's position and standing."

Amanda tried to make sense of the correspondence but couldn't. She couldn't understand why Kurt had hid it in his room or kept it from her. She set Karl's letters aside and reexamined the ones from Heinrich and Johanna.

Heinrich had encouraged Kurt to work hard, make friends, and "integrate himself" as best he could in the Princeton community. In a letter written on September 10, 1938, the day Kurt began work at the Nassau Institute, Heinrich told Kurt to "learn as much as you can as fast as you can." He reminded Kurt that he may "never have an opportunity like this again."

Johanna, good, sweet Johanna, had been less circumspect. In her final message to Kurt, a letter sent from New York on June 5, 1939, she advised him to "keep a low profile," to be true to himself, and to "be cautious around those who might do us harm." She encouraged him to "keep up the fight," to "yield to no one," and to "remember the cause."

"Whatever you do, my dear son, always remember the cause."

Amanda sank as she came to grips with the magnitude of her mistake. She had told a Nazi spy about coming German defeats at El Alamein, Stalingrad, and Normandy and thus given the Nazis an opportunity to change their tactics. She had given Adolf Hitler the knowledge he needed to win World War II and alter the course of history.

She set aside the letters, closed her eyes, and asked herself how she could have been so reckless, naïve, and stupid. Then she remembered another letter and realized that she had more immediate matters to attend to.

"By ignoring my warnings, acting independently, and taking matters into your own hands, you may have put lives at risk. Please cease communications with the Schmidt family and return to Los Angeles immediately."

Professor Bell had wanted Amanda to see his letter of June 22 because he had been rightly concerned she might reveal something important. He had advised the time travelers to keep their mouths shut because he had fully understood the consequences of loose talk.

Amanda started to cry when she considered what she had done. She had put at risk not only the lives of countless strangers but also the lives of her own family.

The Nazis now knew of three time-traveling women who had priceless knowledge of future events. Amanda knew it was only a matter of time before they came for them.

79: SUSAN

Saturday, September 2, 1939

Susan sighed as she stared out a restaurant window and reviewed the most difficult week of her life. In the span of six days, she had comforted a guilt-ridden mother, consoled a despondent daughter, and confronted her own fears, concerns, and doubts about an important relationship, a looming departure, and a world at war.

She had assured Elizabeth and Amanda that they had not given Adolf Hitler the keys to victory or put their own lives at risk. She reminded both that Kurt Schmidt was just one man with a fantastic story and limited access to leaders who would probably not be receptive to predictions of military defeat the day after Germany had plowed into Poland.

Susan turned away from the window, glanced at a menu, and pondered a dozen culinary options described in French and English. She studied the menu until a retired naval officer entered the dining area, walked to their table for two, and returned to his chair.

"Are you feeling better?" Susan asked.

"I am," Jack said. "I guess I just had a case of the nerves."

Jack took a sip of red wine.

"Are you nervous about anything in particular?"

"I'm nervous about a lot of things."

Susan decided not to press the matter. She knew that Jack was nervous about everything from their relationship to his book to developments in Europe that had nearly everyone on edge.

"You look nice tonight," Susan said.

"So do you," Jack said. "You look good in that dress."

Susan couldn't disagree. She *did* look good in a backless red silk gown that seemingly flowed into the plush red carpet. She felt good too. She hadn't felt this good on a date since Bruce had taken her on a surprise trip to San Francisco on their twentieth anniversary.

"Do you need time to order?" Susan asked.

"No. I know what I want," Jack said. "I'm going to get the ratatouille and save the frog legs for another day."

Susan laughed.

"You're not very adventurous."

"I'm prudent," Jack said with a laugh. "I learned long ago to stick with the tried and true at ethnic restaurants. It makes for better eating and fewer trips to the bathroom."

"OK then. I won't push you. You've already made one trip."

The admiral smiled and sipped more wine.

"How is your mother?" Jack asked.

"She's doing great," Susan replied. "She's still a little weak, but she's getting stronger every day. She's lucky. Most people who suffer strokes are never the same."

"I'm glad to hear she's improving," Jack said. He put down his glass and gazed at Susan for several seconds. "Is Elizabeth looking forward to going home?"

"She is. She's looking forward to seeing her friends, resuming old routines, and doing the sorts of things she's done most of her life," Susan said. "She's ready for a change."

"Is Amanda also ready for a change?"

"I think so. She's had enough of Princeton. She's had enough of a lot of things."

"I figured as much," Jack said. "She seemed preoccupied and withdrawn when I spoke to her tonight. She barely said a word to me."

"Don't take it personally," Susan said. "She's still reeling from her breakup."

"Has she heard from Kurt Schmidt since he returned to Berlin?"

Susan shook her head.

"No. She hasn't."

"Is she thinking about his safety?" Jack asked.

"She's thinking about a lot of things. She fell in love with a boy from Germany, a boy who may someday take up arms against this country. That's a lot for anyone to bear."

"I agree."

Susan didn't add that the "boy," a twenty-three-year-old man, was also a suspected spy who had probably monitored Jack's own work and used his position at the Nassau Institute to gather information for the Third Reich. She saw nothing to gain by saying more.

"Let's talk about something pleasant," Susan said.

"All right," Jack replied.

"What's new with you?"

Jack smiled.

"I thought you'd never ask."

Susan brightened.

"Have you heard from a publisher?"

"I've heard from several people."

"Who?"

"Do you really want to know?"

"Yes! I want to know," Susan said.

"Tom Benson of Benson Press called Friday. He wants my book."

"That's wonderful."

"That's not all," Jack said.

"There's more?"

Jack nodded.

"Benson wants to move quickly. He wants to publish in December and start a book tour in January," Jack said. He sighed. "He offered me a five-figure advance."

Susan beamed.

"I'm so proud of you."

"I couldn't have done it without you."

"That's not true," Susan said. "All I did was strike your acronyms."

"You did more than that."

Susan laughed.

"You're right. I did."

Susan was tempted to demand back pay just to get Jack's reaction. She made a mental note to contact Benson Press in 2016. Benson had paid Jack more for a nonfiction book in 1939 than any publisher had paid her for a romance novel in the twenty-first century.

"I'm glad we agree," Jack said.

"So who else called you recently?" Susan asked.

Jack grinned.

"Think of a high-ranking official."

"Can't you just tell me?"

"No."

"I don't like guessing games."

"You'll like this one," Jack said. "Think of someone in the chain of command."

"I don't know. Was it the Secretary of War?"

"No. Try again."

Susan sighed and shook her head.

"You're testing my patience."

"Just guess."

"All right. All right," Susan said. "I'll guess, just this once, that it was the Secretary of the Navy. I know you know him. Did *he* call you this week?"

Jack nodded.

"He did. He called me this morning."

"That was nice."

Jack smiled.

"He called right after his boss did."

Susan's eyes grew wide.

"You're joking."

Jack laughed.

"I'm not. The president called me at ten thirty."

Susan rested her chin on her folded hands.

"Now I *am* impressed."

"I thought you would be," Jack said.

"What on earth did he want?"

"I'll tell you in a minute."

Jack paused as the waiter approached the table and took two orders. The admiral resumed the conversation after Susan requested beef bourguignon and he ordered his ratatouille.

"So why did the president call you?" Susan asked.

"He wants me to be a part of a public relations task force."

"What will it do?"

Jack took a breath.

"It will try to generate public support for several initiatives."

"I'm not sure I follow," Susan said.

Jack paused to look around the room. He continued the conversation when he was apparently convinced that eavesdroppers weren't among the dozens enjoying fatty French cuisine.

"The president is preparing the nation for war," Jack said in a hushed tone.

"What does that mean?"

"It means a lot of things," Jack said. "Roosevelt wants to bring back the draft. He wants to lend ships to Britain, strengthen our treaty commitments, and double the size of our navy. That's why he wants me on the team."

"It appears the First Lady put in a good word for you."

"It appears so."

"When does this task force begin?" Susan asked.

"We meet in October in D.C."

"You're going to be a big wheel, Jack Hicks. I can tell right now," Susan said. "You finally have all the things you've wanted."

Jack sighed.

"You're partly right," Jack said. "I have three books now. I have a job and a purpose. I have many of the things I want, but I don't have everything. I don't have what I want most."

Jack slipped out of his chair and dropped to a knee. He pulled a velvet box from a jacket pocket, opened the box, and presented it to the woman in the red silk dress.

"Oh, Jack," Susan said.

"I know I'm rushing things," Jack said. "That's why I don't need an answer now. I just want you to know where I stand before you do something crazy, like move back to Chicago."

Susan gazed at Jack, wiped her teary eyes, and then looked around the room. She noticed that the kneeling admiral had already gained an audience.

She took the box, pulled out the ring, and gave it a close inspection. She saw more than a diamond solitaire that resembled a ring Elizabeth Campbell had once left on a picnic table. She saw the hopes and dreams of a lonely man making one last grab at happiness.

"It's beautiful," Susan said. "I like it."

"You should," Jack said. "You pointed it out at a store in Asbury Park."

Susan laughed.

"I remember."

Jack gazed at his companion.

"I love you, Susan. I want to marry you and build a life with you."

Susan sighed.

"I know."

"Take all the time you need," Jack said.

"I will."

"I mean it. Don't rush. I'll wait as long as I have to."

"I know," Susan said. She leaned forward and kissed him softly. "I know."

80: AMANDA

Amanda settled into her plush theater seat, gazed at the spectacle on the big screen, and tried to escape. She wanted to let her mind drift to Oz or perhaps to a place where young women worried only about wicked witches and flying monkeys and not Nazi boyfriends, world wars, or the kind of problems that only a talkative time traveler could bring on herself.

She had imagined a different movie experience. Once upon a time, in March, to be exact, she had imagined watching *The Wizard of Oz* with her two best friends. She had imagined watching MGM's Dorothy Gale with *her* Dorothy Gale, having a few laughs at her expense, and then snuggling up to a young man she could take home to mother.

Amanda had sought a memorable evening in the company of friends but had instead found a forgettable afternoon in the company of strangers. She had come alone to the Palmer Square Playhouse to get away from the regret, guilt, and sadness that had haunted her for days.

Amanda looked again at the screen and wondered how she could have ever been so naïve. She wondered how she could have missed signs that even Susan and Elizabeth had picked up. Then she remembered that love was blind. It was Helen Keller, hooded, in a dark room. It was a condition that rendered people incapable of seeing more than they wanted to see.

She took comfort in at least a few things. She had a wonderful mother and grandmother who had smothered her with hugs after she had returned to the rental with Kurt's letters in hand. Each had withheld judgment. Both had assuaged her fears. They had done their best to put a happy face on a situation that seemed to grow more dire by the day.

Amanda did not doubt that she had at least made it possible for the Nazis to change history. She had provided them with information that was potentially priceless. She was less certain that they would actually do something with it.

She knew that Adolf Hitler had been notorious for ignoring sound advice from his more rational subordinates. Perhaps he would do the same if and when Kurt Schmidt was able to tell him what he had learned from a babbling fool from Princeton, New Jersey.

Amanda didn't care. She was reasonably sure the Nazis wouldn't come after her in the next few days or do something that might make a bad month even worse. She would travel to Los Angeles, step through Geoffrey Bell's magic tunnel, and hopefully return to a United States that still flew the Stars and Stripes and not a black swastika.

Amanda looked forward to leaving. She looked forward to starting her new job, reconnecting with old friends, and enjoying all of the creature comforts of the digital age.

She did *not* look forward to leaving Erich, Ella, and Lizzie, who had become a second family, or Dot, who had become a de facto sister, but she knew that leaving them was the price she had to pay to move on with her life. In the grand scheme of things, it was a small price.

Amanda did not envy the people she would leave behind. She could only imagine the struggles they would face in the coming six years. She wondered whether young men like Roy Maine, Ted Fiske, and Bill Green would survive the war. She had learned from Dot in July that Ted had joined the Marines and Bill had volunteered for the Navy. Both men had answered the call of duty even before their country had called for them.

Amanda did not envy her mother either. She felt great empathy for a woman who had less than a week to make the most important decision of *her* life.

Susan had told Elizabeth and Amanda about her big date when the family had gathered for breakfast Sunday morning. She had described Jack's proposal, shown them the ring, and updated them on the admiral's plans as an author and a member of a presidential task force. Then she had asked for their advice on a matter that would surely affect them all.

Elizabeth had encouraged Susan to accept the proposal. She said she didn't mind Susan bringing Jack into the family so long as she brought him into the family in 2016. She did not even want to consider the idea of remaining in the thirties.

Amanda had offered the same blessing with the same condition. She didn't care how her mother found happiness so long as she found it in the twenty-first century. She said she would welcome Jack Hicks as a stepfather even if it required a difficult emotional transition.

Amanda returned to the movie. She smiled when she saw Dorothy, the Scarecrow, the Tin Man, and the Cowardly Lion walk arm in arm down the Yellow Brick Road.

She smiled again when she scanned the audience and saw men, women, and children staring at the Technicolor screen like it was a magic portal to another world. She couldn't believe that the world had once been so naïve, innocent, and trusting. She wished there was a way she could capture the spirit in the theater and take it with her to the more cynical age that waited.

Amanda gave her personal troubles another moment of thought and then surrendered to her surroundings. She dug into her buttered popcorn, sipped her soda, and finished watching and enjoying one of the most beloved movies of all time.

She exited the dark auditorium an hour later, fought her way through a crowded lobby, and stepped into a bright September afternoon. She embraced the daylight and a new mood.

Amanda still felt a little blue about making mistakes, losing Kurt, and disappointing others, but she no longer felt hopeless or directionless. She had new resolve and new purpose.

She thought about that resolve and purpose as she left Palmer Square and started toward Mercer Street, the rental, and her family. It was time, she thought, to stop thinking about the past and start thinking about the future. She picked up her pace and smiled.

81: SUSAN

Friday, September 8, 1939

Y ou're a time traveler?" Jack asked.

Susan nodded.

"We all are. We're from the future. We walked into a magic tunnel in 2016 and walked out in 1938. A professor from Los Angeles, a man who discovered a way to travel through time, sent us here. We will return to California and the future next week."

Jack sat up on the campus bench he shared with Susan, turned to his right, and looked at his friend like she had just declared the world to be flat. He smiled and shook his head.

"It's not April Fools' Day, Susan."

Susan smiled sadly.

"I'm not fooling."

Jack's smile faded. "I can think of many reasons why I shouldn't believe you. Give me one why I should."

"All right."

Susan opened her purse, dug through crumpled receipts, hard candies, and cosmetics, and pulled out a plastic Illinois driver's license. She handed it to her companion.

"What's this?" Jack asked.

"It's my driver's license," Susan said. "Note the birth date."

"You were born in 1967?"

Susan nodded.

"Technically speaking, I'm not even a twinkle in my father's eye."

"You're here though."

"I am," Susan said. "So are my mothers."

"Mothers?"

"You've met both. One is Elizabeth Campbell. The other is Lizzie Wagner. They are the same person, separated by seventy-eight years."

"You can't be serious," Jack said.

"I'm completely serious. We came to Princeton last fall so that Elizabeth could meet Erich, Ella, and Lizzie and be a part of their lives for several months."

"What if I told you I was still skeptical?" Jack asked. "What if I didn't accept this license of yours as proof?"

"Then I would show you some other things."

Susan reached into her purse and retrieved a 1977 Eisenhower dollar, a 2000 Kennedy half-dollar, and a 2016 Roosevelt dime. She gave each to the admiral.

"These are American coins," Jack said.

"They are," Susan replied. "Do you see anything interesting?"

Jack examined the coins and closed his eyes.

"The dates are all from the future."

"Do you notice anything else?"

"Roosevelt is on the dime," Jack said. "We don't put people on coins unless …"

"Unless they are dead. I know."

"This is fantastic."

"Tell me about it," Susan said.

Jack inspected the coins again.

"The man on the dollar also looks familiar. He looks like a young Army officer I met once in the Philippines."

"He'll be a general soon," Susan said. "His name is Dwight Eisenhower."

"What about the man on the fifty-cent piece?"

"You don't know him. He's not important yet."

"He will be though," Jack said. "Is that what you're saying?"

Susan took Jack's hand.

"That's what I'm saying. Each of these men is or will be very important."

Jack smiled.

"I don't know what to believe. My head tells me you're pulling my leg and that you had each of these items custom made for that purpose," Jack said. "My heart tells me something else. It tells me that this is not a joke and that you are doing this for a reason."

Susan looked at Jack with moist eyes.

"I am."

"Please elaborate."

"I didn't intend to bring my license or the coins. The professor asked us not to bring any items from the future, but I brought them anyway. I knew I might need them someday to prove to someone that I was who I said I was," Susan said. "As it turns out, they served another purpose."

"I don't understand."

"Then let me explain. I did two things before deciding whether to accept your proposal. The first was that I told Elizabeth and Amanda what you had done and asked them for their blessing."

"Did they give it?" Jack asked.

"They did. They both like you, Jack. They insisted only that you come with us. They do not want to remain in 1939."

"I think I see where you're going."

"There's more to it," Susan said.

"OK."

"The second thing I did was draw up a list. I wrote down the reasons I should marry you and the reasons I shouldn't. As much as I love you, I wanted to say yes for the right reasons."

"Did the cons outweigh the pros?"

"No. It was just the opposite. It wasn't even close," Susan said. "I found about a dozen reasons to say yes and only two to say no."

"Then why are you crying?" Jack asked.

"I'm crying because the reasons to say no are the most important reasons of all."

Jack sighed.

"What are they?"

Susan paused to gather her strength.

"The first pertains to the coins. When I dug the coins out of my purse this morning, I noticed something about them. Each of the men pictured on the coins played an important role in the war that just broke out in Europe, a war that will eventually involve the United States."

"What does that have to do with me?" Jack asked.

Susan took a breath. "It has *everything* to do with you. Like the men on the coins, you are going to play an important role in defeating the countries that want to crush our liberty and freedom."

"You're overstating things."

"No. I'm not. If anything, I'm understating them. You have a book that is going to sway public opinion at a time it needs to be swayed. You have been asked by President Roosevelt himself to serve our country in an important capacity. I'm sure you'll be asked again."

"But . . ."

"Let me finish," Susan said. She collected herself. "I can't in good conscience keep you from your destiny. Even if I were able to persuade you

351

to join us, I could never feel good knowing that my selfishness led to the deaths of others or even, God forbid, America's defeat."

Susan turned away as the floodgates opened. She did not want to see the hurt on Jack's face any more than she wanted him to see her anguish.

"Do I even get a say in this?" Jack asked.

"Of course you do."

"Then let me tell you what I think. I think I'm the best qualified to determine whether or not my services are indispensable," Jack said. "There are many military men capable of serving this country effectively in a time of war, but there is only one, to my knowledge, who is capable of making you happy. I love you, Susan, and want to marry you. If that means giving up all that I have here and following you to the future, then I'm willing to do it. I don't want to lose you."

Susan looked at Jack and tried to hold his gaze. She scolded herself for even thinking she could walk away from this man and not leave a mess behind.

"I know you don't," Susan said.

"Then give me a chance."

"I can't."

"Why?" Jack asked. "We can be happy together."

Susan wiped her eyes and shook her head.

"We can't," Susan said. "We can't because I'm not ready to marry again."

"I don't understand."

Susan tightened her hold on Jack's hand.

"I know. I don't expect you to understand either. Just believe me when I tell you that it has nothing to do with you. I love you, Jack. You're a kind, decent, honorable man who deserves the best. I am flattered that you love me. I'm honored that you want to marry me and build a life with me, but I can't accept your proposal. I'm sorry."

Jack withdrew his hand and wiped a single tear from his cheek.

"Is this it then?"

Susan nodded. She reached into a pocket, pulled out a velvet box, and handed the box and the ring to a man she would never forget. She leaned forward and kissed him gently on the lips.

"Goodbye, Jack Hicks. Remember me always."

Susan got up from the bench, took one last look at the broken-hearted admiral, and then walked away. She walked slowly and then rapidly across the campus toward a quiet street, a nondescript building, and an unlikely appointment with a man she had never met. She had made The Decision. The question now was whether she could live with it.

82: ELIZABETH

Saturday, September 9, 1939

The long goodbye began with a barbecue in back and progressed through the house toward the front. Erich Wagner wished Amanda good luck with her future endeavors. Dot Gale hugged Lizzie. Ella Wagner asked Susan to write when she returned to Chicago.

Elizabeth didn't even pretend that she would ever see her neighbors again. She knew that she wouldn't and didn't want to say anything that might leave a false impression.

That didn't make the parting any less difficult. There was no easy way to say a final so long to your parents or to an adorable child who had added at least ten years to your life.

Elizabeth stepped past Erich and Roy Maine, who conversed in the living room, and followed Ella out the front door of the rental. The old woman sensed, correctly, that Ella wanted to speak privately before crossing Mercer Street and returning to her home.

"I gather you want to say something," Elizabeth said.

"I do. I want to ask about Susan," Ella replied. "How is she doing?"

Elizabeth guided Ella away from the house. They walked across the front yard until they reached a shady spot under an oak tree that lent itself to private conversations.

"She's not doing well," Elizabeth said.

"I suspected as much."

"How much do you know about yesterday?"

"I know a little," Ella said. "Amanda told me that Susan met with Admiral Hicks and turned down his proposal of marriage. She said they parted for the last time."

"Then you know plenty," Elizabeth said.

"Why did she turn him down?"

353

"She did for reasons she has decided not to share."

Elizabeth tried to mask her lie. She knew damn well why Susan had spurned the finest man she had ever known, but she saw nothing to gain by sharing it now. She wanted a clean exit from a time, a place, and a family that would do just fine without her.

"It is such a shame," Ella said. "They seemed like a perfect couple."

"I agree."

Elizabeth turned her head when Susan, Erich, and Lizzie emerged from the house. She watched Susan maintain a happy face as she talked to her future grandfather and a toddler mother she had come to adore. Elizabeth wallowed in pleasant thoughts until Ella restarted their conversation.

"What is next for your family?" Ella asked.

Elizabeth sighed.

"We pack our bags tonight. We depart tomorrow."

"Are you still taking the train?"

"We are," Elizabeth said. "It leaves at two."

"When will you arrive?"

"We should get to Chicago by Tuesday."

"Are you sure you don't want to take your car?" Ella asked.

"I'm sure."

"Are you sure you don't want to *keep* your car?"

"I'm positive."

"We could sell it for you and send you the money."

"We don't need the money," Elizabeth said. "You and Erich, on the other hand, will someday need a larger car. We want you to have it. Please think of it as a going-away present."

Ella laughed.

"*You* are the one who is going away."

Elizabeth smiled.

"Don't complicate this by reminding me of the rules of etiquette."

Ella laughed again.

"OK. I won't," Ella said. She smiled. "I will miss you."

"I'll miss you too."

The two women embraced. They separated just as Erich said goodbye to Susan and carried Lizzie to the tree on the edge of the lawn.

"Are you two hiding from me?" Erich asked.

"No," Ella said. "We are just discussing matters that don't require your input."

Erich laughed.

"Then I see I was wise to keep my distance."

Elizabeth acknowledged Erich's light comment with a nod and then smiled at the brightest star in the galaxy. Lizzie had lost none of her luster during the course of the evening.

"Do you mind if I hold her one more time?" Elizabeth asked.

"Of course not," Erich said.

Elizabeth held out her arms as Erich lifted Lizzie from his shoulders. She took the child from her father, gave her a hug, and then held her out so she could see her face.

"It looks like this is it, Little One."

"Nana," Lizzie said.

Elizabeth stared at Ella.

"Did she just say what I thought she said?"

"She did," Ella replied. "She has been saying it all week."

Elizabeth embraced the child again and held her close as tears rolled down her cheeks. For the first time in days, she seriously considered staying in Princeton.

"This is hard," Elizabeth said. She sighed and wiped her eyes. "This is much harder than I thought it would be."

Ella stepped forward and placed a hand on Elizabeth's shoulder. Like the seventy-nine-year-old holding her daughter, she fought a losing battle with watery eyes.

"It is hard because you love her," Ella said.

"I do," Elizabeth replied. "I *do*."

"She loves you as well. Sometimes I think she loves you more than she loves me."

"I doubt that."

"I don't," Ella said. She withdrew her hand and stepped back. "You two share something special. I cannot explain it, but I can see it. You have a bond that is as real and as strong as any between a mother and a child."

Elizabeth nodded at Ella and then returned her attention to a little girl who smiled, giggled, and reached out to touch her nose like it was the most interesting thing in town. She would miss seeing herself discover the world at this tender age. She would miss a lot of things.

"Thank you," Elizabeth said to Ella. "Thank you for sharing this wonderful child with me. You have both made an old woman very happy."

"You're welcome," Ella said.

Elizabeth hugged Lizzie one last time. She held her closely for nearly a minute, kissed her forehead, and then reluctantly returned her to her mother. She gazed at the child for another moment, waved to her, and then turned to the man who was her father.

"Goodbye," Elizabeth said. She gave Erich a hug. "Take care of yourself."

"I will," Erich said.

"Take care of your wife and child too. I will know if you don't."

Erich chuckled.

"I suspect that you will," Erich said. "Take care of yourself as well."

"I will. I will for my own sake," Elizabeth said. She laughed. "The last thing I want to do is see the inside of another hospital anytime soon."

"Will we see you again?" Ella asked.

Elizabeth smiled as she thought of all the ways she could answer the question. She looked away for a moment, pondered a reply, and then returned to her mother.

"You will. That is one thing I can promise."

"That's good," Ella said. "I want to see you again."

Elizabeth gazed a final time at the Wagner family, took a mental snapshot, and stored it away in her mind. She did not want to forget this moment.

"I have something to give you before you go," Elizabeth said.

"Oh? What?" Ella asked.

"I guess you could call it my going-away present for Lizzie."

Elizabeth reached into her dress pocket and pulled out an unsealed envelope. She waved it in front of Lizzie like a lottery ticket, waited for her to squeal, and then handed it to Erich.

"What is this?" Erich asked.

"Open it."

Erich did as requested. He reached into the envelope and pulled out several black-and-white photographs from Lizzie's birthday party and a one-hundred-dollar bill.

"These are lovely photos," Erich said.

"I thought you would like them," Elizabeth replied.

"What is the money for?"

"The money is for Lizzie. I want you to open a new savings account for her on Monday and not spend a dime until she is at least twelve years old."

"OK."

"I want you to wait until she is twelve because by that time she will have developed her own interests and preferences. She will know who she is."

"I see," Erich said. "So you want Lizzie to decide how the money is spent?"

Elizabeth nodded.

"I do. Tell her that her Nana Elizabeth once left her some money because she recognized her potential at an early age."

"All right. I will do that."

Elizabeth paused to catch her breath.

"Let her play tennis, Erich. Let her play golf," Elizabeth said. "Let her be the tuba player we know she can be."

"I will," Erich said.

Elizabeth looked at Erich's wife.

"Ella?"

"I will too. I promise," Ella said. She wiped a tear and laughed. "Do you have any more sage advice for two imperfect and inexperienced parents?"

Elizabeth smiled.

"As a matter of fact, I do."

"And what is that?" Ella asked.

Elizabeth sighed.

"Always love your daughter. No matter what Lizzie says or does as a child or as a woman, love her and support her as much as you do now. She will do things that will make you sad and angry and crazy, but don't think it's because she doesn't love you. She does. She *does*."

"Thank you," Ella said. She smiled. "Thank you for your kindness and wisdom."

Elizabeth nodded but did not speak right away. She instead gazed lovingly at her mother until the sound of a passing car snapped her out of a daydream.

"I guess this is it," Elizabeth finally said.

"I guess it is," Ella replied.

Elizabeth reached out, put her hand on Lizzie's cheek, and kept it there until the girl smiled. She withdrew her hand, stepped back, and blew the toddler a kiss. She laughed when the child responded in kind. She waved to Lizzie with her fingers and then looked at her parents.

"It has been a pleasure to know you," Elizabeth said. "I love you all."

Elizabeth forced a smile for the neighbors' consumption, took a deep breath, and then turned around. She reentered the house, walked straight to her room, and fell on her bed. She waited only long enough to take stock of what she had done and then had the cry of a lifetime.

83: AMANDA

Amanda grabbed a soda from the refrigerator and walked across the kitchen toward a door that led to the backyard. She stopped when she saw someone race through the hallway and vanish inside Elizabeth Campbell's bedroom.

"Grandma?"

Amanda waited for a reply. When she didn't get one, she walked slowly to the bedroom door, pressed her ear against the thin wooden barrier, and listened for something that might explain why Elizabeth had run into her room. She winced when she heard sobs.

"Grandma? Are you all right?"

"I'm fine," Elizabeth said. "I just need time alone."

"Are you sure?" Amanda asked.

"I'm sure."

Amanda resisted the temptation to open the door and returned to the kitchen. She knew that her grandmother was upset and knew why. She didn't need a doctorate in psychology to know that she was mourning the loss of some very special friends.

She could relate and knew her mother could relate as well. She had been the first to comfort Susan Peterson after she had come home and announced that she would not marry Jack Hicks.

Amanda exited the kitchen, descended three steps, and walked into the backyard. She expected to find two people standing near a folding table and a barbecue grill but found only the table and the grill. Roy Maine and Dorothy Gale Maine had disappeared.

Amanda called out to her friends. She heard crickets reply. Then she heard a laugh emanate from the front of the rental and decided to follow it. She walked around the side of the house and then around the front until she ran into her party of two.

"There you are," Amanda said. "Where did you go?"

358

"We walked to the front yard," Dot said.

Amanda looked at Roy.

"How do you put up with her?"

"I drink a lot," Roy said.

Amanda laughed.

"You sound like a newlywed."

Amanda handed Roy the soda bottle.

"Here's your cola, Roy. There are more in the fridge if you want them."

"I think this will do," Roy said. "Thanks."

"You're welcome."

Amanda watched with sadness as Erich, Ella, and Lizzie walked across the street. She waved to them when they reached the front door and turned around.

"It looks like the party is breaking up," Dot said.

Amanda sighed.

"The party broke up days ago."

"What do you mean?" Dot asked.

"I mean we've been saying goodbye to people for more than a week," Amanda said. "Dinner tonight was sort of a curtain call."

Amanda and Dot exchanged knowing frowns. Each turned toward the rental when the front door closed. Susan had stepped inside the house.

"How is your mom doing?" Dot asked. "She seems really depressed."

"She is. She hasn't been the same since yesterday."

"I still don't get why she dumped the admiral."

"It's complicated," Amanda said. "It's very complicated."

"It must be."

Amanda didn't even consider explaining the situation. *She* didn't understand it. She had been as surprised as anyone when her mother had come home, in tears, on Friday afternoon and announced that she was leaving Jack Hicks for good.

"What about you and Kurt?" Dot asked.

"What about us?"

"Are you really finished?"

Amanda nodded.

"We're really finished."

Dot frowned.

"He must have done something truly awful."

"Let's talk about something else," Amanda said. "Let's talk about your trip. Are you two still planning to get your kicks on Route 66?"

Dot smiled.

"Can you repeat that in English?"

"Never mind," Amanda said. "I'm just thinking of a song that hasn't been recorded yet."

"You're acting strangely again."

"That's why you like me."

"It is!" Dot said.

Amanda laughed.

"Let me rephrase my question. Are you and this handsome lieutenant planning to drive on the stretch of asphalt that connects Chicago and Los Angeles?"

"We are," Dot said. "I'm so excited too. I've heard so much about it."

"When are you leaving?" Amanda asked.

"That depends," Roy said. He chuckled. "If Dot doesn't fix her hair in the morning, we'll leave at six. If she does, we'll leave next Friday."

Dot elbowed Roy in the side.

"You're not being helpful."

"You two are hilarious," Amanda said. "You've been married eleven weeks and yet you act like you've been married eleven years."

"Bickering is a sign of a healthy relationship," Dot said smugly.

"Did you read that in *Vogue*?"

"No. I read it on a restroom wall."

Amanda laughed.

"Then you can take it as gospel."

Dot lifted her nose.

"I will."

Amanda gazed at her friends.

"What will you do when you get to Los Angeles?"

Dot sighed.

"We're going to pack."

"You're going to what?" Amanda asked.

"We're going to pack our bags. Roy has new orders. He received them yesterday. He's been reassigned to Hickam Field," Dot said. She grinned. "We're moving to Hawaii in October."

Amanda's eyes lit up.

"Oh, Dot, that's wonderful! I'm so happy for you."

"I'm happy for me too."

Both women laughed.

"What will you do there, Roy?" Amanda asked.

"I'll train pilots," Roy said. "I'll train pilots and shuffle papers."

"That's great. Congratulations on your assignment."

"Thank you."

Amanda looked at Dot.

"What about you? What will you do besides lie on the beach?"

Dot smiled softly.

"I'm glad you asked. I have new orders too."

Dot patted her stomach.

"Are you putting me on?" Amanda asked.

Dot beamed.

"No. I'm not. I'm serious for once. I'm due in March."

Amanda hugged her friend.

"No wonder you've been smiling all night. You two are going to have a great time," Amanda said. She sighed. "You're going to have a great *life*."

"I hope so," Dot said.

"This makes my week."

"I thought it might."

"We should go out and celebrate," Amanda said.

"We should, but I think I'll pass tonight," Dot said. "Roy wasn't kidding about the trip. We really do plan to leave at six in the morning."

"I understand."

"I know. We can celebrate in Chicago. Doesn't your train leave tomorrow?"

"It does," Amanda said.

Dot tilted her head.

"Then why are you frowning?"

Amanda sighed. The last thing she wanted to do was explain why she couldn't reunite with her best friend in her hometown in a few days.

"I'm frowning because we're not going to Chicago."

"You're not?" Dot asked. "I thought you lived there."

"I used to live there. I lived there for many years."

"I don't understand. Where are you going then?"

"I'm going to a place that's a really long ways away," Amanda said.

"You're not going to tell me, are you?" Dot asked.

Amanda shook her head as her eyes started to water.

"No."

Dot sank.

"I'm not going to see you again, am I?"

Amanda shook her head a second time. She wiped a tear.

"No."

Dot turned away as tears filled her own eyes.

"Well, that just stinks."

"I know," Amanda said.

"Look at me," Dot said. "You've reduced me to a blubbering mess."

Amanda laughed through her tears.

"I'm sorry. I didn't mean to."

"Give me a hug," Dot said.

"All right."

Amanda gave Dot a long, soft embrace. She felt her friend tremble.

A few seconds later, Dot pulled back, studied Amanda's face, and shook her head. She smiled sadly, leaned forward, and handed out a hug of her own.

"I love you, Amanda," Dot whispered.

"Ditto."

"I mean it. You're the best friend I've ever had."

"Ditto again," Amanda said.

The two women separated. They smiled and stared at each other with watery eyes until Roy faked a cough and interrupted.

"Can I get in on this love fest?" Roy asked.

The time traveler laughed.

"Of course," Amanda said. She hugged Roy. "Take care of my buddy."

"I will," Roy said.

Amanda gazed again at Dot.

"I should let you go."

"I suppose," Dot said.

Amanda took her best friend's hand.

"Have an awesome life, Dot," Amanda said. She sighed. "Find yourself a parachute and take some leaps. I'll be waiting for you at the bottom."

Amanda released Dot's hand and stepped back.

"Goodbye."

84: AMANDA

Sunday, September 10, 1939

If there was one thing Amanda Peterson had learned about Princeton students, it was that they liked bargains. Never mind that many came from some of the wealthiest families in the United States. They liked bargains. So when she placed an ad in the paper announcing that a family on Mercer Street was selling ten-month-old beds, tables, sofas, chairs, and kitchenware at fire-sale prices, she knew she would get a positive response.

Amanda waved as two bargain hunters, physics students named Todd and Nelson, carried her bed, the last piece of furniture in the house, out the front door. She opened a shoebox, grabbed a stack of assorted bills, and walked into a barren kitchen just as her mother set aside a broom.

"That's it," Amanda said. "I sold the last bed."

"Where's the money?" Susan asked.

Amanda lifted her hand and displayed the proceeds from the moving sale.

"It's right here. Take it."

She handed the cash to her mother.

"How much did we make?" Susan asked.

"We made at least a hundred dollars," Amanda said.

"That's good. We'll need every one."

"Are we cutting it that close?"

Susan nodded.

"I have fifty dollars in my purse. That's all we had left in our savings account."

"Then I guess it's a good thing we're leaving," Amanda said.

"I guess it is."

Amanda looked at her mother and saw a shell of a woman. Susan Peterson had said little and done even less since breaking up with Jack

363

Hicks. She had wandered around the rental house all weekend like a lovesick zombie, a person who had forgotten simply how to function.

"Are you all right?" Amanda asked.

"I'm all right," Susan said. "I just needed a couple of days to get my bearings."

"You just seem so sad."

"I am sad, honey. I *am* sad."

"Then why did you break up with Jack?" Amanda asked.

"I did it because I thought it was the right thing to do," Susan replied.

"Making yourself miserable is rarely the right thing to do."

Susan smiled sadly.

"I suppose not."

"You can still accept his proposal, Mom. It's not too late."

Susan reached forward and cradled Amanda's face. She gently pushed back her hair and gazed lovingly at a daughter who had grown much wiser in the past year.

"It is for me," Susan said. "Someday I'll tell you why I did what I did. In the meantime, let's get ready to go. We still have a long trip ahead of us."

"OK," Amanda said. "What do you want me to do?"

"Take all the suitcases out to the front lawn. The cab driver will come to pick us up in about twenty minutes."

"All right. I'll be out front."

Amanda walked out of the kitchen and dining area and into the living room. She grabbed two bags, carried them out the front door, and placed them on the lawn next to the curb.

She repeated the process two more times. When she was done, she pulled out three of the suitcases, stacked them on top of each other, and made a chair. She figured that if she was going to sit and wait for a cab, then she might as well make herself comfortable.

Amanda gazed across the street at the house she considered a second home. She didn't see any activity through the windows, but she didn't expect to. She knew that Erich, Ella, and Lizzie had gone to Mass and wouldn't return until at least one or two. They usually spent most of their Sundays at church or at some church-related function.

She already missed the family. She missed Lizzie most of all. The bubbly toddler was the best sales pitch for motherhood she had ever seen.

Amanda looked to her right, toward the south, and gazed at a block that seemed unusually quiet and peaceful even for a Sunday morning. She wondered what Mercer Street would look like in a few years. She knew it was only a matter of time before a world war and a postwar boom transformed this tranquil neighborhood.

Then Amanda looked to her left, toward the campus, and saw a ghost. Blond, handsome, and six feet tall, he walked with the gait of a man she had once loved, a man who had broken her heart and betrayed his adopted country. She stared at the ghost and froze as he approached a house she had thought he would never see again.

"Stay away from me," Amanda said. "Don't come any closer."

"What's the matter?" Kurt Schmidt asked. "Don't you want to see me?"

Amanda flew off her suitcase chair.

"No! I don't. I don't want to see you!"

"Why?"

"Why? *Why?* I'll tell you why," Amanda said. "I don't want to see you because you're a Nazi spy, Mr. Schmidt, and a liar. You're an enemy to my country and a vile human being."

"I don't know what you're talking about."

"You don't, huh? Well, I'll show you."

Amanda returned to the suitcases. As she opened the bag on top, she glanced at the house and saw her family standing in the doorway. Susan and Elizabeth had no doubt heard the shouting.

Amanda tore through the suitcase and threw clothes and other belongings on the lawn until she found a large manila envelope. The envelope contained dozens of letters – handwritten reminders that even kind, courteous, soft-spoken men could not be trusted.

Amanda opened the envelope and retrieved a few letters. She looked again at Susan and Elizabeth, noted their troubled expressions, and turned to face Hitler's spawn. She waved the letters in his face.

"You see these, mister? I found them in your bedroom," Amanda said. "Yeah, that's right. I found more than boxes in the closet. I found proof that you've been a very busy boy."

"I can explain," Kurt said.

"You can explain? Really? Can you explain your lies?"

"I didn't lie to you, Amanda."

"Oh, yes, you did," Amanda said. "You said you hadn't corresponded with Karl in two years. Well, I have a dozen letters that say otherwise."

"They mean nothing."

"Is that why you locked them in your desk? People don't hide things that mean nothing, Kurt. They also don't lie about 'unshakable bonds' with their Nazi brothers or conversations they insist they didn't have. You said you didn't know the specifics of my encounter with Karl, but he wrote to you and filled you in on every detail. He wrote to you three days before you talked to me on the bridge. Are you saying you didn't know about the letter?"

"Yes," Kurt said forcefully.

"You're lying," Amanda said. "I also read the letters from your father. You want to tell me what your dad meant when he said you should 'integrate yourself' in the community and 'learn as much as you can as fast as you can'? You sought the job at the Nassau Institute because you knew it would give you access to materials you couldn't find elsewhere. You knew you would have contact with people doing sensitive research, people who *trusted* you."

"Don't do this, Amanda."

"Don't do what? Expose you for what you are?" Amanda asked. She watched Kurt as he glanced at Susan and Elizabeth. "Don't mind them. They know. They know everything. They know how you used me and others to pursue a sick agenda."

"I did none of that," Kurt said. "I did not betray you."

Amanda sighed.

"You did though. So did your dad. So did your mom. I think her betrayal hurt worst of all. I thought so much of her. I loved her. But that was before I read her advice to you. Did you keep a 'low profile,' Kurt? Were you 'cautious' around those who might do your family harm? Did you honor your mother and your Fuehrer by keeping up the fight, yielding to no one, and remembering 'the cause'? Yeah, I read that too. I read all of it. I only wish I could tell your mother to her face how much she disappointed me."

"You can't," Kurt said. "She's dead."

"What do you mean she's dead?"

Kurt looked at Amanda with the solemn eyes of someone who had survived a hundred trials. His hollow cheeks told a story of deprivation Amanda had not noticed in her initial rage.

"She died from her cancer last month," Kurt said.

"Then tell your dad," Amanda said curtly. "Tell him how much he hurt me."

"I can't. He's dead too."

"Karl?"

"They are all dead, Amanda. They died supporting things you hold dear."

Amanda felt her hurt-fueled anger subside slightly.

"I don't believe you."

"Then let me explain," Kurt said. He sighed. "Let me explain everything."

85: AMANDA

Madison County, Ohio – Monday, September 11, 1939

L ooking out a window in her train car, Amanda played "Name That Vegetable" as dark green fields went by in a blur. She didn't care if she guessed correctly. She won the game simply by thinking of something less serious than the serious matters before her.

She looked at her mother, who sat beside her at a table for four, and then at her grandmother, who sat directly across from her. Both Susan and Elizabeth had agreed to bring open minds to a conversation Amanda had set up. Amanda had listened to the short version of Kurt's story on Sunday and invited him to present the long version on the trip to Los Angeles.

"Here he comes," Amanda said. "Please hear what he has to say. There will be plenty of time to pass judgment before we get to California."

Kurt Schmidt entered the car like a man fighting his share of personal demons. He frowned as he walked through the coach. He forced a smile when he reached the last table on the left.

"Good morning," Kurt said.

"Good morning," Susan replied. "Did you sleep well?"

Kurt sighed.

"I slept."

Susan offered an empathetic smile.

"I guess we all had a rough night. Please join us."

Kurt nodded and sat next to Elizabeth. He straightened the jacket of his light gray suit before settling into his seat and folding his hands atop the table.

"Are you feeling up to this?" Amanda asked.

"I am," Kurt said. "I want to say my piece."

"That's good. I know Mom and Grandma want to hear it. They know the broad outlines of what you told me yesterday, but now they want

367

details. They want to hear them from you and look in your eyes and know you are telling us the truth."

"I understand."

"Let's start from the beginning then," Amanda said. "Tell us what happened the day you arrived in Germany. I believe that was August 7."

"It was," Kurt said. "Like I told you yesterday, I stepped off the ship in Hamburg and took the express train to Berlin. My brother met me at the station there."

"Where were your parents?" Susan asked.

"They were …"

Kurt turned away.

"Are you all right?"

Kurt looked at Susan and nodded. He gathered himself, took a breath, and continued.

"When I arrived in Berlin, Karl gave me the news. He said my father had been detained and my mother had taken a turn for the worse," Kurt said. "I was not able to see either right away, so I spent three days with Karl at our flat, learning what I could about a grave situation."

"Then what?"

"I went to the hospital. I saw my mother for the first time in weeks and learned that her treatment had failed. She told me she had less than a month to live. She also told me what had happened to my father when he had returned to Berlin."

"What was that?" Susan asked.

Kurt sighed.

"He had been arrested and charged with spying for the United States."

Amanda gave Kurt a supportive smile. She had concluded from that single revelation that she had misinterpreted several letters and unfairly judged an entire family.

"Was it true?" Elizabeth asked. "Had he spied?"

Kurt glanced around the car, as if checking for eavesdroppers, and then turned to face his questioner. He paused a moment and frowned before answering.

"He had. They both had. My parents spied for the U.S. from 1933 until December 31, 1938, when my father learned he was the target of an investigation by the Reich Ministry for Foreign Affairs. For years my parents had collected and leaked sensitive information to the Roosevelt Administration through a contact in the State Department."

"Why did they do it?" Elizabeth asked. "They were Germans."

"They were Germans, yes, but not Nazis. When the Nazis assumed power six years ago, they began replacing key personnel in German embassies around the world. They did not replace my father but told him he could retain his post only if he swore allegiance to the new regime."

"So he swore allegiance to Adolf Hitler?"

"He did, Mrs. Campbell. He did so that he could hold his position, keep his family in this country, and eventually undermine a leader he despised. He knew that by retaining his post at the embassy, he could do considerable damage to Hitler's government and perhaps help America better prepare for a conflict he believed was inevitable."

"So what happened when he learned he was under investigation?" Susan asked.

"He kept a low profile. He ignored his contact and focused solely on his duties at the embassy. He guessed that by doing so, he could persuade investigators to move on. He guessed wrong. Von Ribbentrop's men intensified their efforts to prove his guilt. You may recall seeing men who looked like bodyguards at my father's lecture. They weren't bodyguards at all. They were thugs who had been ordered to watch his every move."

"How did they catch him?" Susan asked.

"The investigators learned the full scope of his activities in May when they intercepted and interrogated an American courier in London. The courier possessed incriminating documents and the names of German officials in D.C. who had provided information to the U.S. government."

"You say your mother was in on this?" Elizabeth asked.

"She was," Kurt said. "She was from the very start. She was the one who kept me up to speed on my father's activities in Washington and the one who updated me on his status when he was arrested, detained, and sentenced to death."

Amanda reached across the table and took Kurt's hand. She held it until he responded to her gesture with a weary smile. She wanted to show him meaningful support before he moved on to the worst parts of what had been a very difficult month.

"What about you?" Susan asked. "Were *you* in on it?"

"I wasn't until my sophomore year of college. My parents tried to keep their espionage secret. When I accidentally learned of their activities in 1936, they brought me into the fold."

"What did you do?" Elizabeth asked.

"I did nothing at first except keep my mouth shut. Later, after I moved to Princeton, I used my position to keep tabs on researchers, visitors, and others who might use the Institute and other research facilities to further the interests of Hitler's regime. My parents asked me only to keep a low profile because they did not want me to do anything that might draw unnecessary attention to my father and his activities in Washington."

"Your brother was not a part of this?" Susan asked.

"No," Kurt said. "My parents loved him but did not trust him. They suspected that his loyalty to Germany was stronger than his loyalty to his family."

"You said you learned about your father when you visited your mother in the hospital," Susan said. "What happened after that?"

Kurt gazed at Susan.

"I saw my father for the last time. Karl and I received special permission to visit him in his holding cell on August 12. We were given an hour to say goodbye."

"I don't understand," Susan said. "Wasn't he given a trial? Even a show trial?"

"No. That was never in the cards," Kurt said. "You must remember that my father was a war hero, one revered even by party members. By publicly trying and executing a war hero, the Nazis would have invited dissent they did not need. So they gave my father a cyanide pill instead. They gave him a chance to preserve his honor and receive a state funeral. My father, naturally, did the honorable thing. He did not want to burden us with anything more."

"Oh, no," Susan said.

Kurt reached into his suit pocket and pulled out a newspaper clipping.

"Here is an article describing his funeral on August 16."

Susan took the press clipping, read it, and then handed it to Elizabeth.

"I'm so sorry, Kurt," Susan said. "What happened after that?"

"Karl and I visited my mother. We saw her after the funeral."

"How was she at that point?"

"She was near death. She was unable to eat or drink or even speak. She drifted in and out of consciousness for several hours," Kurt said. "She regained consciousness the next morning and, during that time, urged me to leave the country. She said it was only a matter of time before the Nazis learned of my complicity and arrested me as well. She told me this when Karl was away. She died before he returned."

"What did you do then?" Susan asked. "Did you leave?"

Kurt shook his head.

"I didn't. I waited a few days," Kurt said. "I wanted to give my mother the funeral and burial she deserved and also try to save my brother's life."

"What do you mean?" Elizabeth asked.

Kurt looked at his questioner.

"I knew Karl would never leave Germany unless I convinced him the country was doomed. He had already turned against the Nazis and hated them for killing our father, but he refused to leave. He did not believe war would come. Nor did he believe the Nazis would come after us. So I told him about Amanda. I told him she was a time traveler who had predicted all sorts of things, including the signing of a treaty between Hitler and Stalin on August 23. When the non-aggression pact was announced on that day, Karl changed his mind. He agreed to leave."

"So you fled?" Susan asked.

"We fled," Kurt said. "We returned to the flat, retrieved maps, documents, and a few personal belongings, and left Berlin. We spent several days on the run."

"How did you get around?"

"We drove. We bought a used car and traveled on rural roads until we reached a checkpoint near Germany's border with Luxembourg. We went there to avoid the more heavily guarded stations near Belgium, France, and Holland."

"Did the guards know you were running?" Susan asked.

"I don't think so," Kurt said. "I had called a cousin from Trier that morning to see if the police in Berlin had come looking for us. She said they had inquired about our whereabouts but had not issued any warrants. She did not believe we were at imminent risk."

"Obviously something went wrong."

"It did. As soon as we arrived at the checkpoint, a junior officer asked us to surrender our passports. He examined the documents, questioned us for about ten minutes, and then sent us on our way. Then a more senior officer arrived on the scene, during a routine changing of the guard, and called us back for more questions. He didn't believe our story that we were mere weekend travelers and made a phone call. That's when things got ugly."

Amanda sighed as she braced for what followed.

"What happened?" Susan asked.

"Karl panicked," Kurt said. "He saw the senior officer motion to one of the sentries and then point at me. He apparently believed the officer had learned something on the phone and was about to order our arrest. So when the sentry entered the office, Karl struck him from behind. He disabled the man, took his pistol, and put him and the officer into a room he could lock."

"Karl did all that?"

"He did. He did all that while I stood there and did nothing. He knew what he was doing. He had taken firearms and martial arts training in Germany. He knew how the Nazis operated and, because of that knowledge, left nothing to chance."

"Tell them what he did," Amanda said.

"Karl saved my life," Kurt said to Susan and Elizabeth. "That's what he did."

"How?" Susan asked.

"He took charge of the scene. He asked me to return to our car, start it, and wait for him. He wanted to make sure there were no sentries on the other side of the building. So I did what he asked while he conducted a perimeter search. When a minute passed, I heard a shot, looked at the building, and saw Karl run toward the car. He jumped in the car, shot a pursuing sentry in the leg, and told me to drive through the gate. I made it as far as the gate itself when the sentry fired at the car. A bullet struck Karl in the head and killed him instantly. I continued driving until I crossed the border into Luxembourg."

"Good Lord," Susan said. "When was this?"

"It was August 31. Germany invaded Poland the next day."

"So Karl saved you?"

"He saved me," Kurt said. "I had wanted to give him a new life in America, but all I could do was give him a Christian burial in Luxembourg."

"I'm sorry," Susan said.

"I am too. My brother did a lot of bad things in his life, but he did a good thing when it mattered most. He put his family before his country. I will never forget that."

"How did you get out of Europe?" Elizabeth asked.

"I took a train to Brussels and Calais and planned to take a ferry to England, but I couldn't find one. All of the ferry services had suspended operations because of the fighting. So I paid a French fisherman to take me across the Channel. The next day, September 4, I talked my way onto a cargo ship that left Southampton for New York. I reached Princeton late Saturday night."

Susan gazed at Kurt like a mother who had finally reached a breakthrough with a headstrong son. She placed a hand on the young man's arm, tapped it a few times, and pulled it back.

"I'm sorry for putting you through this," Susan said.

"I am too," Elizabeth added.

"It's all right," Kurt said.

Susan collected her purse, rose from her seat, and stepped into the aisle. She smiled at the young adults and then glanced at her mother.

"I feel like going to the observation car," Susan said. "Care to join me, Mom?"

"What about Kurt and Amanda?" Elizabeth asked.

"I suspect they want time to themselves."

Elizabeth smiled.

"I suspect they do too," Elizabeth said. She looked at Kurt. "Please excuse me."

"Of course," Kurt said.

Amanda watched closely as Kurt got out of his chair, moved aside, and allowed Elizabeth to pass. She mouthed a "thank you" to Elizabeth when she met Amanda's gaze, stepped past Kurt, and joined Susan in the aisle.

Amanda had never admired her grandmother more than she did at that moment. The woman who had started the journey with a rigid view of humanity had come a long way.

"We won't be long," Amanda said to her mother.

"Take your time," Susan replied.

Amanda waved at Susan and Elizabeth as they walked away. She slid into Susan's seat, waited for Kurt to sit, and then directed her full attention to a man she had clearly wronged.

"I'm sorry I doubted you," Amanda said a moment later. "I should have believed you from the start. I should have judged you fairly."

"You did though," Kurt said. "You acted on the evidence. If I were in your shoes, I would have done the same thing."

"I doubt that."

"Why do you say that?"

"I say that, Mr. Schmidt, because you give people the benefit of the doubt. You see goodness in everyone. You even saw it in your brother."

"That's not entirely true. When I learned that Karl had joined the Nazi party, I did not give him the benefit of the doubt. I assumed the worst and shunned him for two years. He wrote to me. I did not write back. I regret that now. I should have engaged him, like my parents did, and tried to convince him that he had made a poor decision. I didn't follow through."

"You followed through when it counted," Amanda said. "I hope you will do that with me. I still want to build a life with you."

"You do?" Kurt asked.

"Yes. I do. Nothing has changed. The only question is whether you still want to build a life with *me*. You don't have to do this, Kurt. You can get off the train in Dayton, head back to Princeton, and find another job."

Kurt smiled sadly.

"If I did that, I would be more miserable than ever. I didn't leave Germany merely to escape Hitler's oppression. I left to return to you. I thought of you constantly. I still do. I love you."

"That's what I need to hear," Amanda said. "I love you too."

Kurt sighed.

"What's next?"

"We ride the train to California. We ride it until we get to Los Angeles and a magic tunnel you have to see to believe. Then I'll introduce you to a time I think you're going to like."

"I'm looking forward to that," Kurt said.

Amanda reached across the table and touched Kurt's face. It looked older, wiser, and much sadder than the one she had seen in Cape May. She wondered how long it would be before she saw the one she had fallen in love with.

"Are you going to be all right?" Amanda asked.

Kurt nodded.

"I'm going to be fine. I just need time to adjust."

Amanda gazed at Kurt for a minute. She wanted to savor every second of a very memorable moment before moving on.

"I have something for you," Amanda said.

"What's that?"

Amanda pulled back her hands and reached into her purse. She retrieved the rhinestone ring Kurt had worn at Cape May as a "married" man. She placed it on the table.

"I found it in your desk, next to the letters. I almost threw it away."

Kurt picked up the ring and slipped it on.

"I'm glad you kept it," Kurt said. "I like it."

Amanda smiled and lifted her left hand.

"I like my ring too. I put it on this morning."

Kurt took Amanda's hands and pulled them close.

"Perhaps someday soon we can replace these bands with better ones."

Amanda sighed.

"I'd like that."

Kurt gazed at Amanda for a moment.

"I got you something too."

"You did?" Amanda asked.

"I did."

Kurt released her hands, reached into his jacket pocket, and pulled out a flower that looked like it had seen better days. He placed it on the table.

"It's an edelweiss," Amanda said. "You remembered."

Kurt chuckled.

"I guess you could say that."

"What do you mean?"

"I picked it up in Newark."

Amanda laughed.

"You're something."

"I didn't want to return to you unless I could fulfill all of my promises," Kurt said. "I hope this will do."

"It will do," Amanda said. She leaned across the table and gave her blond-haired knight a soft kiss. "It will definitely do."

86: SUSAN

S usan tore through her suitcase like a person looking for a priceless gem, which, in this case, she was. She tossed clothes and toiletries on the sidewalk with reckless abandon and opened pouches and pockets with lightning speed.

"Please tell me you didn't leave it in Princeton," Amanda said.

"I didn't," Susan replied. "I brought it."

"I hope so because I just remembered something."

Susan looked up.

"What's that?"

"*My* crystal is worthless. It lasts 153 days," Amanda said. "We've been gone 365."

Susan felt her stomach drop. The last thing she needed to hear was that the backup to the crystal she couldn't find was now as functional as a brick.

"It doesn't matter. I know I brought mine."

Susan opened her other suitcase and resumed her search. She went through compartments, emptied bags, and inspected anything and everything that might contain a three-inch chunk of gypsum. She didn't stop until she shook a pair of panties and watched her ticket to the future drop to the sidewalk.

Elizabeth, Amanda, and Kurt laughed.

"I guess we know where to find the family jewels!" Amanda said.

"That's enough, smarty pants," Susan snapped. "I can still disinherit you."

Elizabeth looked at Amanda.

"If she does, *I'll* support you."

Amanda giggled.

"Thanks, Grams."

Susan placed the rock in her purse and started putting her belongings back in her luggage. When she finished, she closed the suitcases, stood up, and handed the largest bag to Kurt. She brushed the dust off her dress and looked at her entourage.

"Can we go now?" Susan asked.

"We can go," Amanda said.

Susan checked her watch in the fading daylight, saw that it was seven o'clock, and realized that her long day was about to get longer. She remembered that the time travelers would arrive at about the same moment they had left in 2016. They would enter Geoffrey Bell's basement in the late morning.

Susan didn't want to carry her suitcase another ten feet, much less another block, but she was glad she had asked the taxi driver to drop the four off short of their destination. As she and the others drew closer to the Bell mansion, she saw something she had hoped she would not see: signs of human occupation. She found a late 1930s sedan and an overflowing garbage can in the driveway of the Painted Lady.

"Do you see what I see, Amanda?" Susan asked.

"I do," Amanda said. "What should we do about it?"

"I don't know. Wait here while I get a closer look."

Susan lowered her suitcase to the ground and walked about thirty feet to the edge of the once and future home of a family named Bell. She saw a light in a second-floor window but nothing else to suggest that the house was *presently* occupied. She walked back to the group.

"Did you see anything?" Amanda asked.

Susan nodded.

"I saw a light in a bedroom window but no other signs that someone is home. If someone *is* in the bedroom now, then he or she is probably reading in bed. The light was dim."

"Do you want to keep going?"

"I do," Susan said. "We can reach the backyard by walking between the properties. There are no windows on that side of the Bell house and the passageway is dimly lit."

"Let's do it then," Amanda said.

Susan retrieved her suitcase and looked at the others.

"Are you ready, Mom?"

"I am," Elizabeth said.

"Kurt?"

"I'm ready."

"Then follow me," Susan said. "Be very quiet."

"OK."

Susan led her party to the edge of the Bell property and then veered left. She walked slowly and quietly through a narrow side yard and continued until she reached a backyard that looked like it had changed little in exactly a year.

She waited for Amanda, Elizabeth, and Kurt to catch up and then proceeded to the middle of the backyard. When she reached a spot that looked all too familiar, she lowered her suitcase, turned to face the back of the house, and gave the residence a final inspection.

Susan saw nothing to give her pause. If there were any people inside the Painted Lady, they had pulled the drapes, closed the blinds, and flicked off the lights. She reached in her purse, pulled out the white crystal and the skeleton key, and turned toward the others.

"It looks like the coast is clear," Susan said. "Let's go."

The group leader picked up her suitcase and advanced slowly toward an opening in the lawn that led to a stairway, a door, and a tunnel. She stopped in her tracks when she heard a growl.

Seconds later a German shepherd rushed up the stairs. It stopped on the top step, looked at the trespassers, and growled again.

"I don't want any part of that," Amanda said.

"Neither do I," Susan said. "Back up, everyone."

The four grabbed their bags and retreated to the middle of the lawn. All kept their eyes on a dog that growled two more times, barked once, and then fell to the ground. Fido had apparently decided to cut the intruders some slack but not enough to make a difference. He assumed a defensive position at the head of a stairway that the travelers had to use.

"Now what do we do?" Amanda asked.

Susan didn't have a ready answer. She hadn't expected to find a killer guard dog any more than she had expected to find the house occupied. She vaguely remembered Professor Bell telling her that the mansion would *not* be occupied.

"I don't know," Susan said.

"Why don't you just knock on the door and tell the owner who we are?" Kurt asked. "I'm sure he would let us access the tunnel if we stated our intentions."

"That's the problem though. We can't state our intentions. We have an obligation to keep our knowledge of the tunnel to ourselves. Telling an occupant of the house who is not privy to the secrets of the chamber would invite a lot of problems."

"We have to do something," Elizabeth said. "We can't stay out here all night."

"I know, Mom. I know," Susan said.

Susan pondered possible solutions to the problem as she gazed at a darkening sky. Dusk had already fallen on Southern California.

She looked at the house and then at the stairway and saw no change in the status quo. The windows remained dark and the dog vigilant.

"Grandma's right, Mom," Amanda said. "We can't stay here forever. Let's find a hotel and come back tomorrow. We can wait until the owner brings the dog inside or takes him for a walk. We don't have to walk through the tunnel tonight."

"I agree," Susan said. "There's a hotel a few blocks from here. We can go there now and come back in the morning. I think we're all pretty tired anyway. Let's go."

Susan grabbed her suitcase and once again began to lead the others toward a chosen destination, but she stopped as soon as she saw two figures emerge from the side yard. She recognized both even before she could make out their faces.

"Good evening, folks," Professor Bell said.

Bell smiled as he escorted his wife toward the middle of the backyard. He seemed neither surprised nor upset to see the women or their German friend.

"Hello, Professor," Susan said. "You're the last person I expected to find out here tonight."

Bell laughed.

"That's funny. You're the *first* person I expected to find."

"I don't understand."

"I just picked up your latest letter. It arrived in Los Angeles the same time you did. Mrs. Bell and I collected it before the post office closed. We are just returning from a late dinner."

"So you know everything?" Susan asked.

"I know enough. I certainly know about Mr. Schmidt," Bell said. He extended a hand. "I'm Geoffrey Bell. It's nice to finally meet you."

"You too," Kurt said as he took the hand.

"This is my wife, Jeanette."

"Hello."

"Hi, Kurt," Jeanette said.

Bell turned away from the time travelers and glanced at a German shepherd that hadn't moved. The dog scratched at a flea and looked at the humans with apparent indifference.

"I see you've met Fritz," Bell said.

"You know about the dog?" Susan asked.

"I know about the dog and his owner. I apologize for not telegramming you about Mr. Theodore Pace. He began renting the house two weeks ago."

"Is he inside the house?"

"I believe he is," Bell said. "He usually retires early. He's a heavy sleeper even though his canine guardian is not."

"Do you know him?" Susan asked. "Does he know about you?"

"No. I have managed to avoid his detection."

Susan smiled.

"What about Fritz?"

"I ran into him on my first trip out," Bell said. "I prepared for him on my second."

"What do you mean?"

Bell turned to Jeanette.

"Show our friends the answer to their problem, dear."

Jeanette retrieved a brown paper bag from her purse. She opened it, removed the contents, and handed what looked like a choice cut of meat to her husband.

"Here you go," Jeanette said.

Bell summoned Fritz with a soft whistle, waited for the dog to leave his post, and then threw the piece of meat about fifteen yards to the far side of the yard. He turned toward Susan when the dog ran after his meal, picked it up with his teeth, and ventured even farther away.

"Fritz is partial to pork chops," Bell said. "He also likes to dine alone. We have about five minutes before he returns to the stairs."

Susan held out her white crystal.

"I guess I won't need this," Susan said.

"On the contrary, Mrs. Peterson, you *will* need it," Bell said. "We will all need it if we wish to return to the time you departed. We will all need you to lead us through the tunnel."

"You're right. I remember."

Bell turned to face the others.

"Please follow us into the house, good people. I'm sure you are tired and need some rest. We will have plenty of time to discuss your adventures later," Bell said. He returned to Susan and extended an arm. "Lead the way, my dear."

87: SUSAN

El Segundo, California – Saturday, September 17, 2016

Susan could not complain about the accommodations. Thanks to Professor and Jeanette Bell, she and the others had a plush hotel suite, easy access to the beach, and free use of a meeting room that looked like the private study of a billionaire.

Susan pondered her good fortune as she sat with Elizabeth, Amanda, and Kurt on one side of a long table in the room. Then she gazed across the table at the couple that had set her up in style. She had more questions for them than she could count.

"Thank you for putting us up in this place," Susan said. "I think I speak for all of us when I say we have enjoyed our two days here and look forward to our last day."

"I'm glad to hear that," Bell said.

"I do have some questions though."

"Oh? What are they?"

Susan smiled.

"Why did you send us to El Segundo? Why did you hustle us out of your house?"

"Is that all?" Bell asked.

"No," Susan said. "I have more questions too."

Several people laughed.

Bell smiled.

"Your curiosity is understandable," Bell said. "I sent you here because it is close to LAX. I wanted to shorten your trip to the airport. I 'hustled' you out of my house on Thursday because I had to make room for visitors on Friday."

"They must have been important," Susan said.

380

"They were very important, as a matter of fact. They were and are as important as the four people sitting in front of me."

"What are you saying?"

Bell smiled.

"Do you recall me telling you about the men I sent to the past?"

"I do," Susan said. "You sent a reporter and his son to 1900."

"Well, they are back in the present," Bell said. "They are currently recuperating from their time travels at another area hotel. I expect to debrief them tomorrow."

"Are they all right?" Susan asked.

"They are fine. Like you, they returned in one piece. Like you, they brought back a living, breathing souvenir. They brought back two, in fact."

"So we weren't the only ones to break the rules?"

"No," Bell said. "You weren't."

Susan sipped coffee from a mug.

"Are you upset with us?"

"I was at first. I instructed you to follow my rules for a reason."

"Then why do you seem happy this morning?" Susan asked.

"I'm happy because you acted responsibly for the most part," Bell said. "I read Elizabeth's journal yesterday and learned of the sacrifices you made. I'm sure it was as difficult for you to leave Jack Hicks as it was for your mother to leave her parents and her younger self."

"It was."

"Why *did* you leave the admiral behind?" Bell asked.

Susan smiled sadly.

"I would prefer to keep the reason to myself."

"I understand," Bell said.

Susan turned away and looked out the meeting room window as she pondered the exchange. She considered the professor's question bold but not out of line. He had every right to know why she had discarded an unattached man she had dated for months.

"So if Elizabeth and I acted responsibly, does that mean Amanda acted *irresponsibly*?" Susan asked. "Are you mad at her?"

"I'm not mad at anyone," Bell said. "I expected her to bring Kurt back. I prepared for it, in fact."

"I don't understand."

"Perhaps you should ask your mother. She was on to me from the start."

"I still don't follow," Susan said.

Bell sipped his coffee and smiled.

"When Elizabeth wrote to me on July 5, 1939, she suspected that I was 'up to something.' She suspected that I must have had a reason to advise you to merely exercise caution around the Schmidt family rather than to avoid them altogether."

"Was she right?" Susan asked.

"She was. I did have a reason."

Elizabeth grinned.

"What reason was that?" Susan asked.

"I'll tell you," Bell said. "When I first learned about Kurt, I fumed. I considered traveling to Princeton to bring you back. I thought Amanda was playing with fire. Then I did some research on Kurt's family and decided to let history, a new version of history, play out."

"Please continue."

"I let this new time stream run its course because I wanted to give Amanda the chance to save the life of someone she loved. Had I provided her with specifics about the Schmidt family's transition, I might have created new problems and altered the course of the war."

"So you let my family die?" Kurt asked.

"I had no choice," Bell said. "I had to let your father die because I knew his death would trigger changes in Germany that led to Hitler's defeat. Your mother, sadly, was too sick to save. She had advanced pancreatic cancer. I doubt that even doctors in this time could have done more than extend her life by more than a few months."

"I understand," Kurt said.

"You were a different matter. You were someone I could save without changing history in a significant way. You were someone I could allow Amanda to bring back. That's why I gave her a free hand to follow her heart. I also knew that you, like your parents, could be trusted. I knew about your service to the United States."

"Then why did you advise us to exercise caution around the entire family?" Amanda asked. "Why did you not simply warn us away from Karl?"

"I didn't because I wanted to err at least a little on the side of caution. I also didn't know what to make of Karl," Bell said. "I suspected that he could not be trusted, but I didn't know for sure. I didn't know whether his allegiance to Germany and to the Nazis was stronger than his devotion to his family."

"What about your letter blasting me for withholding a letter from Amanda?" Elizabeth asked. "If I recall correctly, you demanded that we 'cease communications' with all of the Schmidts and return to Los Angeles immediately."

"I did do that. I feared you had acted recklessly and perhaps put your own lives at risk. I was concerned solely, at that point, with your family's safety."

"There is still one thing I don't understand," Kurt said. "You mentioned something a minute ago about letting a 'new version of history' play out. What did you mean by that? What happened in the *old* version of history?"

"I'm glad you asked," Bell said. "I have the answer to those questions and others in this folder. I prepared it for you last night."

Bell opened a manila folder and pulled out photocopies of two newspaper articles. He slid both articles across the table.

"What are these?" Kurt asked.

"Take a look," Bell said. "The first article describes what happened to you in the first version of history. You were killed, along with your brother, in the Battle of Stalingrad."

"That can't be true. I would have never fought for Hitler."

"You might have had you been forced into his army," Bell said. "I don't know what motivated your actions the first time around. I do know that you didn't have knowledge of any time travelers in New Jersey. I know that you didn't arrange to meet a woman named Amanda Peterson on September 10, 1939. I suspect that you stayed with your brother in Berlin, out of family loyalty, until you were both conscripted into the military."

"I see," Kurt said.

"I *don't* have to speculate about your place in history. I know that even though you fought for Germany, you were recognized by the United States, posthumously, for helping to maintain this country's security. You were honored, along with your parents and other German nationals, in a ceremony in 1989 when intelligence records from 1939 were declassified. The second news article explains everything."

Kurt read the article while the others waited. When he finished, he pushed the paper aside, sighed, and looked at Bell thoughtfully.

"Thank you," Kurt said.

Bell smiled.

"You're welcome. I figured it was the least I could do for someone who stuck his neck out for this country and opposed tyranny when it mattered most."

"I do have one more question," Kurt said.

"Please ask."

"How will I become a part of this time? I was born in Berlin a hundred years ago. I graduated from college in 1938. I have no identification or even a personal history I can use in 2016."

The professor smiled again.

"You do now," Bell said. He opened the folder, pulled out more papers, and slid them to Kurt. "I think you will find these documents more than sufficient for starting a new life."

Kurt scanned the papers and then shuffled them together. He grabbed Amanda's hand, gave her a warm smile, and then turned to face the Bells.

"Thank you again," Kurt said. "I don't know how I can repay you."

Jeanette beamed.

"You can repay us by sending us a wedding invitation."

Kurt blushed. He glanced at Amanda, who looked at him with amusement, and then at the woman who always seemed to say the right thing at the right time.

"I'll see what I can do, Mrs. Bell," Kurt said. "I'll see what I can do."

88: AMANDA

Larimer County, Colorado – Sunday, September 18, 2016

Amanda peered through the tiny window and gazed at a hodgepodge of cornfields, lakes, and college towns as the Front Range gave way to civilization. She didn't know if northern Colorado always looked so appealing from 35,000 feet, but today it looked like a little slice of heaven.

She admired the scenery for a moment and then turned her eyes and her attention to other things. She smiled as she thought of a fact only a time traveler could appreciate.

"What's so funny?" Kurt asked from the adjacent seat. "You're grinning."

"I was just thinking about something," Amanda said.

"What?"

"Today is my twenty-second birthday."

"I know," Kurt said. "So?"

Amanda laughed quietly.

"I'm really twenty-three. My body and my mind are twenty-three years old."

Kurt smiled.

"I guess they are. Should I view you as an older woman?"

"It depends, Mr. Schmidt. It depends on whether you want to come home with me today or find a new life at the Chicago airport."

Kurt chuckled.

"In that case, you don't look a day over eighteen."

Amanda laughed.

"You're learning."

"It is kind of odd when you think about it," Kurt said. "You've lived a whole year that only a handful of people will ever know about. So have your mother and grandmother."

Amanda looked over her shoulder and glanced at Susan and Elizabeth. Both snoozed away in the seats directly behind her.

"I suspect they won't care," Amanda said. "Or they will be like me. They will insist on counting birthdays in calendar time and not in real time. There isn't a woman on the planet who would add a year she doesn't have to."

"I'm sure you're right," Kurt said.

Amanda smiled.

"I know I'm right."

"Did I ever tell you that they are amazing people?" Kurt asked.

"Who? Mom and Grandma?"

Kurt nodded.

"When you went to the pool last night, after dinner, they both came up to me, gave me a hug, and said they loved me. I didn't know how to respond. I didn't expect it."

"Expect more of it," Amanda said. "That's how this family works."

Kurt pulled an airline magazine from the pocket of the seat in front of him and started thumbing through the pages. He stopped when he reached a page in the middle and pointed to a photograph of Washington, D.C.

"Is that our next destination?" Kurt asked.

Amanda nodded.

"I start a job at a think tank there on October 3."

"Do you think I'll have any difficulty finding a job?"

"No," Amanda said. "I'll have to give you a crash course on computing and bring you up to speed on the past seventy-seven years, but you'll be fine. You speak four languages, know your history, and look like a movie star. You'll find a job."

"Then I guess I'll leave that matter in your capable hands."

Amanda laughed.

"You're such a quick study."

Kurt put the magazine away.

"When do we go to Washington?"

"We leave on the twenty-ninth. I've already put money on an apartment."

"So I'll get to see a little of Chicago?" Kurt asked.

"You'll get to see a lot of it. I'll make sure of it," Amanda said. She tilted her head and looked at Kurt closely. "Is there anything else you want to see or do while we're on the subject?"

Kurt sighed.

"There is something."

"What?"

"I'd like to travel to Europe," Kurt said.

"You want to go this *month*?"

"No. I'd like to go next year. I'd like to see Berlin again. I've read it's changed a lot."

"You have no idea. It was divided until 1990," Amanda said. "*Germany* was divided until 1990. It's a much different country than it was even twenty-five years ago."

"That makes me want to see it even more."

"Do you want to see your parents' graves?"

Kurt nodded.

"I want to see everything: the graves, our old house, our church. I want to go to Luxembourg too. I didn't do much to honor Karl after he died. I want to do more for him now."

"I understand," Amanda said. "We could go in March or April. I'm sure I could get time off work by then."

"I would rather go in June or July," Kurt said. "I would rather go when the weather is nice."

"Mom and Grandma would love that idea. We could all go."

Kurt sighed.

"Maybe another time. This time, I want to go just with you."

Amanda looked at him with curious eyes.

"You want to travel as a couple?"

Kurt shook his head.

"No. I want to travel as a *family*."

Amanda stared at Kurt as her gentle smile grew into a grin.

"I think I can clear my schedule, Mr. Schmidt," Amanda said. She kissed Kurt lightly on the cheek. "In fact, I'm sure of it."

89: SUSAN

Lake Forest, Illinois

Susan sighed as the taxi driver turned onto her street and began a slow, quiet procession to the house by the lake. Thanks to speed bumps, stop signs, and a fifteen-mile-per-hour speed limit, drivers didn't drive on Sunflower Road. They crawled.

Susan didn't mind. She was in no hurry to get home. She wanted time to reflect on the past year and ponder an uncertain future.

She glanced at the back seat and saw three people who seemed to be in happy places. All three returned Susan's smile, though only one, Kurt, seemed amused. Sitting between Amanda, who held his right hand, and Elizabeth, who clung to his left, he smiled like a man who would forever be captive to at least two captivating women.

Susan thought about Kurt. She admired his defense of liberty, his poise in the wake of tragedy, his dedication to Amanda, and his willingness to make a blind leap from one century to the next. She looked forward to bringing him into the family and being a part of his life.

As the taxicab, a late model Toyota Camry, inched its way toward the sprawling Second Empire mansion with the mother-in-law cottage, Susan thought also about the man she had left behind. She missed Jack Hicks. She missed his smile, his intelligence, and his sense of humor. She hoped that the doubts that had followed her from Princeton to Los Angeles would not be her constant companion in the months to come.

Susan turned her head and gazed again at the oldest occupant of the back seat. She was happy to see Elizabeth Campbell in relatively good spirits. She was happy to have her *back*.

Susan had doubted Elizabeth's ability to recover from several major shocks, but she didn't anymore. She knew now that her frail septuagenarian mother was a tough-as-nails superhero who was capable of overcoming anything. She eagerly anticipated strengthening her bonds with a woman who had always been her best friend and biggest champion.

The driver, a pudgy fortyish man who spoke with an Indian accent, moved his eyes around as he approached a long block of houses that were bigger than national monuments. He glanced at a map on a digital screen, pushed a button, and then turned to face the woman next to him.

"Where is your house again?" the driver asked.

"It's behind that cluster of trees at the end of the block," Susan said. She pointed out the front window. "I want you to stop there though. I want you to stop by those mailboxes."

"Why?"

"I have my reasons."

"OK."

The driver slowed from a crawl to a creep and finally stopped in front of two mailboxes that bore the colors of rival universities. He turned off the ignition and waited for further instruction.

"What are we doing, Mom?" Amanda asked.

Susan turned around.

"We're stopping."

Amanda raised a brow.

"I can see that."

"I want you to get out of the car and walk the rest of the way with me," Susan said.

"Why?" Amanda asked.

"Just do it. The exercise will do us good."

Amanda gave her mother an exasperated look she had honed as a teenager and then turned to the man in the middle seat. She kissed Kurt on the cheek.

"I won't be long," Amanda said.

Kurt laughed.

"Take your time."

Susan smiled at Kurt and then looked one more time at Elizabeth. She saw what she had expected to see: a patient woman who was predictably composed, a quiet person who didn't say a word, and a confidante who returned a knowing smile.

Susan watched Amanda exit the right rear door of the vehicle and then turned to face the driver. She retrieved her purse and opened her own door.

"Give us a few minutes to walk the rest of the way and then drive to the house," Susan said. "I will pay you double for your time."

"I'm in no hurry, lady," the cabbie said.

Susan nodded and exited the vehicle. She shut the door, took a deep breath, and then turned to face a daughter who appeared to be both irritated and amused.

"Did you plan a surprise birthday party?" Amanda asked.

Susan laughed softly.

"No."

"Did you buy me a car? Is it waiting in the driveway?"

"I'm afraid not," Susan said.

Amanda tilted her head.

"Then what's this about?"

"Come walk with me," Susan said. "I'll tell you."

Amanda sighed.

"All right."

Susan stepped forward, grabbed her daughter's hand, and gently pulled her forward. She waved to the driver as they passed the front of the vehicle and continued northward on a sidewalk that separated the narrow street from spacious front lawns.

"Thanks for walking with me," Susan said.

Amanda laughed.

"Did I have a choice?"

"You always have a choice."

"That's not true," Amanda said.

Susan smiled.

"OK. It's not."

Amanda took a breath.

"Are you going to give me some bad news?"

"No," Susan said.

"Then why did you pull me away from Grandma and Kurt?"

"I wanted to talk to you."

"Can't we talk when we get home?" Amanda asked.

"No," Susan said. "I need to say a few things first."

Amanda looked at her mother with puzzled eyes.

"OK. Then say them."

Susan released Amanda's hand. She brought her own hands together under her chin.

"Do you remember the day Grandma gave us a tour of Princeton?"

"I do," Amanda said.

"Do you remember her pointing out a law firm on Prospect Avenue?"

"Yes."

"Do you remember what she said about that firm?"

Amanda gave Susan another curious glance.

"I do. She said it was the oldest in the country."

390

"You're close," Susan said. "She said it was one of the oldest continuously operating firms in the country. More important, she said it was still operating in 2016."

"Is that what you want to talk about? A law firm?"

Susan reclaimed Amanda's hand.

"No. I want to talk about what I did at that law firm."

Amanda sighed again.

"OK."

"I visited the firm the day I said goodbye to Jack," Susan said. "In fact, I walked there right after I said goodbye. I did so to keep an appointment I had made with an attorney named Clarence Pendleton."

"You hired a lawyer?" Amanda asked.

"I did."

"Did you sue someone?"

"No," Susan said. She laughed. "I didn't sue anyone. I simply asked Mr. Pendleton to do a favor for me."

Amanda slowed her step.

"What was that?"

Susan took a breath.

"I asked him to hold onto some letters."

"You mean letters you wrote?" Amanda asked.

Susan nodded.

"I mean ten anonymous notes I wrote and typed in August."

Amanda's hand went limp.

"Mom? What did you do?"

Susan gathered her strength.

"I asked Mr. Pendleton and his firm to hold the letters for seventy-seven years and then mail them to a specific person in a specific order."

Amanda stopped. She withdrew her hand and turned to face her mother.

"Who did you write to?"

Susan tried to hold it together as tears flooded her eyes and her legs grew wobbly. She willed herself the strength to finish what she had started.

"I wrote to a man who lives on this street," Susan said.

"What ... did you say?" Amanda asked in a shaky voice.

"I said a lot of things, honey. I told the man that he had a wife and a family who loved him and appreciated him. I told him that many problems in a marriage could be fixed but others, like adultery, could not. I reminded him that commitments were forever and that vows made on a wedding day should be honored, strengthened, and cherished. I told him all the things he needed to know at a time he needed to know them."

Amanda's face turned white and her eyes grew wide.

"You didn't."

"I did," Susan said. "When I learned about the firm, I knew I had an opening. I knew I had an opportunity to rewrite the future. I had a chance to change my life."

Amanda started to tremble and falter. She reached out to Susan with both hands, held onto her arms, and tried to steady herself. She stared at her mother with moist eyes that revealed fear, wonder, and shock.

"You *didn't*," Amanda said in a barely audible voice.

"I did. I did it for you. I did it for us."

"You mean … he's alive?"

Susan nodded.

"I called him from Los Angeles. He's waiting inside. He's waiting for you," Susan said. She put a hand to Amanda's face. "Happy birthday, sweetheart."

Amanda wobbled and fell to her knees like a boxer going down for the count. She grabbed Susan's legs for support, took a breath, and stared blankly at her teary-eyed mother.

When Amanda finally returned to her feet, she smiled, hugged Susan fiercely, and then turned toward a house that was still a home. She cast her purse aside, sprinted toward the door, and screamed a name that echoed through the street.

"Daddy!"

90: SUSAN

North Chicago, Illinois — Monday, October 3, 2016

Susan walked out of the naval museum and joined Elizabeth on a sunny lawn. She held a sheet of paper in one hand and a souvenir pen in the other.

"Did you miss me?" Susan asked.

"I missed the air conditioning," Elizabeth said. "It's warm out here."

"Do you want to go home?"

"No. Let's enjoy the sun a bit. I just want to rest a while."

"OK," Susan said. "Let's find a place to sit."

Susan scanned the premises until she spotted a suitable location. She put a hand on her mother's shoulder and guided her toward the north side of the lawn. She helped her sit down when they reached a small wooden bench.

"That's much better," Elizabeth said.

"Are you sure? We can go back inside."

"I'm fine."

"All right."

Susan joined Elizabeth on the bench. She didn't know whether she was really all right or simply putting on a brave face, but she gave her the benefit of the doubt. She figured that anyone who had walked the earth for nearly eighty years *deserved* the benefit of the doubt.

"Did the clerk find what you wanted?" Elizabeth asked.

"He found more," Susan said. She handed the sheet, a photocopy of a newspaper article, to her mother. "He dug up a story on a speech Jack gave here sixty years ago. It contains a lot of biographical information."

Elizabeth took several minutes to read the article. When she finished, she returned the sheet to Susan, sat up straight in her seat, and gazed at a flagpole in the distance.

"He married again," Elizabeth said.

"I saw that. He also had a son. He became a father at fifty-eight."

"How do you feel about that?"

"I feel good," Susan said. "I feel good knowing that a man who had endured so much finally found the happiness he deserved."

Admiral John J. Hicks had found more than personal happiness. He had found a place in history. After serving fourteen months as a member of President Roosevelt's task force, Jack had returned to active duty and eventually commanded a carrier group that helped roll back Japan's advances in the South Pacific. He had retired, officially, as a vice admiral in 1948.

"Do you have any regrets?" Elizabeth asked.

"No," Susan said. "Not now. What I have is a measure of peace."

Susan meant it too. For nearly a month she had agonized over her decision to leave a perfect relationship in the past and resume an imperfect marriage in the future. She felt good about what she had done and about what she could still do in the years that remained to her.

"How are things between you and Bruce," Elizabeth said. "You haven't said much to your old mother since we returned to Chicago."

"I know," Susan said. "I haven't because I wanted to see how things developed. The simple truth of the matter is that we're in uncharted territory."

"Does Bruce think you sent him those letters?"

"I don't know. He hasn't even acknowledged receiving them. All I know for sure is that he's more attentive and involved than he was the first time around. He looks at me differently. He looks at me like he did when we were first married."

Elizabeth laughed.

"I don't need the details, dear. I just want to know whether you think this marriage of yours, this second marriage, will last."

"I think it will," Susan said. "I really do."

"Do you know whatever became of that receptionist?"

"It's funny you ask. I called another receptionist at Bruce's firm about a week ago and asked if Brianne was still employed there. She said she wasn't. She said Brianne left the company on March 31. She moved to New York just before the affair began."

"So it appears that your letters had the desired effect," Elizabeth said.

"It appears so."

Susan couldn't complain about the results. She had a live husband and a happy marriage. The only downside to her decision to send the letters had been the loss of six months. By gently steering Bruce Peterson away from a comely receptionist, she had rewritten half of 2016.

Bruce had frequently mentioned spring and summer events that Susan did not remember. He had even shown her photos of their twenty-fifth anniversary, a day spent in Hawaii and not in Chicago. Susan didn't have the answers. She knew only that a stream of time had separated in March and somehow come back together in September.

Elizabeth too had come home to a few surprises. When she pulled out a box of old photos on September 25, she discovered several new additions to the collection.

In two snapshots, one-year-old Lizzie Wagner, sitting in a high chair, posed with an elderly woman identified only as "her neighbor nana." Faded and dog-eared, the pictures matched two new ones that Elizabeth had carried back to the future.

Elizabeth hadn't needed to dig to learn the identity of the neighbor. She had been able to see with her own eyes that Lizzie's birthday party guest on April 23, 1939, had been a kindly Illinois widow, a time traveler who had, for several months, put her stamp on a precious young life.

Elizabeth had also found three photographs of a girl she recognized but didn't remember. In each of the black-and-white high school photos, a perky blonde stood with a group. She held a golf club in the first picture, a tennis racket in the second, and a tuba in the third.

Susan couldn't explain those pictures any more than she could explain time tunnels and glowing crystals, but she was more than happy to file them in a new family record. She pondered the pleasant discoveries until her mother broke a long silence with a not-so-surprising question.

"Have you heard from Amanda today?" Elizabeth asked.

"I did. I heard from her this morning," Susan said. "She called as she left her apartment. She was headed to the think tank for her first day of work."

"Did she take Kurt along?"

Susan smiled.

"Of course."

Susan had laughed when Amanda had told her she was taking Kurt to work. Amanda had taken him nearly everywhere since introducing him to her father as a "blond boy" she had "met on the beach and decided to keep."

Kurt had passed himself off, successfully, as a recent college graduate who had taken time off before returning to Washington, his hometown, to look for work. When Bruce had asked about his family, Kurt had replied, truthfully, that he was an orphan with no living siblings.

"Was Amanda excited when you talked to her?" Elizabeth asked.

"She was ecstatic," Susan said. "I think taking that job and moving back east was the best thing she could have done. She's in her element now."

"Do you think she'll be happy?"

"I know so. She loves research."

"That's not what I meant," Elizabeth said. "Do you think *they'll* be happy?"

Susan smiled.

"I'm even more confident of that."

"Why?" Elizabeth asked.

"I'm confident because of something Amanda asked me to do."

"What was that?"

Susan put a hand on her mother's knee.

"She asked me to call the church and reserve a date."

Elizabeth turned her head.

"You don't mean?"

"We're going to have a June wedding, Mom."

Elizabeth put her hand on Susan's.

"Are you sure?"

Susan nodded.

"I'm positive," Susan said. "Amanda specifically asked for Saturday, June 17."

Elizabeth's lips trembled as her eyes began to water.

"She did *that?*"

"She wants to be married on your anniversary," Susan said. "She wants to wear your ring. Amanda said that ring will get a good church wedding if it's the last thing she does."

Elizabeth nodded her agreement but said no more. Overcome with emotion, she was able to do no more than rest her head against her daughter's shoulder and no doubt think about a wedding she had once said she would never live to see.

Susan pulled her mother close and smiled as she thought about a magic moment, an unforgettable year, and a story that kept playing out in different ways. Life, she had concluded, was not a singular journey down a straight and narrow path. It was a series of adventures with interesting loops, detours, and diversions.

Like her mother, her daughter, and Kurt Schmidt, Susan Campbell Peterson had an opportunity to follow a new course and remake her life. She had a reset button, an opening, a second chance. In the fiftieth week of her fiftieth year, she vowed to make the most of it.